BROWN SHOE

BROWN SHOE

RICK SLONE

RANDOM HOUSE   NEW YORK

Copyright © 1992 by Rick Slone

All rights reserved under International and Pan-American
Copyright Conventions.
Published in the United States by Random House, Inc., New York and
simultaneously in Canada by Random House of Canada Limited, Toronto.

Library of Congress Cataloging-in-Publication Data

Slone, Rick.
Brown shoe/Rick Slone.—1st ed.
p.   cm.
ISBN 0-679-40093-1
I. Title.
PS3569.L66B7   1992   813'.54—dc20   91-35860

Manufactured in the United States of America

First Edition

Book design by Lilly Langotsky
The text of this book is set in Janson.

To Bernard and Selma Slone,
MY PARENTS

"There will always be a cunt or a revolution
around the corner . . ."

FROM Tropic of Capricorn

BY HENRY MILLER

ACKNOWLEDGMENTS

Thanks to Larry Lucchino.
This was his idea.

BROWN SHOE

ilencio untied his boots. They were promised to Truegas. The numbness which had first taken hold of his mind had spread to his fingers so that the simple act of untying the knots required his full concentration. He felt nothing, although he knew his fate, knew without having been told. He was a traitor, not a fool, and he acquiesced. What else could he do? Nor did he blame Roberto. Were the situation reversed—had Silencio the pistol, were Roberto sitting in the dust untying his boots—he, Silencio, would do the same. No, he did not blame Roberto. He was doing what he must. Roberto, too, had acquiesced.

Every death is untimely. When it comes as a blessing, it is long overdue. Sometimes, like now, it announces itself. Even so, few are ever prepared. Silencio was not among them. He was not ready; but given an extra hour, a year, ten years, he still would not be ready. His mind was numb, but not his heart, and in the dung and dust of the corral, surrounded by his compadres, amid those whom he had betrayed, he sobbed. Through his tears he repeated the names of his children while the threads of his life unraveled.

Roberto sat down beside him. Silencio, overcome with shame and weariness, laid his head on Roberto's thigh. They waited together, Roberto stroking the head of the sobbing man. The sky turned light. Clouds covered the mountains down to the lake.

Gavilan, Roberto Gavilan, could not predict how this would affect the men. Not much, he guessed. There were few surprises left. They had marched all night and the wind opposed them the whole climb to the pass. There had been no moon, the trail had been narrow, the snow in places knee deep. Their last meal had been the morning before and the horse had been undercooked. Now they would spend the day in that dung-filled corral waiting for dark. It would rain; or worse, it would clear and they'd have to sleep hidden among the boulders. And later, having learned they'd been wrong about a comrade's loyalty, they would march all night again.

Gavilan sent Paco to guard the trail from below and Truegas back toward the pass. Truegas carried his new boots. Among the men a canteen and a bag of coca went from hand to hand. The coca blunted the sharpness of things—of hunger, and thirst, of dread, regret, and hope. Hope was worse than hunger. Hope was the fist, hunger the back of the hand.

The men sat with their backs against the corral's low stone wall. Their faces told nothing. They waited for their leader to speak, to justify once again the anguish their lives had become. Gavilan began a sentence not knowing how it would end, thinking only that this man's death should not be the waste his life had been.

We become our greatest mistake, he told them. With a single betrayal a man becomes a traitor for as long as he is remembered. Gavilan was thinking out loud, rambling, remembering everything they had ever done for Silencio. The list was long. He picked his memory clean. He mentioned nothing Silencio had done for them, and Silencio had done his share. In Villarica his shoulder had taken a knife meant for Gavilan's back. It was a reflex, what Silencio had learned in the mountains: to live without hesitation, to act with abandon, the lesson for all of them. And their reward as well. A heart can grow to where it dwarfs the mind, it can grow to the size of courage—and bigger, to selflessness and stupendous generosity. But Silencio had become his greatest mistake and now nothing else mattered.

By the time Gavilan had finished it was time to change the guards again. He asked Silencio if what he had said was true. Silencio nodded it was without lifting his head to look at Gavilan or the others. And in a way it was. The way that with a pot on your head you say the world is black.

The men shifted their bodies in search of a comfort which was not to be found. They dipped tenpenny nails into the gourds of lime, catalyst for the coca leaves they incessantly chewed. They pulled ponchos around their shoulders. They needed sleep, food, warmth. They wanted for a thousand things more. What Gavilan

had for them was a newspaper clipping three weeks old, disinte-
grating along the creases.

"Roberto Gavilan, alleged leader of the terrorist Zapato
Moreno, was assassinated in his sleep Wednesday night in his
mountain stronghold. This is the report of Comandante Sanchez
Mosquevera, head of the antiterrorist battalion headquartered in
Huaráz."

Gavilan paused. Without looking up, he could feel their eyes
locked on him.

"The assassination occurred in the central highlands, where for
more than a year Gavilan and a force estimated at between fifty and
two hundred men have conducted a reign of terror." The mention
of "fifty to two hundred men" brought some smiles. "The central
highlands have been designated an emergency zone under the
command of Colonel Escobar Pino Rinaldi. Comandante Mosquevera has declined to release further details of the assassination
pending a full investigation, but he did not deny a report that
undercover agents had infiltrated the Zapato Moreno and were
behind the killing of the rebel leader."

There was more about the murder and sabotage that had been
attributed to the rebels, about their attacks on police barracks,
about their "Marxist" philosophy and their desire to return to the
ways of the Indian past. There was no need to read it all. Little was
true. Gavilan folded the clipping and replaced it in his pocket. He
watched the men. They were waiting for some clue as to how they
should think or feel. He looked from face to face. "What do you
think?" He directed his question to Emilio, whose long legs were
stretched out in front of him and crossed where his bare bony
ankles jutted from his boots. "How do I look to you?" Gavilan
asked.

"Not well," Emilio answered.

"But alive?"

"If I had to say one way or the other," Emilio said. "In this light
it's hard to be certain."

His comment produced a snicker which then ignited arcs of
laughter around the corral until the whole circle was laughing,
except for Silencio. Then the laughing stopped, and once again
they were tired, ragged, hunted, lonesome men. Desperation settled like the dust over all of them.

Gavilan yanked Silencio to his feet. "Look!" he commanded. Silencio went slack, like a cat held by its skin at the nape. His head drooped to his chest. "Look closely!" Gavilan jerked Silencio's head by his hair so the men could see his face. "Study him," he said. "Fix him in your minds. Remember his every feature so that should you see him again, on the blackest night in the blackest cave in these mountains, you will know him. Do it quickly. He won't be here for long." He let go of Silencio's collar. Silencio dropped like rag.

"You may think that you know him already. It's Silencio, you think, your comrade, your brother, but don't be fooled. This isn't the Silencio we know. Another has taken the place of that loyal, unselfish soldier who fought at our sides, who three times was wounded, who shared our food, our struggle, our aspirations. That man has been replaced by a traitor who has turned on his friends and his beliefs for the promise of a paltry reward. That man has been replaced by a weakling without the will to carry out his treacherous obligation.

"Examine him closely, *compadres*. Study him, and when you are finished with him, study yourselves. Search out that part of you which, when faced with a slow, torturous death, would choose, as Silencio did, to betray his friends and his ideals.

"Find it. It is there, I assure you it is there. Dig it out, dig out that part which considers itself more important than the lives of eleven brave men, more important than the cause which has given you the only moments of freedom and dignity you have had in the whole of your otherwise stinking, shit-filled lives. And when you have, when you've got it in your grasp, you must kill it as surely as this imitation of Silencio will be killed today.

" 'But how?' you ask. Whole men, you know how to kill. You aim a gun, you pull a trigger, you stick them with a knife. It is straightforward. Easy. It's sad, isn't it, how easy it becomes? But to kill only part of a man? To kill the weakling, the opportunist, the traitor? How does one do that? How?" He looked around the circle. Even the chewing had stopped.

"No? You don't know how? Let me tell you. You kill it with the only real weapon you have, the only one you have ever had. You kill it with your will. You burn it out with the hot fire of your will, you slice it out with the battle-hardened steel of your will, you strangle it with the irresistible strength of your will. It's the weapon all great men, all great martyrs, all great visionaries have honed to perfection.

"The newspaper claims I have been killed by an infiltrator, an assassin. And who is this infiltrator? You have guessed. None other than our Silencio here. Look at him. Our poor Silencio, who at this moment cannot summon the courage to face the men he betrayed, to look you in the eyes."

Silencio was sobbing again. Gavilan told him to tell the men the plan for the assassination, but he could only shake his head and sob, and so Gavilan, knowing it would have sounded better from Silencio, had to tell the story himself.

Silencio had been given permission to go home to visit his dying mother. On his return he was captured by Mosquevera's men. He was tortured, and threatened with worse. He could, however, they told him, save himself if he did as they asked. They asked him to assassinate Gavilan. His reward would be his life, a hundred dollars, and a commission in the army. He was given a pistol to do the job, and grenades to cover his escape.

An opportunity arose almost as soon as Silencio was back in camp. He asked to borrow a blanket from Gavilan, who told him he wouldn't loan him the only blanket he had, but suggested that they should sleep together under the blanket, and Gavilan would throw his coat over them as well. Silencio thanked him for the offer, then got under the blanket with him, with his loaded .45 and the grenades.

Silencio lay awake all night, unable to bring himself to pull the trigger. Gavilan would not have known except that in the morning he found a safe-conduct pass in Silencio's name issued by Mosquevera on the ground cloth on which they had slept. Gavilan had said nothing of the incident until this morning, although he watched Silencio closely and doubled the guard around himself at night. Silencio did not get another opportunity.

Two days ago a courier had passed Gavilan the clipping. With no information to the contrary, the command apparently assumed the plot had been carried through. Gavilan had given them no reason to believe otherwise. His hope was that if he was thought to be dead, they would relax the overflights and the patrols. San Juan was another lesson in hope: Josélito dead, Córto dead, Valdepenas captured, which was worse than dead.

Gavilan felt nothing for Silencio. His rage at the betrayal had spent itself through the days of continual marching. He had seen enough men die, good and bad, that he felt no more for Silencio's passing than one does for a tick of the clock. They were, he knew, all of them, already dead.

That Silencio would not cooperate in the drama, would not say his lines, frustrated Gavilan. They were not as effective coming out of Gavilan's mouth. In Silencio's version, Gavilan was more generous, more noble. The men, whose attention had been briefly held by the clipping, cared only for food and rest. It took all Gavilan could summon to move them even a little. Their resources were depleted, nearly gone. Nothing, Gavilan thought, should be wasted. Silencio's death should not be wasted either.

"I don't blame you, Silencio," he said to him, not as the betrayed commander, but tenderly, like an older brother. "It isn't hard to understand why you did as you did. In the hands of that shark Mosquevera the best you could hope was that your death would be quick. And then he offered you a hundred dollars, which is more money than you ever imagined, and a commission in the army, which you knew was license to steal thousands more. In your situation, in the hands of that butcher, who wouldn't have done as you did?" He did not mention that the bullets Mosquevera had given him were blanks, that the grenades were duds.

Gavilan squatted and put his face to Silencio's, using intimacy as he had used tenderness a moment before, as a stratagem to squeeze the most from the moment. He lifted Silencio's chin and looked him in the eyes. He smelled Silencio's reeking breath. "Who wouldn't have done as you did? No one, Silencio. And most, just like you, when the decisive moment came would have also lost their nerve, because most are cowards. Most would rather live the hideous lives they live than risk them for a chance at something better. Most choose the familiar even if that is misery and squalor and injustice. Isn't that so, Silencio? We've learned nothing if we haven't learned that."

Gavilan stood, and rising up, swung so hard and with such sudden ferocity that his aim suffered. His hand grazed Silencio's head, merely knocking off his hat. Gavilan's momentum whirled him around and he fell, and the anger he thought had spent itself, the fury he thought he had risen above, broke free. He was no longer acting. The toe of his boot caught Silencio under the chin and lifted him up off the ground. Silencio's teeth were gone. A second kick and the sound of sticks breaking were Silencio's ribs. Silencio curled up, cried out, his mouth a bloody hole.

Two men leapt from the circle, tackled Gavilan, pinned him down. He was no match for them, but on his back he made a show of punching and swearing. Emilio sat on his chest and the other on his arms. Gavilan spat at Emilio, who simply turned his face and sat on Gavilan's chest until Gavilan was exhausted and limp. Then Emilio helped him to his feet, dusted him off, and returned to his seat against the wall of the corral.

Gavilan's calm, only a pretense before, now was real. Drained of anger and frustration, his heart filled with affection for these men who had chosen to share his fate. Even Silencio. He wiped Silencio's face, which was streaked with dirt, vomit, blood, and tears. He held the canteen to the man's swollen lips. He put his mouth to Silencio's ear. Until now it had all been for the others, but what he was about to say was for Silencio alone.

He thanked him for all he had given. It had been everything and it had not been enough. He told him that he understood, and he did understand. He knew the pig Mosquevera and expected no one to withstand his torture. For what? To return and live with hunger and fatigue? To be hunted day after day, to band with desperate men on behalf of people who feared and loathed them, whose wish was simply to be left alone?

Gavilan helped Silencio to his feet. It had begun to snow. The mountain across the lake was hidden in clouds. Placing Silencio's arm over his shoulder, his own arm around Silencio's waist, Gavilan walked him down to the water. The Indians believed gods lived below the surface of this lake in palaces made from silver. The gods were white-skinned, tall, bearded, cruel, and greedy beyond belief. Their demands were unending, their appetites insatiable. In return they were tightfisted with their blessings. At their most generous, they were indifferent.

Gavilan wet his shirttail and cleansed the blood and puke caked at the corners of Silencio's mouth. He offered Silencio water from his cupped hands. He told Silencio that he forgave him, that he knew Silencio was not a coward. Courage is a cat, he said. It can be neither summoned nor courted. It comes and goes as it pleases, favors some more than others for reasons of its own.

"You're a brave man," he said, and he was. Silencio was among the bravest. Not brave enough, was all, not for the choice he had to make. Brave enough for most of life, brave enough even for death, but not brave enough for that.

The two stood below the bank, out of sight of the others. The wind sent small waves against the shore which lapped against the toes of Gavilan's boots and over Silencio's bare feet. They embraced. "My children . . ." was all Silencio could say. His voice trailed off. His children would be taken care of, Gavilan promised, before he placed a hand over Silencio's eyes and put a bullet into his head.

Gavilan walked back to the corral. He had never felt worse. "Bury him," was all he said.

The rest of the day, lying among the rocks, unable to sleep, Gavilan wondered why Mosquevera had taken the trouble to recruit an assassin, then armed him with blanks and dud grenades.

here's a stock market theory that says the public is always wrong. Wrong no matter what. If Joe Square is buying, the smart money sells. You might say the same is true with photography: if the public is looking east, then point your camera west, which is exactly how I got the shot of Inez Pello watching a field of the best two-year-olds in the country romp over her husband Moosh. Every telephoto at the track that day was pointed at him lying in a heap out there like some busted puppet. Meanwhile they miss the expression on his old lady's face, and they miss Azimuth down the homestretch, the saddle empty, stirrups flapping.

I know what you're thinking. Anyone who's seen the picture says the same identical thing. How could I be so in*sen*sitive? What about her *feel*ings? Look at her *face*, they say to me. Yeah, I say, *look* at her face!

Maybe they'd feel different if they knew Inez like I do. Normally, when a person's getting some on the side, I say more power to them. Of all the things people do to each other in this world, I can think of plenty worse. Except Moosh himself was a decent sort of guy. His big problem was he had blinders on where Inez was concerned.

Then again, nobody bought the picture, which probably goes to show you. Maybe it *was* in bad taste. No one would touch it. That much I know. Of course half of them didn't even look at it. They have their own photographers, they told me. Or they bought their photos from the agencies, I should hook up with an agency, they said. The agencies told me get some experience, go see the papers, they had trouble enough getting work for the guys they already had. I don't know. Maybe I'm meant to be a cook, maybe I should forget this photography stuff. Could be I'm getting a message here.

Nothing wrong with cooking for a living, I suppose. After all, where would I be if it weren't for Blacky? Tapped out, visa expired, couldn't go home if I wanted to. That's where I was when I met him. Couldn't even speak the language. Took me three months to figure out that *sopa* wasn't soap and *ropa* wasn't rope and *dinero* wasn't your dinner. Then Blacky—he doesn't know me from Adam, I'm one of a thousand gringos came down here to climb or for the beach or to make a connection, decides to stay, or *has* to stay—Blacky gives me a job busing tables and eight weeks later I'm standing at his elbow at the stove. Nah, I've no complaints with cooking. Some people would even call me a chef. I've been in the kitchen, what—two years? But I'm no chef. A lot of carpenters can build a house if you hand them the blueprints. That don't make them an architect.

But Blacky, now, he *is* a chef, *and* a carpenter, and he could be an architect or any other damn thing he put his mind to. He fixed up this falling-down dump of a house on a back street in Miraflores, turned it into a three-star restaurant. Red tile roof, high beamed ceilings, hardwood floor, wrought iron, courtyard in back where we serve lunches, flagstones, shady, got a fountain, herb garden, nice. Best place to eat in the capital. Everybody knows Blacky's. And Blacky, he did it all by himself.

All over the walls is art, Blacky's collection, stuff done by his friends and patrons of the place, some pieces taken in trade for bar tabs Blacky let run, others by artists from New York, or France or Germany. He's got two of my photographs, I might add, one is hanging right there as you come in the door, the very first thing you see: the one of the people at the bus stop. Probably cost him a hundred bucks just to have it framed. He told me he liked it, which is why I gave it to him, but I didn't expect him to hang it in the restaurant, knowing how particular he is, and all his ideas on art, what is and what isn't.

Then he went and *bought* the second one from me, the sneezing nude, although all he's done for me, I offered to give it to him for nothing, a present just like the first. But Blacky insists on paying me. Told me he wanted to be the first to actually buy one of my pictures, and besides I'd given him one already. Name your price, he says, and I did, of which he pays me exactly half. You don't get to be where Blacky is by paying the asking price for anything. Then again, I asked triple what I wanted. You don't hang out with Blacky every day for a couple of years without picking up a trick or two.

Wine is something else Blacky knows. He's got the best cellar in the city. For me the distinctions between one bottle and the next are blurry when I'm stone sober. Wine tasters are the other group of people where you have your spitters and your swallowers. Cruz told me that out at the track one day. Inez Pello, Cruz told me, spits. I pretended I didn't know.

I like cooking fine, working at Blacky's and all, but living down here has been an adjustment. I look around the city, millions of people, millions and millions, it gives me the same kind of feeling I get looking at an ant farm. Interesting, yeah, but the whole thing falls on the floor, who cares? Get out the bug spray and the broom. All those people out there—sick, poor, lonely, this, that, you start to worry about them you'll only eat yourself up. There are people who can talk about brotherhood and not sound like fools or saps, and I don't know that there's some of them even believe what they're saying, it's a noble thing, but if you say to me you care about everybody, as in Humanity, I say you don't care about anybody, as in Nobody. There's no trick to loving someone a continent away.

I never thought about any of this until I came down here. Actually, it was a couple months after I got here that I really began to think about it, after the money ran out and my cameras got stolen and my surfboards, and living under a tarp at the beach didn't seem as great an idea as it did back up in Baltimore. People who say we're all the same are wrong, we're not, but I don't have the time or the patience to make decisions case by case. I got my prejudices: I'm for the Orioles. I'm for the American League against the National League. I'm for the East against the West, and the North against the South. I'm for the underdog against the favorite. I'm for my family, I'm for my friends. I know where I stand.

This is neither here nor there. Blacky is how I got off on this tangent. What's important to him is the restaurant. He's here all day, works here, sleeps here, has a bedroom upstairs. You pass by day or night you'll see his car in the lot, a '62 Chevy Impala convertible that doesn't convert anymore because as long as he's had it he never once put the top up and now he can't, the mechanism's seized, totally rusted out. The only time he leaves is first thing in the morning to do the buying. More often it's the last thing he does before he goes to bed. He plans the menu from recipes he invented or stole. He selects the wines. We work side by side. He lines me out on every dish, tastes everything that leaves the kitchen. When things get slow he sometimes leaves the cooking to me and goes out to entertain. Plays piano. By ear. Can't read a note. Classical, jazz, bossa nova, does a great Jerry Lee Lewis and Ray Charles even better, dark glasses and all. Got a baby grand, a Chickering, out front. I'll never forget the name because single-handed I was the one who moved it in. Almost single-handed. The other two guys had trouble lifting their feet. We could fit four tables in the space it takes, and we could use those tables, too, small as the place is. If you don't call by Thursday, you don't get a reservation for Saturday night. Keep it hard to come by, Blacky says. The place seats thirty. We do two sittings, fifty, sixty dinners on weekends, a little slower during the week.

It's been no different tonight. I'm searing the lamb for dinner fifty-one. A regular customer. He likes it so rare it's cold in the middle. "Pittsburgh blue," they call it cooked like that. You sear it first, then pass it across the open oven door, it's done. Blacky's out front schmoozing, playing piano. I'm back here by myself, or almost. The salad guy is gone, and the prepster, which leaves just me and Peregrina. She's going through the dirty dishes like a John Deere through a wheat field. She only stops to toss her braids back over her shoulder when they drop into the suds. Peregrina's like most of the Indians you see in the city, life seems to chew them up from the inside out. They age like dogs, seven to one.

First thing I do once the meat is set on the plate, side of white beans, a crème-fraîche mint sauce drizzled over top, I toss my apron into the hamper, put my head under the tap. The kitchen is 110 degrees in the shade. I sweat through my clothes every night. The sweat rolls off me. I change my shirt, towel off, run a comb through my hair, pour myself a Scotch, and take a seat in the back of the dining room where I can listen to Blacky and watch the customers eat. You handle ten pounds of raw meat a night, three pounds of butter, garlic, black pepper, fish, devein shrimp, up to your wrists in olive oil, have a taste of this, a bite of that, you lose your appetite, but watching other people eat something you cooked, well . . . Once in a while you get somebody shows a spark of appreciation. For the most part they can take it or leave it, but what do you expect? These people are only as hungry as someone can be who hasn't eaten since lunch. A truly hungry person, I guarantee you, will not send his meal back to the kitchen, even if it is a "fishy" fish. One of these times some fussy broad sends her plate back, I'm going to stitch her lips shut and see what that does to her standards.

Two A.M. The customers are gone and the busboys have wiped the tables and put up the chairs and Peregrina's polished off the last of the dishes and there's only me and Blacky left. There's a bottle of red on the table. He pulls out the coke, lays four lines on a saucer, and offers all four to me. I was ready to call it a night, but now I'm good for another hour. Blacky lays out an hour's worth for himself.

Sometimes after everybody leaves we'll stick around and play music together, I play a little guitar myself, Blacky on the Chickering. Sometimes we'll throw darts, or we'll cruise the clubs, see who's around. Mostly we just shoot the breeze. I would have thought I'd of heard Blacky's whole rap by now; anything he had to say about himself I would have guessed he'd have already said to me. He told me about his mother, who was a cook herself, and about the people she worked for, rich, rich people, but nice, and how they moved them out of the barrio and sent Blacky to some swank private school and then picked up the tab for his college. He told me stuff about his ex-wife, the things she used to like to yell while they were doing it, and he told me about whose palms you had to cross to accomplish this or that in the capital. He told me what it was like to grow up in a barrio, the gang wars and all. He gave me the skinny on about half the women in Miraflores. He showed me his checkbook one night to prove a point which I've since forgotten. This is all to say I thought I knew the guy pretty well. In fact I thought I knew everything there was to know about him: what he'd done, what he was doing, what he hoped to do, and I would have bet you any amount I could predict what he was about to do next. But what he tells me while he's uncorking the bottle of wine, I couldn't have predicted in a hundred years.

"Bobby," he says, twisting in the corkscrew, "you heard of the Zapato Moreno?"

This is a rhetorical question. Who hasn't? They do half the stuff the papers claim they do, they're very busy people, not to mention nasty, but you can't trust what you read in the papers. It's no different here than it is back home.

"You contemplating joining up?" I ask. We're doing drugs, drinking, it's late, and I'm not attuned to a serious political discussion.

Blacky raises an eyebrow. He starts a sentence, stops, starts again, stops again, takes a swallow from his glass, takes a breath, exhales. "You know what a bagman does?"

"Bag man? Yeah, let's see. Bag man, bag man . . . Sure. Bag man: wears three coats even in summer; totes rubbish around in a shopping bag, hence the name. Usually a lady, though, babushka on her head, men's shoes, no laces, talks to herself . . ." I'm still not synched to the proper conversational tone.

"A bagman collects money," Blacky says. "For illegal purposes. For clandestine organizations." He says it like he's reading the dictionary. I want to believe he's building to a punch line, some variation of a joke he's told me a dozen times, like the one about the Polish terrorist who blows up a bus and burns his lips on the tailpipe. "I work for the Moreno," he says.

First I don't know what to think, and then I think what a fool he played me for, and then what else has he lied to me about? I remember a time I danced with a slim boyish girl. Turns out she's a slim girlish boy and everyone knew but me.

Some part of me is saying, hey, what's the big deal? You got stuff you don't tell Blacky. What is he, your wife? Another part, the part of me that had Blacky figured, had him down pat, knew all his moves and has just been juked, *that* part wants to duck this whole scene. "Did I tell you I saw Eddie Arcaro out at the track this afternoon? Surprised me how tall he is." I feel if I don't make a joke out of this, I'm going to be very pissed off. Last time I even remotely felt a burn like this coming on is a big reason why I'm down here in the first place. "Yeah, I was talking horses to an American out at the track this afternoon, tall, lanky guy, which is probably why I don't recognize him right off, I mean this is *Eddie Fucking Arcaro* I'm chatting with! In the paddock at Montesucre!

Be like you bumping into Toots Shor in the Belgian Congo or whatever they call it now. Zimbangwe. Anyway, we're waiting for the start of the sixth race, and I'm explaining my theory of handicapping, and he's listening to me, very polite, a real gentleman, had a harelip, very tall, wore a bow tie as I remember, blue, and he says to me, after he listened to the whole spiel beginning to end, he says to me, looks me directly in the eye, probably the only guy in this whole goddamn country tall enough to look me in the eye, he says, 'If you're a handicapper,' he says to me, 'My name is Eddie Arcaro.' "

Ordinarily that'd break Blacky up. If I know anything, it's how to make the guy laugh. Now he's watching the blue smoke from his cigarette. "Listen to me, Bobby," he says. *Bow-bee* he calls me, like they all do down here.

I don't want to. I don't want to hear this.

"I'm a contact in the capital for the Moreno," he says, talking right through me. "I pass information between the mountains and the city. I collect money."

I go for my wallet, pull out a fiver. "I hope I get a lapel button at least."

"Bobby, listen . . . ," he says.

"Five not enough?"

"Dammit, Shafto, will you shut up and listen to me? Please? Just shut up and listen for once!"

I shout right back. The volume's way up, the anger's coming. I feel the rumbles down in my chest.

"You read in the papers that Gavilan's dead?" he says, suddenly calm.

If you lived in the capital and you were blind, deaf, and illiterate, you read where Gavilan was dead. Gavilan's everywhere. Newspapers, magazines, TV, radio, everywhere. Remember when James Dean died? Roberto Gavilan, same deal. They can't ever get enough of Gavilan down here. Far as I know all the details aren't out of the mountains yet, Gavilan is like Bigfoot in a some ways, lots of people hunting him, reports of sightings, fuzzy photographs of his back from a distance, hard to take any of it seriously, but sure, I read where he's dead. Two, three weeks ago already. "So?" I tell him.

"So he's alive," Blacky says.

What's this got to do with me is what I'm wondering, but before I can fully formulate the question, while I'm still *rehearsing* in my mind the sneering sort of tone I plan to use, he tells me what this has to do with me, and maybe it's because he seems to have read my mind, or maybe because I can sometimes read his, I get this *feeling* low behind my rib cage which I associate with the time I was fourteen and the firecracker went off inside the pocket of my shirt.

Blacky answers the question I hadn't had to ask. "Gavilan needs a favor."

"Hey, whoa, don't look at me, pal. I don't even know how to play bridge," I tell him, "let alone blow one up." Another thing I don't know how to do is shut my yap. I want to, but I can't.

Blacky stands up, walks away, turns around, comes back to stand right over me. He points a finger in my face. He's shouting now. In two years before tonight I never heard him shout. "You can't lay off for even a minute, can you? Not for a single goddamn minute. You're acting like a first-rate asshole. If I had any idea what an asshole you are, I never would have said a word. You're making me regret I ever mentioned this to you. You're not the only photographer in the capital. You're not even the only one I can trust. I just thought I'd ask you first. I thought you'd like the chance, asshole."

He walks around the table, snorts "Asshole" under his breath. Then he sits down, sliding his chair in close, leaning his round dark face toward me, talking low and slow. Cool. Back in control. Blacky again. The Blacky I know. "Gavilan's never been interviewed. Never been photographed. Never. He wants you to do it. The interview. The pictures. People all over are interested in Gavilan. You want to be a photographer, right? A photojournalist? This is your chance."

"Me?"

"You." He pointed.

"Hold on a second here, Blacky, boy. I think I'm missing something. All the journalists there are in this city, must be hundreds, from the dailies, the magazines, the wire service stringers, the foreign correspondents, the agency guys, and you're telling me Gavilan wants me, yours truly, Bobby Shafto"—I pointed at myself with both hands—"a goddamn *cook*, to take his picture?"

Blacky nodded.

"Get real." I leaned back and folded my arms across my chest.

"What's so hard to understand? He's a friend of mine. You're a friend of mine. He knows about you. I recommended you."

"Because we're such good friends, you and me."

"Other reasons, too."

"We're such good friends, how come all this time I think you're Joe Ordinary Blow you're running a fucking revolution out of the restaurant?"

"And you're a total asshole." Blacky stands again and walks away. He paces back and forth with his hands in his pockets. Silent. Thinking. Walks over to the Chickering. Slams his fist on the keys, *Plong. Plong. Plong.* A minute later he sits back down across from me, lights a smoke, lights another for me. My anger, which a moment ago was kicking up dust out on the horizon, seems not to be coming closer. Just like that, he hands me a smoke, I begin to remember we're friends, Blacky and me, that all my other friends are memories.

"You know what you remind me of?" he asks.

Yeah, I do know. A jealous broad.

"You remind me of a jealous broad." I smile. He smiles. "What's so funny, asshole?"

Nothing, I tell him, but now I'm smiling big. I have to pee. I push myself away from the table, stand up, and not too steady, Freddy.

"Choke the dragon," Blacky says.

"Wring out the monster," I finish the routine.

The bathroom's not made for a person my size. My two fists fill the sink. What I can see of myself in the mirror is my chest. I splash some water on my face. Blow my nose. Back to the table, Blacky's opened another bottle, filled my glass. I take a mouthful, slosh it around.

I ask him why me. That's the thing I don't get. He hasn't said why me.

"Couple of reasons. Gavilan hates the press. He vowed to never let a journalist near him."

"What's the big beef with the press? Without the press he's nothing. The press made him what he is."

"Exactly."

I still didn't get it. What was he up to if not attention? For himself, his cause . . .

"It's horseshit, Bobby. This whole guerrilla business is complete and total horseshit."

"You mean he's not who they say he is?"

"I mean they *made* him what they say he is." Blacky could see I wasn't catching on. "Suppose you tell me what you think you know," he said. "And I'll tell you if you're right."

I told him. I knew what everybody else knew. Had something to do with the Indians. How shitty they're treated and all. How they've been screwed since Pizarro. An Indian rights kind of trip, only instead of the marches and demonstrations that tied up traffic, and all those flyers they hand you on the streets so by the time you get home at night every pocket is stuffed with crumbled sheets of paper, and the spray-painted slogans everywhere—you won't find a wall within a hundred miles that isn't scribbled on—instead of all that annoying inconvenient bullshit, the Moreno were into blowing stuff up. Terrorism. And they hung dead dogs from the street-lights, the crazy fuckers. Kind of their calling card. But mostly the Moreno were up in the mountains and didn't bother you. It wasn't their fault twice a day you could be stalled in traffic holding your joint in your hand while a bunch of priests and college kids and other political loonies paraded down the middle of the street shouting and waving banners and shit.

Blacky covered his face with his hands.

"You telling me I don't know what I'm talking about?" I acted indignant. "What about last week when some of those whacked-out bastards made me late for the track? Missed the first race." I chanted and stomped my feet to give Blacky an idea of what I had to sit through. "Waited twenty minutes for them to pass. Right there where Ochoa hits the Avenida? By the brewery? Crazy sons of bitches cost me money. Frankie gave me a tip on Pasta Fazool. Went off at seven to one."

"What an asshole you are," he said, but he was smiling.

"If I'm such an asshole, why don't you wise me up?"

"I don't have the time. There may not *be* enough time. All you need to know for now is that Gavilan wants to tell his side of things. He wants a photographer. He wants someone at home in the mountains—he knows you climbed all through there—and most important he wants someone he can trust."

"He doesn't know he can trust me. He doesn't even know me."

"*I* know you."

I chewed on that a moment. Had to admit the idea excited me. A photojournalist. Had a nice sound to it. On the other hand it was hard to get a grip on any kind of reality here. I couldn't connect. Blacky a Moreno? Me in the mountains with Roberto Gavilan? I put those thoughts aside on account of a resolution I'd recently made: Good or bad, don't question your luck. I tried to think of something to say besides how crazy this was. "Seems to me it's to his advantage to have the army think he's dead. They'll stop chasing him."

"That's the point. The army knows he's alive. But nobody else. And if Gavilan's dead, so is the Moreno. He *is* the Moreno. No Roberto—no recruits, no support, no money."

"Maybe Jerry'll do you a telethon," I said and regretted it immediately. Sometimes my mind was a step behind my mouth. Usually.

Blacky let the sarcasm slide. "He asked me to find him a photographer. I found you."

Blacky laid out some lines, opened another bottle. He sat at the piano and I pulled my guitar off the wall where I hung it. We played. I thought about what Blacky had told me. Blacky and Gavilan. I try to put them together in my mind. They didn't go easy. You'd think, come the revolution, they'd put the torch to the restaurant first. Any day of the week you'll find the lyingest, cheatingest, thievingest, most corrupt bastards in the country, in the whole hemisphere probably, eating at Blacky's. I stopped in the middle of that Jerry Jeff song about desperadoes waiting for the train. "Just out of curiosity, how do you get to Gavilan?"

"From the barrio. I was Moreno before they called themselves Moreno. We were Los Sultanos back then. Gavilan was a little kid who used to hang around me and the older guys."

"Robbin' and stabbin' and lootin' and shootin'." I knew the story. "Ratchet in your waist."

"I stayed in touch after my mother and I moved out. The Sultans became the Zapato Moreno, Gavilan was sixteen or so, he wasn't a little kid anymore. He became their leader, El Jefe. Everybody knew what had happened to me, what I'd done and where I was. They knew I'd escaped the life. Sometimes some of them came to see me. To talk, ask advice, but mostly I think to see for themselves the living proof that someone had made it out. Gavilan came a couple of times. You sensed he was different right away. Special. Had a bigger view of things. The others saw my car, or the clothes, the money, just the surface. The effects. Roberto looked past appearances. He looked *into* things. He was interested in the abstractions. He wanted to find the source of whatever it was. And part of what made him special was that he could pull you along. I got to know him. One thing led to another . . . Okay? Now, are you interested in the job or not?"

"One thing I don't understand. How does a gang from the streets become guerrillas?"

"A long story. I'll tell you, but first I need to know. Are you in or out?"

"Where do I sign?"

"You'll leave within a week or two. I'm not sure. We have to arrange a place to meet."

"Don't you think I need to know more about the guy? Maybe do some research? The pictures, yeah, but an interview?"

"A photo essay, then. And I *told* you I'd fill you in. Everything you need to know. But later. Tomorrow, maybe. I'm wiped out."

"Tomorrow . . ." I look at my watch: almost seven. "Today is already tomorrow, and today's my day off."

"The next day, then. And one more thing," Blacky said as I got up to go. "Do the buying for me this morning, will you? San Isidro market. You know the routine. The list is on the wall by the walk-in. Any later than nine o'clock the good stuff is gone." We shook hands. Mine was sweaty, I don't know from the drugs or the wine or what, and I wiped my palm on my trouser first. "And one more thing, Bobby . . ."

"The market was your 'one more thing.' This is two more things."

"I didn't make a mistake here, Bobby, did I?"

"I think you did," I say. I'm putting on my jacket, black satin, orange bands on the shoulders. Orioles. "They give double coupons at the market at San Miguel."

"Bobby?"

"You mean if they wire electrodes to my balls do I tell them what I know?"

"C'mon, Bobby. Ease my mind here, man."

"Two-twenty or regular house current?"

"You truly are an asshole, you know that?"

"Take it easy, Blacky. I'm your boy."

A low gray ceiling hangs over the capital without interruption from May until the end of August. September shows morsels of light to a city grown accustomed to life without shadows, to muted colors and hazy outlines.

The house was on Venice, a narrow, curving, shady street in Miraflores. At one time the carriage house for the mansion beside it, it had been converted into an apartment with a living room and kitchen downstairs, and a bedroom and bathroom up. French doors off the living room opened onto the grassy yard. In the fountain a stone maiden poured water from a pitcher, and bougainvillea climbed the walls. A breeze rattled the palms. There was the splash of the fountain and the singing of morning birds. Jacaranda twined around a wrought-iron trellis up to a porch off the bedroom where a man, the morning paper folded in his hand, drank coffee at a glass-top table.

"Nin*aaa!*" he called through the open bedroom doors. He was in his fifties. He combed his thinning hair back from his high forehead. His glasses were tinted rose, the frames black, heavy, and rectangular. He wore the uniform of an army colonel. He looked away from the morning edition of *El Observador* into the bedroom. "Nina!"

Her wet bare feet left prints on the porch's wooden floor. Holding her white terry-cloth robe closed with one hand, she leaned over his shoulder and kissed him lightly on the cheek. She took a slice of bread from the table, moved to the railing, and tore small pieces to throw to the birds down by the fountain. Her wet hair, pulled back like a ballerina's, was brown and thick and just long enough to be gathered by a blue rubber band. Her small ears were flat against her skull, the lobes pricked with tiny diamonds.

"Well, Rinaldi, what great problem is eating away at you today?" she said in a tired, mocking tone.

"What makes you think something is, as you put it, 'eating me?'"

"Something must be on your mind." She sat on the railing and leaned against a post. "Something always is." A finch, bolder than the others, took a piece of bread from her fingers.

"It so happens you're right. It's Elena," Rinaldi said.

Nina tilted back her head and closed her eyes at the mention of the name. She had heard this before.

"It's been nearly two years," he said.

"Twenty months," she said to the birds quibbling down on the ground.

"Two years is a long time, don't you think?"

She tore another piece and threw it into the yard. "He was her son, Rinaldi. Her *son*. Why is that so hard for you to understand?"

"He was mine, too. Terrible things happen, yes, they do, they happen all the time. But life goes on."

"What do you want me to say, Rinaldi? That a mother shouldn't grieve?" She took another slice of bread from the table and sat down on the railing, her back against the post, one bare foot on the floor.

"She still refuses to come to the city. She used to love to come to the city, now she won't leave the ranch. And her garden, did I tell you? She had Luis take out all the roses and cover the beds with gravel. Luis told me this. He told me she hasn't been out to see the horses in weeks."

Nina, rather than throwing bread to the birds, was now throwing bread at them, not with any force or accuracy, the bread was too light, but the intent was there. She rolled a compact pellet between her thumb and forefinger and threw it hard. The birds seemed not to notice the difference.

"And time has only made it worse," Rinaldi went on. "Time and her seclusion. I can't be going back there every week, Nina. You know that. The ministry has been very fair to me, wouldn't you say? But their patience with me is wearing thin. I don't know what I'm going to do."

Her ammunition gone, she folded her arms across her chest, hugging herself. She looked down at the floor, at her footprints, retracing her steps around the table to Rinaldi and then back into the bedroom from which she had just come, from where they had spent the night together, and her thoughts tracked further back in time, twenty months, and then forward again to the present, to how weary she had become of their relationship, weary and impatient—with him, and with her dependence on him. "I haven't noticed that you've been suffering so terribly," she said, not looking up. She hated when he whined. He never used to whine. There was a time when she believed there was nothing which could ruffle him, no problems he couldn't solve, even hers, especially hers.

"I don't expect you to understand. How could you? Elena and I have been married twenty-eight *years*. We've lived a lifetime together. I have an obligation to her." Nina turned her back to him. Two birds by the fountain were pecking at the same crust of bread. "Twenty-eight years is longer than you've been alive."

Nina watched the birds maneuver for the crumb. The winner carried it away into the trees. She heard Rinaldi fold the paper, heard the rattle of his cup. She sat at the table, poured herself some coffee. Rinaldi offered her the bottle of brandy, but she covered her cup with her hand. He shrugged and poured some into his own. She lit a cigarette.

"You smoke too much," he said.

That was great, she thought, coming from him. He'd given her her first cigarette, but she didn't suppose he remembered. Not exactly her first, but the first she didn't have to smoke in the barn or bathroom. She held her robe closed with one hand and watched him read.

"And stop staring at me!" he shouted. He slapped the newspaper down. The paper toppled the creamer. He jumped out of his chair and, backing away from the table, examined his jacket and pants for cream. She watched the puddle spread to the table's edge and drip onto the floor. She made no move to clean up the mess. "I can't turn my back on her, Nina. I can't and I won't." He put a cloth napkin over the spill. "I love you dearly. I would do anything for you, you know that, don't you? Happily. Eagerly." She watched the cream drip onto the high black gloss of his shoe. He swore under his breath. He put his foot on the chair and wiped his shoe with another napkin; then, dropping it, mopped the floor, pushing the napkin around with his toe. He went into the house. She could hear the water running. He came back, drying his hands on a towel. She hadn't moved except to raise the cigarette to her lips. Rinaldi picked up where he had left off. "I've given you everything, haven't I? Everything you wanted. And you have paid me back many times over. But I'm not a lovesick puppy, Nina. I'm not so . . . so . . ." He searched for a word on the ceiling. "So *bedazzled* that I do not see that one day, sooner or later, you'll . . . What are you smiling about?"

"Nothing," she answered. The quick sardonic smile was gone.

"You were smiling. I saw you."

"It was nothing."

"Where was I?"

" 'Bedazzled,' " she said. "I mean 'not bedazzled.' " The smile reappeared. She hid it behind her brimming cup. The liquid was scalding and she put it down.

"Someday, Nina, you'll know what I mean. You'll understand. Someday you are going to find someone else, someone with whom you will want to make your own life, a life like I had with Elena, like your mother and father, God rest their souls, had together. I accept that fact. I am resigned to it. I neither like it nor look forward to it. I can only say that when the time comes I hope you will find someone who will mean as much to you as Elena does to me. Whether we live together or not, I don't deny the part she played in my life, and I won't desert her now."

Nina stirred her coffee. She blew on it. It was he who was staring now, waiting for her response.

"She was a beautiful woman," she said absently, staring into her coffee. She leaned over to sip from the cup without picking it up off the table. The coffee was still too hot. Despite her seeming indifference, she felt defeated. She did every time Elena was discussed. She crossed her legs, pulled the robe down over her knee.

"Please, Nina, try to understand. Think about my position."

He was always asking her to think about "his position" as if it were the only thing that mattered. She didn't want to think about his position. "Everyone loved her. I was foolish to think I could ever replace her," she said. She felt the onset of self-pity, and struggled to elude it. "I never truly believed I could. Maybe I *am* too young to understand."

Whether it was because she loved him, or because she needed him so badly—and she was unsure anymore that there was a difference—she found she could not remain angry at him. In his absences, which seemed now more frequent and more prolonged, she argued endlessly with him in her mind. But in his presence her anger disappeared. Was it the man himself, or what he provided? She didn't know. She wasn't sure she even wanted to know. But of one thing she was certain: she wasn't ready to face life without him.

She stubbed out the cigarette she had just lit and looked up at him. "Is there a reason for telling me this?" The edge was gone from her voice. "I mean now, again, this morning. Is there something I can do?"

He avoided her eyes. He adjusted his tie.

"There is, isn't there?" She pulled another cigarette from the pack, and left it on the table.

Mindful of the spill, he leaned across the table and placed his hand on hers. "I can't go myself," he said. "I would if I could, but I can't, and there's no one else I can send. She won't see anyone else, but she might see you."

As what he was saying began to sink in, Nina tried to pull away, but he closed his fingers and held her there. "Me? Why me? She hasn't spoken to me since before . . . before I moved away!"

"She always loved you, Nina. From the time you were a little girl. She saw a lot of herself in you. If she had had a daughter she always said she would have wanted her to be just like you, and then when you and Alejandro were engaged—"

Nina yanked her hand away. She picked up the cigarette, walked to the railing, and staring out across the yard, struck a match. "And what's the matter with you? Why can't you go?" She wondered what it was going to be this time. Another fishing trip with General Archuelo? "What is so important you can't go visit your wife?"

"I hadn't wanted to tell you before," he said. He was suddenly, unusually diffident. "I don't know why. Afraid of jinxing myself, I guess. I wanted to walk in one day with the stars on my shoulders and the braid on my hat. I wanted to wait until it was certain . . . so often things fall through . . . no fault of your own . . . It's my lifelong ambition. You can't know what it means, a boy from the streets to come up through the ranks . . . In any event, I've word they're reconsidering . . . the Gavilan thing and all. They're giving me a second look. The answer could come any time. So you see, I don't dare leave the capital. I wouldn't have asked you otherwise, if it weren't so important to me, if there were someone else who could go . . ."

"So now you want me to visit her," she said distantly. "Don't you think that that's a little much to ask of me? That it may even be a bit . . . peculiar?" There was little conviction in her protest. Rinaldi sensed her compliance. He took the cigarette away from her and ground it into the ashtray. He reached for her hand again and this time she did not draw away.

"It's not as if she knows about us. To her you're still the girl from the farm up the road, Alejandro's fiancée, the daughter of her closest friends. You'll remind her of better times. As soon as things quiet down, I'll go myself. I wouldn't ask you if there were anyone else. Think about her."

"Her? Think about *her?* What about *me!* I don't think I can face her, Rinaldi. I honestly don't think I can face going back there at all. After what's happened, how could I?"

"I'll have someone drive you to Huaráz, if you want. Luis can pick you up there and take you the rest of the way. Please, Nina. Do this for me."

"I need some time."

"You'll do it, then?"

"To prepare myself."

"Whenever you feel up to it. But soon. She's withering away," he said.

"Oh, Rinaldi! I can't believe you've asked me to do this. It'll be so awkward. What would I say? She doesn't want to hear from me. If she wanted to she would have called, or answered my letters. And even if it weren't to see her, I don't know if I could go back there now. So much has happened. So much sadness. I've spent all this time trying to get it out of my mind, I don't want to be reminded. I don't want it all stirred up again. The ranch, Father, Mother, Alejandro . . . It's so unfair of you to ask, Rinaldi. Anything but that."

"It won't be so bad. You'll see. You forget how beautiful it is. It will be all right, I promise. You'll visit Elena, you'll see the mountains again, maybe you'll visit some of your friends. It'll be fine. You'll see."

The colonel stood behind her chair. He had expected more trouble convincing her. He hoped he could be as persuasive with the Minister. She leaned her head back against him and closed her eyes while he smoothed her hair. A horn honked out on the street. He backed away, looked around for his hat.

"Do you have to leave this instant?" she asked.

"My driver is waiting."

"Just a few minutes longer. Please."

"The meeting with the Minister, remember?"

"But you said it wasn't until later."

"I have a briefing first," he said, which was, in a manner of speaking, true. "I can't inform the Minister until I'm informed myself, now can I?" He placed his hands on her shoulders. "Can I?"

She turned in her chair. "Why not have the person who's briefing you simply brief the Minister? Then you can spend the morning with me. We could go to the beach." She reached for her cigarettes.

"That would be the way to do it, I agree. Shorten the chain, one less link to distort the facts. Except . . ."

"Except what?" She stood and faced him. "We could go to the market together. I could fix you lunch. We could go to the beach. We never go to the beach anymore."

". . . except it isn't the way it's done. Half the government would be unemployed."

"What about tonight?" she asked, putting her hands on his lapels. "Oh, I forgot. The Uruguayan Embassy is tonight."

"Paraguayan." He put on his hat, adjusted it carefully.

"To hell with the Paraguayans, and the Uruguayans, too," she said. She pulled his hat down over his eyes. He let it stay that way, askew, then smartly saluted, making her laugh. She lifted the visor. She remembered something of what she had once found appealing about him. Why she loved him. It was at Mirasol, after dinner, everyone sitting around the table. Father, Mother, Elena, another rancher and his wife, Alejandro . . . Rinaldi, it was Captain Rinaldi back then. Uncle Rinaldi. She'd been sitting beside him as she always did, rearranging the seating if she had to. Dinner was over. He'd opened his silver case, and as if it were the most natural thing in the world, offered her a cigarette, flicked his lighter in front of her face. She was fourteen. Mother looked apalled. Father sputtered a moment, but Uncle Rinaldi distracted them with a story he was telling. After that she no longer had to sneak. He always treated her like that. Bought her her first low-cut dress to wear at the Stockmen's Cotillion. She was sixteen then. Her parents didn't approve of that either, but Uncle Rinaldi somehow convinced them. Though she was a child, he treated her as if she were a contemporary, with the same seriousness, the same consideration. He didn't tease her, or patronize, or call her "Teddy" like the others.

"And what's your agenda? Lunch with one of your friends? Where's Inez?"

How ironic, she thought, how now that she was an adult, and they were lovers, he treated her as a child. She brushed imaginary lint from the lapel of his jacket. "Inez has gone to Miami. With her lover. She won't be back until a week from Thursday. She's shopping, or so she says."

"You doubt the word of your friend?"

"Last time she went 'shopping' in Miami she came back with bigger, perkier breasts. Besides, Inez is more your friend than mine."

"Do I detect a note of jealousy in your voice, Nina, dear?"

"I'm perfectly happy with my breasts."

He laughed. "As am I. I'm speaking of my relationship with Inez."

"You know me better than that."

"I see her at the Jockey Club. I feel sorry for her, is all." He pushed up his sleeve and looked at his watch. "Well, if not Inez, something else is on your mind. I can tell. Come now, what is it? Quickly, I haven't all morning."

"As long as you're asking, there is a tiny something . . . ," she said.

"You needn't be coy. My car is waiting." He picked up his briefcase.

"Thursday night. Callao plays San Sebastian. I already have the tickets. Midfield. High up. What do you say?"

"Nina! You know what I think of your going to football games.

The crowds are completely out of control. Especially the San Sebastian crowd. They're maniacs. It's dangerous. Every game ends in a riot. People are always getting killed. You remember what happened last year when Callao played San Sebastian."

"But it's not like I'd be going alone, you'll be there, and besides, the game decides who goes to the play-offs. Please, Rinaldi."

"Even if I wanted to, which I don't, I still couldn't go. The Red Cross benefit is Thursday night."

"The papers say Eusebio is back at 100 percent."

"Nina, I'm on the *board*. I can't very well skip the dinner. I have a seat on the dais. I'm expected to be there. I've an obligation."

She pounded his chest with her fists in mock frustration. "Oh, dammit, Rinaldi. All I hear is about your obligations. To your job, to Elena, to the Red Cross. What about your obligation to me?" She realized the futility of her position, and the contradiction. Part of his attraction had always been who he was, his rank, his money, and the powerful circles in which he was accepted. "I'm sorry, Rinaldi." She smoothed the front of his jacket. "Of course you can't go. It just seems we have so little time together anymore. I don't mean to be bitchy. I understand. I do, really I do. I just wish it were different."

"It isn't easy for me either, Nina. Remember that. But I'll tell you what. I'll make it up to you. Saturday the Argentine Rodeo is in town. I'll get us tickets. We'll have dinner first. Do we have a date?"

She hugged him. She held his head and kissed him on the forehead. "Promise?"

He held up his hand as if he were taking an oath.

"And none of your friends tagging along?"

"Just the two of us."

"Oh, you do know how to make a girl happy, Rinaldi." She winked at him. "I've an idea. I'll go to the market, buy some fresh fish, and make us lunch. Just in case your appointment is canceled."

"I would say that that is highly unlikely."

"Then I'll eat the fish myself, and maybe the sun will come out and I can sunbathe in the yard." Her mood had brightened. "Are you sure we can't have dinner together tonight?"

"Not naked, I hope, Nina. Someone could see through the hedge."

"And tomorrow is out too?"

"Tomorrow is the Red Cross. But Saturday, you have my word. And I still don't like it you lying here in the nude. Someone could get the wrong idea."

"Someone else, you mean."

Rinaldi's face reddened. "Good-bye, my love," he said, and kissed her on the lips. It was he who had to raise his face to hers. He reappeared in the yard below the balcony and paused at the opened gate. She returned his wave with a salute. "I left a check for you on the dresser. Don't forget the rent is due," he yelled.

I won't, she thought. Her resentment flooded back, making her weary.

Twenty minutes later the gate opened again. She emerged in jeans, T-shirt, and dark sunglasses. Across the front of the shirt, CALLAO was printed above a drawing of the team mascot, a snarling puma, one paw resting atop a soccer ball. She carried a large straw handbag.

The cabbie held the door for her. "Where to, señorita?" he said, pulling away from the curb and throwing the arm on the meter.

"San Isidro market," she said settling back onto the seat and closing her eyes. "I'm in no hurry. You can take your time."

alixto Morro rubbed his shoulder and watched the other boy part the bushes to look again at the hut fifty yards up the path. "I don't know how you can see with those glasses you wear," Morro said.

Without taking his eyes from the hut, the boy, Tomás Weiss, whispered back, "Are we going in or aren't we?"

"The one lens is completely busted out and the one that isn't busted out is cracked. I don't know how you do it."

"We've been hiding here all day. I can't take it anymore."

"A little bit longer."

"We've got to get some food." Weiss contorted his long, bony body to stay concealed behind the bush. A bandanna, more like a filthy red rag, kept his blond hair off his forehead.

"At least we had that bread the old guy gave us. Think about them guys up at the mines," Morro said.

"That's what I mean. We're overdue already and we're, what— five hours away?"

Morro was sitting tailor-seat, his gun across his lap. His pock-marked skin showed through his sparse, scraggly beard. "You look really weird with those glasses, man. I'd think you'd be better off with no glasses at all." He rested his back against a tree trunk. This was his seventh month in the mountains. Weiss was relatively green, and Morro, remembering his own first weeks—the paranoia, the physical strain, the effort to prove himself, and the struggle to master the thousand tricks of survival—sympathized with his comrade. "You ever stop to think about what people might think if they see a person wearing a pair of glasses like that? They'd think there goes a person who doesn't have all his marbles."

"We got a job to do here, Morro."

Morro rolled onto his hands and knees to place his mouth near Weiss's ear. "Go ahead," he hissed. "Be my guest. Walk up the path, walk past that dog, knock on the door, you don't know who's inside there, could be anybody, could be ten armies inside, but you want to go? Go!" He rolled back onto his rear end. "Look, Weiss. I'm hungry just like you, tired just like you, I'm just as wet and just as dirty and just as cold, and I say we wait."

"We got a mission."

"Our mission is to stay alive. Ask Roberto."

"You got to eat to live. It's not like there's a hut every ten feet. If they don't have any food to sell, maybe they know someone who has. We'll never find out hiding in these bushes. We've been here an hour and all we seen was a woman and couple a kids."

"And the dog," Morro said. "Don't forget the dog."

Weiss squatted beside Morro. "I'm going. I'll find out one way or the other. You coming with me?"

Morro pushed Weiss over onto his seat. "Patience, man. Relax. Breathe. Remember what happened the last time we barged into someplace." Morro opened his shirt to show Weiss the purple bruise. "Almost took my head off with that goddamn shovel."

"You can't count that guy. He was pissed off to start with. Had nothing to do with us."

"That's my point. They're all like that. That's what I'm telling you. Wait a few more minutes. Try thinking about something else. Take your mind off your belly. Think about those college babes back in the city."

"High school. I was in high school. And I thought you were going to be a priest."

"I was thinking about maybe being a priest, yeah. So what?"

Weiss stood up. "I'm going."

"What're you going to tell them?"

"Tell them the truth. We want to buy some food."

"Suppose they ask who for?"

"They're not gonna ask who for. They know who for. They just got to look at us to know who for." Tomás Weiss put his arms out to the side and held his rifle out for Morro to examine him. Weiss walked up the path. Morro let him go. Weiss walked past the dog and knocked on the door. When no one came he knocked again. He listened. Hearing nothing, he pushed the door open and went inside. It was one room, a dirt floor, a table, chairs, a pot on the fire. Through the window in the back wall he saw a woman running away from the hut over a newly turned field. There was a baby on her back and another in her arms and two more children holding on to her skirt. They were little and the ground was uneven and they stumbled every few steps. Morro joined Tomás Weiss inside and they watched the woman until she had disappeared across the field.

"All we wanted was food," Tomás said.

"She don't know that," Morro answered.

"She didn't wait to find out, either."

"What'd you expect? Her last guests strung up her dog."

"It wasn't us." Weiss sounded hurt.

"She don't know that either. She knows a bunch of guys look like us, dress like us, shouting slogans, come up here and hang her dog for no reason in the world she can think of. She knows last week the mayor from Viracocha disappeared, and probably she heard about the guy got shot up at Santa Cruz. Same guys, same outfits, same slogans. She don't know if it's us, the army, or who, and she don't care. Maybe we can scrounge something to eat. See what's in the pot."

"You know what Roberto says about that."

"We'll leave her the money. I didn't mean we was going to steal it. Shit, I'm starved. Aren't you?"

"I'm OK. It's for the others. Up at the mines."

"How about the dog? I heard dog's not too bad you cook it right. We'd be doing her a favor we took the dog."

The dog was big and its fur was thick and matted where it had fur, and where it didn't, where the mange had gotten it on its belly and down one flank, the black skin was stretched over its bones. Only by looking at the bare flank could you see how skinny the dog really was. Its lips were drawn back over long, yellow teeth. The noose had worn a deep, bloody groove in the flesh of its neck. It turned slowly in the wind. Weiss cut the rope with a knife and the carcass dropped to the mud. It landed stiff and toppled onto its side. Tomás pushed his blond hair off his forehead, fixed his glasses on his nose, and put his knife away. "Must've been a pretty mean bastard," he said, nudging the dog with his toe.

"Not as mean as the bastard who hung him."

"Mean and ugly."

"They're all that way up here. Comes from eating corn. Comes from living at the end of a very short rope all your life," Morro said.

"I dunno. Maybe. Maybe it's just the breed."

It was already late in the day and cold and the rain that had stopped for a few hours was falling again. They hadn't slept since the camp at Blue Lake twenty-four hours before and had eaten only a few slices of bread. But they had had water to drink and they knew they could go without the food if they had to. It took an hour to skin and butcher the dog. They wrapped the meat and the organs in a rag which Morro stuffed in his pack, and while Morro went off to bury the head and hide, Tomás Weiss sat down. Aside from queasiness he felt from the gore, and the cold, fatigue, and hunger that were almost normal for him now, he was dizzy. He thought he might have a fever, but by the time Morro returned the dizziness was gone, and the fever—he would get some aspirin from Rivera back in camp.

They agreed Morro should return alone with the meat, since they were already overdue and something to eat was better than nothing at all. Tomás himself had suggested it. He would continue the search for food and return by the following day whether he'd found any or not.

He walked in steady rain through the evening with only a vague idea of where he was going, west, out of the Cordillera Blanca. He suspected he would come to a town, all the paths out of the mountains came to a town or a village eventually, but then the terrain started to climb again and he knew that he was lost. He was wet, tired, hungry, he had been for hours, for days, and then came this dizziness and fever, and now he was lost; even so, he knew that as bad as things seemed, he ought not to think about them, that thinking would only make things worse.

He'd come across a lean-to not far from where he'd split from Morro. Hours later, he wondered if he shouldn't have spent the night there out of the weather, if he shouldn't go back. His mind wandered as he walked, and thoughts came to him of food, steaming platters of food, his mother's peppery stew, meat simmered in wine, tomato paste, and garlic, carrots, red pepper and pintos, plenty of pintos. Time and again he slipped on the muddy track. He cut his hands and arms and stubbed his toes on rocks in the trail. Brambles scratched his face. They tore his clothes. At one point they grew so thick he had to crawl on his belly to get through. He was sure he was going in the wrong direction, but he knew there was nothing for hours behind him and he hoped he would come across something not too far ahead. Then he reminded himself not to think, and especially not to hope.

He came to a peasant's house. There were no lights and he didn't see it until he was on top of it. A man opened the door, and seeing the tall blond boy and the rifle he stepped outside under the dripping eaves. From inside, a voice yelled, "Who is it, Ramón?" and the man closed the door behind him. He was very nervous. The woman called to him again. He spoke in a hushed voice. The words came out quickly. He told the boy that he wanted to help, but he wasn't brave enough, that he knew what the army did to anyone they even suspected of helping the Moreno. He had his wife to consider and his children. He said if his wife knew Tomás was at the door she would have a heart attack. She was old and quarrelsome, he said, but he loved her, and he didn't know what he would do without her. There was another house not too far up the path, he said, where he thought maybe Tomás could find some food and a dry place to sleep.

Tomás wanted to lie down right there, to sleep under the eaves— at least it was out of the rain. Instead he walked out into the night. He walked until he came to the end of the path where, as the man had told him he would, he found a hut. The door was open and Tomás, who no longer thought nor hoped and now no longer even feared, walked in.

"Sit down," someone said, he didn't see who. The room was dry and warm and the boy went directly to the fire. He stood close to the flames until his pants began to steam. He pulled off his torn, sopping tennis shoes. His toes, revived by the warmth, began to buzz and ache. He massaged his feet, which were white and wrinkled and blistered. He watched the steam rising off his skin. He turned around to warm his back and faced into the room.

She was working at a table with her back to him, a dark shape outlined by the lantern. Her hair was glossy and black and hung in long braids. "You need to eat," she said without turning around. Her voice was familiar, like someone's he'd known—youthful, a girl's, he wasn't sure whose. He watched her work at the table. His head was swimming, his teeth were chattering. His stomach and chest were cold and the fire scorched the backs of his legs. "Take off your clothes," she said over her shoulder. Her voice made him jump. He knew who it was she reminded him of—not a girl, but his mother. He hadn't seen his mother since when? He tried to remember. The effort seemed to make him dizzier.

"There are blankets over there," she said. She pointed to a bed in the corner of the room. He peeled off his shirt and pants and laid them out by the fire. He wrapped himself in the blanket. He was shaking uncontrollably.

When she had finished at the table she raised herself from her chair and with halting steps walked to the fireplace. She looked nothing like his mother. She braced herself on the stones and lowered herself to her knees beside him. With a wooden spoon she stirred the pot. "Stew," she said. She no longer sounded like his mother, either. She held the spoon for him to inspect. Her hand was trembling. "Meat," she said. She put the spoon in again and poked around. "Pintos in here somewhere, too. You like pintos, don't you, boy?"

Still, there was something familiar about her. He looked, but his eyes wouldn't focus. He thought it was his weariness or the smoke from the fire or the steam on his glasses, and he took them off and polished the one good lens. He saw her skin was wrinkled around her neck and her face was deeply lined. Her eyes were like shiny black buttons. They transfixed him. He couldn't blink or shift his gaze. It was something she was doing to him with her eyes, he didn't know what or how. His panic was intense. He couldn't focus his thoughts. His ears were buzzing, his eyes were tearing profusely, yet he couldn't blink. He saw her lips move, but he heard only the buzzing in his ears. A chill went through him, he shuddered, then the buzzing stopped. His vision returned to normal. He had the thought that she had given him his vision back, that somehow she had captured it, held it, and now she had returned it to him. He wiped his eyes. His forehead was burning. She was stirring the pot, a frail old woman sharing her supper with him. He decided the fever was stimulating his imagination.

She handed him a bowl of the stew, which he accepted gratefully and ate quickly, burning his tongue and the roof of his mouth. He ate a second helping before she helped herself. When he gave her back his empty bowl, he accidentally touched her hand. It was soft and smooth and he felt surprise at its softness, and then revulsion. He pulled his hand away. She laughed, showing stumps of teeth. She wore a silver band on each of her fingers and silver combs in her hair, and silver earrings which tinkled and chimed when she moved. She used his shoulder to get to her feet. She took the pot of water from the fire. "For tea," she said. "You want some tea, don't you, boy?"

He watched her take a chair away from the table. It seemed to require all her strength to drag it just a few feet and position it under a high shelf on the wall. She put a knee on the seat and then a foot, and then, holding on to the back of the chair, she stood and reached with both hands for a jar on the shelf. The chair wobbled and she lost her balance. He thought she would fall. She held the jar against her bosom and by inches lowered herself back to the floor. The boy watched her drag the chair back to the table.

She tried to unscrew the lid. She closed her eyes with the effort. "Here," she said, handing it to him. "Open this for me." She sounded annoyed. He tried but couldn't. The metal lid was rusted. He wiped his hands on the blanket and tried again, without success. After he handed it back, she twisted the lid. It came off in her hand. "You must have loosened it," she said. She thrust the open jar under his nose. "Smell." He jerked his head away and fought the urge to gag. "Ha!" she laughed. "You ate too much, boy. You wolfed it down. No wonder your stomach is upset. Now you've got to take your medicine." She laughed again. "Everybody's got to take their medicine sooner or later. But where is mine, boy? Where is the medicine for me?"

She dumped some of the stuff from the jar into the pot on the fire. After it had steeped a while, she filled a cup to the brim and handed it to Tomás. "Take it," she said.

Tomás made no move to take the cup.

"Here," she repeated. "Take it. Go on . . . ." She held the cup up to his face. "Take it!" Her hand shook and a few drops of the scalding liquid spilled on his bare thigh. He screamed, and jumping up, swung his arm, knocking the cup out of her hand. She leapt to her feet in a single swift motion. Fragments of clay lay in a steaming puddle on the floor. "Clumsy fool!" she shrieked.

He ran out the door holding the blanket around him, one hand at his throat. He didn't know where to run, except away from the house and the woman and the fright he had felt inside. Cold hard rain slapped his face. The panic pushed him forward while the rain and darkness pressed against him and slowed him but did not stop him. He ran blindly down the hill. He heard her call behind him, and at the sound of her voice terror rippled through his body. He looked back and saw her in the light from the doorway running after him. He slipped, fell, got up, ran again, fell again, got up again running. He heard her feet splash in the rivulet that flowed down the path. The blanket snagged on a branch, was ripped from his hands, and he ran on naked with his arms in front of his face to keep the branches from scratching his eyes. He heard her close behind him. Then something grabbed his ankle and he was flying and he fell hard and there was a crack. He skidded, and the pain tore through his leg up to his stomach and through his skull and he screamed. He rolled onto his back and he squeezed his eyes shut against the pain. His fingers clutched his leg and they found the ooze that was blood and water and mud and they found the long deep tear in his flesh and then they touched the sharp jagged edge of bone jutting out from his thigh. He groped for his glasses and tried to drag himself away. He clawed handfuls of mud. She held him by the ankles. Her grip was incontestable. The pain ripped through him and he fell back, dizzy and sick with pain and fear. She pulled him to his feet. He felt he was spinning. He passed out.

She lowered his body onto the bed in the corner. He was unconscious, his breath came in erratic shallow spurts. Blood and mud ran off his body in watery streaks. She tied a rag around the wound and washed his body with warm water. She cleaned him and dried him. Blood soaked the rag around his leg and leaked from the scratches, cuts, and tears in his skin. She lit candles and placed them all around the bed, humming while she worked.

When he awoke, she held his head and put a cup to his lips. Tea dribbled down his chin. "Sooner or later you have to take your medicine," she said, cradling his head.

His face began to burn, and sweat beaded on his forehead and upper lip and on the wings of his nose. Gems of sweat glistened on his scalp, which tingled, and then his balls began to tingle, and then he felt a burning in his penis. There was an itching in the pit of his stomach. His toes and his hands and feet grew cold and numb and the numbness spread up his legs and from his fingers to his shoulders. His abdominal muscles clenched in spasms. He turned his head and retched. She cleaned him again and pressed cool rags to his forehead.

His lips turned blue black. The flesh collapsed on his cheek-bones. He could no longer feel or move his arms. She arranged them across his chest. The pain in the bad leg stopped. He couldn't feel his legs at all, couldn't move them or feel them.

She had put candles all around him and he saw the flickering light and he heard her humming. He followed her with his eyes. He heard scratching noises in the wall behind his head. He heard the sizzle of rain falling into the fire. She put something into the fire that filled the room with dense, pungent smoke. He was para-lyzed now, but he could think and he could feel and tears began to roll down his cheeks.

With a knife she shredded his clothes and burned the pieces in the fire. She sat beside him on the bed. Her eyes were slits, and when she opened them they were moist and dark and reflected the light from the candles. Her eyes shot a jolt of fright right through him. His hair stood on end. She held the knife in one hand, gath-ered a handful of his hair in the other, and lifted his head off the bed. Convulsions shook his body. With a single slice of the blade she cut a hank of hair and laid it on his chest. She shaved his skull while tears rolled down his cheeks. His stomach twisted and he retched and heaved again. Spit, hair, and foam mixed in the corners of his mouth. When she finished cutting she put the blond hair in a pouch and put the pouch away.

In the light from the lantern she threaded a needle with coarse black thread and in close, tight, even stitches she sewed his lips shut. With the same needle and thread she sewed his eyelids shut, but by that time Tomás Weiss was already dead.

A Cadillac limousine circled the Plaza de Armas in the evening traffic and pulled to the curb in front of the Gran Hotel Belén. Before it had stopped completely, the white-gloved hand of the hotel doorman was already on the handle of the car's rear door. He stood at military attention in his long green coat with double rows of brass buttons, gold braid, and epaulets. His downcast eyes fell first on the flawless shine of a black Italian shoe, then on the knife-edge crease of the dark blue trousers. He noticed the fit of the jacket, how it hung without a wrinkle across the back of the shoulders. After closing the limousine door he hustled across the sidewalk and up the steps to the hotel entrance to arrive a step ahead of the colonel. "Good evening, Colonel, sir," he said, but the colonel didn't seem to hear.

Despite two invitations from acquaintances seated at nearby tables, the colonel drank his double pisco sour standing alone at the bar. He drank another, paid his tab, then took the corridor past the currency exchange, pushed open a side door, and once again was out on the street.

The sidewalks of the Avenida Colonial were normally crowded at evening rush hour, but this night a solid wall of people lined the curb. Across the street and over their heads, the colonel could see, had he chosen to look, the flashing purple neon Varig sign, and below that the red banners and bobbing placards of demonstrators marching in the direction of the Plaza de Armas. Their chant rose above the honking of cars and trucks in the side streets waiting for the parade to pass. The colonel hugged the buildings and walked against the flow of the demonstration. He was impervious to his surroundings, sealed in the privacy of his thoughts. He was always distanced from the life on the streets by his position and wealth, but now he walked as if in a trance. Amazon tarantulas, mounted on cardboard like black, hairy fists, and cobalt-blue butterflies big as saucers passed beneath his recognition, as did paintings of the blond, blue-eyed Jesus, and the black Jesus, the mounted conquistadores, and the array of sad Indian faces, all of them done on black velvet from the same phosphorescent palette. He was as oblivious to these as he was to the choking fumes of thousands of idling motors stalled in side streets waiting for the demonstration to pass.

He turned a corner and walked up a one-way street into the oncoming traffic. As the pall of exhaust began to lift, it exposed the sharp underlying stench of piss that in the city's arid climate never washed away. He passed shells of abandoned buildings and rubble-filled lots. He looked up once before he turned again at the Church of Our Lady of the Compassionate Heart, as if to get his bearings. An old woman slept propped against a wall behind which a statue of Mary rose out of plumb. Bricks showed through the peeling plaster. "Gavilan lives" had been painted along its length in letters three feet high.

No doorman stood at the entrance to the Three Crosses Hotel. The wrought-iron gate was heavy and creaked as if it weren't opened often. The colonel walked through a dark archway into a courtyard where tables were set around a chipped cement fountain painted aquamarine. A boy with tangled hair and a beard sat among the empty tables drinking a beer and writing a postcard. He wore blue jeans and a brown wool poncho. His backpack leaned against his chair. An Indian swung a mop over the cracked mosaic tile, then wrung it out in the fountain.

The manager dozed behind the registration desk, his chair tilted back against the wall. His tie was crooked, his yellowed shirt collar curled at the points. The slap of the colonel's palm on the register awakened him. The startled clerk searched without success for his glasses, which were propped on top of his forehead. He held the slip of paper that the colonel had handed him an arm's length away, pulled it back under his nose, squinted, then put it under the cone of light from the desk lamp. "What does it say?" he asked, handing the paper back.

"Mosquevera," the colonel answered.

"Two thirty-one. Up the stairs and to the right. Is he expecting you?" But the colonel was already crossing the courtyard. He walked up the stairs and down a dark hallway, checking the numbers above the doors.

A short, wiry man in a sleeveless undershirt, his pants unbuttoned at the waist, the ends of his belt hanging loose, stood in the open door. Beyond him a bed, nightstand, and armoire filled the room. He stepped aside for the colonel. The door to the bathroom was closed. Amid dirty plates and greasy napkins, a chicken carcass sat on the bedspread. The man rolled the threadbare green chenille into a bundle, chicken bones, plates, and all, and threw it into the hall. The plates clattered and broke. He locked the door, wiped his hands on his undershirt, and sat on the bed. He swung his feet onto the sheet, crossed his ankles, and leaned back against the headboard. His shoes were untied. He wore no socks.

Captain Mosquevera's personal habits filled the colonel with revulsion—not that Mosquevera gave two shits either way. It was one of Mosquevera's pleasures to irritate his superior officer, and tossing the dishes into the hall was a way he had of showing his contempt for Rinaldi and his aristocratic pretensions. He had planned the scene as he waited for the colonel to arrive. Later, drinking with his friends, he would brag of how he had taunted Rinaldi with impunity.

"A drink, Colonel?" Without waiting for an answer, he poured two glasses and held one out to the colonel, who, although a drink was what he badly wanted, made no move to accept. It was actually an expensive aged Scotch Mosquevera had poured into another bottle of a less prestigious brand. He had been hoping Rinaldi would, on the basis of the label, disparage the liquor and give Mosquevera yet another opportunity to sneer. He hadn't counted on Rinaldi's turning it down. Mosquevera shrugged. Next time he would know better, he would put the cheap stuff in the expensive bottle. He settled back on the pillows and put his hands behind his head. "What's the matter, chum? Somebody hang your dog?" A wooden match bobbed in the corner of his mouth.

"They gave me the Cross of the Order of Bolivar," Rinaldi said flatly.

"Well, now. Congratulations." Mosquevera raised his glass. "To the Order of Bolivar," he said, and drained it off. He looked amused.

"They're sending me to La Paz," Rinaldi said, barely loud enough to be heard above the noise coming through the open window from the street. Mosquevera put his hand behind his ear and gave Rinaldi a questioning look. "La Paz," the colonel repeated. Mosquevera had heard, but pretended he hadn't. Anything to jerk Rinaldi around, like putting the room's only chair in the hall so Rinaldi would have to stand.

"La Paz!" Mosquevera lifted his glass again. He picked his teeth with the match to hide his smile. He pictured himself telling some of the boys, and it became harder to keep himself from laughing.

"They passed me over," Rinaldi said, as if he could not comprehend such a thing.

Mosquevera thought for a moment that Rinaldi might cry. The boys would get a kick out of that. Because of their conspiracy, Mosquevera could be familiar, insolent, even insulting, but he was keenly aware of the line he was treading. He knew Rinaldi to be a weak, self-indulgent man, whose inflated opinion of himself made him at once an easy target and extremely dangerous. He had seen what an angered Rinaldi could do.

From the beginning he had known Rinaldi's ambitions were futile. A man from Rinaldi's background could only progress so far in life, even in the army, which was considered to be the country's most democratic, egalitarian institution. Ruthlessness could get you only so far up the ladder. Cunning, perseverence, and force could take you further, and nothing would take you as far as money, but the very highest places were reserved for those with a birthright. It was a simple fact of life. Short of a coup, Colonel Rinaldi, regardless of his accomplishments, had no more chance of becoming General Rinaldi than Mosquevera had of becoming Archbishop. The top ranks of the army and the church were exclusive clubs entry to which the likes of Mosquevera and Rinaldi would always be denied.

"After Gavilan's assassination I was certain I would get the promotion. I was sure of it," Rinaldi said.

"So was I." Mosquevera allowed Rinaldi his illusions. He encouraged them. They had made Mosquevera richer than he had ever thought possible. He had been a sergeant when fate had brought them together. Gavilan and the Zapato Moreno provided them both with the means to their separate ends. "A shame, Colonel. I'm sorry," Mosquevera said.

Rinaldi snapped out of his mood. "I'm sick of your condescension, Mosquevera. I don't need your pity. Who do you think you're kidding? I know you aren't sorry."

Mosquevera raised his glass and toasted the colonel again. He wasn't embarrassed by the accusation. He always felt better when all the cards were on the table, when everyone knew where he stood. It was no secret he cared little for the status of rank, only for the opportunity for profit it afforded. He had never tried to mask his contempt for officers in general, and had shunned their company as much as possible, choosing his friends from among the underworld from which he himself had risen.

"You ought not be so smug, Captain," Rinaldi said. He seemed to have regained his composure. "Mine was not the only bad news. Perhaps you've heard the rumors already? No? I guess not, you wouldn't be lying there like a contented pig if you had already heard. Allow me to be the first to tell you. The Minister wants to disband the unit. He plans to restore civilian control to the province."

Whatever shock the news held for Mosquevera, he appeared unaffected. For one, he didn't want to give Rinaldi the satisfaction of seeing him off-balance. For another, he had long known they couldn't keep fighting both sides of the war forever, that sooner or later someone would realize the Zapato Moreno were not the threat they had been portrayed to be. Someone, in fact, already had, and that was a piece of news he had been saving for Rinaldi.

"It gets even worse, chum," he said. "You might find yourself living in La Paz on a little less income than you had previously expected. The cocainistas cut the payments. Since the Moreno disappeared they don't see where they need our protection anymore."

"None of this would've happened if Gavilan were still alive," Rinaldi muttered.

"It was nice while it lasted. We couldn't stand the bums up forever."

"I told the Minister there were Moreno all through the mountains. I told him it was too early to end martial law. And what did he say to that? He said that the Moreno without Roberto Gavilan was a snake without a head."

"Well, if that's what he thinks, now comes the good news. I've been saving it for you. You ready for this? Gavilan ain't dead, not really, no more than you or me."

Rinaldi blanched. He stood in disbelief while Mosquevera told him that the assassination had never come off, that the Moreno they had turned and inveigled into doing the job had bungled it and had been killed himself. Coincidentally, this was true, but Mosquevera had no knowledge of what actually had happened in the mountains. What he knew and didn't tell Rinaldi was that the bullets he had given the man were blanks, that the grenade he had given him was a dud. Mosquevera had shelled out thirty thousand dollars for his captaincy, an investment that had paid off many times over. He saw no reason to jeopardize his paycheck in the attempt to earn Rinaldi a promotion that Mosquevera knew wouldn't be forthcoming anyway. He had simply appeased Rinaldi with the assassination plan, never intending to murder the man who Mosquevera knew was the key to the cocainista treasure chest, and who, unless he had been bludgeoned with the .45 or force-fed the dud grenade, was still alive. Why Gavilan hadn't shown himself was unclear to Mosquevera, but he had seen it as a lucky happenstance. Now the point had been driven home to Rinaldi: to wipe out the Zapato Moreno would not win him his promotion, and would, as Mosquevera had predicted and as events had borne out, kill the golden goose. The cocainistas had already cut off the protection money, and now the ministry wanted the show shut down completely.

Rinaldi listened in silence. All he could think was how foolish he would be made to seem, having announced the death of Gavilan, having personally taken responsibility for its planning and execution, having accepted the Order of the Cross, to have to admit now that the plan had failed. "This was all your idea, Mosquevera." He meant it as an accusation.

Even now Rinaldi didn't get it. Mosquevera took it as a lesson in how self-importance could blind a man. It would have to be pointed out to him, Mosquevera thought, he would have to be led to see the significance, but not before Mosquevera had his little bit of fun.

Rinaldi walked to the window. "I'll be the laughingstock of the army," he said. "Why did I listen to you?"

Mosquevera ignored this lapse in memory. "We had to do something, right?" he said. "It was getting harder and harder to convince the ministry to keep us up there. You think teaching a coupla dumb Indians the alphabet is a reason for martial law? They weren't even messing in the trade much anymore."

"This was your idea," Rinaldi insisted. "Everything was going along fine. Another six months I'd have had the promotion."

"Even before that, half the stuff we say they did they either didn't do or we did it for them," Mosquevera said.

"I never should have trusted you. I was a fool to trust you. It was a stupid plan concocted by an idiot. We could've kept on going just like we were. In another six months they would've promoted me. They would've had to promote me."

"We didn't do too bad," Mosquevera said. "For a fool and an idiot we did pretty damn good. What's wrong with being a colonel? Colonel ain't so bad."

"What do you know, you ignorant peasant? If it weren't for me you'd still be strong-arming pimps for quarters," Rinaldi said.

"And you, you still think they're going to put your statue in the Plaza de Armas, don't you?" Mosquevera felt himself losing control. "With your big estate and your polo-playing asshole friends, you think you're better than me. But I know about you, Rinaldi, I know . . ." He stopped himself. Don't blow it, he thought. Stay cool. Back off. "I know if Gavilan's alive, we're still in the ball game. I know when the word gets around, the cocainistas are suddenly gonna want to make the back payments they owe us."

"First I tell them we killed him, and then I tell them we didn't." Rinaldi was stewing again. "They'll think me an imbecile," he said.

"Then you'd fit right in up there. They might promote you on the spot."

"Fuck you, Mosquevera. What do you care if I look bad?"

"I don't, you're right, but it's your last hope of getting that promotion. Could be what you say is true. Could be another six months of Gavilan they'll change their minds."

Rinaldi perked up. His mind began to play on the possibilities. He would tell them Gavilan hadn't been killed, but he'd been wounded, seriously wounded, which is why they hadn't heard from him. That's not so farfetched. Gavilan was alive, and he was as great a threat as ever, he would say—maybe greater, because while Gavilan had been recovering from his wounds, the Moreno had been gathering strength, preparing for a new offensive. He would tell the Minister that, but he would need proof.

"Proof!" sneered Mosquevera. "There wasn't no proof to begin with except what we gave them, what we invented. Not that they gave a shit anyway. The only thing made a difference was when one of the mules got hit. They didn't like nobody disrupting their business."

"Why doesn't he show? What is he up to?" Rinaldi paced to the window.

"Maybe they've disbanded, gone home, gone back to the barrio, wherever they come from, the sewers. Maybe they finally wised up. It was hopeless from the beginning. The indios wanted nothing to do with them. The indios jacked them around."

"We're the ones who turned the Indians against the Moreno," the colonel said. "That was our strategy. Let them do the work for us."

"Even before us, the Indians weren't going for the Moreno program—Chairman Mao and all that bullshit. Half of them never heard of China, and they're telling them Mao Tse fucking Tung. Dumb fucking commies. All them Indians want is to be left the fuck alone."

"The Minister believed Gavilan was Castro's second coming. He believed it with his heart," Rinaldi said.

"He believed shit. The Minister didn't want nobody messing with the cocaine. He could give a flying fuck about a bunch of weirdos talking Mao Tse Tung."

"I tell you he believed Gavilan was Castro's second coming. Those were his words."

"Perfect. Now all you do is tell him he's rose up from the dead."

"I want proof," Rinaldi said. "If he isn't dead, where is he?"

"I dunno and I don't care. You want to press our luck? We can't keep it up forever. I thought we did pretty good up until now." He knew Rinaldi had bought the idea. Now he would let Rinaldi think the idea was his own.

"I didn't go to all this trouble to retire a colonel. We have to find Gavilan."

"Or we can just pretend we found him. Same thing," Mosquevera said, but Rinaldi seemed not to hear.

"Gavilan will convince the Minister that we're still needed in the mountains, that to pull out now is premature. Gavilan is the only one who can do that. Before this assassination scheme of yours, no one would have even considered pulling out."

"I don't know what went wrong." Mosquevera scratched his head. "He depends on publicity even more than we do. At least we can write our own. What do you think we ought to do?"

"We start a new flow of intelligence." Rinaldi was animated now, pacing back and forth to the window. "We document sightings, propagate rumors that Gavilan has been seen in various villages. We stage some disappearances, public officials, judges, teachers . . ."

"Hang some dogs from the streetlights, paint 'em up with commie slogans . . . ," Mosquevera egged him on. "The newspapers eat that shit up."

"We plant a cache of weapons."

"Hit the cocainistas ourselves. Disguised as Moreno, of course. Bring the trade to a standstill. Then we up the cost of protection."

"That's a beginning," said Rinaldi. "But we need a public outcry. We need something to galvanize public opinion. An atrocity, an attack on the public that can't be ignored."

"Sounds to me like you have something in mind," Mosquevera said. "You do, don't you? Another bombing? I don't know, Rinaldi. Last time was pretty fucking messy, remember?"

Rinaldi shot him a murderous look.

"Of course you remember. I only wanted to know if you thought the situation was that desperate."

Rinaldi straightened, ran his palms down the front of his jacket, tugged at the hem. "Obviously, Captain, you've never been to La Paz."

Rule number one: the public is always wrong. Rule two: even a blind pig gets an acorn once in a while, which is why I carry a camera with me anywhere I go. I've got it with me now walking along the bluff above the beach to the San Isidro market. It's too late to go home to sleep and too early to drive, and if I walk I'll get there about the time the market opens. I can walk and take some pictures and try to sort through what I just heard from Blacky. If anyone but the man himself had told me Blacky's a Moreno, I'd have laughed in his face.

San Isidro market is open-air, a couple dozen stalls—fruits, vegetables, fish—with a wall on three sides and the bluff on the fourth. The thing of it is everyone there is enrolled in Blacky's trip, in the restaurant. The best of everything, the vendors set aside for Blacky. Even before the big hotels, the Belén, the Crillon, or the Sheraton, they take care of Blacky first. For his part, Blacky is very appreciative, to the tune of twenty dollars here, soccer tickets there, a bottle of booze, maybe a necklace for a vendor's daughter. Because of Blacky I don't have to inspect every melon in the crate. I tell them what I want, I get the best they've got. If it isn't grade A, they tell me. I don't have to be on guard someone's going to slip in a carton of eggs half the shells are cracked.

I'm among the first people there and I zip down the shopping list. I tell them what I want, they show me the goods, they wrap it up to deliver it later on. Meanwhile, I've got the time to shoot a roll of film or two.

I love this light. It's so dependable, even, shadowless, I don't even have to check my meter. I shoot a lady hosing down the asphalt, the hot pink of her sweater against the wet shiny black of the pavement. Some I take wide open at a thousandth, freeze the spray in sharp, focused droplets. Then I slow to a quarter-second, stop the lens way down, the water will look like smoke steaming out of the nozzle. There's a vendor with a wide smile and gold front tooth, the brim of his hat hides his eyes. There's a boy asleep on a pile of cassavas. A gull drops down on a tub of mackerel. He misses and so do I. I finish the roll on a tray of peppers, and drop in some black and white. I'm working with a medium telephoto, scanning the scene through the viewfinder to see what catches my eye, and she does.

These folks down here are no race of giants to start with, but they look like school kids next to her. I don't see her face, just high heels, these legs in blue jeans, a T-shirt, a big basket of produce— lettuce, squash, bananas, melons. I swing in a wide arc around her, keeping my distance, I don't want to make her self-conscious or scare her off. Sunglasses hide half her face and I can't tell where she's looking, or whether she sees me or not. I wish she'd take them off, but maybe it's just as well. If her eyes are up to the standard set by her skin, her nose, her cheeks, her melons, it'd be too much. I finish off the one roll and change the film. When I'm ready to find her again, I don't have far to go. She's standing right in front of me, arms crossed, glasses on top of her head. Her eyes are gray and narrowed. A straight thin scar cuts across her eyebrow, skips over the socket and trails off onto her cheek.

"What's this all about?" she says, catching me unprepared.

I start to tell her that I'm a photographer, then I get sidetracked onto the produce. Where I'm headed is how much I'd like her to pose for me, but before I get anywhere near that part, she pulls down her shades and storms away. I'm left with my mouth open and half a dozen people watching my face turn red. I call her some stuff to her back under my breath, but my anger only lasts a little longer than the embarrassment, because, I think, I may have gotten a couple frames that will have made it all worthwhile.

There's this lady, Marlena, she runs a lunch place at the market, a stall with a propane stove behind the counter is all it is, a refrigerator, a couple of stools to sit on and all of it under an awning. She's the Marlena of Ceviche Marlena, a fixture on Blacky's menu. Blacky's contribution is the à la carte price, seven bucks and change. Some credit comes my way, but all I do is ladle it out, the praise belongs to Marlena. The shame of it is Marlena's ceviche doesn't travel well. In the three miles between here and Blacky's it loses its shine, which is not to say it's bad, in fact it's considered a specialty of the house, it's only to say there's something about eating at Marlena's that makes it twice as good, even at ten in the morning. I order the big bowl, the fifty-center, and I'm eating and listening with half an ear to Marlena talk about this, that, and the other, and what I'm thinking is how I blew it with this chick.

Probably she was a model already. Nah, maybe not, not with that scar, but I can imagine she's had guys come on to her like that before. There's plenty of girls who go for that story, and plenty more who could care less that there's actually film in the camera. But this one, she's one in a million. That's why I can't believe I see her taking a seat on a stool three down from me. She asks for a cup of joe and lights up a smoke as if I weren't even there, or at least the run-in we had hadn't occurred.

I sure don't want another public beating like the last one she gave me, you can bet, but something inside me won't let it rest. I ask can I pay for her coffee?

No answer. She drags on her smoke.

Can't say I blame her. I try a new tack. I think I owe you an apology, I say, and she turns her head, though not quite far enough to actually see me. It's more like she cocks an ear.

"Well?" she says. "Do you or don't you?"

"I do," I say.

"I accept," she says.

This throws me because I'm unprepared for anything but an all-out battle to win her forgiveness, and then she adds, "I over-reacted. Freaks should get used to gawkers." She spins the stool around, looks at me over her shades, looks me up and down. Then she pushes her glasses back onto her nose and spins back to her cup of coffee. "You, of all people," she says, "should understand."

If I lower my guard for a minute, the smart-ass in me takes over. I don't even want to say what I'm saying. "Gawking? Nah, that was no gawk," I say. "A gawk is different. For your bona fide gawk the mouth has got to be open, wide open. See, this"—I let my jaw drop —"is a gawk. What you saw earlier, and Marlena might be able to back me up on this, is ogling." I roll my eyes.

A hint of maybe the most meager possibility of a smile crosses her face. Not giving her the chance to object, I run through my rap, everything I wanted to say before. After she hears me out she can think I'm feeding her a line, she can think it's all a ploy to get into her pants, she can think whatever she wants. I just don't want to strike out with the bat on my shoulder. She listens. She doesn't interrupt. She doesn't say anything. "Well? What do you think?" I ask, as if this were a person who needed an invitation to speak her mind.

"Out of the question," she says. She puts out her smoke, takes a last hit from the coffee cup. "Please excuse me," she says. She picks up her basket. A red pepper drops out. I field it, fall in step beside her, put the pepper back in. I run back to leave some money for Marlena, and catch up with her across the market.

"Ever had Marlena's ceviche?" I'm looking for common ground, but she keeps walking, eyes straight ahead, doesn't miss a stride. "You should try it sometime." She's being a jerk, playing a parody of hard-to-get, her with her fuck-me shoes and her fuck-you attitude, although I can't blame her, a total stranger giving her the rush. Whatever attraction I had for this person, aside from my desire to photograph her, is being clubbed to death. I'm surprised by my own persistence. "It's like Guinness, though. They say Guinness doesn't travel well either, that outside of Dublin it isn't the same . . . Me grandfodder was Irish, y' know. On me mum's side." I'm annoyed with myself for so badly wanting this woman, but I know I'll feel worse if I let her walk. She steps out into the street to hail a cab and I go right on talking. I'll say any damn thing to keep the connection. A taxi pulls to the curb. "Miraflores," she says to the driver.

"Whaddaya know?" I say. "I'm going to Miraflores too." I just came from Miraflores. Really I'm going the other direction—Callao. Home. She slides over to make room for me. I have to wriggle in, Japanese cars aren't made for a body like mine, or hers—if she's not six feet tall, she's close to it. I'm still talking about the ceviche, telling her the secret is in the marinade, that most people don't know you can let it marinate too long. The driver hasn't wound it out into second before she tells him stop the car.

"I'm sorry," she says. "I've made a mistake. I can't allow this to continue. Nothing can come of it. It would be best for both of us if we ended this right here and now. The mistake was mine. I'll find myself another cab." She grasps the door handle, but I hold her arm. No, I tell her. It was me who pushed myself onto her. She did her best to discourage me. I'll get out, I tell her, and I do.

"No hard feelings," I say. She extends her arm, I think to shake hands, and I hold out my own, but she's just reaching out to close the door, and I'm left standing in the street with my hand out as the cab lurches off. I shoot her a few more times through the rear windshield, hoping she'll turn around, but she doesn't. The cab turns the corner. She's gone. Well, not entirely. I still have the film. I go back to Marlena's to ask if she's ever seen her before, but she hasn't, and a person like that, you'd remember. I write down my address and phone number, in case she comes back. You never know.

I rent the upstairs of a two-story warehouse in Callao, right on the harbor. If you have to live in the city, it's not a bad place to be. I've space for my studio and darkroom, and access to the roof where I got a couple of potted plants and some folding canvas chairs. When I moved in it was all one big room, windows the length of two of the walls. I built partitions, made a studio/gallery out front, and a living space and darkroom in the back.

Darkroom work is a lot like cooking: you follow a recipe, so much of this, so much of that, a couple parts water, then you drop in your film, stir it up, let it stew. The instructions are very precise. They give you temperatures plus or minus a quarter of a degree. It would seem to require a lot of attention, especially the part you do in the total dark, but after you've broken the rules enough times you begin to notice it doesn't make all that much difference. For openers, try to find a thermometer that reads plus or minus a quarter degree. I use a meat thermometer I took from the restaurant. When the needle's past poultry but not yet to veal, I know the developer's right. Ham's cold and roast beef is hot.

Photography has been around long enough you take it for granted, but if you think about it, it's an amazing trick. Miraculous really. You aim a little box at someone, push a button, and two hours later floating face up in an inch of a brownish liquid, there she is again. One of the pictures is as good as I'd hoped. A vendor is holding a fish by the tail for her inspection, and she's looking at it very intently, and the people around the stall, they're looking at *her* very intently, and dead center is this glassy eye of the mackerel. There's this triangle happening, everyone eyeballing everyone else and the fish, he's eyeballing you.

I tack the pictures up on the wall. It's plain I missed an opportunity. I'd like to find her again. There must be a way, she's no everyday woman. I run down a list of options: one, I can hope she goes back to Marlena's, reads my note, and calls me; or two, I can stake out the market, wait for her myself. Not a very extensive or promising list. Then it occurs to me: the second roll, the one still in the camera, has the pictures of the taxi, and taxis have numbers, and if I got the number, I could find the driver and he could tell me where he left her off. She had a bag of groceries, she was probably going home, somewhere in Miraflores is what she said. Inside half an hour I'm at the office of El Segundo Cab.

I've seen plenty of detective movies, read my share of novels, the thing that gets me is this is exactly the kind of information Perry Mason sends Della out to get. Why do you suppose, then, I've been sitting in this shabby office for an hour—me, the receptionist, and the dispatcher—and I'm no closer to who was driving cab 189670 than I was when I came in? The receptionist has a beehive hairdo and the same answer for every question I ask: "The supervisor will be in at four." She never looks at me directly, although she checks me out with quick glances out of the corner of her eye.

The place smells of dead cigar, and there's constant static from the radio interrupted by loud raspy exchanges I can't understand a single word of. The supervisor struts in at four on the dot. He's short and dark with sixteen ballpoint pens clipped onto his shirt pocket. He leads me into his office. "At your service," he says. I tell him what I'm after. "Impossible," he says. "The regulations." He waves his hand as if to dismiss the whole matter.

"Of course," I say. "Regulations."

"This is the modern world," he says. His voice is sympathetic. He is shuffling through a pile of papers. He doesn't look up.

"Of course," I say. I take my money out of my pocket, slide the paper clip off, lay a twenty down on the stack. He stops his shuffling. "The modern world," I say.

"There are ways, however," he says. He folds the money, creasing it with his thumbnail. "Perhaps next week—"

I peel off another bill, smooth it out, put it down. He lets it lay. The fluorescent bulb is blinking and ticking and the static crackles over the transom. He looks at it. Twenty bucks. It could take him a day to make twenty bucks. I can hear it calling to him.

"—or at the earliest, tomorrow afternoon—"

I drop another bill on his papers.

"It could cost me my job," he says.

I let him know how much I appreciate the risk, but this time he waves me off. Tomorrow, he says, and pushes me through the door. I don't want to leave without what I've come for, but I don't know what else to do. He may even be telling the truth.

The door to the warehouse isn't locked, which is normal, it never is. It's on the steps up to the second floor, when I reach for my wallet where I keep the key to the studio, that I realize my wallet isn't there. I slap my thighs, my hip, slap my shirt, slap my hip again—no wallet. Even if you've never lost your wallet you can imagine what it might be like—all your cards, your identification—that is, unless you lost it down here, in a country like this, then you can't. A driver's license, for instance: to get a driver's license they make you apply for the application. Plus, I'm illegal. I sink down onto the steps, hold my head in my hands, pity myself a minute or two.

At least I'm not locked out. I keep a spare key hidden up on a beam above the door. I leave a crate there in case I need to reach it, and now, when I get to the top of the stairs, I see there's somebody sitting on it. A cook doesn't make many enemies in the course of his day, and you're strong enough to bend the handle on a cast-iron skillet, you don't worry much about the occasional guy who's unhappy his fillet is overcooked. I can't see who it is on account of there's no light in the hallway except a window way at the other end behind him. Hey, I say, still fifteen feet away, and my answer is sparks on the floor. Whoever it is has tossed down his smoke, which takes a hell of a lot of nerve, I think, to use my floor as an ashtray; and with what's happened today, on top of no sleep, and this is supposed to be my day off, I'm starting a burn. I had a lousy afternoon, and here's the guy gonna pick up the tab.

Turns out it's her. You might think she was just who I was expecting, that's how nonchalant I act. "Hey," I say.

"Hello," she says, getting up off the crate.

"Been waiting long?"

"Not long." There are five or six butts on the floor at her feet. It seems I wasn't the only one ready to stretch the truth.

"I had a feeling I hadn't seen the last of you," I tell her, leaving out the part about the steps I had already taken and the steps I was willing to take to bring that about. "That's why I left the note with Marlena. I had a hunch." She starts to say something but I cut her off. "No need to explain. I don't blame you. Must be a thousand guys hitting on you every day." I'm talking a mile a minute, just jabbering away. I push the crate under the beam and, standing on it, feel around for the key. She's watching me with her arms folded across her chest. "My secret hiding place," I tell her. "Do you mind closing your eyes?" She gives me a funny look. "That's exactly the problem, isn't it? You don't know me, I don't know you . . . You could be anyone. You could be here casing the joint. How's a person to know?" I step off the crate, wipe my hand on the back of my jeans, put the key in the lock. "You *don't* know. You can't. You trust your luck. You take a chance." I open the door.

"I think there's a misunderstanding here," she says. "I don't know what you're talking about. I don't know any Marlena, and I certainly haven't received a message from her. I would have phoned, in fact I did, but no one answered."

I reach in, flip on the lights, kick open the door all the way. Gentleman that I am, I'm waiting for her to go first.

"I still don't think I've made myself clear," she says. "I'm here because I have found this." She hands me a tooled brown leather wallet says "El Paso" in little colored beads. "It's yours, I believe. You left it in the cab."

My wallet! I hold it like a bird you could squeeze too hard and break its bones.

"I went back to the market, but you were already gone, and then I tried to phone, but there was no answer. I thought you might be out looking for it, so I brought it here. It's only what I would hope someone would do for me. I feel somewhat responsible for your having lost it in the first place."

She turns and starts down the hall toward the stairs. "No, wait!" I grab the sleeve of her T-shirt, and right away let go on account of the dirt from the beam. She looks down at the fingerprints and then she looks at me, and then her eyes jump past me through the open door into the studio. I don't know what exactly caught her attention, but directly opposite the door is a mural-size blowup of a bull goring a picador's horse. The detail's sharp enough to see the stitching on the saddle. The sunlight, the colors in the crowd, the way the horse is rearing, his nostrils flared, the way the bull has laid its belly open—I'm really proud of that picture. I step aside to let her see. She walks slowly into the room. Her eyes rove over the walls, over the bullfight pictures, the racetrack pictures, the kids at ballroom dancing class. I close the door, lean against it, questioning my luck like I had just promised not to do.

No, she couldn't, she told him, she couldn't have dinner with him, she wasn't dressed to go out.

"Who's going out?" he'd said.

But she had fresh fish waiting at home, she said. It would spoil if she didn't get home to cook it.

"Plenty of fish in the sea," he'd said.

He had an answer for everything, she thought, but what was the harm? She had nothing planned for the evening, which lately seemed more and more her situation, and it was easier to give in than to argue with him. It reminded her of her and Rinaldi, with the roles reversed, and how tiresome it was to have to plead for companionship. For Bobby's part, he looked thrilled, which made her think he didn't hear yes very often, and set her to wondering why. If you overlooked the impulsiveness that most men either had outgrown by his age or had had subdued by life, he had no glaring shortcomings she could see, and you didn't really have to overlook it, the impulsiveness, you could just as easily call it zest and let it go at that. He was almost handsome in a careless way, and as for his size, it was rare to find herself with anyone with proportions scaled to her own. At the market was one thing, but to be in the same room with him was something else again. She noticed herself taking inordinate interest in his whereabouts. He was alluring and scary at once.

She wandered around the studio looking at the photographs, which in places were tacked three layers deep on the walls. She glossed over the muscle men, unable to see what was it about those oily bulges that people found attractive. She averted her eyes from the one of the bull goring the horse, and loved the children in dancing class, boys who couldn't be older than eight or nine in suits and ties, and the girls in petticoats with bows in their hair, and especially the girl in patent leather shoes with white anklets whose chin was resting on top of her partner's head. She saw the picture of Inez which, judging by the look on her face, must have been taken the time her husband the jockey was trampled, and she wondered what kind of a person would intrude at a moment like that. Inez made her think of Rinaldi, stirred vague suspicions, and these thoughts of Rinaldi in turn made her feel disloyal and guilty, and she quickly moved on.

She stopped at the pictures he'd taken of her at the market. She'd never seen a picture of her she liked as much as the one of her and the mackerel. It was because she didn't know her picture was being taken, she thought. She looked as long as she dared. She was leery of appearing immodest and absorbed with herself in front of this stranger, and she wandered on before she was really ready to. Among the things she disliked about herself, vanity was near the top of the list, especially since it was founded almost wholly on hearsay. Whatever time she spent in front of the mirror was out of curiosity as much as narcissism, a search for that which others admired in her.

She was looking at a nude frozen mid-sneeze when he called her into the kitchen to ask if she wanted beer or wine with her dinner. She preferred beer, but told him wine without thinking about it or knowing why.

"I was hoping you'd choose the beer," he said. "I don't actually have any wine."

When she said she truthfully preferred the beer anyway, she could tell that he didn't believe her, that he thought she was being polite. "Really," she said. "I never drink wine. It's wasted on me."

"Then why did you say you wanted it?" he asked.

"Why did you offer when you didn't have any to serve?" Her tone of voice matched his.

She followed him up a ladder through a trapdoor onto the roof. He carried a salmon steak wrapped in foil, the plates, and utensils. She carried the bottles of beer. They sat in folding canvas chairs. The breeze off the ocean blew the paper napkins off the tray and scattered them over the roof. He climbed back down for more napkins and returned with two sweaters as well. The one he handed to her smelled of baby powder and was big enough to pull over her knees, which she hugged against her chest.

Probably it was the effect of the beer—she was on her second—or maybe the changing colors in the sky, or the breeze, or the pleasant sense of anticipation with which she awaited the meal. Whatever it was, she couldn't recall what had provoked the resistance she had felt so strongly in the taxi that morning. She had practically thrown him out of the cab. What could she have been thinking? Rinaldi wouldn't mind her having dinner with another man, she didn't think. He certainly wouldn't've objected to her sharing a cab. He always encouraged her to meet new people, to make new friends, but her devotion to him had always been such that she hadn't the time or the inclination.

Again she deliberately put Rinaldi out of her mind. The morning was over, and now was right now, and if what had happened between them earlier didn't bother Bobby, she wasn't going to let it bother her. As for Rinaldi, let his uniform and his medals and his decorations charm them silly at the Uruguayan Embassy. He could charm them to tears. With the gulls overhead, with the sun going down, and the freighters anchored in the harbor, with the tantalizing smell of fish on the grill, the clean wholesome smell of the baby powder, with the way he was looking at her, the excitement of being desired and feeling desirable, at that moment Rinaldi seemed not to matter so much. She watched the sun go down and drank cold beer from the bottle, and when Bobby finally spoke, he startled her.

"Up here I can see what the surf is doing from La Punta all the way to Agua Dulce and La Herradura. It's one of the reasons I took this place. I could look at the ocean forever. And it has all the space I need. A place this big anywhere else would cost an arm and a leg. Admittedly, the neighborhood isn't the greatest. Downstairs is a woodworking shop and you have power saws whining all day. And sometimes the smell of fish can gag you."

She pushed her brows together and because her arms were pulled inside the sweater, gestured toward the charcoal grill with her head.

"Oh no, no, no," he said. "From the fish meal factory a few blocks back. When there's an offshore wind."

It was nice, she thought, to be taken seriously. Then she laughed, and he caught on and he laughed at being teased. She liked that. Rinaldi hated being teased. He endured it when there was something he wanted, like this morning with the hat.

"Don't thank me," he said. "It was nothing."

She'd complimented him on the meal and he spent five minutes telling her that he didn't have to catch the fish, or grow the vegetables, or brew the beer, and that he didn't have to invent fishing, or agriculture, or the process of fermenting grain into an alcoholic beverage, and on and on about how incredible it was to think there was a way to turn sand into glass, and glass into bottles, windshields, and zoom lenses, and how lucky civilization was not to have had to wait for him to discover it, because he hadn't a clue as to where to begin. "In a roundabout way," he said, "the point is that the part I played in making this dinner is pretty small, but on behalf of Archimedes, Balboa, and the rest, I'm glad you liked it."

In a roundabout way, she understood.

He brought up a pot and brewed coffee on the coals. Lights shimmered on the water. She remembered consenting to see Elena, and she couldn't fathom why she'd agreed to do such a thing. The picture it conjured filled her with dread. Bobby talked in spurts, long monologues interspersed by equally long silences. Sometimes he asked her questions, but he didn't interrogate her like Rinaldi did, and he asked her nothing about her past. He said that as soon as he saw her he thought she was a model, or maybe an actress, and that if she weren't she ought to be. It was flattery and she liked it. That he wanted her to pose for him he made very clear. She was noncommittal. She said that she'd never done any modeling, but that once a photographer took her picture at a soccer game and it appeared in the Sunday magazine. As for acting, she'd joined a theater group when she'd first come to the capital, had had a part in one of their productions, but had quit at Rinaldi's request. In telling the story to Bobby, she dropped out the reason she'd quit. Not that she had had aspirations, at least none to which she was willing to admit. But she had liked being part of the group, had enjoyed performing, and had considered herself modestly talented. She sometimes thought about returning and, remembering how much she'd liked it, wondered why she had acquiesced without so much as a word of protest. Thinking about it now, she resented Rinaldi for having had the gall to even ask such a thing of her.

Bobby offered to drive her home, but she insisted on calling a taxi. She preferred to avoid a scene on the doorstep. While they waited, she looked at more of his pictures. She decided the one of Inez was terrific. She could see where someone might think it cold, but there was no denying its power. Even if you didn't know the story, it was all there in her face.

Bobby stood to the side and watched her, pleased at her obvious pleasure. Inez was his favorite, too. He wanted to ask her what exactly she was seeing and thinking and feeling, and then reminded himself not to question his luck. Tonight she was his luck. "You and Blacky are the only ones who see anything in it," he said. "Maybe you'd like to go out there one day with me. To the track, I mean. Tomorrow, for instance. You want to go tomorrow?"

She said no, and she lied, she told him that she had plans for the afternoon. She didn't *want* to say no. In fact, not an hour earlier she had promised herself to give the word "yes" more of a chance.

Bobby said that he was going early to take some pictures, that he'd get her back in plenty of time for whatever she had to do in the afternoon. He thought she might like it, he said.

How would you know what I would and wouldn't like? she wanted to say. Rinaldi did that to her, too, tried to dictate her tastes. She wanted to be indignant, but she remembered the promise she had made to herself, and besides, he had only made a suggestion. "Pick me up on your way," she told him instead.

They arrived at the racetrack early enough to catch a groom still sleeping outside Agua Fria's stall. Bobby took the picture, but dropped his lens cap, which rolled into a dim corner. He swore under his breath, and bent down to pick through the muck to find it. She found the light switch before he had sorted through too much manure. "Don't thank me," she said before he had actually thanked her. "I didn't invent the incandescent bulb, all I did was turn it on." Bobby laughed.

They wandered around the stables and through the empty grandstand. He photographed a man sweeping the trash from the prior day's races—soft drink cups, racing forms, cigarette butts, pari-mutuel tickets. Bobby pointed the lens toward the ground, cropping around the push broom, the man's bare feet, and the litter. He asked her to get in the picture and took several shots of her refusing. They started back to the stables, then Bobby walked back to put something into the Indian's hand—money, she assumed. He closed the man's fingers around it.

He took shots of a hot walker and a big roan colt still steaming from its workout. The colt was covered with a navy wool blanket with JGB sewn on in gold satin letters. The hot walker's coat had just the one sleeve. He was an Indian, too. She could understand Bobby's interest in the subject, but for her, having lived there all her life, the irony in that sort of contrast was trite.

Bobby asked her to pose with some jockeys he knew, and her initial response was no. In fact her tongue was already up against the roof of her mouth to form the letter *n* when she switched to yes, which came out "Nnnyess."

Bobby mimicked her. His teasing had no edge, and she was already glad she'd come, doubly glad, it turned out, because there weren't any jockeys around, and she was able to keep her pact with herself without having to pose for the pictures. She had seen enough of the visual ironies in his photographs, the contrasts he looked for and so frequently found, to guess he would ask her to dandle a jockey on her knee, or something she would find equally embarrassing. She liked the muscle men more than she liked most of the rich/poor, old/young, big/little pictures he made.

"I'm thinking about the beach today," he said walking back to the van. "I've got another day off. I know you have plans, but maybe you can change them, I mean if you want."

"What plans?" she said without thinking.

"The plans you said last night you had for this afternoon." He stopped to look at her.

"Oh, *those* plans," she said remembering her lie. "They've been canceled."

"Canceled?" he said.

"Annulled," she said. He smiled and started walking again. "Expunged," she said and put her arm around his waist. "Erased. Scuttled. Finito."

*   *   *

The beaches she was familiar with were to the south of the capital, which is where Rinaldi had his place, at Santa María del Mar. Bobby drove north from the city, beyond the harbor, past the airport, beyond the slums and the factories, beyond the resort at Tula, a two-hour trip to a grubby little place called El Barro, which straddled the Pan American Highway between her family home in the mountains and the capital. She'd passed through it many times, but never stopped because she never saw anything but the crowded sidewalks and cheap shops along the commercial strip through the center of town. From the car she never saw anything that enticed her to even slow down.

A block off the highway, the street to the beach turned to dirt. The single-story houses were painted an array of pastels, and dusty geraniums grew in flower boxes under shuttered windows. Nearer the beach, the paint on the houses wasn't so fresh. Walls were crumbling. A three-legged dog nosed through rubbish in a vacant lot. A boy flew a kite from a rooftop. Bobby took a picture of the boy. She was surprised he bypassed the dog.

The beach was a half-mile crescent from the whitewashed church at one end to the rocky point at the other. Fishing boats were drawn up on the sand. Beside them their owners, agreeable subjects for Bobby, were mending their nets. In front of a row of padlocked cabanas, boys played soccer with a ball of rags bound with twine. The three-legged dog watched from under a bench.

They walked the length of the beach and back. She carried her shoes, letting the cold water rush around her ankles. They spread their blankets near the rocks, where, protected from the wind which kicked up stinging swirls of sand, she felt warm and drowsy. She'd been awake since four in the morning, when Bobby had picked her up for the trip to the track.

Bobby was talking. He could talk more than any man she'd ever known. From what she could gather in her torpor, he was talking about his brother, but her mind was on Rinaldi. Rinaldi owned a beautiful house on the beach and they never spent any time there at all. He had no time for the beach. He was an important man, Rinaldi. She should have felt flattered that he gave her as much time as he did when he was in such demand. She *should* have felt flattered. She didn't. It was neglect she was feeling instead. She fell asleep.

When she awoke, a slice of orange sun lay on the water. To the north, a storm left a smudge on the sky. The wind churned white-caps across the bay and the waves were breaking point to point. She was cold and Bobby wasn't there. She wondered for an instant if he had thought her rude enough to have abandoned her there, on the beach in El Barro—no purse, no money, just jeans, a T-shirt, and rubber thongs. She had a moment of panic before she saw him waving to her from up on the rocks.

They were wet from spray, green, hairy with algae, slick. They were tricky to climb. Near the water line, retreating sea exposed sharp barnacles. Bobby grabbed her hand to bring her up to his perch.

"For a moment I thought you'd deserted me," she shouted over the wind and the surf. He moved closer, put his ear near her lips. "I thought you'd deserted me," she yelled. "I FELL ASLEEP." Bobby let his chin drop to his chest and closed his eyes. He made a pillow with his hands. The way he moved his mouth, she guessed he was snoring. "You were talking about your brother. YOUR BROTHER!"

He thought for a moment. "BLACKY?"

She wanted to tell him that falling asleep was the sort of thing you did only in the company of people you trusted, but the noise of the wind and the surf killed the impulse. Talking was too difficult. It was hard enough for her to say that kind of thing just once, quietly, let alone to have to repeat it at the top of her lungs. They abandoned the conversation. They sat and watched the storm pro-gress north along the coast. Waves bashed the rocks, and the wind misted them with spray. Nina was cold.

"Ready?" he yelled.

She climbed down carefully. He handed her his camera and peeled off his shirt and handed her that. He took off his pants, army pants with lots of pockets. He was wearing a bathing suit underneath, a skimpy, gaudy, flowered nylon thing. He tied his clothes in a bundle and pointed to where the boats sat on the beach. What she understood was that he wanted her to wait for him there. She thought he wanted a moment to be by himself by the edge of the ocean, to meditate, commune with the sea or some-thing. She didn't know what to think. She walked down the beach and left him alone.

When she reached the boats she looked back, and even as she watched she didn't believe what she was seeing, it simply didn't register. He had somehow climbed down to the water line. He was poised on a rock. Then she saw it coming: an enormous wave. She saw it, but he didn't—obviously he didn't, or why would he still be standing directly in its path?

The wave hit him and knocked him backward. Before he could get to his feet a second wave, bigger than the first, rolled in and knocked him back again. The next wave was bigger still, and out behind it line after line of waves, light green on the darker green of the ocean. Somehow he got to his feet. He stood and steadied himself to dive.

She ran toward him, was still fifty yards away when he dove. She could see red lines down his back from where he had scraped himself on the rocks. She searched for him in the foam and yellow scum that floated out in front of the rocks. At first she couldn't find him, and then she did, she saw his head, and then he was gone again. Seconds later she saw him forty yards farther away, swept out in the riptide. He looked tiny. The rip took him farther and farther from shore, pulling him out to where the next wave was rising out of the deeper water.

The wave rose and, moving toward shore, sucked water up from out in front of itself, increasing its height and mass and its power, exposing the black, barnacle-encrusted rocks of the reef. Plumes of mist blew from its crest as the moving green wall tilted past vertical. The wave lifted Bobby straight up its face, sucked him up along with the foam, scum, and floating debris, then pitched him out in an avalanche of water. The wave collapsed like a building, with Bobby underneath. Nina felt the impact through the sand.

She watched him swim slowly away from the rocks, way out into the bay, out beyond the breakers a quarter-mile from the beach. She could see him rise as the swells passed beneath him, and then he'd drop into a trough and she'd lose him again. She remembered to breathe. She followed him along the beach as he swam toward the center of the bay. The fishermen watched him, too. They wouldn't take a boat out after him, even when she pleaded. There was no discussion. "If we were to go after him, who would go for us?" one of them said.

She took a rope from one of the boats and waded into the surf herself. A wave knocked her down, and the cold took her breath away. A fisherman picked her up. His grip hurt her arm, but she was glad he was there. He held her arm and they stood thigh deep in the surf together.

Bobby was making no progress toward shore. The current seemed to be moving against him, taking him back toward the rocks, forcing him to swim continuously to stay in the same place. He floated on his back. He treaded water. When he wasn't swimming, the current pushed him back toward the rocks.

Then he seemed to be drifting inshore, closer to where the waves were breaking. He started swimming hard, kicking his feet and stroking fast. There was no break in the oncoming waves, and she couldn't see how he hoped to get through. If anything, the waves were getting bigger. A huge wave overtook him. He angled across the smooth, unbroken face, rode it a hundred yards before he dove beneath the surface. He reappeared swimming into the following wave, and he rode that one the same way. The third wave brought him into shallow water, and he stood and walked toward Nina and the fisherman. He was smiling. He said something she didn't hear. Watery blood rolled down his back. He draped one arm over her shoulder and the other around the fisherman's neck, and the three of them came out onto the sand.

It was cold, windless, and starry, and their fire was the only light on the beach. They had wrapped the blanket around themselves. The fishermen had gone, leaving the jar of wine for them to finish. Bobby said he was fine and asked her please not to ask him again. He put his arm around her. He talked. How he could talk! He was telling her about how close you could get to something before you actually touched it. He told her he had given the matter a lot of thought.

"As long as you haven't touched the thing yet," he was saying, "then there must still be some space between you. It stands to reason. If there's still some space, then you can get even closer. Get it?"

She didn't. She wanted to ask him something that had been on her mind for hours: Why had he dived into that raging water? "It wasn't for my sake, was it?" she asked. "You didn't do that for me?" He had a puzzled look on his face. "To impress me or something crazy like that?" He laughed at that. "You didn't, did you?" She was incredulous. "You went out there for me?"

He threw some driftwood onto the fire. "You get closer and closer," he said. He held his hands ten inches apart. "But there's still some distance between you, so you move five inches, halfway. But there's some distance still, and you want to get closer, so you come halfway again. And again. And again." His palms came almost but not quite together, a gap of an inch between them. "*Now* do you get it?" he asked.

"There's still closer to get."

"Right."

"So?" she said.

"So!" he said.

"So what?" He hadn't answered her question. She didn't know what he was talking about.

"So you'll never get there going by halves." And then he clapped his hands. "It stands to reason." He clapped his hands again.

The road from El Barro to the capital runs adjacent to the sea, but at night that is something you have to know. You can't see it or hear it, although all that separates you from the water is a guardrail and five hundred feet of air. Bobby played a tape of Hawaiian classics, glancing over at Nina half a dozen times to see if she was enjoying the music. It was for him a test of their compatability. He had decided he could never really love a woman who didn't really love Gabby Pahanui. She seemed to well enough. And she said she did when he asked.

"Really?" There was a plea in his voice.

"Really," she said, sensing how much it seemed to mean to him.

At her door the invitation he was hoping for wasn't extended, but she gave him another instead: dinner and the soccer game the following night. The game'd been sold out for weeks, she told him. It wasn't only Callao–San Sebastián, it not only decided the league title, it was Eusebio's final game. Seats were being scalped for a hundred apiece. "Midfield," she said. "High up."

He told her he'd love to go, but he might not be able, he might be out of town. He heard how lame his answer sounded, how vague, like "plans," so he said "Huaráz" to beef it up, make it more specific, more credible. He wasn't thinking. It just slipped out, and he was immediately sorry.

"I was born near Huaráz," she said. "I may be going soon my-self." Her tone was distant. Her eyes turned down. They were suddenly back to square one.

He wanted to explain, but he couldn't because of his promise to Blacky. Further conversation could only lead him to further eva-sions. Awkwardly, quickly, he kissed her. He'd call in the morning, he said. He climbed into his van and pulled away from in front of her house, too much in a hurry to notice the man in the black Mercedes parked in the shadows on the opposite side of the street.

Sweet Jesus, Antonio thought, his must be the hardest piece of ground in the whole sierra.

With a pair of oxen—a pair of oxen would make him a wealthy man in Viracocha, he himself owned only two sheep, a cow, and one calf—he could have had the field ready to plant in a morning, but a hammer and chisel would have been faster than that plow of his. He recognized that there were times, like now, when having so little was a blessing: they would never appoint a poor man mayor. To be appointed was an honor, surely, but it was a great expense as well, and some years, like this, when it was Viracocha's turn to host the Feast of Santo Rosario, the expense was enormous, far greater than the honor, most would agree. Not that they would ever appoint him anyway. No matter how much money he had.

But money was why Theofilo, mayor-to-be of Viracocha, would have to leave for the coast and the sugar plantations right after his inauguration. If there were an inauguration. Because of the money and because of what had happened to his predecessor, Justinio, Antonio doubted Theofilo would be found in time for the ceremony. Were it me, Antonio thought, I would not be found. Dominga would bury me first. That is, if I hadn't been murdered and buried already, which according to the rumors had been Justinio's fate—killed and buried in the *puna*. Some said the Moreno had killed him, who knew why?

It had been six months since the Moreno had first come to Viracocha requesting a meeting with Justinio and the village council. Their leader spoke for an hour or more, and the point, as best anyone in the village could tell, was that they were defending them against the army and the government in the capital, whom they called "the enemy." The soldiers, who had been to the village the preceding week, had claimed to be defending them as well. Except for the weather, which was by turns too hot or too cold, too wet or too dry, and the land itself, which was steep and rocky, a better habitation for goats than people, and except for history, which had consigned a once brilliant, rich, and powerful culture to stagnancy, poverty, and impotence—aside from these things and the dog-eating bastards from Copa Chica, with whom they'd been feuding for longer than anyone could remember, the people of Viracocha had no enemies of which they were aware. But between the Moreno and the army, the consensus among the men of the village was that the army had the better boots.

The army had also slaughtered a ewe, pregnant with twins, it turned out, but the soldiers hadn't cared that it was pregnant or that it had cost its owner a year's worth of wages. Nor did they offer to pay. The officer said one ewe was a cheap price to pay for protection from the Moreno. At that time Viracocha had seen nothing of the Moreno. Since the Moreno arrived, it had seen nothing of the army.

The Moreno had also taken a sheep. When its owner asked for double the animal's value, thinking the Moreno would bargain if they were going to pay at all, they paid the asking price. Without complaint. Thus the village remained undecided as to whether the Moreno were generous, foolish, or both. In fact, almost everything about the Moreno was a mystery as far as the Indians were concerned.

Antonio's opinion was that since no one knew what the Moreno were after, and since the Moreno were still somewhere around, it was likely they hadn't yet gotten it. Whatever "it" was. They might have held Justinio responsible; he was missing almost a week. Justinio's wife said that he didn't return from his fields Friday night, and on Saturday they found their dog hanging from the tree.

Antonio didn't know why the Moreno would kill the mayor if they didn't want his money or if he hadn't been caught with one of their women, much less why they would hang a dog. Justinio had no money. This Antonio knew because Justinio had come to him for a loan, money for Santo Rosario. Antonio guessed that Justinio was down on the coast in the sugarcane fields, and that he had hanged the dog himself before he left. It was a mean dog and Antonio didn't blame him if he had.

Antonio's plow was homemade and crude, but it got the job done. Antonio shoved the share into the earth, Augusto jumped on it to sink it into the ground, and together they levered it down. Dominga turned over the clod so the grasses would rot, and then pounded it with her adz to break up the soil. Their field wasn't so big that one couldn't spit clear across it, but so far it had taken the three of them three days to get it ready. Antonio guessed they would finish in time to go to Marcara that evening and see the inauguration.

Dominga had fallen behind. Hers was the harder job, breaking the clods, especially there, high on the hillside, where the soil was stonier and the earth more compact. Antonio told her to sit for a while and rest. He handed her the coca and the gourd of lime, and gave her water from the pot. Then he and Augusto took turns pounding the overturned earth. Augusto, strong for a boy of twelve, could almost do the work of a man. He sang while he worked, something Antonio never did anymore, at work or at any other time, at least not sober, but he was not yet to the age or the state of mind where the singing of others annoyed him.

Theirs was the highest field where corn could still be grown, although until Antonio had first begun to cultivate this particular plot (after he'd been cheated out of the land he'd inherited from his mother), the fields just below his had always been thought to be the highest where corn could still be grown.

Antonio agreed with the new assessment, and no one knew better than he. He'd scoured every inch of the sierra within Viracocha's jurisdiction for arable land. Everything in the warmer, more fertile valley was either not for sale or too expensive. Higher, the land became too steep to plant, and farther back into the canyon it was too cold for corn. He'd searched beyond the communal pastures, even beyond the *puna*, the grassy plateau which the village still referred to as the savage land, all the way to the limit of the Viracochan world, the glaciers of Nevada de Copa. Beneath them was Blue Lake, by whose shores Antonio, in defiance of village taboos, sometimes took his sheep to pasture.

The tune was something Augusto had learned in church, but the words—he was making them up as he went along—were about a puma. Antonio noticed that lately Augusto had a one-track mind. The boy had somehow learned that when his father had been his age, he'd killed a puma with a rock. This was true, and certainly not something of which Antonio was ashamed. But now it was pumas all day long: pumas in the bushes, pumas in the storage room, songs about pumas, rhymes about pumas, games with pumas. Antonio wished whoever had told Augusto—most likely Eduardo Guzman—had kept his big mouth shut. He carefully explained to his son that the incident had happened twenty-five years ago, that even in those days pumas were rare, that it had been blind dumb luck, and that it could just as easily have been him as the puma who had been killed. He wasn't even hunting at the time. He'd been chasing a lamb which had wandered up into the rocks. A young male puma, as it happened, was stalking it too. Until the cat hissed at him Antonio was unaware of its presence. By then it was ten feet away, and Antonio was too scared to breathe.

The puma was torn between its fear of Antonio and its appetite for the lamb, and while it made up its mind—a long, long time to a frightened twelve-year-old boy—Antonio picked up a rock. He only wanted to scare it off, he told Augusto. Killing it never entered his mind. His throw would have missed by a mile if the puma hadn't leapt right into it. Now, ever since Augusto had heard the story, all the boy thought about was pumas.

Antonio sat beside Dominga, sharing the coca, their backs to the wall they'd built with stones they'd dug out of the field. They could've built a wall twenty feet high with the stones they'd dug out of that field.

September. Cold afternoons. They sat shoulder to shoulder facing the western sun. The sun was one of the pleasures of their lives. The stones at their backs were warm and blocked the wind coming down off the mountain. They inhaled the smell of freshly turned earth and soaked in the last heat of the day while Augusto finished breaking up the clods. He lifted the adz by heaving it to his chest and pushing it up over his head from there. It seemed to require all his strength, and the weight of it nearly pulled him over backward. When it fell, he fell. He checked to see if his parents were watching before he spit on his hands and hefted it again.

Marcará. The streetlight in front of Luna's store was, for a change, on. The rest of the plaza was lit by candles and lanterns. About sixty villagers had assembled there in front of the church. Señor Cesante, the oldest and most respected man in Viracocha, himself appointed mayor seven times, stood on the church steps with the rest of the village council. He was holding the mayor's staff, which was tipped with a silver cross and said to be two hundred years old. Antonio suspected its true age was probably closer to a hundred. On the table in front of them were the chalice, the candles, a heavy brass crucifix, and a puma skull. Everything necessary for the inauguration was present—everything except the new mayor, Theofilo. If he didn't go to the coast, Antonio thought, he should have. Either way, that's where he would find himself before too long.

Augusto stood between his father and mother. Alberto, Antonio's middle son, ten years old, climbed onto his father's shoulders to search for his other brother and his sister in the crowd, but Julia found them first. Even after a full day's work and a ten-mile walk from the *puna* where she had watched the sheep with her little brother Marcellino, she seemed happy. The inauguration meant there would be a Feast of Santo Rosario after all. To Dominga, Julia looked tired, unwell, and under her breath she murmured a prayer, asking not only Jesus but the local saints Mama Rosa and Mama Limpiay to protect her daughter and allow her an easy childbirth. The baby was due in a little more than a month, about the time of Julia's fifteenth birthday. At Dominga's urging, Antonio had left offerings of cigarettes for the gods. To Antonio it seemed a waste of good tobacco, but Dominga had her own beliefs, and he'd given up trying to talk her out of them.

Julia told them Marcellino had stayed up in the *puna* with the sheep. Even knowing how seriously Marcellino took his responsibility to care for the animals, it was surprising to them he'd consented to stay. He was only seven and afraid to sleep in the *puna* huts alone. Especially this particular hut, which was right by the bank of a stream, despite the fact that, as everyone knew, demons often lived in *puna* streams. It was Antonio's opinion that the damp which rotted the thatch and settled in your lungs made the hut bad, not demons. Antonio didn't believe in demons. He thought perhaps the watercourse had changed, which would explain why the hut had been built and then abandoned.

Julia laughed when she described the way Marcellino had looked when she'd left him. It seemed to Dominga that teenagers feared nothing, except the judgments of their peers, and seeing Julia laugh at her little brother's fears, she was worried to think that this particular hut was where Julia had slept with the father of her child.

Shouts came from the far side of the plaza, and from atop his father's shoulders Alberto reported that Theofilo was leading a crowd of people into the plaza. And how strange! He was walking backward! Theofilo's wife was being carried in, an injustice in Alberto's mind, because it was Theofilo who was to be the mayor, after all, not Señora Teresa, and shouldn't he be the one allowed to ride? In any event, seeing the way she screamed and struggled, Alberto sensed she didn't really appreciate the experience in the way he thought Theofilo might, and certainly not the way he, Alberto, would if he were being carried atop the crowd to the steps of the church.

The crowd parted to let them through. Theofilo didn't trust himself to climb the steps backward, and he turned around to see Señor Cesante extending him his hand. Teresa was set on her feet. She also reached for Señor Cesante, but was quickly restrained. She sprayed spit at him instead, which the village elder, whose eyesight was failing, and who now stood on the top of the steps with his palms upturned and his face to the sky, took as a signal to skip the invocation in order to speed the ceremony along.

Unlike his wife, Theofilo seemed to have surrendered to his fate. Slowly he ascended the steps. He took his place beside Señor Cesante just as the frail old man, who was nearly deaf as well as blind and had missed all of Teresa's prior calumny—against himself and the council, against Justinio, against her husband, against the village itself, and the Feast of Santo Rosario for which, as mayor, her husband was obligated to foot the bill—heard himself called, unbelievably, at a solemn public ceremony, before the door of the house of God, with the entire village as witness, and loud enough to penetrate his anxiety over the impending downpour and his dim musings over the fate of his village saddled with the likes of a Theofilo for mayor, Señor Cesante heard himself called by no less than the wife of the mayor-to-be, a "senile lump of green guinea pig shit."

No one had ever addressed Señor Cesante that way, at least not to his face, and in the ensuing stillness Theofilo made his bid for financial solvency. He knew there was no place to run, and with a logic borne of desperation he thought he might barricade himself inside the church. He bolted for the door. In the attempt to block Theofilo's escape, a councilman accidentally whacked Señor Cesante on the temple with his staff. The clunk on the head knocked the old gentleman onto the table, spilling the chalice, toppling the candles, and sending the puma skull bouncing down the steps. Teresa cheered her husband and urged the councilman to "hit the old bastard again."

Theofilo pulled at the door with all his strength. Had he attended church more often he might have known that the door opened inward, and that not even a man with the strength of the legendary Copa Chican, Dominguez, could have pulled it open. Theofilo braced himself with his back to the door. He was trapped. The council blocked his escape. They forced him to his knees and dragged him before Señor Cesante, who raised the brass crucifix and struck Theofilo a blow which would have knocked him unconscious had Theofilo not been wearing a hat which absorbed some of the impact. The first part of the ceremony had been concluded. The Viracochans cheered.

Theofilo was helped to his feet. He was glassy-eyed and his hat sat cockeyed on his head. Someone pinned his arm behind his back. The kissing of the staff, the symbol of the acceptance of the responsibilities of office, was to be the concluding ritual of the abbreviated inauguration, but Theofilo averted his head and retracted his lips. Eduardo Guzman impatiently twisted Theofilo's head back around as if it were a melon on a vine and pinched Theofilo's cheeks, forcing him to pucker. Then Señor Cesante, wobbly even on his better days, offered the silver tip to Theofilo's lips, not quite hard enough to break his teeth, but with enough authority to bring about a nosebleed, and the job was done. Theofilo stood alone on the top of the steps, the staff in his hand, his head tilted back, pressing his finger to his bloody nose. Officially mayor of Viracocha for the term of one year, he was released to assume the duties and the expenses of office. And, thought Antonio, if what they say happened to Justinio was true, the danger as well.

Blacky chose a table by the pool. He had his pick. A waiter in a white coat brought him his drink. Blacky signed the tab with Bobby's name and reached into his wallet for a tip. The waiter refused. He pointed to a line on the bottom of the check which read "No Tipping Allowed." Blacky slipped the folded bill into the boy's coat anyway, pointing to another line at the top of the check: "Malibu Beach Club, Members Only." "I'm not a member," he said.

The day was overcast and the pool deck almost deserted. There were two women, bikinied, sunglassed, drinking white wine coolers at a table under an umbrella. A boy dangled his feet in the water and played with a sailboat on a string while a gang of children chased each other around and through the orderly rows of empty lounge chairs. Blacky sipped his Scotch and watched the surf wash onto the beach.

Bobby came out of the locker room, his hair wet, carrying a black and orange Baltimore Orioles gym bag, the tail of his Hawaiian shirt hanging out of his jeans. By that time Blacky was drinking his second and the women from the bar were sitting at the table with him. Blacky introduced them to Bobby as they were getting up to leave.

"You put your drink on my tab, didn't you?" Bobby asked.

"They pretend money doesn't exist around here," Blacky answered. "No tipping, no prices on the menu . . ."

"You did, then," Bobby said. "Good. I want you softened up. I need a favor. I want the night off. Nina's got us a couple of tickets for the game tonight. Midfield. High up."

"She the one from last week?"

"Which?"

"With the Great Danes."

"Siberian Huskies. Nah. Nina's from San Isidro market. She's—" Bobby switched into a put-on French accent "—How do you say . . . ? Special." He kissed his fingertips. "Very special. How about something to eat?"

Blacky held up his glass. "Another of these."

The waiter came as soon as he finished serving the gang of children who had given up tag and were sitting, all nine or ten of them, two tables away. "I'll have a burger, Ramón," Bobby said. He jerked his thumb over his shoulder and shook his head. The kids were throwing french fries at one another. "And a beer for me and another Scotch for Blacky. Have you met Blacky?" The two shook hands.

A moment later, chairs scraped on the cement and there was a howl. Bobby turned to see a blond doughy kid who looked thirteen and older than the rest holding a skinny dark kid, the same kid who'd been playing with the sailboat, in a headlock. The skinny kid was crying. The bigger boy pushed him into the pool. Then they all ran off toward the tennis court. The skinny kid trailed after them, squooshing water in his shoes.

"Cancel the sandwiches," Bobby yelled at Ramón's back. "Just bring the drinks." Bobby went to kids' table, put a couple of sandwiches and a handful of french fries on his plate, and brought it back. "You sure you're not hungry? There's more," he said to Blacky.

"How in hell did they ever let someone like you into someplace like this?"

Bobby started to answer, but his mouth was full of food. "Remember a tall blond girl—"

Blacky tossed him a napkin. "Ketchup on your mouth."

"—volleyball player—"

"I remember. Her father's a diplomat or something?"

"And chairman of the membership committee. Sigrid was her name."

"But why?"

"If you want to know why, you must not remember Sigrid." Bobby fitted his mouth around the sandwich.

"Not 'Why Sigrid,' you jerk. I know why Sigrid. Why here. *This* place." Blacky looked around.

"Great gym. All the equipment—"

"Mirrors all over the walls."

"—steam room, private surfing beach, pool, certain other attractions . . ." He wiped the corner of his mouth with the back of his hand and indicated the ladies at the bar with a tilt of his head.

"And Sigrid?"

"School. Geneva."

"Junior high?"

"I just wrote her a letter."

Bobby ate his lunch. Blacky sipped his Scotch. The kids returned and ordered ice cream and disappeared again before Ramón brought the food. "So what's the skinny with Gavilan?" Bobby asked, dipping a spoon into an unclaimed sundae. "I could sponsor him if he wants to join."

"You ever hear of the Missing Tooth?" Blacky asked. He pointed to the corner of his mouth. "Chocolate syrup."

"Moose's Tooth, up in Alaska, some buddies of mine climbed it four years ago." He jutted his chin. "Did I get it all?"

"Yeah, you got it. If you know some of this already, bear with me."

The Missing Tooth was a barrio built on the dunes back of the city. There were a series of shallow caves in the sandstone cliffs which had been periodically inhabited for years. The municipal authorities were forever going up there to evict the inhabitants, but as soon as the police would leave, the old tenants or new tenants would move back in. The city's solution was to brick up the entrances. It wasn't long before someone knocked the bricks out of one of them, probably someone from another barrio in need of building supplies. From the city, the gap in the sandstone resembled a missing tooth, and thus the name. Ultimately the squatters were more persistent than the city. The fact was that campesinos were coming to the capital in such numbers, and the pressure to expand became so great, that the city acquiesced, and what with the bricks already there, and the caves, another squatter settlement was founded, the Missing Tooth. Within a year the Missing Tooth was home to fifteen thousand people.

Blacky and his mother came from the mountains to live with

relatives in the Missing Tooth when Blacky was nine years old. The relatives, from his father's side of the family, had no room for them, it turned out, and so they had to fend for themselves, like everyone in the Missing Tooth. Blacky scrounged in the garbage dumps first, then sold penny candies and cigarettes from a cart on the streets of the city, working himself up to where the company, which had hundreds of carts and hundreds of boys in its employ, gave Blacky a cart of his own. He earned sixty cents a day, fifteen of which he returned to the company for use of their cart. In addition, he had a quota to meet which required that he be on the street for twelve to fourteen hours every day. If he missed the quota he didn't get paid, and if he missed for three days another boy would get his cart.

His mother, on the recommendation of her sister-in-law, got a job as a maid for a European family, the Marchamps, in Miraflores. Blacky used to meet her there after work and escort her home. Mrs. Marchamp, impressed by Blacky's devotion, offered Blacky a job. He was a good-looking kid, always clean, neat, you wouldn't know that every morning he left a house that was nothing more than grass matting tacked to a makeshift frame of pilfered two-by-fours. But because Mrs. Marchamp didn't want to take Blacky, who was eleven at the time, out of school, she arranged for him to work only on the weekends. She didn't know he'd never been to school. Blacky did nothing to correct this misunderstanding.

Nor did he tell his mother he had quit his job. While she thought he was selling candy from a cart, he was running with a street gang known as the Sultans. His specialty was ripping the earrings right off the ears of women in the Plaza de Armas, but he did other things too, almost exclusively preying on tourists, not only because they had the money but because they were either frightened or sympathetic. Either way they were vulnerable. Nor was everything he did illegal. He wasn't against working if he thought he was fairly rewarded. He liked the airport, which was new and clean, and he found that if he paid the police a share of his tips he could carry bags or call cabs, or even present himself as a tour guide, which was good work when he could get it. Weekends he worked at the Marchamps'. He looked forward to the weekends, since there was very little to actually do, the food was good and plentiful, and the house was surreal in its opulence. It cost him out of pocket—had he spent his weekends hustling, on average he'd have netted more—but money wasn't everything.

The truth was he would have worked just for the chance to spend time in the Marchamp household. It was an existence completely unrelated to the life he led in the barrio, not just in another part of the city, but another world altogether. It was exotic. It was clean, quiet, safe, comfortable, and for all of that he had to admit, after the novelty had worn off, also somewhat boring. Not so boring he wanted to give it up, however. He tried to make himself indispensible, not just to the Marchamps, whom he rarely saw even when they were at home—and they were often out of the country —but to the other employees from whom he took orders, and whom he recognized as holding the real power in the household. He washed the cars, weeded the gardens, ran errands. He asked for chores. He thought it was only a matter of time until they would discover how unnecessary he was.

Not long after his thirteenth birthday he lost his virginity to one of the older girls who worked in the kitchen. She led him to the music room on the top floor of the house. Among its features were a stereo, skylights, a window seat, oriental rugs, a harp, and a grand piano. Sex and the piano were simultaneous discoveries and for him held almost equal fascination. He learned piano by diddling upstairs. He was worried Mrs. Marchamp would find them out, but he couldn't help himself. When he could find nothing else that needed to be done, he sat at the grand piano in the large, bright, quiet room, listening to records and working out the fingering on the keyboard. And because of the girl, he became a fixture in the kitchen. Almost by accident he learned to cook.

He worried that Mrs. Marchamp would somehow discover that he'd lied to her about going to school. She asked him about his studies whenever she saw him. From hanging around the airport he had picked up phrases in several different languages, and he had a worldly air that made him seem more educated than he was. His greatest fear was that he might be called upon to read—a recipe, directions on a bottle of pesticide, a shopping list—so he asked the chauffeur to teach him, persuading him with a pair of earrings Blacky knew were too valuable to be fenced in the ordinary way. He studied on the window seat in the music room, borrowing books Mrs. Marchamp was only too happy to loan him from her library. On the weekends he worked, he read, he made love, he played the piano, and during the week he ran with the Sultans.

Blacky at sixteen was an accomplished kid: he was astonishingly well read, he could pull a transmission, he could hang a door, he played piano by ear; but it was in the kitchen where he found his place. He had a natural talent for cooking. From time to time he would be loaned out to cook for people in Mrs. Marchamp's circle. Or entertain on the piano. Blacky became her cause. She offered his mother a live-in job as well as a job for Blacky in the kitchen. She offered to send him to private school. He was reluctant to leave his friends in the barrio, but smart enough to see where the graduates of the Sultans went as opposed to the graduates of Notre Dame Academy; and besides, there was no comparison between their grass mat shanty and the servants' quarters at the Marchamps'.

Predictably, he never really fit in at Notre Dame. For one, while he could fool Mrs. Marchamp he couldn't fool his teachers, and he was given extra work to fill the wide gaps in his knowledge. If he was behind the other students academically, he was by an equally wide margin more worldly. After all, he had been more or less on his own since he was nine. His classmates seemed petty, childish, and unbelievably naive in comparison to his friends in the barrio. What's more, they possessed an arrogance that was all the more galling since it was totally unwarranted. Their sole achievement was to have been born in a particular neighborhood to a particular set of parents. And if they accepted the son of a maid in their classroom as their gesture toward democracy, they drew the line at the other places where they gathered—the Malibu Beach Club, for instance. Blacky preferred the Sultans, and he returned to his old neighborhood every chance he got. He was drawn to the risk, the excitement, and the freedom the streets represented to him. There, boldness mattered, cunning and nerve mattered. The cynicism and apathy cultivated by his classmates were without value on the streets.

Blacky had finished his Scotch. Bobby ordered him another, and another beer for himself. A guy came over and sat down uninvited at their table. He was carrying a couple of tennis rackets and a leather bag over his shoulder.

Bobby introduced the newcomer, Felipe Vonderahe, to Blacky. Blacky stared into his drink. "Howzit going, Phil?" Bobby said.

"For shit," Phil said.

Bobby gave Blacky a wink.

"I don't know what the hell I'm going to do." Felipe slumped back in the chair and closed his eyes. "Son of a bitch," he sighed.

Ramón came to the table. Felipe slid his Ray-Bans up onto his forehead.

"Heineken Dark, a glass of ice, and a twist of lime," he said. "Quick. I'm dying." Ramón came back a moment later shaking his head. Felipe sighed again. "What next? I can't hit a decent back-hand all morning, my goddamn serve abandoned me, and now this clown tells me they're out of Heineken Dark."

"There's Heineken Light, and in the dark we have Guinness and Negra Modela . . ." Ramón rattled off five or six brands.

"Forget it," Felipe said, disgusted.

"Would you care for—"

"I told you forget it!" And then, after Ramón had walked away, but before he was out of earshot, he added, "Where the hell do they find these guys?" Blacky pushed away from the table. Bobby stood up.

"Hey, where're you guys going? I just sat down."

"Next time, Phil," Bobby said, chasing Blacky across the deck. He followed him through the air-conditioned lobby to the portico at the front. The attendant brought Blacky's car around, sputtering and belching exhaust. The portico filled with smoke. Blacky slid behind the wheel, but the passenger door didn't open, so Bobby tossed his gym bag in the back and vaulted into the seat as Blacky gunned it out of the driveway. "I don't know how you can stand it," Blacky said. The busted muffler dragged, shooting sparks.

"Where we going, anyway?" Bobby asked. Blacky didn't respond. "Hey, Phil's not such a bad guy."

"Phil's an asshole."

"You heard him. He had a tough morning. His backhand abandoned him."

"He's an asshole."

"You got to get to know Phil a little bit before you can really begin to fully appreciate what an asshole he is. You just met him. You got no right to make a judgment like that."

"I got a right." Blacky said, and then he told Bobby the story.

At Notre Dame Academy, Blacky and Phil Vonderahe were classmates. Blacky wasn't any closer with Phil than he was with any of the others, Blacky was always an outsider, but there was an incident involving Phil that crystallized Blacky's feelings toward the whole bunch of them. One Saturday when Blacky was on his way back to the barrio, Phil surprised him by getting on the same bus. Phil was with a girl, a very pretty girl whom Blacky didn't know. Blacky never went back to the old neighborhood in the blue blazer, gray slacks, and tie he wore to school, just as he never wore his barrio clothes—old pants, sandals, and a soccer jersey—to school. Phil and the girl sat down directly across the aisle facing Blacky, and although Phil's eyes passed over Blacky several times, Phil didn't acknowledge him. At first Blacky thought Phil didn't recognize him in his barrio clothes—it was possible, the bus was crowded, people standing between them—and then Blacky thought, no, Phil recognized him all right, it was that Phil didn't want the girl to know that he knew a boy from the slums. Blacky was an embarrassment.

"Nah," Bobby offered. "He was probably just scared you were going to bird-dog his girl."

"If that was it, he had good reason to be. She was a great-looking chick. I got a hard-on just looking at her."

"I used to get them on the bus all the time. It's the vibration, I think. From the engine. Some mornings on the way to school I had to get off with a book in front of my crotch. Once I didn't have a book and I had to ride a couple of miles past my stop."

Blacky said that he came finally to realize it was more than Phil's not recognizing him, worse than Phil's being embarrassed to know him. The truth was Phil *didn't even see him.* Dressed as he was, Blacky was invisible, and not just to Phil, but to the girl too, and to that whole segment of society from which the two of them came.

It was not much different in the barrio, he admitted, which was why he never went back in his slacks and loafers. They were nearly exclusive worlds. No one in the Sultans showed any interest in where he was Monday through Friday. Guys who went to school were stiffs to them, one stiff indistinguishable from the next. If they had any interest in his other life, they never expressed it. They treated him the same as ever. In contrast, at school they asked him all about the barrio, but they didn't believe what he told them.

Blacky drove to the eastern edge of the city, a commercial district of factories and warehouses backed up against the dunes. He parked near the conglomeration of buildings, garages, and stalls that comprised La Parada, the market cum truck and bus terminal which occupied four square city blocks. Immediately some kids approached them and held out their hands. Blacky gave the oldest a quarter and with no more than that passing between them, the kids assumed posts around Blacky's car.

"Cheap insurance," Blacky said. "But I'd take my stuff if I were you."

"I got my camera, but I thought I'd leave the gym bag. Nothing in it but sweaty shorts."

"Listen to me," Blacky warned.

"Then what're you paying them for?"

"The policy covers the car, but not its contents. Let's go. The stuff should be waiting. Shouldn't take me a minute."

"What stuff?" Bobby asked, instantly alert. He narrowed his eyes.

"You know, man. The *stuff*," answered Blacky. "The spice." He winked.

Bobby didn't mind a little toot from time to time, but he wanted nothing to do with the buying or selling of it. He wished Blacky hadn't brought him along. Dealers were wacko. The idea of making a buy in a public place made him sweat. Looking right and left and over his shoulder, he followed Blacky through the crowd.

There was row after row of stalls selling meat and produce, cheese, fresh fish, beer, pop, booze, bottled water, notions, potions, lotions. There was the smell of rancid cooking oil, sizzling meat, propane, fish, diesel exhaust. There were long lines of people at the ticket windows with suitcases, trunks, paper bags, cardboard boxes, straw baskets, packages wrapped in newsprint and tied with twine. There were people on benches waiting for buses, porters wheeling dollies, cages of chickens and ducks, cattle in pens. There were horns, whistles, loudspeakers, radios, air brakes, bleating goats, and revving engines. Bobby followed Blacky through the tumult.

A boy in a tattered coat with the bus company's insignia sewn on his sleeve waved a bus into a parking slot. The bus was half again as large as a normal bus, ultramodern, with a second level for sight-seeing and dark windows all around. What caught Bobby's eye was the customized paint job done in brilliant colors and minute detail: down one side a chain of snow-covered mountains, conquistadores down the other. A condor sailed under the windshield. The Huandoy Empress reminded Bobby of a luxury liner docking in a dingy, smoky, smelly port. Glad for an excuse to duck out of the buy, he told Blacky that he'd meet him back at the car when he finished taking pictures. He put his gym bag over his shoulder and shot the bus from all angles—the sleek twenty-first-century stratocruiser discharging passengers from out of the Middle Ages. He liked the shiny newness of the bus, and the people in their bright primary colors stepping off with bundles, with babies tied to their backs, with shopping bags, burlap sacks, cartons, and pack-ages wrapped in newsprint and string, with buckets, with baskets, with chickens. Their anxious, expectant faces. He quickly shot a roll of film.

A boy positioned himself in front of Bobby's lens: ten, eleven years old, ragged, brash. "Take a picture of me," he demanded. "Hey, mister, take my picture." He mugged for the camera. "Hey! Mister!" Ordinarily, Bobby would have told the kid to hit the bricks, or if the kid were persistent, he might have pretended to take the kid's picture, looked through the viewfinder and not snapped the shutter, just to get rid of him, because on principle he didn't like aggressive kids like this, who were only going to hit you up for money afterward, who posed stiff and puffed-up with pre-posterous, unnatural smiles. Ordinarily he would have told the kid to get lost, but this kid, in a coat so ragged the patches had patches, and tennis shoes with the toes cut open, without laces or socks, this kid said take my picture in perfect, accent-free English.

"What did you say?" Bobby asked, thinking he hadn't heard him right.

"Take my picture," the kid repeated. He could have been from Iowa. So Bobby took him over to stand between the headlights of the Huandoy Empress, posed him beneath the talons of the condor so it looked as if the giant bird were swooping down to snatch him up and take him away. He gave Bobby his best puffed-up smile, and while Bobby composed the scene in the viewfinder, rotated the zoom in the attempt to decide how much of the boy and how much of the front of the bus he wanted in the frame, and whether to include the little window above the windshield which indicated the bus's destination and now read TERMINAL, while he turned the frame from horizontal to vertical and back again, while he focused and adjusted the settings, the boy stood still and patient, grinning like a banshee, his hands on his hips, his feet spread wide.

"OK," Bobby said. "One . . . two . . ."

He squeezed the shutter. As he did, he felt a tug at his shoulder and the weight of his gym bag was gone. He spun to see another kid racing away with it through the crowd. In a flash of realization he turned back to see his subject sprinting away in the opposite direction.

Bobby ran as if he had jewels in the gym bag instead of a sweaty jock. He chased the kid down the narrow aisles, around the stacks of boxes, between stalls, through the maze of passageways, dodging people, bumping them, shoving them out of the way. The boy burst through the confusion and into the relative open of the street, giving Bobby, who was not as agile but who was faster in the straightaways, the room he needed to run the boy down. Perhaps he thought that Bobby wouldn't bother to chase him at all, or that he would more easily lose him. He was definitely surprised to see Bobby bearing down on him. He picked up speed, but with nowhere to hide, out on the street amid traffic moving in both directions, he could only count on Bobby's endurance giving out before his own.

They ran for a block, two, three, Bobby's camera swinging on the strap and banging into his chest. Bobby closed the gap. Running full speed, he reached out and grabbed the boy's collar, but it tore away in his hand. The boy tossed the gym bag away, but Bobby didn't stop. The bag didn't matter. He'd been made a fool of by a couple of kids. He was insulted and angry, and his anger drove his legs. He ran the kid down, held him by the back of the neck, held him hard because the kid was fighting to get away. He was no taller than Bobby's armpits. Bobby's hand nearly encircled his neck. He was choking him. The boy punched and kicked and twisted in Bobby's grasp. Bobby squeezed tighter. The kid gasped for air. He coughed and gagged. Afraid his hold was strangling him, Bobby released his neck, grabbed the kid's biceps, and lifted him up off the ground. The kid kicked wildly. He twisted and screamed, and Bobby held him at arm's length where the kicks couldn't reach him. The kid spit in his face, then kicked at Bobby's crotch. This one connected. The jolt made Bobby let go. He thought the kid would run, but the kid leapt right back at him, swiped at Bobby's face with his fingernails. Bobby grabbed him again, pinning his arms, lifting him off the ground. The kid thrashed wildly, ferociously.

A crowd had gathered, its sympathies clearly with the kid, but no one was yet willing to get between them. Bobby felt the dark pressure of rage surge into the muscles of arms. He ignored the demands to let the boy go. He held the boy in a bear hug. He squeezed, holding him immobile, squeezed harder, wanting the boy to submit, knowing as he crushed him against his chest that the boy would never surrender, that he would die before he'd surrender, that this was a fight to the death.

Bobby wasn't willing to see it through to its conclusion. He knew he had lost. He relaxed his grip. Quick as a cobra, the boy sunk his teeth into Bobby's shoulder, biting through the the Hawaiian shirt into his skin and then swinging his head as if trying to tear away a chunk of his flesh. Bobby screamed in pain and surprise. He threw the kid to the ground. The kid jumped to his feet, whirled, and crouched. From somewhere he pulled a knife. His eyes burned with an intensity of hatred Bobby had never before seen or known. Bobby braced for the attack, held out his hands to defend himself.

The kid beckoned to him. "Come on, you motherfuck."

Come take take me now, he was saying. He circled and the crowd moved back and Bobby knew that if he was going to stop the boy, he would have to kill him. He dropped his hands, backed away, turned, and parted the crowd. He walked quickly in the direction of the car, the kid taunting him the whole way down the street.

"Hey, *hijueputa!* Hey, you! You yellow gringo homo motherfuck! Hey, you! Motherfuck!"

Bobby was in the passenger seat when Blacky returned. The guards were still at their posts. Blacky dipped into his pocket for another quarter. "What the hell happened to you?" he asked.

"Let's just get out of here," Bobby said, unwilling to get into it.

Blacky eased away from the curb, inched through the people

milling in the street out into traffic. Bobby stewed in his humiliation. They drove through a part of town new to Bobby, and though ordinarily he would have been interested in the landscape, would have tried to fix the place in his mind, proud of his knowledge of the city, he registered nothing of the view beyond the windshield. He replayed his defeat, trying one interpretation after another, searching for one he could accept. He switched on the radio, but switched it off right away. "Goddamn little bastard," he muttered. "I wasn't going to do anything to him, wanted to teach him a lesson is all. Now I'd like to break the little bastard's neck." He told Blacky the story of the gym bag.

"You think you ought to have that bite looked at? Maybe we should go to the hospital," Blacky said.

"Probably has rabies, the little indio spic bastard. Lucky I didn't kick his ass for him."

"Forget it, man. It was nothing personal."

"He doesn't need you to defend him."

"It goes on every day. It's no big deal. You should've let him go. You're nuts to risk your neck over a gym bag. Unless you have to. That kid has to. What's your excuse?"

"You saying I ought to feel sorry for him? For all them little slimy bastards?"

"Feel sorry for *them?* That's a joke. They feel sorry for *you,* man. It's *you* they pity. Dumb, bored, overfed gringo, paying for what they take for free, taken advantage of by everyone. You're prey to them. They laugh at you."

The thought that some dirty little skinny ignorant kid was laughing at him brought blood to Bobby's face. "I coulda crushed him. I was choking him. I coulda broke him in two, but I let him go. Then the little fucker bit me." He looked at the tear in his sleeve, pulled it back to reveal a ragged tear in his skin.

"You did the right thing letting him go. Forget about it."

Bobby cooled down enough to allow himself some admiration for the fierce little fucker, who couldn't be cowed, who wouldn't back down. The kid had risked his life, had put it on the line, was willing to die—for what? A gym bag.

Bobby changed the subject. "Well, you scored at least, I hope," he said. Blacky didn't seem to understand. "The spice," Bobby reminded him. Blacky hefted the brown paper bag beside him on the seat and grinned. Bobby looked inside. "These are red chiles," he said.

You couldn't drive into the Third of July. There was a road around the perimeter, but all the paths through it were too narrow for cars. Close to forty thousand people were squeezed into less than a square mile of land. They lived in mud-brick houses if they were among the more fortunate, and in shacks, shanties, or lean-tos of cardboard, corrugated iron, tar paper, tin, sticks, rags, canvas, packing crates, newspaper, flattened cans, grass mats, or palm fronds if they were not. Whatever they could find to protect them from the weather and provide some measure of privacy from their neighbors was used.

Built on a dune back of the city, the capital spread out below it, the Pacific visible in clear weather in the distance, the squatter settlement had a postcard view. But that was all to commend it. Since in the government's opinion the land had been settled illegally, it provided none of the municipal services available to other residents of the city—no garbage collection, no fire department or police, no electricity, no hospital, no schools. No sewers. Raw sewage ran in the streets and collected in open ponds. Water for the whole of the settlement was pumped in through two standpipes that were the foci of the settlement life. Often a person could stand a whole day in line waiting for water. Bobby had never been inside a barrio. He had an idea it was something he didn't want to see, and he let Blacky go alone to Peregrina's house. He couldn't imagine how seeing where and how she lived would make him feel any better. "I'll watch the car," he said. "Save you the premium." Blacky parked on the perimeter road and disappeared into the warren that was the Third of July.

Bobby sat on the fender looking down at what he could see of the city through the overcast. He reminded himself to bring a camera up here on a day when it was clear. A little girl came by, leading a puppy on a rope. Bobby asked her if she would pose for him and she agreed even before he offered her the money. He finished off a roll, shooting with the lens wide open so that the girl and the puppy would be in focus but the background would blur. Blacky came back with Peregrina—as long as he was in the neighborhood, he thought he'd save her the bus ride to work—and they started back down into town with Peregrina sitting squarely in the middle of the backseat as if the car were a rowboat she might cause to tip.

"You missed the turn," Bobby said when they were once again within the city proper, back on paved city streets.

"I'm not finished with the story and there's someplace else I want you to see. You in a hurry for something?"

Bobby was looking ahead to his date with Nina. He looked down at his watch, which he noticed for the first time was gone. He exploded. "Son of a bitch!"

"It was junk," Blacky said trying to derail him before he could work up another head of steam. "I'll get you another. A good one, not like that piece of crap you had."

"Ripped it right off my wrist!" Bobby let his righteous anger rise. "Little Indio bastard—" He cut himself off, remembering Peregrina in back, and muttered an apology over his shoulder.

Blacky turned off the pavement again, talking while he drove the convertible over the deeply rutted road, dust swirling up behind them.

La Parada, with millions of dollars of goods moving in and out every day, was a rich mine for criminals of every sort—pickpockets, hijackers, con men, prostitutes, muggers, labor racketeers, shoplifters, purse snatchers, they all made their livings there. And since the Missing Tooth was close to La Parada, it was considered to be the Sultans' turf, just as the airport belonged to the Lords. Of course La Parada was too valuable to be the sole possession of juvenile delinquents. It belonged to the Sindicato, but the Sultans, considered a sort of minor-league farm team for the big-time thugs who really controlled La Parada, were permitted the Sindicato's leavings. Six months before Blacky left the barrio, the Sultans hijacked a truck that had broken down along the Río Carrillo Road, which runs along the western side of La Parada. The driver hadn't been gone an hour before the Sultans had picked it clean. The cargo was shoes, thousands of pairs, all of them wingtips, all of them brown, molded from a single piece of rubber, complete with phony laces, like rubbers you wear in the rain. Within the week a substantial portion of the population of the Missing Tooth, men, women, and children, including all of the Sultans, were wearing molded brown rubber wingtip shoes.

About that time a twelve-year-old began hanging around the

Sultans, and he drew the attention and the affection of the older
kids because he would do anything on a dare. He would fight at the
least provocation, would take on anyone regardless of size or age—
even one of the thieves at La Parada, who tried to shoo him off a
mark the thief had reserved for himself. The kid attached himself
to Blacky, and they used to work La Parada together, scouting for
unlocked doors and windows, or for people who obviously didn't
belong—tourists looking for local color, or anyone who wasn't
alert or who was too weak to resist or too slow to give chase.
Blacky gave him a pair of rubber wingtips and the kid stuffed newspaper in the toes to keep them from falling off. Although officially
still the Sultans, since the hijacking the gang had become known
around the barrio and around La Parada as the Zapatos Morenos,
the Brown Shoes, and later they adopted the name themselves,
dropping the final *s*. Blacky's protégé was accepted into the gang,
not that there was any formal procedure or ceremony. The new
Moreno took the name Gavilan as his nom de guerre.

Blacky stopped the car to remove a barricade, then continued up
the dirt road until the slope tapered off and they reached a broad
plateau the size of three football fields. The city was in front and
below. Behind was a sandstone cliff where there was a row of caves
with the entrances bricked over. Blacky and Bobby got out of the
car. Peregrina stayed behind, listening to the car radio.

"The Missing Tooth," Bobby said. The ground was sandy, hard,
and flat. He picked up a stone and sailed it out over the city.
"What happened?"

Blacky was in college, working part-time at the Marchamps' and
part-time in the kitchen at the Crillon. He still kept in contact with
his boyhood friends in the barrio, those who hadn't died or been
killed or jailed or hadn't moved away, gone into the army or the
Sindicato. Blacky was the only one to have gone to college. If you
didn't count the classes Padre Elio held, and a kid only attended
those because the padre made it a requisite to play basketball,
Blacky was the only one to have gone to a school of any kind. With
his success, his job, his money, Blacky became a sort of counselor
emeritus to the Zapato Moreno.

It was January, summer vacation between his junior and senior
years—Blacky remembered because the kitchen at the Crillon was

sweltering. The Missing Tooth, like the Third of July, got its water by tapping into the city lines. This was illegal and was managed through bribes that began with a maintainance crew and spread upward into the pocket of the assistant commissioner of the Department of Public Works. It wasn't very much money, but it wasn't very much water either. It was pumped through a single four-inch pipe which hooked into the city system below São Paulo Street. Beyond the city limits the pipe came above ground and ran alongside the barrio road to the Missing Tooth, where it branched into four separate standpipes.

The residents could do without sewers, and they could do without electricity, and they found they did very well without the police, but they could not do without water. The pipe was their lifeline and the community leaders had established procedures for the distribution of the water and regulations on its use. There was a round-the-clock patrol to prevent vandalism and a full-time volunteer maintenance crew. Occasionally the pipe sprang a leak or the pump broke down, but the repairs were always top-priority and the water was restored within a day. Two days was the longest the Missing Tooth had ever been without water. No one had more than a two-day reserve. The next nearest source was down in the city, and naturally the people from the other districts objected to long lines of squatters using their water. And who had time or energy for a five-mile round-trip twice or even once a day with a heavy jug? Even when you lived in a packing crate, there were conveniences you got accustomed to.

That summer the Missing Tooth lost its water for over a week. The problem was at the source. Publicly, the city denied any obligation to repair the break. Officials claimed that the squatters had no rights to begin with, that they were trespassers, in effect stealing the water, and that the city owed them nothing. Privately, they let it be known that the so-called break in the line could be repaired with a judicious application of cash. Led by the padre, the barrio leaders decided to take a stand.

In what was a catastrophe for their community, the Zapato Moreno, never known for its civic spirit, saw an opportunity for profit. Gavilan has been given credit for the idea, although the facts have been lost or distorted in all that has transpired since. He was seventeen years old, and a Moreno leader. The story is that

Gavilan broke into the municipal maintenance yards, stole a fully loaded tanker—the kind of truck the city used to water the streets in San Isidro and Miraflores—and drove it up to the barrio. He was received like a hero. No mention was made of the guard he had allegedly bludgeoned. Originally, the plan had been for the Moreno to sell the water by the bottle, but Gavilan, claiming it was his to do with as he liked since he alone had actually stolen the truck, insisted on giving it away. In the barrio he became an instant celebrity. The city called him a criminal and issued a warrant for his arrest.

The story made the front pages, was picked up by the wire services, and was distributed all over Latin America. Sought for grand larceny and aggravated assault, Gavilan disappeared. When the police came to repossess the truck, they found the road up to the settlement blocked. Padre Elio, the Moreno, and thousands of others formed a human barricade.

After three days the tanker ran dry, the press had found itself another story, and the situation in the barrio turned from festive to desperate. Barrio leaders, behind the padre's back, agreed to the increase in payments. A deal was made. The guard from the maintenance yards, it was reported, died from his injuries. Some said he died of a heart attack, others said he didn't die at all. In any event, Gavilan was now wanted for murder, and instead of turning on the water as they had agreed to do, the city brought up the bulldozers and leveled the place.

The residents scattered, most being absorbed into the other barrios. Some had lived there for twenty years and the razing of the Missing Tooth was as devastating to them as an earthquake. The police declared the Moreno a criminal organization and arrested as many members as they could find. They stepped up the hunt for Gavilan, who had been hiding in Blacky's apartment. He had been a petty hoodlum, no different than thousands of boys in barrios all over the city, but assisted by the press, the police made him first a local hero and then a national symbol. Unofficial Moreno gangs sprang up, even in middle-class neighborhoods. In the name of Roberto Gavilan, chaos, always simmering, always rattling the lid of the pot, boiled over in every barrio in the capital and spilled out into the provinces.

From Blacky's, Roberto went to the mountains, where he

hooked up with Padre Elio, who'd gone up there himself to start a
new ministry after the demolition of the Missing Tooth. The police
were looking for the padre as well. He wasn't truly a priest, hadn't
taken the vows, been ordained, or any of that, was more a kind of
activist, a do-gooder crank, but he called himself Padre and he
attracted a following. For months Gavilan did little more than lie
low. Feeling sorry for himself was the way he later described these
days to Blacky. Out of boredom he began to accompany the padre
on his circuit of the mountain villages. A person couldn't hide
forever. Motivated by the same impulse that brought him to steal
the truck and then give away the water, he was gradually drawn
into the life. He learned he could be useful. If the padre needed a
shovel, Roberto would get it. A sack of cement, a pair of pants, a
bottle of aspirins, send Roberto. It was minor-league crime compared to what the Moreno had been into in the barrio, but there
was a Robin Hood aspect Roberto enjoyed. And besides, what was
he going to do? He was wanted by the police, apparently not so
badly that they were willing to chase all over the sierra in order to
find him, but wanted nonetheless. Six years passed in the mountains that way.

Everything changed when Padre Elio decided to build a clinic
for the Indians. It was more of a wish than a concrete plan, but the
clinic was where Roberto saw his chance to make a real contribution. You could get away with the theft of some tools here and
there, some lumber, but not with what a clinic would take to build,
supply, staff. A clinic required an ongoing source of cash, and Roberto knew where one flowed.

The cocainistas were operating freely within the sierra at this
time. Indians cultivated the coca plants, and sold the leaves to others who manufactured and exported the drug. Massive bribes en-
sured that the traffic could proceed unimpeded. The conspiracy
extended into the highest levels of the military, the judiciary, and
the federal government. With the protection of the most powerful
institutions in the country, with no enemies to speak of, and with
such a wide margin of profit, the cocainistas ran a very careless
operation. The locations of their factory, the routes their couriers
took in and out of the mountains with cocaine and money were
common knowledge among the people who lived there. These
people, Indians, turned their heads the other way. Even if they had

the means, they hadn't any desire to interrupt the trade. Coca was the important cash crop, and if a few crazy whites chose to kill each other over who got how much, what was it to them?

Gavilan got word back to the capital and several of the old gang came to join him. The cocainistas, sloppy and overconfident, were easy prey, no more a problem to the Moreno than the tourists in the Plaza de Armas. They were surprised how easy it was.

The clinic was built, a doctor was found to run it, some medical supplies were purchased to supply it. It was rudimentary, and the Indians, always suspicious, for the most part avoided it, yet it was a start.

A minor incident in a barrio was one thing, but the cocaine trade was another. People in power, people whose pockets were directly affected, took notice. There was renewed interest in the whereabouts of Roberto Gavilan. And the cocainistas weren't the only ones who had come to see him as a threat. Ranchers in the sierra and plantation owners nearer the coast blamed Gavilan and the Moreno for the labor problems they were having. Without a source of cheap labor, they could not operate. They claimed the Moreno were agitating the Indians, putting ideas in their heads about unions and land redistribution and agrarian reform. There were, in fact, many groups who advocated these measures at this time—legitimate political parties, student activists, labor leaders— but it was the Moreno who were, depending on your point of view, given the credit or the blame. That they had nothing to do with it was irrelevant to those with a strong enough need for a scapegoat.

At a ranch outside Huaráz a bomb destroyed a stable, killing a valuable Thoroughbred. A boy was also killed, a college student from an old sierra family, the son of a career military officer. The government accused the Moreno, said they themselves had claimed responsibility. Gavilan's name was back in the papers. The uproar made by the powerful ranching families prompted a declaration of martial law. A curfew was imposed. Suspected Moreno were given summary trials and imprisoned. Others simply disappeared. The bombing was followed by other acts of violence. There were attacks on rural police stations. Policemen were killed and weapons were stolen. The government now called it rebellion and sent the army to quell it. What had been an impromptu barrio uprising staged by a handful of juvenile delinquents over a broken water pipe had become, through a combination of circumstance and several lengthy and almost wholly fictitious army intelligence reports, a conspiracy which threatened to overthrow the government. The purported rebels were the Zapato Moreno, led by a charismatic twenty-five-year-old named Roberto Gavilan. In truth, the only threat was to the profits from cocaine.

Blacky finished the story as he was pulling under the portico of the Malibu Beach Club, where Bobby had left his car. Bobby climbed out, told Blacky he'd see him at work the following night. His head was spinning from what he'd heard.

Nina's wearing faded blue jeans, a white sweater, and running shoes. She has a blue and gold button pinned on her chest. "Arriba Callao" it says. A second button pinned on her purse has a picture of a black man wearing a blue and gold jersey.

"Another Eusebio fan," I say. I'd already told her about the scratch on my face, but not the truth. The teeth marks I don't figure to have to explain unless I luck out.

"You know him?" she says.

Eusebio might be the most well-known man in the hemisphere. "You?"

"Sort of," she says. "I've seen him on a few occasions." She corrects herself: "Two occasions."

"You went out with Eusebio?" She goes out with *him*, what does she need with me? "He has a place down the coast in Chorrillós," I say, nonchalant. I read it somewhere.

"I saw him at a party. I couldn't keep from staring," she says.

"He's only five-seven, five-eight, something like that . . ."

"There were lots of people there, a hundred people, maybe three of whom I knew. He asked me to walk outside with him."

". . . I don't think he's even as tall as you are."

"In the garden."

"Short little dude. Tiny, really. Itty-bitty fella."

"I went, of course; how could you refuse a person like that? I couldn't. And listen to this: while we were talking he unbuttoned my blouse. Can you believe it? He unbuttoned my blouse and put his hand on my breast. What nerve!"

"Probably had to stand on a chair," I say.

"I couldn't believe it. I was stunned," she says.

"What did you do?"

"I let him. He called me a few days later and we went to a Chinese restaurant for dinner. Some *chifa* dive out by the airport. He said he liked to go there because the owner never made him pay. When the food arrived he said he wasn't hungry. Then he took me home."

"What did you do?"

"I had an egg roll."

The game was a tie, one–one. Eusebio didn't score. The crowd, for a Callao–San Sebastián game, was relatively well behaved. No shots were fired. Someone made it over the fence and across the moat, but she was stopped by a mounted policeman. We stood the whole game—everyone did. Walking back to the car in the crowd, Nina held my arm.

She has dinner for us at her place. It's the first I've been inside, and while she's upstairs changing clothes, I take the chance to nose around. I check out the framed photographs on the walls—Nina at twelve or thirteen with who I guess are her parents, pictures of the farm with Huascarán in the background, her on horseback, Huascarán in the background, her with some campesinos, Huascarán in the background. There's that famous picture of Eusebio scoring the only goal against Chile a couple years back in the Cup quarter-finals. Written across the bottom is "To Nina, with love, Eusebio." There's an old print of two guys, one with his shirt off, the other in uniform, their arms over each other's shoulders and laughing. And more pictures of Nina, all with this same guy in the uniform, although these are more recent and the guy is much older: at a table in a nightclub; holding hands with Rio spread out behind them; with the President, no less.

I didn't hear her come down the steps, but when I turn around she's behind me seated on the sofa, her legs curled up under her. Her hair is pulled back off her face and tied in the back. She's wearing eye shadow and lipstick—dark red lipstick—a black velvet jumpsuit, gold hoop earrings, and a wide gold choker around her neck. Her feet are bare.

"I thought we were eating here," I say.

"We are," she says. "Would you like a drink before dinner?" I follow her to a low cabinet where she keeps the liquor. She bends, allowing me a glimpse of what Eusebio had his hands on in the garden. There's twenty different bottles lined up on the shelves. "And there's beer and white wine in the refrigerator," she says.

"I'll take a beer," I say, not sure how a drink can improve the way I'm feeling.

"Sorry, all out of beer." She laughs, leaves, and comes back with two.

"There's something I want to know," I tell her. I do want to know, although why I'm not sure. If the answer's what I think it is, knowing can only bring me down.

"Let me guess," she says. "You want to know if I have a boyfriend." "Boyfriend" isn't the word I'd have used, but, yeah, that's the question I had in mind.

"How'd you know?" I ask.

"I was wondering the same about you."

"I don't have any boyfriends. Girls, they come and go. You?"

"There's no shortage of candidates," she says.

"I wouldn't guess there would be, but the question I'm asking is, is there an incumbent?" She nods. "Him?" I point to the guy in all the pictures. She nods again. "Where's he at?" Dead is the answer I'm hoping for.

"Busy," she says.

She excuses herself to finish the dinner and refuses my offer of help, which is fine with me. I phone Blacky at the restaurant, but I keep getting a busy signal and after that dinner is ready. Cheeseburgers with lettuce and tomato, french fries, the cold bottles of beer, coffee with anisette, ice cream for dessert. We do the dishes together and go into the living room for another cup of coffee. She offers me a cigar from a dark polished humidor, Uppmanns, which I refuse. She takes a cigarette from her pack.

A breeze comes into the bedroom through the double doors off the porch. The top sheet is turned back on the bed. Nina's in the bathroom. There're two things I'm glad for: the mattress is hard, the bed is king-size, and there're no stuffed anythings anyplace. Three things. I take the right side of the bed, the side away from the bathroom. When you're used to sleeping alone, sleeping with anyone's tough, the actual sleeping part I mean, and you don't have to station yourself along the shortest lane to the toilet to make it any tougher. There's a bowl of gardenias on the table beside the lamp. I pull the cord, not wanting to go into the marks on my shoulder, lie back on the cool pillows, wondering for the second time in a week what I've done to deserve such good luck. It must've been something huge.

Her nightgown goes to her thighs, sheer lacy flimsy thing, and the bathroom light shines through, showing the curve of her hip and some of the rest. She wants to know before she turns out the light if I'd like pajamas, which I don't, or anything else.

"Like what?" You never know. It could be exotic.

"Like a toothbrush," she says, "Or a blanket, a drink . . ."

"Nothing, thanks," I say.

"Take the toothbrush," she says.

Against her skin my hands are cold, cold and rough like stones. I apologize and rub them together before I reach for her again. I've got a case of goosebumps. Her arms go around me, we're belly to belly, her palms on my back, and I can't stop shaking, it's the damndest thing. She pulls the sheet over our heads, I hold her closer and press my face to her neck. Our breathing warms the air, which is filled with the smell of her, and after a while the shivering stops.

We pull the blanket down to the cool night and gardenias. I warm my hand between her thighs. Her hair is damp there. Her moving fingers brush my chest. My nipples pinch. "I don't know what's wrong," I say while she kisses my neck. She kisses my cheek, my eyes. I pull away and sit up.

"Are you sick?" She sounds alarmed. "Not something you ate, I hope." She gets up on one elbow.

I don't know whether I'm sick or not. I know I'm not hard, which is enough to make me sick. I fall back on the pillow and stare at the ceiling. "I'm sorry," I say. This is the worst luck ever. I fold my arms across my chest. Nina rolls toward me and slides her hand over my stomach and down, but I push her away.

"Ooo, sorry," she says to me softly. She combs my hair with her fingers.

Of all the goddamn things. I always took it for granted. I try to think of a reason why. And tonight of all nights. Shitfire. I picture her telling her friends.

"Well there's one good thing at least," I say. The good thing is that she isn't laughing.

It's good when a person can tell a joke on himself, even a lousy one. Sometimes it's the only way out. But don't let them kid you—the joke's always better on somebody else.

"Would you like something to do while you're moping?" she says. "To take your mind off yourself?" She takes my hand, instructs me in a quiet voice: lower, gently, small circles, not so hard, right there, keep it there. I keep it there ten, fifteen minutes. Just like that, she says. Keep it right there, yes, that's right. Ah, she says. Ahhh. She's coming, I think she is. I hope she is. My fingers are cramping. She's breathing fast, sips of air. She bites her lower lip, her eyes are closed, and she's very wet. She's coming for sure. Big sigh. She opens her eyes. I wiggle my fingers, and she laughs, pushes my hand away, and covers herself with her thigh. She takes my hand and lays it on her breast.

"Your turn," she says. She pushes me onto my back, and rests her head on my belly. She says she loves how it feels when it's soft, not the thing I need to hear. I can't bring myself to say this is something that never happened before, even though it's never happened before. I decide it would be cowardly to leave. She turns on the lamp on the nightstand. I pull the sheet to my neck. "I may have a remedy here," she says. She opens the drawer and pulls out a small wooden box. "Medicine," she says. She lights one and hands it to me. "I'll be back in a minute," she says.

It's hard to say how long she is gone. I've put on my T-shirt. "Chilly," I tell her when she comes back. She hands me a drink in a mug. She has a drink for herself and two paperback books. She gets into bed beside me. "How's the patient?" she says.

I look underneath the covers. "Resting quietly, thanks." The wine is sweet and warm and spicy with a stick of cinnamon.

"Are you feeling better? Really?" she says. I suppose I am. I remember what's happened, of course. This isn't a case of amnesia here. It's true this limp dick is out of commission, who knows for how long, but he's also stoned enough it doesn't seem so crucial anymore.

She opens one of the paperbacks to a place marked with a scrap of paper and starts to read out loud. I don't remember the last time I was read to. My mom probably, but I don't recall that she read me the story of Serena and how much it pleased her to have a penis or two jammed into her every orifice. With all the manpower Serena required, lucky for her her father was a general.

Nina reads without smiling about gleaming scimitars and Serena's glistening swollen snatch. Her voice is deep and serious. Her hand slides over my crotch. Beneath the sheet something is swelling. She reads a sentence more, closes the book, and turns out the light.

She sleeps with her head on my arm. My elbow has pins and needles, my hand is numb, my body's too long for the mattress, the footboard cuts into my Achilles tendon, the blanket goes only as far as my ankles, my feet are cold, I have to pee bad, but I don't move. I like holding her while she's sleeping.

When I wake up in the morning, a hot pot of coffee is on the table on the porch off the bedroom. Nina has already showered. She has on a white terry robe and her hair is wrapped in a towel. Her feet are bare. "It's probably not a good idea to talk about what happened last night," I say, "but . . ."

"You know how it is," she says. "We barely know each other. One can anticipate a certain amount of . . . awkwardness. When we kissed, my nose got in the way. Next time it will be better."

"I'm getting a second chance?"

"You make it sound like a tryout," she says.

"And the dope in the nightstand, the books . . . ?"

"Belong to Rinaldi. The man in all the photographs? The 'incumbent,' as you choose to call him."

"None of my business," I cut her off. I don't want to hear about Rinaldi. He's probably got a million bucks and a dick a yard long.

"His job is very demanding. Sometimes he needs something to relax him, or to stimulate him, or both. Have you heard enough, or do you want to know more?"

"That's plenty," I say.

"Now there's something I'd like to ask you."

"About last night?"

"About today."

"What about it?"

"That's exactly what I want to know," she says.

During the time it takes to set up the lights, the reflectors, the canvas backdrop, to set up the tripod, load the camera, make the electrical connections, test the system, take the readings, Nina doesn't say a word. She looks like she's in the doctor's waiting room.

"Hey," I say. "You ready? I point to the stool. You'd think with the look she has on her face that I'd told her to slip her feet into the stirrups, hitch up her skirt, and I'll be along soon as I scrape the cat crap off the speculum.

First there were lines between her eyebrows. I tell her she's frowning and she says she's not. I say she is. I bring her a mirror so she doesn't have to take my word for it. Once her brow is smoothed out, I see her lips are pressed into thin straight lines, there are droplets of sweat on the wings of her nose, and her makeup's wrong. I shoot eight or ten frames anyway, wooden expressions, wrong makeup and all, and then the flash conks out. It's one thing after the other.

"This is all my fault," she says. "I'm sorry. I hate to have my picture taken."

"What about the ones at the market?"

"That was different," she says. "I wasn't having my picture taken, I was shopping. I'm comfortable shopping."

She has an answer for everything.

This is a different person than the one who chewed me out in the San Isidro market. What happened to the aloof, self-possessed woman who tossed me out of her cab? Where's the candor she showed me last night? I try every trick I know to coax her out of herself: I ask her to fantasize, I turn on the music, we two-step to a whole side of Johnny Gimble, I tickle her under her arms. Nothing works. After an hour she's convinced herself she has no talent for modeling.

I'm frustrated, annoyed, blaming myself for the way it's worked out. "Listen," I say. "This is no easy thing. You have to put yourself out. It's risky. You have to make an effort. You have to work. You know that word, don't you? 'Work'?" It sounds worse than I'd intended it to be. Sarcastic. But there's something about her expression that tells me that if what I want to do is goose her a little, I'm on the right track. Nothing I've said or done up till now has jarred her out of her self-consciousness. But there's no call for me to say what next pops out of my mouth, none whatsoever. As soon as I said it I knew it was a lousy thing. I didn't know her well enough to say a thing like that. "Of course we can forget the pictures and you can go shopping, where you're *comfortable*, or whatever it is you normally do all day while the colonel is away."

I fire three frames before she's off the stool. The motherless strobe only works for the first. My immediate problem is what to do with her now that she's hurt, angry, and on her way out the door. She blows by me, high heels rapping on the wooden studio floor. I grab her arm. "Whoa!"

She spins like a discus thrower, and with her open hand she catches me flush on the cheek. Her follow-through takes her around, throws her off balance, and she goes down hard. My face stings like flames. I taste blood. My fist stretches and closes. I feel my anger taking over, galloping with me toward the edge, but something helps me to rein it in. I pull back hard, get a hold of myself. One second is all it takes. I bring my hand to my cheek and, seeing me raise my hand, she draws back, eyes wide, her arm ready to fend off the punch she thought she saw coming, the one I might have thrown and didn't.

She hesitates before she takes the offer of my hand. Whatever it was that came over her a moment ago is gone. My anger's gone too. "Jesus," is all I can think to say. Her eyes dart around. She holds the wrist of the hand that slapped me like she's taken it into custody, like it's a culprit could at any time twist out of her grasp. Then she tosses her head and swings the hair out of her eye. "I'm sorry," she says.

I don't think she is. Sorry isn't how she feels. She never guessed she had it in her, to stand up for herself like that. She's learned something about herself today, and my guess is it's come as good news.

In the bathroom mirror the one cheek is scratched and the other is red around the imprint of her hand, which is raised and white. I'd been an inch away from laying her out—pure reflex. She'd coldcocked me, hadn't she? No matter that I had it coming. Neither of us says a word for a couple of minutes, maybe two minutes, which is a long time not to talk if you're anywhere except in a movie. She presses a cool damp cloth on the place, and from behind me watches my eyes in the mirror. If I were the man of my imagination, I would have stood and looked until she had to look away, or until I took her in my arms. The man of my imagination is steady and silent, he doesn't hit women even if he's provoked. He's a man of few words. "I—" I start to say something, I don't know what.

She shushes me. She has my attention. I think she may be the woman who will make me into the man I want to be. She takes my hand, leads me back into the studio. She sets the stool upright and sits on it. I pick up the camera and start to shoot. The strobe fires without a miss. In twenty minutes and fewer words I have four rolls of film. An hour in the darkroom confirms what I had seen through the viewfinder: here's a face could wear out shutters, give rewind levers metal fatigue. Here's a person you could photograph for a lifetime.

She is smoking a cigarette and looking at the contact sheets. She could be sorting the mail. Her eyes fix each of the faces an instant, then move to the next. She tosses the sheets on a table.

"Do you have more time?" she says.

First she sits tailor-seat, her back straight, arms straight, hands flat on the floor beside her. Then she kneels, sitting back on her ankles, her hands on her thighs—nothing cutesy, but fresh. Then, like a catcher, squatting. All open poses, frank expressions, no pouting, jutting lower lip, no come-hither shit, nothing like that. She stands up, at ease, legs shoulders' width apart, feet flat on the floor, then hands on her hips, then over her head, then folded across her chest, and then the phone rings.

My finger stays on the shutter. She changes with every click, and we both ignore the ringing. After it's rung twenty times I start for the phone, but she stops me and pulls me to her and holds me until the ringing stops. She steps back in front of the camera. When the phone rings again I tell her it's Blacky wondering where I am. I'm supposed to be at work, should've been there already. She doesn't stand in the way again like I was hoping she would. I count fifteen rings before it stops. It could only be Blacky, ring fifteen times.

I pack my gear away. She showers. When I'm done she's adjusting her slip in front of the mirror. Her dress is hiked up. "I'm hungry," she says. "Do you know somewhere good?"

THE KIND OF KID SHE WAS

The restaurant is jamming, which is both good and bad: good because it's always good to do business, and bad because me not showing for work wouldn't be any big deal if the place weren't quite so busy. I figure that Blacky, the all-time, all-world trim-master, will, when he sees Nina, recognize the quality of my excuse. In fact, I pretty much expect Blacky to choke when he gets a look at her. Generally speaking, he doesn't think much of my taste in women.

We take a table in back. I tell Nina I'm going to get us some wine and I head toward the kitchen and Blacky. I've felt better than I feel tonight five, maybe four times in my life. Blacky's got the skillet in one hand and a glass of Scotch in the other. The bottle is on the cutting board. "Nice of you to show," he says.

I say, "Take the fish off the fire, my man. There's someone I want you to meet."

"No time, my man," he says, laying it on. "My chef crapped out on me tonight." The wine he pours in the skillet hisses, steams, flames until the alcohol burns off. He hasn't looked at me yet.

"I apologize, all right?" I say. "But when you see the reason . . ."

"It's arranged," Blacky says. "You leave tomorrow. You better be ready."

"Ready for Freddy," I say.

The meeting is set for Marcará, a town fifteen miles north of Huaráz. I've been there before: a church, a school, a store, bus stop, Luna's Hotel—Mr. Moon's.

"Leave tonight, you can be there by morning," Blacky says. "If anyone asks, you're a trekker."

"Nobody treks this time of year," I tell him. "Rain in the mountains this time of year."

"Maybe no one will ask. Wait on a bench by the fountain in the plaza. Someone will meet you there and take you to the man. Be there at three Saturday afternoon and stay until five. If no one comes for you by five, come back again at three on Sunday. If no one comes on Sunday, the meeting's off. You come back here."

"How will they know it's me?"

Blacky shoots me a disgusted look. "You mean suppose there's *two* six-foot-four gringo assholes sitting on the bench in Marcará at three Saturday afternoon?" Blacky pulls the pan off the fire, slams down his Scotch. He grabs me by the arm and pushes me backward into the pantry. "First you blow off work and then you don't answer your phone, and then you waltz in here asking stupid questions. What is with you, Bobby? Whatever it is, you better wise up. Now isn't the time."

"OK," I say. "OK. All right. Let go my arm. Jesus H. Christ. All I did was ask a question. Anything else I should know? Do I need a gun?"

"You plan on shooting something?"

"What about if the army comes?"

"As far as the army's concerned, if they find you up there, you're Moreno. On the other hand, if the army shows up, the Moreno will think you brought them. Either way, pal, you've poached your last trout. You didn't tell anyone about this, did you?" He doesn't give me time to answer. "I'm telling you, Bobby, all of them in the mountains—the Moreno, the army, the cocainistas, the Indians— they're all wired real tight. They're edgy, you know what I mean? The prospect of sudden, violent death is something they live with day in and day out. They've seen it up close, they've some of them brought it about. They don't have the patience for a wise-ass Norteamericano up in the mountains. None of them do. You get me, Bobby?"

"Sure, sure, sure, yeah, yeah, yeah," I say. "No, wait, not 100 percent. Something's been bugging me about this business. I'm going up there to take pictures, right? They don't care their faces are going to be in the paper, in a magazine? They're not worried they're going to be identified, or there's going to be reprisals against their families? That's the part I don't get."

"You don't get any of it," Blacky says. "Do you? So don't worry about it. You're there to take pictures. You're a photographer. This is your chance."

That's straightforward enough. Crazy, but straightforward. I take him by the arm, back him out into the kitchen. "C'mon into the dining room a minute," I say.

Blacky peels my fingers off. "Listen, asshole," he says. He points at the end of my nose. "Don't fuck up."

"Hey, this is me, your old buddy, Bobby, remember? You got something to say, come out and say it."

"You heard me, asshole. You fuck up, it isn't like you're in the kitchen and you burned a couple of chops."

"I read you loud and clear."

He slides the fish onto a plate. Anchors the parsley sprig with daub of ancho-chili butter. Adds a lemon wedge. Looks perfect. "Don't try to get over on him, Bobby," he warns me. "Your cornball charm won't work on him." He goes back to his cooking.

I came in here feeling great and here is my good friend Blacky wrecking my mood. I grab the first bottle of wine my hand falls on and go back to our table. Santo is standing there talking to Nina. Santo's a busboy.

"*Shumaq warmi*, eh, Santo? What do you say?" Santo's taught me a few Quechua words. *Shumaq warmi* means "beautiful woman." Santo winks; I taught him to wink. He excuses himself, which in Quechua sounds something like "crabby padlock." I open the wine. Nina orders: rack of lamb, winter vegetable puree, pheasant wonton salad, and shoofly pie. Afterward, since it's obvious Blacky isn't coming out, I take Nina back in the kitchen to see him. I introduce her to Peregrina first, and the two of them, very formal, exchange a few words in Quechua—Nina talks some Quechua. Then I take her over to Blacky.

"Enjoy your meal, Miss DeBettencourt?" Blacky says.

"You *know* each other?" I say, surprised.

"I've been here before," Nina explains.

"You chose a good night to come," Blacky says. "The regular cook didn't show."

"I think I'm to blame for that," Nina says.

You know how it is when there're people you like, and you want them to like each other, only it doesn't take a clairvoyant to see that that isn't going to happen here, and I push Nina back to the table on the pretext Blacky has a lot of work to do, then I excuse myself, crabby padlock, and go back to the kitchen to see what's eating Blacky.

"I haven't missed a day in six weeks, if that's what it is," I tell him. "Except for yesterday."

Blacky swallows Scotch. I've seen him drink a fifth in an evening. Most evenings. "I put my ass on the line for you, Bobby," he says.

"Yeah, so? Spell it out for me."

"It's the girl."

"You don't like her. What else is new? I just didn't know I needed your permission."

"The only thing worse than your taste is your judgment," he says. "Do me a favor, Bobby. Do whatever you want, only wait until after this business is over."

"If that's what's on your mind, I got some bad news for you, chum. She's coming with me."

"Great, that's just great," Blacky says to his shoes. "Shit."

"No big deal. She's going along for the ride, just to Huaráz, that's all. Visit some friends. Besides, I thought she might be of some help. She talks the talk. You heard her."

"She didn't happen to mention she was the mistress of Escobar Pino Rinaldi, did she? *Colonel* Escobar Pino Rinaldi? No, I guess not."

"Who told you?" I say, surprised for the second time.

"And did she also mention that he's the man in charge of the emergency zone?"

"So she knows a guy in the army, so what?"

"So what is you tell her the trip is off."

"Just like that. The trip is off."

"Right."

"Just like that?"

"Just like that.

"I'll tell you what," he says. "Let's forget the whole thing. Forget Gavilan. Forget the photographs. Forget I ever mentioned this to you. That woman out there you're messing with is the mistress of an officer in the army, and not just any officer, but the officer in

charge of the emergency zone, and if that weren't enough, a corrupt, murdering son of a bitch to boot. You want to take her with
you, and you can't see how there might be an objection, which
makes you either very stupid or very naive, or both. And I'm even
worse for involving you in the first place."

"He's gonna call out the troops because I took his squeeze out to
dinner, right? You think maybe he'll lob a few mortars into the
kitchen, soften me up before they storm the place?"

"I think he'd take it personally, yeah. There are some guys,
Bobby, who don't treat things like this as lightly as you or me."

I can't believe he's telling me this, Blacky telling *me* I ought to
back off because some other guy has made a prior claim.

"And that's the least of it," he adds.

I turn him away from the stove. "What's the big deal? I told her
she could come, I can just as easily tell her she can't. If she asks
why, I'll tell her the truth: I got an invitation from Roberto Gavilan, but I'm not allowed to bring a date. Simple as that."

"It's off," Blacky says.

"I'll do it, I'll do it, I'll tell her. I'll take her home tonight and
that will be the end of it. I'll tell her I can't take her to Huaráz. I'll
make up some excuse. She'll have to find another way. Okay? You
satisfied?"

"This was a mistake, a big, big mistake. I had to be an idiot. It's
not as if I didn't know you," he says. "It's off."

Blacky thinks just because I goof around a little, I can't handle
this. I can handle this. I was *made* for this. I'm the guy who photographed the bullfights from *inside* the ring. "Shitfire," I say to him,
"what's a raggedy-ass guerrilla and some old limp-dick colonel to
me?"

"You're proving my point for me, Bobby. You think this a joke.
This is not like picking up girls on the beach with that 'You could
be a model' rap of yours. This is not making pals with the exercise
boys at the track. This is serious business. Lives at stake here. You
think it's a joke."

He's right. I do. I don't say I do, but I do. A couple of dozen
guys in camouflage suits along with the cokehead owner of a restaurant are undertaking the violent overthrow of the government.
Right. Sure thing. Blacky, if I wanted to, I could take over my knee
and spank. Even if he *weren't* into it, I could put him over my knee,

that's how dangerous a dude *he* is. The rest of the guerrillas better
be a whole lot fiercer than Blacky. And then there's the part about
my photographs. Me, Bobby Shafto, in *El Tiempo*, or *Newsweek*. Or
Life! Sure, I think it's a joke, Blacky's right, but it'd be fine this
time if the joke were on me. I've been *waiting* for this. I wasn't cut
out to bake blueberry muffins all my life. I feel like the contender
who just got a shot at the title. I'm ready to roll. Let me at the
greaseball. Meantime I've got to smooth it over with Blacky. "Can
I be frank with you here for a minute . . . ?"

"Spare me your horseshit, Bobby, please, Bobby, because this is
serious business, and to you it's all a game."

"Just hear me out, OK? I listened to you, now you listen to me.
It's Nina. She . . ." The fact I'm involved with Nina will explain
something to Blacky. A woman's always been at the bottom of his
biggest problems. In his mind, any unusual behavior, there's a
woman involved in it somewhere. It's weird, I know, and it's the
way Blacky thinks. If you heard him talk about his marriages, you'd
understand. "I really think she's special."

"Save your idiot psychology for somebody else," he says. "I
could give a rat's ass about the broad. I want some evidence you're
responsible enough to be trusted where there're people's lives at
stake. Not to mention your own."

"All right," I say. "You win. You offered me a chance. Don't
yank it away from me now. I won't let you down."

He holds out his hand, shakes mine, holds it in both of his. I put
my other hand in. I really do love this guy.

"Now what about the girl?" he says.

"Which girl is that?" I say. I untangle my hands from his, relieved he didn't try to hug me.

Blacky can go to hell. It's not as if I was out every day beating
the bushes in search of Miss Right. Blacky knows. He could tell
you. All that ever interested me was Miss Right Now. But that was
before Nina came along. I got the feeling that there's a finer person inside of me a hair to the other side of my all bad habits, and
Nina, she's the one could coax that person across. Thinking about
this, and how to tell her about Huaráz, is the reason that backing
out of the restaurant parking lot, I plow the van into Blacky's car. It

takes the sound of metal on metal to bring me back to the everyday world and things like what rearview mirrors are for.

Blacky, the asshole, he leaves his goddamn wreck in the middle of the parking lot, it's no wonder I back into it. The piece of shit's already so damned dinged I don't know which dent I made and which were already there. I do know my taillight wasn't busted in a hundred pieces until a few seconds ago. Fuck Blacky's goddamned car, and fuck the asshole who parked it there. I give it a kick and my boot goes clear through the fender, which makes me laugh despite myself. What a guy. Drives that rusted-out piece of shit, he never once put the top up on it since the day he bought it, sits out in the rain, puddles on the floor, beer cans, water sloshing in the convertible well, he doesn't care. Now it's got a hole in the fender the shape of my foot.

The case I've built against Blacky is too feeble for me to stay worked up about, and Nina, she and I don't go back far enough for me to show her how petty I can be. That's why when I slide back behind the wheel, all I say is "The taillight broke," and I throw it into gear, as if I'm this placid, together person, it takes more than a broken taillight to set me off.

"How'd you like the shoofly pie?" I ask, to turn my mind from Blacky. She wants to know why they call it shoofly pie, the answer to which I tell her—me being a chef, she came to the right person because I'm not only a chef, I'm a gastronome.

"Is that with a *g-n-o-m-e?*" she says.

I like that. I like somebody who can joke around. I like somebody who makes the attempt. That's a high state as far as I'm concerned, when a person is able to joke around. What she says next is funnier, that we've been invited to Colonel Rinaldi's for drinks.

"You what!" I can't believe what I heard. She repeats herself. She's accepted. I swerve across two lanes of traffic and slam on the brakes in a no-parking zone in front of the Alhambra Theater. People standing in line for the movie turn to stare. "Are you crazy?" What a night! First Blacky, now Nina. What next?

"My God, Bobby. I had no idea you'd react this way."

"Didn't I just hear you say plain as day that you accepted?"

"I wanted you to meet him. You wanted *me* to meet Blacky, didn't you? What's so crazy about that? I'm sorry, Bobby. I had no idea . . . If I had known . . . But he's expecting us. We'll only stay a few minutes."

My van is blocking the lane. Someone leans on his horn. I glance in the rearview mirror.

"Can we find someplace else to talk, Bobby? Other than right here in front of the Alhambra? We're causing a scene."

The horn blares, a long, uninterrupted blast. I turn around to look. "The part that gets me is how did he know about me to even invite me?" The horn again. I roll down my window, stick out my arm, give the guy the finger.

"I told him, of course," Nina says. "I talk to him almost every day, and I told him. I told him we met at the market, I told him we went to Montesucre . . . He asked all about you. He was interested. He said he wanted to meet you. I wanted *you* to meet him. He said come over for drinks. It was a very natural thing to do."

"Natural my ass."

Now there is a whole line of cars behind us, all of them honking. The early show is over, the sidewalk crowded. People are leaving the theater, others arriving.

"Can we carry on this discussion somewhere else?" Nina asks. "Besides, he's expecting us. We're late as it is."

"Let them honk. We're not moving an inch."

"I'll just get myself a cab, then. I don't want to keep him waiting." She opens the door.

"Hold on. Can you wait one second. *Please?*"

She shuts the door. "Are you coming with me or not?"

Horns are honking. People are watching from the sidewalk.

"Give me a minute," I say. "I can't think with all this racket." I open the door, slide off the seat. "Say you'll stay until I get back, OK? Is that a promise? Be right back."

I shut the door, walk down the line of cars behind me. I stand in the oncoming lane. Traffic stops. I motion the cars stuck behind me to pull out and go around. I'm a regular goddamn traffic cop. One guy thinks to have a word with me. I don't wait to hear his spiel. I grab his little matchbox of a Nipponese piece of shit and rock it back and forth. I've got it by the rain gutter, got half a mind to tip it over on its side. The lady in the passenger seat is holding on to the dashboard and shrieking. The guy's glasses come unhooked from one ear. He quick rolls up his window. I step out in front and pound my fists on the hood. He lays rubber in reverse, quick throws it in forward, and swings wide around me. I chase him a ways, but the exertion has cooled me off.

Back in the van, before I've even closed the door, she's telling me that a person can't behave that way, that you have to control your temper, that violence is wrong and crazy, and that if we don't leave this instant she is getting out. I rest my head on the steering wheel. I've heard it all before.

The way I see it, a person makes his case the best way he knows. Take Nina, for instance. There's such a thing as an attractive nuisance, something you have to put a fence up around, like a swimming pool, because people can't always help themselves, they might jump in and drown. You got to protect them from themselves. It's the law. Now Nina, if she had thick ankles, beady eyes, you think there'd be any problems? Which is why I suppose the Arabs make them wear veils. Somebody's bound to get hurt, guaranteed. But who's going to blame Nina? She's just using her looks to get what she wants, and looks are totally fair and legal according to the rules.

There's other people can talk their way out of anything, tell us black was white and we'd buy it. Mostly they're politicians. Talking's allowed in the rules. And what about the guy with a truckload of cash? Money is very persuasive. Money's allowed. Then there's me. Nobody'd call me pretty, and my tongue's thicker than my wallet. So how do I get what I want? What's for me to use?

Me, I've got big arms. The thing of it is, go and swing your fists sometime, even if they're asking for it, even if they deserve it, see where swinging your fists gets you.

People never stop to think that in all the ways you can hurt a person, knocking them down is one of the least. My nose was busted four separate times. I've had stitches, concussions, sprains, dislocations, a couple of acres of black-and-blue. There was the time I broke both hands in one night. All those things more or less healed, but there are other things, things people do behind your back, things people say to you, or about you, some of those things never heal.

"I've had enough," Nina says. "I'm leaving. I'll give Rinaldi your regrets."

"The old goat." I still have my head on the steering wheel.

"You don't know him at all."

"I know what you told me. I know he's Alejandro's father."

"Why are you making such an issue of this? Rinaldi's a friend of mine, you're a friend of mine, I like you both, I thought you might like to meet each other. Is that such a far-fetched idea?"

I put the van into gear and pull out into traffic. "A person doesn't have to be Sherlock Holmes to see what this is all about."

"Forget I ever mentioned it. Just drop me off at his house. I'll tell him you couldn't come, that you had other plans. It's no big deal. I should never have accepted without asking you first. It's all my fault."

"Let me get this straight," I say. "You're telling me this guy genuinely wants to get to know me?"

"Not 'this guy.' His name is Rinaldi. And yes, he does. Can you drive a little faster, please?"

"I move in on his woman, and he invites me for cocktails."

"You wouldn't understand."

"Then do me a favor. Clue me in."

"He's my closest friend. I told him about us. I tell him everything. Now he wants to meet you."

"Aw, shit, Nina. You didn't. Everything?"

"I didn't tell him *everything*."

"The man isn't stupid. Even if he is, he can't be *that* stupid."

"Grow up, Bobby. Not everyone is as possessive as you believe. Rinaldi doesn't think like that."

"I just wish you hadn't of told him."

"I *didn't* tell him. Why won't you listen to me?"

"OK, try me again," I say. "I'm listening."

"It isn't all that complicated. Don't you remember how he's looked after me, everything he's done for me? Do I have to go through it all again?"

Breakfast this morning was when she'd told me the story. How they'd lived on adjacent ranches, how Rinaldi and her old man had been buddies in the army, how growing up she'd spent as much time in Rinaldi's house as her own. And then the stuff about what a bum businessman her father was, one wild scheme after the other —llamas for export, the dude ranch—Rinaldi bailing him out time and again, until finally the old man'd sunk all he had left into an Arabian stud that got killed the same time Alejandro did. And then her father committed suicide and her mother died not long after that and she was left with the ranch and a lot of bills and Rinaldi came to the rescue again. Bought the ranch himself so it wouldn't be divided up among the creditors, and paid her a price above the market value, so that while Nina came out with nothing in the end, at least she didn't owe anybody, either.

Nobody but Rinaldi, that is.

And then he took her to the capital. She was a mess—her fiancé dead, her father and mother, her home no longer hers and not a place she wanted to live in anymore anyway. She couldn't do a thing for herself. A basket case. Totally unprepared. The only thing she knew was the farm. How to set the timing on a tractor, how to shoe a horse were skills of little value in the city. Other than that her father had always managed every part of her life, or tried to. She didn't even know how to write a check, although it wasn't an issue since she had no bank account either. Rinaldi set her up in an apartment and offered to send her to school if she wanted to go, and he took her out to dinner and to parties because if he hadn't she would have just sat alone in the house. He gave her money for clothes and money for rent. He looked in on her every day. He brought her food, fully prepared meals because she'd had a cook, and cooking was another thing on that long list of things she didn't know how to do. They became lovers. How this happened she didn't say, but it didn't take much of an imagination. And while she didn't think it was exactly "natural," a spontaneous gesture of affinity or mutual attraction, it wasn't as if she were a virgin either, and given what she felt she owed him, and how badly he seemed to desire her, she went along. The least she could do.

In truth she was flattered, she admitted that much. An important man like Rinaldi, who seemed to know numbers of beautiful, self-assured women, he wanted *her*. She liked the way she thought his attention reflected on her, propping her up, even if it was in a sort of artificial way. Bolstered her self-esteem. It was desirable to feel desirable. And if by her association with him she gained no real self-confidence, she learned at least how to fake it. She began to come out of herself, is how she described it. She enrolled in acting classes. She took a job selling cosmetics in a department store. Neither the job nor the classes lasted very long. Rinaldi asked her to quit, he didn't feel they were "right" for her. He couldn't say why; or if he could, she didn't remember his reasons. It was enough that he'd made the request.

They spent a lot of time together in those first few months. He took her to Rio. He took her to Hong Kong. He introduced her to all sorts of interesting, important people. He took care of her and in turn, she did what she could to take care of him. Alejandro was his son as well as her fiancé, it was his loss too; and Elena, absorbed by her own grief, remained a recluse at the ranch. Nina sometimes thought about Elena and Alejandro, but she tried not to. She justified her behavior by reasoning that if they could know the true nature of her relationship with Rinaldi, they would somehow understand and approve, or at least not condemn her for it. She was helping him through this difficult time, as he was helping her.

Personally, I didn't buy a word of it. But sex is a touchy thing, sex makes people crazy, let me tell you about it sometime, and if she wanted to talk about it in terms of "debt" and "true nature" and "coming out of herself" when it looked to me like a straightforward case of some old fart wanting to get it on with a young buttery babe, and willing to foot the expense, who was I to say it was something different? She'd told me the kind of kid she was: smoking, drinking, teasing the ranch hands, strutting around outside the bunkhouse, getting a kick from turning them on until one day she got one of them so turned on she couldn't turn him off. I didn't know her as a teenager, but judging from what I see sitting beside me right now, I can't say I blame Rinaldi. You had to credit him for his foresight, an eye for what little girls grow into. And he was patient man—lecherous, but patient. That didn't mean I liked him, and for sure it didn't mean I wanted to have a drink with him. But it's where we seem to be headed.

She'd sung a long, low, sad song this morning, and I listened to every word. She said it was important to her to let me know where things stood. Knowing that about her, I don't know why I should have been so surprised she also told Rinaldi where things stood vis à vis me, but I was.

"I *care* about him, Bobby. I really care about him, about his feelings, about his opinions, his thoughts, what he thinks about me. I go to him for advice. I trust his judgment. He *knew* the time was coming, Bobby. He knew about you before I did—not you, Bobby Shafto, per se, but somebody like you. He knew it. He told me, and

I didn't believe him, but he was right. It's how I let this happen. That's why I told him."

"What exactly did he know?"

"He knew I would . . . meet someone. He always said it would happen, that one day I would meet someone, not like him, someone younger, someone with life ahead of him. He thinks his life is in the past."

I drive the final few blocks in silence, then turn into the drive. "I can't help thinking that if you cared as much about him as you say you do, you wouldn't have said a word to him about us. Either that, or you wouldn't have gotten mixed up with me in the first place. That's the way my mind works. But I also know there's plenty of things in this world that I don't understand. You tell me I'm wrong about Rinaldi. OK, I'm wrong."

"You don't really believe that."

"No, I'm willing to admit it. I might be wrong."

"Then you're coming in with me?"

KISSING YOUR SISTER

I pass by Rinaldi's all the time. I'd thought it was an embassy. This is nuts, coming here, I don't know what Nina was thinking accepting his invitation, but I'm here now and I'm going through with it. A guard opens the gate for us, we pull into the turnaround, somebody else opens the car door, and a third guy takes us to Rinaldi. He's waiting in the library. The colonel in the library with the gun. Seems like we woke him up. He kisses Nina's hand, shakes mine, breaks the connection quick. Nina disappears to the bathroom, leaving him and me alone. Like I predicted, the vibes are weird. Could be me, but they are very weird.

"What can I get you to drink?" Rinaldi says, the first words out of his mouth. I can spot an alcoholic when I meet one, being so close to Blacky has taught me what to look for: every occasion calls for a drink. He doesn't wait for my answer to pour himself something over ice. "Pisco sour," he says, holding up his glass. "Are you sure I can't make one for you?" He eases himself into a dark leather chair and sets his drink on the armrest. I look around the room—ceiling two stories high, balcony all around, dark paneling, alcoves, stained glass windows, books wall-to-wall and floor-to-ceiling. I fidget, try to think of something to say, if only to see if he isn't asleep in the armchair, his head back against the cushion. "Did you see where they held Eusebio scoreless last night?" I say.

"I didn't," he says. His glasses are on his forehead. He massages his eye sockets.

"They put a man on him who dogged him all night, and they stalled, the same tactics Chile used in the Cup quarterfinals. It makes for a lousy boring game, but it worked."

"Yes," he says. "Very dull." His eyes are still shut. He puts the glass against his cheek. "Frankly, I detest the game."

"But you do appreciate winning tactics, don't you? Being a military man and all."

"Chile lost, as I recall, and San Sebastián apparently was happy to settle for a tie. I don't approve of playing for a tie. If one is going to play, then one must play to win."

"A tie is like kissing your sister," I say.

He sips his pisco sour, but doesn't open his eyes. "I didn't say that," I tell him. "Well, I did just now, yeah, but I didn't say it first. I think it was Darrell Royal said it after Texas tied Oklahoma." I ramble on, about Jimmy Saxton who played for Texas, little guy they said could chase down jackrabbits, and the Michigan State–Notre Dame game that Parseghian played for a tie, and back to Eusebio and the game last night. "Coach Royal hit it on the nose: like a kiss from your sister." Through all this Rinaldi is in kind of a torpor, a snake out in the cold. "Of course, I don't have a sister, so I got to use my imagination here. Have you got a sister, Colonel?"

"Only a brother, I'm afraid." He opens his eyes and shuts them again.

"Then you can't vouch for it either." Rinaldi takes a sip of his drink, his head is still resting on the back of the chair. Some vivacious host. He just couldn't *wait* to meet me, right? Nina isn't back from the bathroom yet. I feel like I want to wake him and shake him. "If you don't know about kissing your sister," I say, "then maybe you could give me the dope on what it's like to screw your dead son's fiancée." He gets to his feet and starts over to where I'm waiting for him when Nina walks in and prevents him from breaking his nose. He blows right by me to the bar, like that's where he was headed all along.

"Bobby and I were just going out to the stables, weren't we, Bobby? Would you like to join us?" he says. I've got to admire the old goat's reflexes. "You spoke about his interest in racing. I thought he might like to see Kid Pro Quo."

"Bobby can speak for himself, I'm sure," she says. "I'll be fine here. You two go on without me."

"I love the stables, reminds me of the ranch. There's a bench out there where I do some of my best thinking. I often go there to be alone . . . ," Rinaldi is saying to me. Where before he was morose, suddenly he's animated, very congenial. I wink at Nina on the way out. ". . . And then there's Kid Pro Quo. Quite an interesting story . . ." He shuts up the second we're beyond the library door, but I *do* happen to know Kid Pro Quo, and he *is* an interesting story. You might say I know him personally, only I didn't know he belonged to Rinaldi.

The Kid's trainer, Paco Arturo, was one of the first people I met at the track. I got to know him and I got to know his groom, Frankie Agramonte, and since they didn't mind me hanging around taking pictures, I hung around a lot. Kid Pro Quo was Paco's only horse at the time and I got to know him pretty good, too. I knew he liked his oats with molasses, for instance, that he was a cribber, and that you didn't want to turn your back on him, he'd try to nip you for sure, or worse.

I was at the track for his first start as a two-year-old. He showed early speed, but tired in the stretch to finish seventh. The next time out he broke fast and faded again, finished twenty-one lengths behind. In his third race he started slow but rallied to fourth. Something was funny there, no consistency, and Frankie confirmed it for me: Paco's holding him back, Frankie said. He doesn't want to win with him until the odds are right. Sure enough, his fourth start Paco drops him in class, which according to Frankie is the signal he's ready to let him run. Me and Blacky put down two hundred apiece. Kid Pro Quo goes off at fifteen to one.

I went from the track directly to the restaurant with my pockets stuffed with cash. After work that night Blacky and I didn't get home until the next afternoon. I sprang for the hotel, the champagne, and the caviar, even though I don't much care for champagne or caviar. Blacky brought the coke and the girls. Well, that's not quite true; Blacky did bring the coke, but it was the coke that brought the girls. Their story was they'd been fashion models in Paris, and how they looked you could believe it. I'd seen them around, they'd been to the restaurant a couple of times, and I ran into them at the club, but they never said boo to me before. None of them was the one to turn my life around, but the three of them together pointed my week in the right direction.

I was also there the afternoon the Kid went down. Just before the clubhouse turn Beau René stumbled and the Kid had to jump to clear him. Beau René, the five-horse, the jock had white and blue silks, I remember it very clearly because it happened right in front of me, and I have the picture I took to help me remember. I sent it to *El Observador* Sunday magazine, and they printed it minus my credit, and then they stiffed me for the twenty-five bucks to boot. So Beau René is down on the turf and the Kid jumps, and his front hooves clear Beau René easy. It was his rear hoof on the driver's side that landed square on Beau René's head. From where I was on the rail, even above the sound of the forty or so other hooves hitting the turf, the shouts and whistles of the jocks, the noise from the crowd, you could hear the crack of metal shoe on bone. The track vet saved himself a bullet on Beau René. Kid Pro Quo broke his cannon bone just below the hock. In a case like that often as not they'll just put the horse down, but I'd heard somebody bought Kid Pro Quo and saved his life. It seemed unusual because he had mediocre bloodlines, and in seven starts he only finished in the money that one time, which led me to ask Paco if he really did set up a betting coup. To this day he swears the win was a surprise to him.

The grounds are dark, and very quiet. I don't know what Rinaldi has in mind. I can't picture him wanting to duke it out over Nina. The two of us walk the gravel path to the stable. Inside the stall he flips on the light. A second later a soldier, seventeen or eighteen years old, with pimples and an automatic rifle, steps through the door. Before I get the chance to really panic he salutes and fades back into the dark.

Kid Pro Quo whinnies. He's very skittish. He backs into the far corner of his stall. Rinaldi tries to approach him, but the horse rears as much as the ceiling will allow and then turns his hindquarters toward us. He snorts and watches us over his shoulder. Rinaldi retreats to the door. I make soothing noises, come to him slowly. I pull a brush from a hook on the wall even though he's already brushed to where his coat shines like a sports car. It must be Rinaldi who bothers him, because me he doesn't seem to mind. He nibbles my shirt collar, and puts his muzzle up to my ear. I wonder if he remembers me. His breath is warm and sweet. I do his neck and stroke down his chest and foreleg, moving the brush in long, hard strokes. He watches over his shoulder and takes the chance to nip me good on the hip, for which I slap his nose. He straightens up and lays back his ears. I run my hand along his neck. "Thatta boy, easy boy." I rub his back leg, the one he broke. I act absorbed, but I haven't forgotten the look on Rinaldi's face back in the library. I'm waiting. His court, his ball, it was him who invited me.

He unwraps a cigar, punctures the tip with a toothpick, puts the whole thing in his mouth, licks the wrapper all the way around, and pulls it out slowly. He turns out the light. He rolls the cigar in the flame from his lighter, sucking little puffs. On the wall behind him his shadow balloons and shrinks. The same soldier steps inside the stall again, and again Rinaldi dismisses him. I can't see Rinaldi's face, just the red point of his cigar. He speaks slowly, softly, never raising his voice or changing his tempo. "If I learn," he says jabbing his cigar, "that for any reason whatsoever, you see, or even so much as speak to Nina DeBettencourt again after tonight, I will see to it that you, Mr. Shafto, Mr. *Bobby* Shafto, disappear. And lest you misunderstand me, I do not mean deported, although that is also within my power to arrange." He puffs his cigar, watches the smoke disperse. "I mean vanish, as smoke vanishes into the air." Kid Pro Quo fidgets and prances. He snorts.

I square around to face Rinaldi. "You want to go? You and me? We'll go right now." I drop the brush.

Rinaldi laughs. "Very amusing, Mr. Shafto. Of course I don't want to 'go,' as you put it. I don't need to. I have influential friends, indebted to me, men for whom the disappearance of an individual is quite easily accomplished. Subversives, radicals, Moreno, addicts, all manner of undesirables, here one day and"— another puff of smoke—"gone the next. In the case of a person such as yourself, Mr. Shafto, a cook, a man without means or connections, a foreigner who is, in fact, illegally residing in our country, a fugitive from the law—in the case of a person like that, it would be laughably easy. Are you surprised, Mr. Shafto? You shouldn't be. Yes, I know quite a bit about you. Arrested for assault in Baltimore, Maryland, having beaten a man to within an inch of his life. Your wife's lover, I believe he was, isn't that so, Mr. Shafto."

"Ex-wife."

"Precisely. Nor did she, your *ex*-wife, escape without injury. Her vision, I remember from the report, has been permanently impaired—"

"That's what her lawyers called it."

"Oh? And what do you call it, Mr. Shafto?"

"I call it a black eye."

"In any event, you took it upon yourself to punish the poor woman merely because you disapproved of her behavior."

"She was sucking his cock while the kid was sleeping five feet away. Did the report mention that?"

"And you took it upon yourself to punish them both. With your own two hands. According to the report, you broke your fists on the man's face."

"On the door, busting down the door, not on his face. And it wasn't my fists, either. It was my thumbs."

"And then you proceeded to beat the man senseless. When your own thumbs were already broken? Can that be? It's a pity the incident didn't happen here, Mr. Shafto. We Latins understand that sort of behavior. It's considered justifiable. Some might argue it's expected of a man. A man with a temperament such as yours surely understands a man like me. You have only to examine yourself to know without doubt that I mean what I say."

Kid Pro Quo tried to lift his forelegs, but I was holding his halter. He swung his hindquarters toward Rinaldi. Rinaldi backed toward the door of the stall. "Unlike you, however, I need not bloody my hands on your skull. As I said, a phone call is all that's required. Such are the benefits of being well connected. Nor is your exact fate something over which I need trouble myself. There are men who undertake such chores with, ah—relish. I think I make myself clear, do I not, Mr. Shafto? Mr. Bobby Shafto? Yes, I do. I believe I do."

Nina's drink is going watery on the table under the lamp. She's listening to music. Coming into the room, we startle her. Rinaldi freshens Nina's, pours one for himself and one for me. What he'd said to me in the stable still has me backpedaling. My brain is stalled. "I think I make myself clear," he'd said, and then, "Now let's go inside the house and have ourselves a drink."

Where Rinaldi was almost asleep when we arrived, now he's fully awake, in high spirits. He tells a joke and laughs at it himself. He's positively giddy. He lies when Nina asks what we talked about out in the stable. He talks about Kid Pro Quo. He says the Kid's his favorite.

"Even though he's thrown you twice?" Nina asks.

"Three times," Rinaldi corrects her. "I admire that about him. He has his own mind."

Rinaldi changes the subject. He talks about Blacky's. He tells Nina there's a package he had put into my van, something she's to take up to the farm with her when she goes. Sprinkler heads, he says. For Luis. From Chicago.

Nina checks her wristwatch. "It's after eleven. Bobby and I should be going. And you have to be at work in the morning, Rinaldi. What time will you pick me up tomorrow night?" She turns to me. "We're going to the rodeo tomorrow. I'm so excited. I can't wait. The Argentine National Rodeo, the best in the world."

"Ah, Nina, darling," Rinaldi sputters. "My dear, I—I don't know how to tell you this. I know how much you were looking forward to going, and I meant to tell you earlier, truthfully, but with all the goings-on down at the ministry—forgive me, dear, I feel terrible, I feel truly awful, but I've been so wrapped up in my work . . ."

Nina's face goes hard. All straight lines. She crosses her arms.

"I'll make it up to you somehow. I promise. I'd fully intended to get us the tickets, I meant to, I even had it penciled in on my calendar, I can show you, Saturday the twenty-fourth, the Argentine National Rodeo, and then the Minister called, and one thing led to another, and, well, you know how it is."

"You forgot," Nina says.

"Worse than that. I accepted another invitation. I hope you understand. You do, don't you, my dear?"

Roderigo Clemente Quispe had been Indian once. Because "Indian" was not a racial designation, having less to do with a man's genes than where he lived, the style of his shoes, his name for God, the music he played, or the language he spoke, he was Indian no more. Unlike Roberto Gavilan, however, whose grandparents were Indians, and whose parents had lived in the mountains, but whose speech and mannerisms were unmistakeably of the barrio, Clemente was not so far removed that he couldn't pass, which is why Gavilan had chosen him. In sandals, homespun pants, sweaters, and raw felt hats, their weapons hidden, the two of them left camp at Blue Lake.

Emilio had been left in charge. Gavilan had instructed him to scatter the men among the rocks through the day, and then to move at night to the abandoned mines at Sestre. They were to remain there until Gavilan returned with the photographer. Emilio was not to reveal their destination to anyone. Gavilan himself had not told Clemente the true rendezvous. Instead, he said it was the construction camp at San Gerais.

The trail wound down from the lake through the paper-barks—short, twisted, sparsely foliated trees. They encountered no one there. The Indians considered the land this high on the mountain to be the uncivilized domain, a belief that no doubt colored their opinion of the Zapato Moreno. Once clear of the paper-barks, the two would surely be seen, but the Indians' natural reticence and their acquired aversion to strangers would keep them at a distance. Gavilan's story, should anyone be aggressive enough to ask or foolish enough to need to, was that they were miners going to town for provisions.

It was unlikely they would encounter any army patrols. That part of the mountains was still considered Moreno territory, although it had been months since there was any substance to the claim. Even then, Gavilan had known that the army only halfheartedly wanted to reclaim the province, that they couldn't have been as cowardly and inept as they appeared.

Three hours' walk brought them to the cairn marking the upper boundary of Viracocha. The marker was no more than a pile of stones on which passersby had placed coca, cigarettes, and some *trago* in an old beer bottle, offerings for the gods who ruled the mountains, and to whom all the land, crops, animals, and destinies of the people belonged. Clemente gathered up the coca and cigarettes and tucked them inside his shirt. The bottle he threw in a high end-over-end arc over the spiky tufts of grass. The ground was marshy and the bottle landed soundlessly.

"Our luck's running shitty enough as it is," Gavilan said, referring to Clemente's theft of the offerings.

Clemente denied himself no opportunity to scoff at his heritage. "Piss on luck," he said.

"Luck" had been the wrong word to use, Gavilan thought. He wasn't afraid of bad luck either, although he respected the role fate played in one's life. And if he doubted the eventual success of their undertaking, something he did more and more frequently, he never expressed it. He considered defeatism no less a betrayal than the one Silencio had perpetrated, the one for which he had paid with his life.

They came to a shepherd's hut surrounded by a low stone wall, and when no one answered their call, they crawled through the entrance. Inside, there was no one and nothing but dust and the rank odor of urine on rotting straw. Gavilan backed outside before he had to draw a second breath. The huts were built for the use of the shepherds, but Indian kids used them to get drunk and screw. Outside, Clemente handed him the coca he'd taken from the cairn. The dry, bitter leaves absorbed the little saliva he had. He felt the tingling on his tongue and gums, and as he walked and chewed he thought about the coca, the cocainistas, and how greed preyed on weakness. It was something he knew firsthand.

The trail entered a eucalyptus grove. The buttresses of Huascarán appeared for the first time to the north behind the ridges of Hualcán. Again they stopped to rest. It was midafternoon. The sweet smell of eucalyptus was on the wind, a respite from the sage and dust they had inhaled all morning. Gavilan dipped his hat in the stream and offered Clemente a drink. They rested and drank and looked across to the mountain. A woman had been one of the first ever to reach the summit, maybe the very first—an American, of course. For the women there, in the valley below the mountain itself, the simple tasks of living demanded more than what was required to climb ten Huascaráns, but from where Gavilan and Clemente sat in the eucalyptus grove, one would never know. From there it looked like the artist's ideal of rural life: streams rushed through plowed and planted fields, sheep grazed, smoke rose through the thatched roofs of small, neat cottages and dispersed against the sheer, white, monumental walls of the mountain. Only a blue sky was missing from the scene, a blue sky and the filth, squalor, poverty, disease, and despair which couldn't be seen from that distance.

An Inca Cola bottle partly filled with *trago* and a package of Inca cigarettes had been left on the cairn which marked both the lower boundary of Viracocha's grazing land and the start of the cultivated fields. Clemente pocketed the cigarettes, but Gavilan ordered him to return them. The trail widened here and joined a dusty road along which potatoes grew in tiny plots and cows were penned in corrals fenced with brambles like concertina wire. From there the two men saw a dust cloud up ahead. "Workers in the fields," Clemente said, reading Gavilan's mind. Gavilan had learned to trust Clemente's sight. Maybe because his eyes had adapted to the scale of the mountains, or maybe because he had never read a book or watched TV—whatever the reason, Clemente could see a crow blink a hundred yards away. They had to walk another quarter mile before Gavilan could see the line of campesinos, twenty of them or so, men, women, and children, stretched across a field.

Gavilan weighed his caution against their need for provisions and started toward them. They ceased their work. They drew into a knot and stared at him through the settling dust, twenty dark, sullen faces under wide-brimmed hats. A woman shoved her way to the front to meet him. Her skin was as wrinkled as the paper-bark.

She held a four-foot tree limb, a tool she had been using to break up the clods of earth, and screamed at him in Quechua, a language Gavilan's mother had spoken at home, one which he could understand when spoken slowly, and couldn't speak at all. The woman shrieked into his face, and the men stood behind her and the children watched from behind skirts and between legs. He had walked the fifty yards across the field with a smile on his face, but he couldn't hold it any longer.

Clemente stepped between them and spoke to her in her own language, which only seemed to fuel her tirade. The others formed a crescent around them. Clemente pulled at Gavilan's arm, pulled him away and yelled at the woman. For every step backward the strangers took, the campesinos took a step forward. "Tell her all we want is to buy some food," Gavilan said.

"They want us to leave," Clemente said, pulling on Gavilan's arm.

"Tell her we'll pay," Gavilan said.

"They don't want our money." The woman was still yelling, still advancing.

Gavilan jerked from Clemente's grasp, turned away from the crowd to look Clemente in the face. "Tell them we'll pay," he insisted. Clemente wasn't listening, he was reaching inside his poncho. Only after seeing Clemente's gun did the woman lower the tree limb she had raised over her head, but she didn't stop her shouting and her shrill voice followed them across the field.

The road passed through flat, marshy ground. The stream had split into half a dozen channels, slow-moving rivulets of oily muck amid bushy hummocks of grass. Fifty yards off the road, a man and a boy struggled with a cow. At first it appeared the animal was merely stubborn, but then, closer, they could see its legs stuck in the mud.

"Forget it, Roberto. We don't have the time," Clemente said. "They probably don't want our help anyway." Gavilan mystified Clemente, and Clemente never troubled himself to figure out Gavilan's workings. He watched, he observed, he wondered. He had learned to sometimes anticipate the man without understanding him, as on a sunny day he could feel the rain still a day or two away.

Gavilan jumped from hummock to hummock and finally across a

yard-wide arm of dark water. He waded in and took the rope alongside the boy. The mud sucked at his sandals and he sank in to his shins. They pulled together, the man, the boy and Roberto. The cow bellowed. She tried to rise up, but she couldn't free her hind legs. She mooed pitifully as a trickle of blood dripped from her nostrils. On the bank her newborn calf paced and cried. Gavilan and the boy pulled on the rope, and the man pushed with his shoulder underneath her tail. "It's no use, mister," the boy said. "She's got no strength left to help herself."

From the bank, Clemente said, "See?" as if he had known all along this was another futile side trip.

"Maybe with the four of us we can get her out," Gavilan said to Clemente. "You can probably lift her out yourself." Clemente was skinny, but proud of his strength.

The four of them pulled together, and the cow's hind legs moved several inches out of the mud. They pulled harder and she rose up a little more, her feet working in the mud now, searching for footing. Clemente pushed from behind alongside the man while Gavilan pulled with the boy from in front. The cow, her neck twisted by the rope, seemed to give up and then, bellowing with sudden effort, climbed up onto the bank. The calf reached underneath his mama for her muddy dugs.

A line of mud crossed their clothes at their thighs. Mud was caked on their arms, spattered on their faces, in their hair, and on their teeth. You could see it when they smiled. The man said he and the boy had just about given up, that the cow, their only cow, would have died had not Gavilan and Clemente come along to help, and if the cow had died, the calf, being so young, would have also died. It would be his pleasure, he said, considering the great service they had done him and his family, if the two of them would come to his home for a meal.

Antonio's house was on the hillside overlooking the road to Viracocha. Outside the doorway, a baby wrapped in a shawl on her back, his wife was grinding corn, but when she saw the two strangers she hurried into the house. The boy, Augusto, having tethered the cow, led them down to the stream. He whistled a tune which Gavilan had taught him on the way down from the pasture. The boy and his father changed clothes in the bushes and washed only their hands and faces. They both saw the guns the strangers took out from under their sweaters. Without a change of clothes, Clemente and Gavilan waded into the stream fully dressed. Not an hour before, this water had been part of the glacier. Its force and the rocky bottom made standing tricky. Knocked over twice, Clemente gave in and lay down, his head upstream, the water foaming over his shoulders. The boy and his father laughed out loud.

There was little daylight left when they reached the house. They had to duck through the doorway. Inside, with just the fire smoldering under a blackened pot, it was dark and smoky. The dirt floor sloped. Clemente and Gavilan sat close to the fire to dry their clothes. Augusto told his younger brother Alberto and his mother about the cow. They laughed at the part where she spattered them with mud. While she listened, Dominga squatted by the fire and stirred the pot, the baby still wrapped on her back. A smaller, younger boy came through the doorway and, surprised by the guests, hurried to sit beside his father. He was covered with dust. His hat was battered, his jacket was shredded at the sleeves, his pants were in shreds at the cuffs. Gavilan recognized him as one of the children he'd seen among the workers in the field.

Augusto told the story again from the beginning. He, his father, and Alberto laughed again in the places they had laughed before, where they were in the mud, and where Clemente sat in the ice-cold stream. The youngest, the newcomer, sat stonefaced holding on to his father's sleeve. Dominga ladled out the food—boiled potatoes, cornmeal with water and sugar, and *cancha*, roasted kernels of corn. They ate with their fingers off squares of newsprint.

"Your boy," Gavilan said indicating the youngest, "I saw him today in the fields above the village."

"Marcellino is his name. He's shy, but a good worker," his father said. He hugged his son. The little boy hid his smile in his father's chest.

"They ran us off," Gavilan said.

"Hah!" Antonio laughed. "Of course!" He explained that it was the normal way to treat strangers in Viracocha and the surrounding mountain villages. Clemente shot Gavilan a knowing look. Although he had come to Viracocha as a boy, Antonio went on, and was now past forty, he himself was still regarded by his neighbors as a stranger, a foreigner, with suspicion. But not so they were excluded from contributing labor to community projects, like the clearing of the irrigation ditches, or the planting of the communal fields, to which he had sent Marcellino as the family's representative. "Ask me," he said. "I know all about what it's like to be a stranger."

Clemente could have eaten everything there was to eat himself, but following Gavilan's example, he declined a second helping. After a portion was set aside for Julia, the oldest child, not yet home, the pot was scraped, the wooden spoon was licked, dropped kernels of *cancha* were picked off the floor and eaten. Because firewood was scarce and expensive, on cold nights the family ordinarily went to sleep after dinner, but this was a special occasion, and although they knew that having shared their food they would be a little hungrier tomorrow, and having thrown more wood on the fire they would perhaps be a little colder, they were glad for the break in the routine, and thankful to the strangers for their cow.

Augusto and Alberto sat on either side of their father, Marcellino between his father's legs, and Dominga held the baby inside her sweater. Clemente borrowed Alberto's flute and played songs from his village, the notes high, sad, and clear in the quiet night. Augusto asked his father to tell about the puma. Antonio, embarrassed, at first declined, but then allowed himself to be persuaded. "Gusto has a one-track mind lately," Antonio explained.

After all the talk—about the puma, the tale of which the boys made their father tell and retell in the smallest detail, about the cow and the bath and the incident up in the fields, about Clemente's village, and the Missing Tooth, about the Feast of Santo Rosario still a couple of weeks away, and school—and hours after Clemente had fallen asleep, his poncho pulled to his chin, they heard a voice calling from outside.

Julia stumbled in through the doorway and collapsed sobbing in her father's arms. "They made me wait all day," she said when she was calm enough to speak. "I told them, I told them it hurt, but they didn't seem to care." She began to cry again and they had to wait until she could continue. "There was no place to sit, and they wouldn't let me sit on the floor unless I paid them some money, and I would have, but I didn't have any except what I needed to take the truck home. Then a nurse let me sit on the floor outside the door, but I had to give her my bracelet. I couldn't help it, Mama. I had to sit down. I sat and I waited and people came in and people left and they walked past me and I tried to tell them about the baby and the pain and they told me I had to wait my turn, and after I'd waited all day they told me it was too late, the clinic was closed, they told me to come back tomorrow. And then the ride in the truck, and the walk up the hill, four hours it took me to walk tonight from Marcara! My stomach hurts so bad, Mama."

Her mother stroked the girl's hair while her father rocked his daughter in his arms.

"I warned her," Antonio said to Gavilan after Julia had been put to bed. Bed was a pile of blankets on the floor against the wall. "I told her it would be a waste of time. But she had to find out herself. I know her. I know the pain must be bad if she went to the dogshit bastards in Huaráz for help. Sometimes I think I understand why there are *guerrilleros* in the mountains." Augusto, who had been staring into the fire, looked up.

Antonio, Dominga, and the children slept together under their blankets like a litter of pups. It was one of Gavilan's principles never to sleep in a house, especially one where there was only one way out, and he woke Clemente and the two of them went outside to sleep under the eaves.

Before there was even a hint of light in the sky, Dominga was up starting a fire. She heated watery cornmeal and a boiled potato for each of them. Julia slept through breakfast. In the same dusty, frayed clothing in which he had worked the day before and in which he had slept, his bare heels crushing the backs of his laceless, too-small shoes, and half asleep, Marcellino turned in the doorway to wave good-bye. His mother handed him two potatoes and a handful of *cancha* wrapped in a square of paper. "Save the paper, my good, sweet son," she said to his back as he disappeared through the doorway into the dark.

BLUE VACANT RECTANGLE

People trickled off the hillside paths in twos and threes to join a larger stream of people flowing down the road from the smaller, higher villages toward the market in Marcara at the foot of the valley. Men led donkeys loaded with burlap sacks, and others, their backs horizontal under the weight, carried the sacks themselves. Women with babies tied in shawls around their shoulders walked in clusters. One led a sheep on a rope, another a goat, a third carried a chicken under her arm. They talked and those with free hands spun wool on drop spindles.

The sky was double diamond blue. In cool, deep shadow, the road followed the stream. Augusto ran beneath the overhanging branches. He threw stones at birds, he whistled, sang, made side trips down to the stream, up onto the hillside, and into the yards of the houses along the way. Antonio, Roberto, and Clemente followed behind.

In the center of Viracocha the dirt road circled a crumbling dry fountain. A dozen mud houses faced each other across a dusty plaza. One of them was the school. Antonio could afford to educate only one of his sons, and since Augusto, the oldest, chose to work with his father, the privilege had fallen to the next in line, Alberto. It was for the best. Gusto understood that his father needed his help, help Alberto was still too young to give. Besides, Alberto was better suited for school, Gusto being far too restless, and slow-thinking Marcellino would've made no student. Augusto whistled and tossed stones into the stream while he waited for his father and the two strangers to catch up. He threw four times at something he eyed in a bush on the stream's far bank. All four rattled the stiff stalks and dry leaves. Roberto asked him why it had taken a hunter such as himself four rocks to down a puma.

"There were five," he said. "And I got them all."

The sun had just topped the ridge. The valley became a bright trough of light. The thermal baths at Chancos were reputed to have curative powers and drew people from all over the province. Already there were several cars and a bus parked by the roadside. Vendors sold soda pop, oranges, papayas, bananas, bread, soap, and shampoo. There was a stone patio and a restaurant, thatch-roofed and open on all sides. Big pots sat on propane burners, fly-spotted meat hung from a beam, and bruised papayas were piled beside a blender and a tray of cloudy glasses.

Gavilan bought pop and bread for the boy and his father. They sat on the wall in the shade. "Do you want to take a bath?" Gavilan asked Clemente, who had never had a bath in his life. He said he'd give it a try. "What about you, Antonio? Augusto?" The father said no, and the boy, watching his father, also said no. Gavilan made the offer again, making it clear that he was going to pay—a bath cost three cents—but still the answer was no.

All the cubicles were occupied, and they sat together on the wall waiting their turn. Gavilan asked if they wanted more to eat. Augusto looked at his father, who said yes, please, and then the boy said yes, please, and the four of them took seats at a table. Music blared from the radio. In the sunlight a girl combed and braided her friend's long wet black hair. Women washed clothes in the stream and spread them out to dry on the bushes. A boy sold ice balls from a cart. Yesterday he'd walked the twenty miles to the snout of the glacier below Hualcán and returned with a block of ice he'd hacked out himself and carried back wrapped in burlap to make the ice balls he sold at the baths for two cents apiece.

Antonio and Augusto wolfed down plates of rice and chicken. The food was gone in minutes, and when Gavilan asked if they would like more, they carried their plates back to the woman dishing food out from the big pots on the stove. Part of the second helping they ate, and part Antonio scraped into a plastic bag which he put underneath his sweater. Whistling the tune Gavilan had taught him, Augusto walked to the stream to wash his hands and returned to the table to find an ice ball waiting for him.

Their numbers were called. Two rows of five cubicles faced each other across a narrow aisle. Clemente took the first, and Gavilan the last on the same side of the aisle. The cubicle was ten by ten, with a small glassless window high in the wall opposite the door. There was a bench, and above it were nails on which to hang clothes. The tub itself was concrete, four by six, and three feet deep. The attendant drained the water from the previous bather, dumped a bucket of water on the floor, and swabbed the tiles with rags wrapped on the end of a broomstick. He plugged the drain with more rags, then lifted a wooden slat to allow the hot water to fill the tub.

Gavilan thanked the boy, tipped him, latched the door, undressed, wrapped his pistol in his jacket, and laid his clothing on the bench. He sat on the crumbling concrete floor of the tub and waited for the water to climb up around his body. The level inched up. In ten minutes it was not yet to his belly. He lay back and looked out the window at the bright blue sky.

Clemente's tub, closer to the cistern, filled more quickly. He had hung his clothes on the nail and placed his gun in his hat on the bench. The water, hot and deep, stung the cuts and scratches and sores that covered his skin.

The boy and his father sat in the shade at the table. The boy nursed his soda, swirling each mouthful around until the fizz was gone, then sucked awhile on his ice ball. They watched the people get off the buses. Every so often, Antonio touched his pocket where he had put the money for the mule he was planning to rent to take the provisions back to the mountains.

Three jeeps moved up the road against the traffic of people and animals going down to the market. The driver in the lead jeep pressed his hand to the horn while an officer, standing, yelled and waved a rolled newspaper at whoever impeded their progress. Outside the baths, the parking spots taken, they simply abandoned the jeeps and blocked the road entirely. From their features there was nothing to distinguish these soldiers from the people going to market, or from Antonio at the table in the restaurant, or from Gavilan or Clemente. They had the same dark eyes and skin and hair, the same broad face and broad nose, the same high cheekbones. Their uniforms set them apart, and their swaggering manner. Their pressed fatigues were tucked into their polished high black boots. And each had an automatic weapon.

There were a dozen of them, and not enough seats in the restaurant. Antonio and Augusto relinquished their table without being asked, and walked across to the opposite side of the patio to watch and wait in the glaring sun. The soldiers ordered their food. They propped their weapons against the tables, slung them over the backs of their chairs. The officer sat alone. Conversation around the patio ceased, which made the radio seem all the louder. The women gathered their laundry, and the girls, only one pigtail having been braided, followed the stream up the valley until they were out of sight.

"Hey, kid!" the captain yelled. "Ice!" A blue-tipped match bobbed in the corner of his mouth. The boy chipped off a piece from the block. "How much?" the captain asked. The boy held up a pair of fingers. "Then I guess I need some change." The boy held the twenty in his hand, looked from the bill to the captain and back to the bill. He reached into his pocket. He counted the coins in his palm, and counted them again. Less than a dollar. He gave the twenty back and shook his head. "What kind of a businessman doesn't carry change?" The soldiers watching laughed and the captain laughed and then returned the bill to his wallet. He unfurled his paper and sipped his Coca-Cola. The proprietress, watching from behind her pots, wiped her hands on her apron.

Gavilan lay back. The tub was filled to his ears and the water muffled all sound. His thoughts drifted in the steam rising off the water. He no longer smelled the sulfur, nor felt the sting of the sores on his legs and arms. He'd forgotten the irritating crumbs of cement on the bottom of the tub. He soaked and gazed through the steam at the vacant blue rectangle of sky.

The captain called for the check while the soldiers mopped the last of the food with slices of bread. The proprietress handed him a scrap of paper torn from a larger sheet. "For everything," she said.

"Ah," the captain said, examining the bill. He studied the paper as if there were more than the single figure written there. "Are you sure you counted everything?" She assured him she had. "The Coca-Cola?" Everything, she said. She wiped her hands on her apron. "Good," he said and folded the piece of paper carefully, unbuttoned his shirt pocket, put the paper inside, and rebuttoned it. He resumed reading his newspaper. The proprietress looked around as if expecting help. She wiped her hands on her apron, and waited. "Well?" he said, looking up from the news.

"Please, excuse me, Captain, but we haven't been paid yet for the food you ate here last week," she said.

"Haven't been paid?" The captain put down his paper.

"For last week or for the week before that," she said.

"I don't understand. I filed the requests myself. Do you have copies of the invoices?"

No, she didn't, she said. Was that a problem?

"No," he said. "If you don't have them now, I can pick them up next time we come." The soldiers looked at their plates and fingered the silverware. The captain handed her his glass. "Another, thank you," he said without taking his eyes from the page.

For Clemente, a bath was unprecedented, hot water miraculous, shampoo a foreign substance. He squeezed a drop from the tube, sniffed it, tested its slipperiness between his fingers, sniffed it again, tasted it with the tip of his tongue. Then he emptied it all into his palm and, grinning with pleasure, worked up as much lather as the mineral-laden water would allow.

Captain Mosquevera finished reading his newspaper. He pushed up his sleeve to examine the watch which he wore with the face on the underside of his wrist. Out on the patio, the men threw rocks at empty bottles they had lined up on the wall. Someone got the idea to put rocks on the wall and throw the bottles instead. Within minutes the patio was littered with broken glass.

The attendant's appeal to the captain, who had been smiling at the antics of his men, was taken as an insult and unpatriotic. "What!" he shouted. "You keep us waiting fifteen minutes, twenty minutes, half an hour, we who everyday risk our hides to protect the likes of you, and now you want me to stop my men when they are having some harmless fun? You're wasting my time. We can't wait any longer. We have a mission to perform." He signaled one of his men to come. "The attendant tells me the baths are free," he said. "The tubs simply need to be emptied."

"Who's that?" Clemente called at the sound of the door being forced. There was lather over all of his body, thick mounds in his hair. He opened his eyes and the stinging forced them shut again. "Who's that? What do you want?" There was alarm in his voice. The flimsy latch gave way, the door flew inward and slammed against the side of the tub. Soldiers rushed into the room. "Who's there?" Clemente still couldn't open his eyes. They grabbed him under the arms, lifted him out of the water, and shoved him, eyes shut, stumbling, soapy, and naked, into the sharp sunlight. He fell to the ground, skinning his knee and his palms.

"Your time is up," said one of the soldiers. The other tossed Clemente's clothes out after him. In midflight, the pistol separated from the hat and landed in the gravel near Clemente's leg. The hat landed after. Clemente's fingers groped in the dirt. A boot stomped on it.

The shriek brought the bathers in the other cubicles to their doors, and sent the ravens nesting in a nearby tree into the scorching afternoon sky. Captain Mosquevera picked up the gun. Soldiers grabbed Clemente's ankles and dragged him naked over the stones of the patio, clutching his broken hand and screaming in terrified, blind, searing pain.

Submerged to his ears, Gavilan heard nothing but the rumble of water slowly filling the tub. His eyes were fixed on the blue vacant rectangle on the opposite wall, his thoughts off in reverie, so when Augusto's face appeared in the window, it was a second or two before he comprehended what he was seeing: the face of a small boy in a window eight feet off the ground. He sat up in the tub.

"Mister!" The boy reached his arm through the window. "Your pistol. Give it to me. Hurry!" The urgency in Augusto's voice, and the piercing scream of a man in undeniable pain convinced him to act. He unrolled his clothes and put the gun in Augusto's outstretched hand a moment before the weight of a shoulder was thrown against his door.

"All right," he yelled. "I'm coming, I'm coming. No need to bust it down." The thud hit again. He looked up at the window. The boy was gone. Gavilan danced on one foot, trying to get the other through his pant leg. Holding his sweater, hat, and sandals under his arm, he opened the door. A soldier grabbed him by the neck and pulled him outside, and another took his wrist and wrenched it up behind his back.

"Jesus Christ," he said, "I stay a couple of extra minutes and they call out the army." The soldier twisted his arm further.

The bundle was pulled from under his arm, each item examined then thrown to the ground. They released him with a shove and a

kick. He gathered his clothes and dressed slowly in the aisle between the rows of cubicles with the others who had been similarly
evicted. His shoulder ached. He heard engines rev and tires spin.
He didn't know if Clemente would talk, if the indifference to pain
he'd acquired as an ignorant brute of an Indian was armor against
the practiced, relentless, pitiless cruelty of Mosquevera. He suspected it wasn't. Not that it would do Clemente any good were his
capacity for pain infinite and his courage impeccable. But at least
he had no secrets to tell. The story about rejoining the others at
the camp at San Gerais was invented for just such a possibility.
Whatever else they would pry from Clemente would be information they already knew, or would never believe: that there were
only a dozen of them left, that they were tired, hungry, and out of
supplies.

Gavilan walked alone down the road to Marcara. A few hundred
yards above the town, Antonio and the boy, leading a donkey, fell
into step beside him. They walked down the road into town together. Gusto, unaware that he was a single green bud on a dying
limb of a people, strode out ahead. He cracked the animal's rump
with his stick. *"Ashnu!"* he yelled. "Donkey!" And the boy and the
beast led the way into town.

A crumpled cigarette package flew out the speeding van's window, sailed momentarily in the turbulence, then skittered along the two-lane blacktop. Before it came to a stop, a man with a bundle of sticks tied to his back trotted barefoot onto the road, trapped the paper under his foot, picked it up, smoothed it out, and put it in his pocket.

Nothing has changed, she thought. Still the same. Squinting through cigarette smoke, she saw herself in the rearview mirror. Look at me! Damn! With one hand on the wheel, the cigarette between her lips, her eyes on the mirror, she combed her hair with her fingers. She overturned her purse on the passenger seat and sorted through tissues, keys, coins, and cosmetics, then flipped the cigarette out the window, and did her lips as the van hurtled through the cool morning air of the Santa Valley with no appreciable loss of speed. She put her eyeliner pencil between her teeth, pulled the cover off, and did her eyes while steering with her knee. Then she readjusted the mirror and searched the pile on the passenger seat for another cigarette. Finding none, she swore.

The road was straight and smooth and level and she drove seventy miles an hour, passing an occasional person on the side of the road. Got to have a smoke, she thought. And a cup of coffee. She wondered why she'd agreed to do this. It was an insane thing to agree to do, to visit your lover's wife, especially when your lover was a perfect grade A, number-one shitheel. She turned to see if she had the package for Luis, and the thought of Luis brought back a welter of memories, of her parents, the farm, Alejandro. Tears came to her eyes. Damn. She pounded the wheel with her palm.

Damn, damn, damn. She looked in the mirror to see if her mascara had run.

She reached for her purse and remembered she was out of cigarettes. She thought about Rinaldi and how casually he had dismissed their date. He'd *forgotten*. Forgotten! At least *my* word is good for something, she thought. When *I* say I'm going to do something, I do it. *That's* what I should have said. Instead she had said that of course she understood, he was a very busy man. Immediately afterward, furious with him for his lack of consideration and with herself for her unwillingness to stand up to him, she'd hopped into the van with Bobby to drive up to the mountains. She hadn't even bothered to ask why they had to leave on the spur of the moment, in the middle of the night, which was why she looked such a mess this morning, why she was out of cigarettes. They drove from Rinaldi's to her place, where she threw some things in a duffle, then to Bobby's to collect his gear. They had driven all night, stumbling into the Luna Hotel before the sun was up. It wasn't until now that she questioned the wisdom of what she had done and of what she was doing, driving to Mirasol Farm. But she had said she was going to do it, and she *was* going to do it. Mixed with her anxiety was the righteousness she felt in keeping her word despite the fact that he hadn't kept his, and pleasure at having for once acted spontaneously. This was to be an adventure, and she didn't want her promise to Rinaldi, the inconsiderate bastard, hanging over her head to spoil it. Nor did she want to lose her resolve. She'd gotten up at first light, written a note for Bobby, and left him asleep in the hotel.

She saw a little girl behind a crate on the shoulder of the road. She hit the brakes, put the van in reverse, and backed up until she had reached the roadside stand.

"Cigarillo?" Nina called out the window. She climbed out, left the car in the middle of the road, left the door open, the motor running. The girl handed her a single cigarette from an open pack of unfiltered Incas.

"This is all you have? Incas?"

The little girl struck a match. Nina put the cigarette in her mouth and, holding her hair back, bent to the flame.

"Gracias, *nena*," she said. She gave the girl a coin. She started back to the van and came back. "Better give me the rest of the pack," she said. She gave the girl more money. "Thanks, again," she said. She felt better, and she waved as she pulled away.

She knew from the barbwire fence on both sides of the road that she had reached the Rinaldi farm. From the first fence post it was 1.3 miles to the gate. She lifted her foot off the accelerator, shifted into neutral, and let the van coast down the level road. It was a game she had played with Alejandro, trying to see if the car could coast the whole 1.3 miles.

She remembered the last time she had been to the farm. She saw in her mind the procession go up the hillside behind the house, up to the eucalyptus brake. Huascarán was covered in cloud that day, too. She remembered Rinaldi, how shaken he looked, walking behind the casket. Elena didn't attend the funeral, had stayed in her room for days, seeing no one, not her daughter-in-law-to-be, not even Rinaldi. In the next ten weeks everything changed. Alejandro, her father, her mother, all gone. Nina left for the capital. She wrote Elena a long, intimate letter, waited months for a reply. When it came it was brief, impersonal, and addressed itself to none of the heartfelt disclosures that Nina, with so much difficulty and so many misgivings, had expressed in her own letter. The message was clear, and she did not write again. She had, in fact, neither seen nor spoken to Elena at all since before Alejandro had died.

She was thinking about when they had last been together— Nina's bridal shower, she remembered—as the van rolled to a stop, the gate still more than a quarter mile away. Alejandro had been the only one able to coast the entire way, and he'd been going over a hundred when he pulled his foot from the gas at the start of the barbwire fence.

"Slow—Horses" the sign said. "No Trespassing," and underneath, "Mirasol Farm." A straight dirt road split two rows of poplars. After half a mile it passed corrals, a barn, stables, then the garage. Graveled here, the road curved around to the front of the main house, which sat shaded in a grove of willows. Before she had shut off the motor, Luis was walking down the steps from the porch to greet her.

The sight of the small, neat, white-haired man somewhat eased her apprehension. They embraced on the path between the rose beds, or what had formerly been the rose beds, and now were long, rectangular beds of gravel, carefully raked, set in the wide, green, close-mowed lawn. They held each other at arm's length so that they could examine each other.

"The trees in the capital, are they as good for climbing as the ones on the farm?" Luis asked.

"They must not be," Nina said. "I haven't had the urge to climb a single one." She looked around. There wasn't a fallen leaf, nor a blade of grass growing up through the flagstone, nor a pebble kicked onto the lawn. The fence posts were plumb and the wire was taut, the barn and stables freshly painted. A black Labrador puppy ambled over to sniff her shoes and she bent down to pet it. "And you, Luis," she said. "I can tell by the run-down state of the farm that you're still spending your afternoons in town at the bar. Don't you ever feel even the tiniest twinge of guilt?"

"The whiskey helps some," he said. "Come into the house. I'll tell the señora you're here, if she doesn't know already." She followed him up the steps and then ran back down to the van, returning with the brown package from the backseat.

"The colonel asked me to bring this up for you. He said it was too important to trust to the mail. He said you'd been waiting for it."

Luis took it out of her hands. He looked for a place to set it down, choosing a wicker chair. She noticed Nick's bed wasn't by the front door. She wanted to ask Luis where the dog was, but she was distracted. "A fuel pump," he said. "For the tractor. Come in and wait while I find Mrs. Rinaldi. I think she's in her room."

A minute later he returned. "She said to make yourself comfortable, she'll be a few minutes. As you can see, nothing has changed. I'm going to take that package out to the garage. It's nice to see you home again."

"Thank you, Luis," she said. "It's nice to be home." So far, anyway, she thought. She'd meant to tell him the thing in the box wasn't a fuel pump, but the mention of "home" sent her thoughts elsewhere. The screen closed quietly behind him and she watched him walk lightly down the steps. Then she went to the bar in the living room to pour herself a glass of club soda. She hoped it would settle her stomach.

She sat on the piano bench. Everything *was* exactly as she had remembered it, the polished wood floors, the Indian rugs, the windows with the view of the mountains, the piano. She picked up a framed photograph of herself and Alejandro. She wanted to re-hearse what she would say to Elena, but something would not let her mind focus on the subject. Wherever her eyes came to rest touched off memories. She saw her parents sitting on the couch under the windows, the same couch where she and Alejandro as teenagers had kissed until their lips were chapped. Under the piano was where Queenie had had a litter. In this same room she and Alejandro were to have been married. This was where she'd waited for the doctor to come to stitch up her eye. She took the pack of Incas from her shirt pocket, shook one out, and lit it. She was looking for an ashtray when Elena came in. Nina didn't notice her standing in the archway, and when she did the sight of the older woman startled her.

"Teddy," the woman said softly. Just Teddy. She made no move to come any closer. She stood in the archway in tan jodhpurs and riding boots, a white shirt and a turquoise scarf tied around her neck. Her silver hair was pulled back and tied in a French braid, her fingers were interlaced in front of her.

Nina put out her cigarette. She tried to wave the smoke away. She looked around for someplace to set the ashtray down. She wiped her hands on her jeans and brushed her hair from her fore-head with her fingers.

"Mrs. Rinaldi, Aunt Elena, I . . ."

"Elena is all right now. Call me Elena. And you? Is it still Teddy?"

"No one calls me Teddy anymore."

It wasn't just the inherent awkwardness of the situation, or the memories the room brought back to her, or even the way Elena had seemed to materialize in the doorway. From the colonel's de-scriptions, Nina had been expecting a different Elena, an invalid, a recluse, a dispirited, melancholy rag. If anything, this Elena was more vital, more radiant, more poised and self-possessed than Nina had remembered her to be. She was the woman Nina had admired and emulated since she had been the tomboy from the farm down the road. Elena had been for her the model of grace and charm, glamour, beauty, confidence, and competence. For a moment, Nina stared.

"Is everything all right, dear?" Elena asked, coming toward her. "You're not sick, are you? Sometimes the altitude is a problem the first few days after you come up from the city. Perhaps you'd like to lie down." Elena took both of Nina's hands in hers.

Nina listened for irony in Elena's voice, looked for mockery in her eyes, and found only concern and affection. "No. Nothing, I'm fine," Nina said. "It's just these cigarettes, these Incas. I'm not used to them."

Elena pulled Nina into her arms and hugged her. Nina's arms hung at her sides. "Thank you for coming to see me, darling," she said. Nina looked over Elena's shoulder into the foyer in time to see the heel of a boot flash past the archway. Elena stepped back to look at Nina's face, then she hugged the girl again. "I was hoping you would." This time Nina returned her hug. "I know it can't be an easy thing for you to return to this house, to come back and be reminded of all that's happened here." Nina found herself crying. She hugged Elena hard. She was surprised at how little there was to her body, as if Elena's bones were balsa.

They sat side by side on the sofa, their knees almost touching. "I've been wanting to talk to you for months now." Elena still held Nina's hands. "I have to tell you how hurt I was when I didn't hear from you after . . . afterward."

"I tried to see you," Nina said, "but you weren't seeing anyone, and then I wrote, but you didn't answer, and when you finally did, well, I thought you didn't want to see me. Didn't you get my letter?"

"I'm sure I would remember if I had."

"Something must have happened to it," Nina said.

"Did you send it to the farm? Sometimes the mail gets lost coming all the way out here," Elena said.

"That's just it. I didn't put it in the mail. I gave it to—"

"To whom?"

"It's not important anymore," Nina said. She reached into her shirt pocket. "You should have let me know if you wanted to see me. You knew how to reach me. I had no idea. I wish you had let me know," Nina said. She fingered the unlit cigarette and slid it back into the pack.

"Well, here you are, and all the rest, that's behind us now. Besides, I think it's best things worked out this way. I needed time. I wasn't ready, and I don't think you were ready, either. I thought that when you finally came to me, *if* you came to me, it would be the signal I needed. That you had put it behind you. That you were ready to hear what I had to say."

A surge of anxiety overtook Nina, as if her worst expectations of this meeting were about to be realized. She stood up quickly, excused herself, and went to the bathroom. She splashed water on her face. She looked at herself in the mirror. What have I let myself in for? she thought. She had been prepared for distance between them, or hostility, but this unexpected intimacy, this affection had shaken her. She felt lightheaded; maybe it *was* the cigarettes, or the altitude, or both. She felt out of her depth.

She returned to the living room. Through the window she saw Luis sitting on the porch off to the side with his back against the house. If she had remained sitting beside Elena, he would have been out of sight, but from where she stood she could see him, or part of him, his arm and his legs. She sat on the piano bench where he was still in her sight.

"Maybe I'm rushing things a bit," Elena said. "You're really quite pale."

"I'm feeling better now. What is it you wanted to say?"

"I've gone over it and over it in my head, but now that you're actually here, I hardly know where to begin."

Nina watched the figure on the wicker porch chair lean toward the open window. She stood up. "Whatever it is, it can wait, can't it?" Nina said. "I think you're right. I could use some fresh air. Would it be all right if we went for a walk?"

"I was on my way out for a ride when you drove up. I would love for us to ride together, like we used to. How long has it been since you've been up on a horse?"

"Forever. Do you have a pair of boots I might borrow?"

"I'm sure I can find you something, if you don't mind that they're men's. I'm afraid mine would be much too small. First I'll ask Luis to saddle another horse. You remember Araby?" Elena called for Luis through the front door several times before he came in the back through the kitchen.

"I thought I heard you calling me, Mrs. Rinaldi. I was out by the shed," he said as Nina watched him lie.

The path led up the hill behind the big house. Araby was full of energy. Nina held him back. He'd been an unbroken yearling when his sire, Sekunder, was blown to bits, along with Nina's own mare, Clea, and two other Arabs unfortunate enough not to be out in the pasture that afternoon. And Alejandro. Now the remaining horses that once belonged to her father were owned by Mirasol Farm.

Neither woman spoke until they had crested the hill and passed through the eucalyptus brake, where they dismounted and tied the horses. The headstone, of course hadn't been there when Nina had last been to the knoll. She thought she would cry when she read the inscription, 6 July 1948–9 April 1971, but she surprised herself, and when she turned to where on a clearer day one could see the bulk of Huascarán, her eyes were dry. "I miss him," was all she said.

They remounted and followed a path along a stream. "You heard they killed the man responsible, I'm sure?" Elena said, pursuant to nothing.

"Gavilan, you mean? If you want to know does it make me feel any better, the answer is no," Nina said. "I hated him, it's true, but do I feel any better? I can honestly say I don't."

"I don't feel better, either," said Elena. "It may be surprising to some that a mother should feel no satisfaction in knowing the death of her son has been avenged, but I don't."

Nina was silent. She marveled at how the clouds could hide so completely anything as big as Huascarán. If you didn't already know it was there, you would never guess.

"The reason may be," Elena continued, "that the man they have killed isn't the man responsible." She paused to let her statement sink in. She watched Nina for a reaction. "I'm not sure how I would feel if the man actually responsible were dead."

Nina's stomach tightened as if anticipating a punch. No, of course she wouldn't be raving, she thought. No wild-eyed accusations. Hers would be more subtle than that, a twisting of her perceptions. The isolation, the brooding, would do that. "No one said Gavilan did it himself," Nina answered. She tried to seem offhand. "But it doesn't matter now," she added, as if the question were settled, as if there were no need to discuss it further.

Elena wasn't deterred. "That, dear girl, is exactly what they hoped we'd believe."

Nina had braced herself for an outburst. That would have been fitting somehow, healthy, she thought. The outburst hadn't come and she'd been lulled by Elena's tranquillity and warmth. Now it seemed Rinaldi had been right after all: Elena had lost her grip. Everyone knew the Moreno had planted the bomb. Who else would have done such a thing? Whatever Elena was thinking, Nina didn't want to know. Tears and accusations were preferable to quiet paranoia. The two women rode together in silence, the horses' hooves kicking up small explosions of dust on the path. Nina searched for something to say, some way to derail the conversation.

"You think I'm mad, don't you?" Elena said, after a while.

"No," Nina answered too quickly. "Not at all." She tried to control her voice.

"Perhaps 'mad' is too strong a word," said Elena. She searched in the trees overhead for a word. "Unbalanced, perhaps?"

Nina unbuttoned the flap of her shirt and fumbled for a cigarette. "No. Not that either," she said. She reined in her horse, struck a match, struck another, returned the unlit cigarette to the pack. "I think you're . . . distraught. It's understandable. Anyone would be . . . your only son . . . a terrible thing, and being up here alone for months, isolated . . ." She lifted her head and looked at Elena for the first time. She mustered all the sympathy she had to offer. "It must have been terrible for you."

Elena cut Nina short with a brusque wave of her hand. "Oh please, Teddy, not from you, too. I thought you of all people might understand."

"It's bound to have some effect on a person."

"Enough, Teddy. Stop. Excuse me, but I've already heard so much of that sort of thing." Then, seeing how she'd wounded the girl, she changed her tone. "What has Rinaldi been *telling* you? In the first place, I pray to God you never find out what a terrible thing it is, and—"

"It takes time—"

"Teddy!" Elena's patience broke. "Please! I know when I'm being patronized." She put her hand to her eyes, paused, then shook her head as if she were trying to erase the words she had just spoken. Her composure regained, she began over again. "With all due respect, my sweet Nina, how could you possibly know what it might or might not take to get over the loss of your son? Or for that matter, your husband?"

Nina felt the urge to spur the horse, to let Araby run.

"I'm sorry, dear," Elena said quickly. "Please forgive me. I hadn't planned to be so blunt. It isn't even what I'd intended to tell you, but now that I've begun . . ."

"Aunt Elena, I—"

"No, Nina, allow me to finish."

"I don't know. I—" Nina put her face in her hands.

Elena handed her a handkerchief. "Use this. Go ahead. It's clean. Now listen to me, Nina. To begin with, I have no anger toward you. Not anymore. Rinaldi and I were lost to each other a long, long time ago. Before you were even born, I'd say. Our marriage was a formality carried on for the sake of appearance." Nina looked up. "Oh, don't be so shocked. We each had our reasons. I believed I was doing it for Alejandro's sake. As for Rinaldi, he felt divorce would have damaged his precious career, that it would be a blotch on his record. And he was right, of course. In the army, the proper wife, from an approved background, with the full complement of social skills, was as important to one's advancement as anything else. More important, perhaps. I don't think it would be an exaggeration to say that Rinaldi—from an undistinguished family, and to be honest, a man of mediocre ability, with an inadequate education, beset by insecurity, and at times overpowering feelings of inferiority—would not have risen to his rank without me. It's true, you know. It is, after all, why he married me. Of course I didn't know that at the time. I was madly in love. I can say this because Rinaldi himself would be the first to admit it. Well, perhaps not the first, but he appreciates the contribution I have made. He's told me as much.

"This ability he has to convince others to subordinate themselves to him is his greatest asset—that, and his boundless ambition. And I do not for a moment underestimate his personal charm, an attribute of which you, among many others, are well aware. The point is Rinaldi and I didn't have a marriage as much as a kind of unstated agreement through which we each pursued our own individual interests. Mine was the farm, the horses, and Alejandro. His was the army. So you see, Nina dear, you weren't the one to come between us, because there had been nothing of that sort between us for years. You weren't the first, and in my opinion, you won't be the last, and if I had to say one way or the other, I'd be surprised if you weren't sharing him with somebody else right now."

Nina again found herself speechless. She stared at the swirling cloud hovering over the mountain, revealing fragments of its features one moment and obscuring them the next. She was no longer crying, but when she spoke her voice was small, unsteady, a little girl's. "I don't know what to say."

"There is nothing that needs to be said. I didn't expect an admission, and I certainly don't want an apology. There's nothing to apologize for. But it is important for you to believe me. I need that. *Do* you believe me, Nina?"

"That there may be others? I don't know. I don't know what to believe."

"I'm not talking about Rinaldi's mistresses. That's unimportant now. And you won't have to take my word for it. You'll figure that out on your own. He'll begin to find himself extremely busy, tied up with his work, with his causes. He'll become forgetful. You're not a stupid person, you'll figure it out."

Nina turned, eyes wide, to look at the older woman. Elena smiled. "See, you're beginning to piece it together already. No, I'm not talking about his women. I only brought it up to demonstrate that I am not the deranged, grief-stricken person Rinaldi portrays me to be. You see, I know about that, too."

Nina felt a wave of relief. Her worst imaginings of the meeting with Elena had come to pass: she'd been confronted with her affair with Rinaldi. She had dreaded such a moment, but it had been not at all like she had imagined. She felt . . . relieved.

They were coming to a rise. Nina pressed her heels into Araby's flanks, eased up on the reins, intending to let him run, but Elena reached out and held his halter. "Nina," she said. "There's something else. It's time you knew."

A lizard spooked Araby, he reared, but Elena held tight to his halter. "Take control of your horse!" she ordered.

Nina found she was holding her breath. Her thoughts were confused.

"Nina!" Elena shouted again. "Take control!" Nina reined in. Araby tossed his head. In a moment he calmed down. Elena released his halter.

"Are you ready?" Elena asked. "Listen to me carefully. I want to tell you who killed our Alejandro," she said. "And why."

* * *

It was another hour before they returned. Luis was getting into the truck. "I'm going into town, Mrs. Rinaldi. A gasket for this fuel pump. Something I can get for you?"

"Nothing thank you, Luis."

"And you, Miss DeBettencourt? Anything? Licorice?"

Nina smiled that he had remembered. She shook her head. "I'll be gone by the time you get back," she said.

"You don't mind unsaddling the horses, Mrs. Rinaldi, and turning them out?"

"Since when do I mind anything having to do with horses, Luis? No, you go ahead. We'll make out fine."

Luis gunned the engine and drove off down the road between the rows of poplars, the tires spraying gravel. "He always was a bad liar," Elena said as she tied her horse to the fence.

Τhe sounds from the street started early—the shouts, the clack of horseshoes hitting the pavement, engines revving, babies, dogs, roosters. As tired as I was, I couldn't sleep through all the racket, and my guess is Nina couldn't either, because by nine, when I woke up, she was already up and out. There was a note on the nightstand: "Gone to visit a friend, borrowed the van, back by late afternoon. Love." Even her handwriting was terrific. I understood why Rinaldi would threaten me, and for all the same reasons, threats weren't enough. I couldn't take the guy seriously, at least not from three hundred miles away.

We'd arrived in the dark, the power was off as usual, and we'd been led to the door with a candle, so my first good look at the room came when I opened the shutters. After driving all night over twisty mountain roads—no painted lines, no guardrails, no road signs, highballing truckers, cars without taillights, cars without headlights, sheep on the road, whole families out on the road— after all that on top of dinner at Blacky's, and drinks with Rinaldi, believe me when I say I didn't care too much that there wasn't a waterbed or color TV. But then I'd stayed at Mr. Moon's before, and I knew what and what not to expect in the way of accommodations.

Our room had a double bed, seven sacks of cement, a small ceramic collie on the nightstand, and a pile of potatoes three feet high in the corner. The earthy, moldy smell I smelled all night was, I could see now, a blend of the potatoes, mouse droppings, and damp plaster on the wall. Out in the courtyard you had to look close to tell if they were renovating the place or tearing it down.

Windows boarded up, a ladder instead of steps to the second floor, where you didn't see weeds, you saw rubble, but there were still lots of things I considered worth saving: the red tile roof, the palm tree, the terrazzo, the balconies, those slatted shutters, bougainvillea . . .

Vendors were setting up in the plaza and on the sidewalks all around. People pouring into town. Buses, trucks, horses, donkeys. Mr. Moon, robber baron, mayor, a grandfather thirty-nine times, Marcara's loan shark and leading citizen, kept an eye on things from the doorway of the Moon General Store, Enrique Moon, Propietario. He combed his silver movie-star hair (cut twice a week in Huaráz) and his bushy salt-and-pepper eyebrows, adjusted the blue beret I'd never seen him without, and struck a pose for the camera: a profile, chin tilted up, arms crossed, serious, dignified, befitting a man of his prominence. On the other hand, nothing could coax the señora, who habitually wore her dresses a size too small, to pose. She turned her back every time I pointed the camera her way, and as soon as I put it down again, she'd go back to sweeping the sidewalk in front of the store.

After breakfast I wandered back to the market, now in full swing. A quick look around told you all you needed to know: wrinkled tomatoes, wilted dusty lettuce, bent and rusty nails, a piglet tied on a piece of blue yarn (made a nice picture), dented cans with missing labels. But then again, the market was the place you went to see your friends, catch up on the gossip, buy your salt and sugar, get your corn ground, drink a beer, buy an ice ball for the kid, and maybe catch the evening mass before heading home.

For me it was a great place for pictures, especially since I learned the way to get the shots I wanted. The secret is, it's one thing if a stranger points a lens in your face, but a customer, a *paying* customer, now that's another matter.

I bought a corroded brass lock that didn't have a key in exchange for a picture of a teenage girl with shiny black braids and silver barrettes, silver earrings, and a slew of silver rings and bracelets. I generally go for the pretty ones. There're plenty enough pictures of haggard faces, and the same goes for bums, cripples, freaks, and skinny kids got runny noses and flies in their eyes. Another good one I got, an older lady, hard to tell exactly how old, but not decrepit or anything, sitting behind what must've been fifty burlap sacks rolled down so you could see what was inside them. Twigs, seeds, berries, buttons, leaves, bark, petals, nuts, beans, roots, peas, powders, flowers, you name it, fifty at least. I asked her if she had anything to make a woman fall in love with you, and I got a shot of her weighing out a mixture of stuff on a little balance scale and all those sacks fanned out around her. She warned me the stuff was potent. I said maybe she ought to sell me the antidote just in case. I left with the love powder in a little leather pouch on a string around my neck and another shot of her laughing about the antidote. And then there was the guy under an awning sold me six different dyes—chartreuse, purple, pink, and three others—folded up in small squares of newspaper. I figure he jacked up the price, but for seventy cents I got my pictures, a present for Nina, and a nickel change.

I made a circuit of the plaza, shot three rolls of film. Over by the church where I had gone to change my film in the shade was a guy brewing a vat of their local beer. *Chicha*, they call it. The way I understand the process, they chew up the corn, spit it out, and cook the mixture with sugar. The saliva supposedly makes it ferment, which I don't know whether is true or not, but ever since I found this out I can't bring myself to drink the stuff. I wanted the picture, though, the big black cauldron, little tongues of flame underneath, and the guy behind with the paddle—a lean, tough, unsmiling guy in a torn sleeveless T-shirt, muscles like knotted rope, and all this steam off the yellow bubbly *chicha* rising up around him. I was right out front about what I wanted. I offered him money.

"Keep your money," he said. "Should I smile or not?" I told him to ignore me, just go about his business, and I walked around him, took a bunch of pictures. "Do you really make that stuff with spit?" I asked.

"Do you know a better way?"

"Not very appetizing," I said.

"Not supposed to be. Supposed to get you stoned. Anyway, you think nobody spits in your—what kind of beer do you drink?" he asked.

"Pabst," I told him.

"Never heard of it," he said.

"Pabst Blue Ribbon."

"I guarantee you, they spit in it, probably piss in it, too," he said.

I didn't doubt it. You work in a restaurant, you know sometimes something gets into the food.

"Come back later," he said. "Try a jar of this. Make you change your mind about *chicha*. Make you forget about—"

"Pabst Blue Ribbon."

"Pasburibbin."

There was a soccer game on the playground which sits between the school and Luna's store. It was just a bunch of kids playing pickup. The moment they saw me, the game was forgotten and they crowded around, pushing each other for the place in the center of the picture. I used the Polaroid, and a minute later I showed them the print. I held it up over my head, not to tease them but to protect the picture, which takes a few minutes to dry, and they jumped for it like puppies after a biscuit. They picked out each other's faces, insulted each other, then ran back to their game. All but one ran back. Sad little kid. He said his name—Baptismo. Baptismo? I asked him three times to be sure. Who names a kid Baptismo? I gave Baptismo the picture, which he thanked me for and folded in half and then in half again and put in his pocket. I asked him what he was doing standing on the sidelines while the other kids were playing and he said the ball was his and he had to, his dad would kill him if he came home without the ball. I said you mean they're using your ball and they won't let you play? He could play if he wanted, he said, he just didn't want to.

I took some pictures of Baptismo. I let Baptismo take some pictures of me. I took some of the game. You can tell when you get something good, and I knew I didn't—of the game, I mean. I couldn't focus fast enough, couldn't follow the ball or predict where it would be. After that I said good-bye to Baptismo and went back to my room, which was cool and dark—a good place for storing potatoes—and like most everyone else, kids excepted, I napped through the early afternoon.

The plaza was empty at three, the vendors were gone, the buses gone, the doors of the houses were closed and the shutters closed, Moon's was closed, no one on the benches, no one by the fountain, or on the steps to the church, but over in the school yard the game was still going on. Blacky's instructions were to sit on a bench in the plaza and wait. I picked the one closest the fountain, and for the first five or ten minutes I watched very alertly, expecting any second to see whoever it was I was waiting for come walking up, or maybe whistle from one of the doorways, but all I heard was the fountain, and all I saw was Baptismo standing by himself on the sidelines and the rest of the kids playing ball.

I dusted my lenses. I reorganized my camera bag. I studied Copa's summit through a telephoto. I estimated what the light readings would be in different parts of the plaza and then checked them against my meter. I sat until I couldn't sit any longer, and then at 3:30 I walked over to watch the game. I wasn't there a minute when a blocked shot bounced wild and rolled under an old junker of a VW beetle parked in front of Moon's. The ball wedged under the axle. The kid who went to retrieve it only jammed it under worse.

It was really no big deal. Anyone who can dead-lift three hundred pounds could do the same thing, but when I lifted the car off the ball, the fuss the kids made, you'd have thought I'd picked up the back where the engine is, which is by far the tougher thing to do. Then they each tried to do it, and then all of them together tried to do it, but there are only so many holds on a VW bumper. I got some shots of them trying to lift the thing, and another of all of them sitting on it with sad little Baptismo up on the roof holding the ball.

On one end of the playground, next to the church, a basketball hoop was nailed to a pole. It was a rusty rim without a net and a warped delaminating sheet of plywood for a backboard. Baptismo, who stuck with me after the other kids had left, told me the padre had put it there a couple years ago. The padre was Italiano, he said, and a basketball player, but since he'd hung it there and tried to teach them the game, no one had used it, not even the padre anymore.

Baptismo's soccer ball was heavy, underinflated, and smaller than a basketball. Its leather cover was scuffed to suede, but it was round and it bounced, more or less. I dribbled it twice before I went in for a lay-up. The rim sagged in front, which is what gave me the idea I might be able to dunk. I came in from the side so my momentum wouldn't carry me into the pole and, palming the ball, swung it over my head and slammed it through, something I'd never been able to do with a regulation ball and ten-foot basket, even when I played the game a lot.

Baptismo played hoops like he'd been issued a pair of hands just the day before yesterday and hadn't quite gotten the hang of them yet. His hand-eye coordination was all in his feet. The closest he came to sinking a shot was when he tried to head in a rebound. Every couple of minutes I looked at my watch and looked at the bench in the plaza, but nobody came, and nobody looking for me could have missed me. Baptismo and I were the only ones around.

Blacky had told me to wait until five. I had another half hour to go when Baptismo decided he'd had enough, it was time to take his ball and go home. I asked him if it'd be all right to borrow it, since I had some time to spend on the bench with nothing to do but wait and think about what I had to think about. I told him I'd leave it for him at Moon's, or take it to his house if he'd tell me where he lived. He let me borrow the ball, but he changed his mind about going home. He said he'd wait until I was done, and sat on the Volkswagen's bumper to look at his photo and wait.

I shot fouls for a while, getting the feel of the ball, getting back my eye before moving farther out to a place that would have been about the top of the key, if there were a key. I retied my laces, spun the ball in my fingers, bounced it twice, breathed deep, zeroed in on the rim, set myself, jumped, and sent up an air ball—on target, but way way short. The ball hit the pole and bounced off at an angle.

I don't know how long he'd been standing there, couldn't have been very long. He let the ball roll onto his foot, flicked it up off his toe, and caught it on his instep. With the sun behind him I couldn't see his face, and I thanked him before I recognized who it was. The *chicha* man. He passed the ball from instep to instep, flicked it up, caught it on his thigh, balanced it there, let it drop to his instep, flicked it up, bounced it up off his forehead, then caught it on his other thigh. You see guys down here do stuff like that all the time. They do it on street corners. Plenty of guys down here could probably knit with their feet, but like Baptismo, if they had to use their hands, forget it. That's what made it so surprising.

He sends up a twenty-five-footer which was just a hair short, so with the soft rim and the mushy ball, it thumps and lays on the iron. Before it falls, he leaps and taps it in. I was as surprised to find

a hoopster in Marcará as I would've been had the gimp-legged
mutt which at that moment was pissing on the steps of the church
come over and introduced himself in French.

He tossed me the ball. I bounced him back a pass that sent a puff
of dust off the court. He missed a twenty-foot jumper. I passed the
ball back out again. You had to see this guy to believe him: sandals,
funky pants, sweater full of holes, beat-up old hat, the felt kind
they all wear down here. He takes four more shots from twenty
feet, makes three, changes his spot, and makes another three for
four. Then it's my turn. I move out to the corner, and with the rim
suddenly looking bigger than a hula hoop, hit five in a row with
him feeding me passes in between. He strips down to his sleeveless
tee, folds his jacket and sweater, takes off the hat, and steps out of
his sandals—the kind with the tire-tread sole and the straps cut
from an inner tube? If you ever wondered where they send your
old 70 R 15's, now you know. "One-on-one?" I ask.

"To ten," he says. "Have to win by two."

"You don't have shoes." It just occurred to me.

"Visitor's ball," he says.

You have to actually slam the ball down to get it to bounce as
high as your waist. I dribble twice to my right, try driving around
him, switch back left, feeling him out, seeing what kind of defense
he plays—pretty good, it turns out, because before I get off a shot
he snakes in a hand and bats the ball away. It rolls clear over to
where Baptismo is still sitting on the car in front of Moon's. He's
got the gimp-leg mutt on his lap. My ball, and I take it in again,
dribble right, go up for a shot, only to have him slap it back in my
face. Still my ball. I drive right at him, pull up, jump, and shoot
over his head. The rim hasn't shrunk from hula-hoop size.

"USA, one," he says.

He swishes a two-handed set shot from twenty-some feet. One–
one.

With my height advantage, I should have worked him inside, but
the ball was too tough to dribble, and I had a hot hand, so I take
him into the corner and put up a jumper from there. He screens
me from the rebound, takes it back to the foul line, turns, and
pumps it through. This is unbelievable. "Where'd you learn to
play like that?" I ask.

My ball and I take it right to him again. I have five inches and forty pounds on him, and I push right through and lay it in.

"USA, two," I say.

His shooting went cold after that and I put in five in a row, all the same way, by backing in until I was close, falling away, and shooting over his head. He was quick, but as dead as the ball was, it nullified his speed. The one time he did get around me, I came over his back and rode him into the pole, accidentally, but hard enough to knock the wind out of him. He was down on the court a minute or two, sucking air. I helped him to his feet. I thought I'd go easy on him after that, lay back, shoot from outside, give him a chance to get back in the game, but he swiped at the ball and got my finger, jamming it bad. While I was holding my finger, he laid the ball in.

"Stove my goddamn finger," I said. I pulled on it, and the knuckle popped. Jesus, it hurt—but I bit the bullet.

"Seven–three," he says.

I'd been thinking the game was over, I'd had enough. The knuckle was already swollen and turning blue. "Seven–*two*," I correct him. "You got my hand."

"I got the ball."

"You got my goddamn hand."

My left is useless, so I dribble with my right, work my way in, keeping my body between him and the ball. When he reaches around me for the steal, I spin, beat him bad, and with a clear lane to the hoop, figure to slam it in. What I don't figure is for him to recover as quick as he does, and at the top of my leap, with the ball in one hand over my head, I feel him underneath me. There's no way to avoid him. I flip in the air and land hard on my shoulder.

I bat his hand away, get up without his motherless help. My shoulder hurts, and my finger's stoved, and my forearm is scraped and bleeding, but I'd been dumped plenty of times before, and on asphalt, too, and this wasn't any big deal, except that the principle of the thing was beginning to piss me off. I wonder what kind of belligerent cocksucker this is, what he's trying to prove. I reach for him, but the shifty son of a bitch slips away. I want to crumple him, the sleazebag peasant asshole campesino. He jams my finger, lowballs me into the weeds, and now he wants to help me up.

What stops me from slam dunking the fucker is I see Nina drive into the plaza and park my van in front of the Beetle. I yell to her wait a minute, I want to finish the game. She sits on the bench by my cameras.

It's closer to twenty minutes before the game is over. The guy plays every point as if it really were the Pan American Games. He never lets up, presses me on every point, in my face, not an inch between us. On offense he runs me around, working the ball until I give him his shot just so I can stop and catch my breath. He closes my lead to nine–eight before I put him away with a drive that leaves him flat on his back and me with an easy lay-up.

"Nice move," he says. It wasn't. It was a blatant charge, but he doesn't call it on me and I'm sure as hell not about to call it on myself. My finger hurts, the knuckle is bluish yellow and twice the normal size. I'm dirty, sweaty, out of breath. Got a headache. The altitude always takes some getting used to.

"I wish I had a picture of that," he says as he's pulling on his sweater. I think he means that last drive of mine, and I couldn't understand why, but he's talking about the time he took my legs away and dumped me. "The expression on your face," he says. "You should've seen it."

"Pretty funny, huh?"

"I'll go get that beer," he says, and he trots off across the playground. I'd forgotten about the *chicha*.

Past five o'clock. Siesta is over. Moon's is reopened. A couple of people are in the plaza. Whoever was coming to meet me isn't. I walk over to Nina. Grubby as I am, she turns her cheek and lets me kiss it, which I take as a good sign, although she doesn't look so pristine herself, and the kiss isn't returned. "How was your day?" I ask.

Her answer is to put her arms around me and hug me hard. I hold her with my one good arm.

"Oh, Bobby," she says. "You have to take me with you."

"Take you where?" I ask, but I know where.

"To Santo Rosario. Will you?"

That's the reason I gave for my coming up here: to photograph the Feast of Santo Rosario. I invent some reasons why she can't, but she is quick with an answer to every one. She says she wouldn't mind camping out even in the bad weather, and that she's a strong hiker, she's certain she could keep up, and that she can be of use to

me, she can speak the language, she'd act as my interpreter. Another time, I say. I didn't bring enough food for two people, and
her answer to that is she'll eat what there is in the village, potatoes
and corn are OK with her, and anyway she could stand to lose a
few pounds. Please, can't she go? I'm out of reasons, except for the
real one. I'd sworn an oath to Blacky I wouldn't tell her. It'd be
best, I say, if she takes the bus back to the capital like we had
planned.

"I can't," she says. "Not now." She won't say why, only that
something had happened that morning and now she can't go back,
and she has noplace else to go. She held my wrists. Stalling, I ask
her again what happened, and she says it has to do with Rinaldi and
she can't go back to him and she can't explain it all to me now, but
sometime she will. I'm out of everything but the truth.

I'm saved by the *chicha*. "Here it is," he says. He's come back
with a jar of the stuff, big glass half-gallon jar. "All we need now is
something to drink it from." He looks from one of us to the other.
"Pardon me," he says. "I interrupted something."

Nina assures him he hasn't and wipes her eyes with a handkerchief. "I think I saw some paper cups in the van," she says. "If you
don't mind that they've been used." She gets up to get them.

"I'll go with you," he says.

I get up, too, with Baptismo's ball. He's waiting on the VW
bumper hugging the crippled pooch. I notice the van's headlights
are on and I'm racking my brain to think of something to tell her,
some plausible explanation why she can't go with me, if I really *am*
going someplace after all. I don't know. She'd said she didn't want
to go back to Rinaldi, and I sure as shit don't want to send her
there. It might be easier to take her with me and think of something to tell Blacky later on. That way at least I'd have a couple of
weeks to figure it out.

We have to walk around the fountain. Nina, a few steps ahead of
us, stops suddenly, turns, and puts her hand to her forehead to
shade her eyes. "I was waiting for Bobby to introduce us," she says.
She holds out her other hand. "My name is Nina DeBettencourt."

"I know," he says. He shifts the jar into the crook of his arm.
"Gavilan," he says. "Roberto."

I see the flash an instant before the blast of hot wind flattens me.
Pieces of metal and flame are falling all around the plaza. A hubcap

bounces on the sidewalk, cinders hiss in the fountain, fall on my back, and burn holes through my shirt. I roll in the dirt. The two of them are in a heap together five feet away, him on top of her, protecting her head under his body, covering his own head with his hands.

The Beetle is a ball of flame. Everything from the fire wall forward is gone, blown away. The door hangs on a hinge, the windows are blown out. Baptismo is nowhere. In front of the bug my van is burning in dense black smoke, the streetlight lying on top of it. The van explodes, lifting itself clean off the ground. I press my face to the dirt and cover my head, and there is another shower of metal, cinders, and glass.

My head is ringing, but other than that and a few holes in my shirt I seem to be OK. I shout to Nina. She's not hurt, and neither, apparently, is he. He gives me thumbs up. I don't see Baptismo and try to convince myself I'd seen him wander away before the blast. I go back to the bench for my camera. I shoot the burning cars and the black hole that was the front of the store and then, as close to crying as I'd been in I don't remember when, I walk over to the charred smoking lump of nothing that had been something a minute ago, that had been waiting for me to return his ball.

It was a deep slice through the meat of his palm, like a gill, Bobby had said. Gavilan sat on the edge on the bed and held his wrist while Bobby did what he could to clean it out, peering underneath the flap of skin as if it were the hole card of a blackjack hand, then dousing it with iodine and wrapping it with gauze and tape. Within minutes the bandage was sopping red.

Gavilan was silent. "Hanging tough" was the way Bobby had put it. Bobby chattered nonstop, but Gavilan's mind was elsewhere. He knew he couldn't safely remain where he was. He was thinking where he might go, wondering if he'd be able to go, given the blood he'd lost and how weak he felt. He'd watched Rivera too many times to kid himself about his wound. His wound . . . this wasn't a wound. A wound you got in a fight. This was a simple cut, an accident a drunk might have stumbling to the can. Wouldn't Rivera get some mileage out of this? Survives the bomb, falls on a bottle of beer and slices his hand.

Bobby, who was telling them about the Feast of Santo Rosario while rooting through his gear for another roll of bandage, saw Gavilan's smile and thought it was at something he'd just said. He was relieved to see some expression, any expression, on Gavilan's face. "It's the truth," Bobby said. "I read it somewhere." He couldn't tell if Gavilan was really hanging tough or in shock. A cut he could deal with, even a bad one like this, but if Gavilan flipped out he wouldn't know where to begin. And it didn't seem like Nina was going to be much help. The bomb, and all the blood, and who he turned out to be and all—she had her reasons, he knew. But then again, whatever she'd thought of Gavilan before this afternoon, he had just saved her life, or at least he had risked his own protecting hers, and that should count for something. Bobby found a roll of adhesive tape and tore several strips with his teeth. He went on with his story. "Seriously, instead of holy water, he sprinkles everyone with pee."

"This is the village priest?" Nina asked to keep Bobby talking. Bobby's tone reassured her, as if a moment ago they all hadn't been nearly blown to bits, as if this man sitting three feet away, a man who until this morning she had been led to believe had murdered Alejandro, whom she had despised, who she thought had been murdered himself, as if this same man weren't bleeding to death in front of her eyes. With Bobby's knife she tore another strip from the bed sheet.

"Not the priest," Bobby said. "Somebody *dressed up* like a priest. And another guy pretends he's a devil and he runs around scaring the kids, and somebody else puts on boots, pins cardboard medals to his chest, wears sunglasses, and with a riding crop he rides around town on a horse whacking anybody dumb enough to get close to him. He's the general."

Rinaldi. Nina's stomach knotted at the thought of him. What was she going to do? After what Elena had told her, she couldn't go back where she knew he would be waiting, not until she found out if it was true. She didn't know what to believe. Her whole experience with Rinaldi belied what she had heard. The Rinaldi Elena had described Nina didn't know and didn't want to know. She might have been speaking of a different man altogether, except there were hints, certain indications, currents in their relationship that opened her to the possibility. And there was Elena. So poised, so confident, convincing. You couldn't dismiss her. "Don't take my word for it," Elena had told her. "Find out for yourself."

Nina unwound the bloody gauze and replaced it with a strip of bed sheet, careful to keep her eyes on Gavilan's hand, careful not to meet his gaze. Her fingers were sticky when she was through. There were smears on her shirt and cheek. She tried to tape the bandage. It was too wet, the adhesive wouldn't stick. She applied a fresh piece of gauze. Yesterday, she thought, she would have stood by and watched him bleed.

Bobby rambled on about Santo Rosario while Nina ripped more strips and Gavilan, pale, sat pressing the bandage on his hand, wondering if by all this talk Bobby was trying to distract him—he himself had done the same thing for others more than once—or if this was his normal behavior. As for the girl, he knew he would try to speak to her as soon as word had reached him that Shafto might be bringing her. He'd recognized her immediately. She was just as he'd remembered her from the pictures in the papers. Her presence had brought out the boldness in him, and the scent of her brought back with an ache almost as bad as the pain in his hand a part of his life he'd left in the barrio. Like basketball, and beer. He'd told her his name, yes, he had, but that was the point, to live boldly again, own up, to hide behind nothing. It had felt good to say his name out loud. He'd told her because he wanted her to know, to set the record straight. Whether or not she believed him, he'd wanted to tell her that it wasn't the way they'd made it out to be. He'd just played his first basketball in he didn't know how long, and he had played pretty well considering, and for a time there was only the court and the rim and the ball, the freedom that comes with forgetfulness, and Shafto, whom Blacky had told him he'd like and he did. And then, his body warmed by the exercise, his mood lifted by the competition, he sees her come into the sunny plaza, tall and pretty, sees her sit by the fountain . . . he wanted to talk to her, needed to. Besides, where was the risk? He'd planned to be gone within half an hour. The closest phone was fifteen miles away. It didn't seem they were all that interested in the Moreno lately, anyway, or in him. Now she knew and he had to trust her. He pressed on the bandage. He thought possibly he'd severed some tendons. He knew that they needed to stop the bleeding soon. He felt needles of panic shoot through the thickening haze.

Bobby hadn't gotten off of Santo Rosario. "Happens every year about now. Someday I'll take pictures of it. In fact, if you didn't show," Bobby said to Gavilan, "I was thinking maybe I'd go up there instead."

"There *is* no Santo Rosario," Gavilan said, his voice subdued, a monotone.

"Huh?" Bobby said.

"No Santo Rosario."

Which? "The village or the feast?"

"The village is there, but the people aren't. The army drove them out. Harboring Moreno, the army said. I don't know about the feast."

Nina cut in. "And what do *you* say?" It sounded like an accusation.

"No Moreno in Santo Rosario. Never were. Maybe the army wanted to keep it that way. Maybe they wanted to set an example."

"Are you telling us the army drove people out of their homes for no reason?" Another accusation.

"They always have a reason. It isn't always what they say it is."

Bobby tried to derail the confrontation. Things were bad enough. "I sure as shit am going to miss that van," he jumped in. "I remember a surf trip I took up north in it a couple of years ago. You couldn't believe the mosquitoes . . ."

Gavilan knew he couldn't travel, he certainly couldn't make the long hike back to the mountains, not right away, not even if they managed to stop the bleeding. In a day, maybe two his strength would return, his head would clear. He struggled to focus his thoughts. For now he was dependent on Shafto and the girl. He didn't know how reliable either of them were, especially the girl. He would have thought she'd have left by now, which would have forced him, ready or not, to leave as well. Something was keeping her, he didn't know what. The room seemed airless to him, and he stood to go to the window, but standing made him dizzy and he had to sit back down.

". . . Ninety-nine degrees and a hundred percent humidity," Bobby was saying as he opened the shutters, "and all the van's windows are rolled and the doors're closed and I'm completely zipped in my sleeping bag, you know the mummy kind, zips all the way around your head, and, picture this, I'm breathing through a snorkel . . ." He looked across the street into the plaza where Moon's store was burning and the cars were smoldering and there were people watching in a group near the fountain. Off to the side he saw the soccer ball and the body which had been moved onto the grass and covered with a blanket. "So there I am, soaked in sweat, and those motherless mosquitoes . . . flew down the snorkel . . . bit my tongue . . . my throat . . . I swear . . . Shitfire." He shut his eyes and pressed his face to the shutter and fought to hold back, but his body heaved with crying and the effort to stifle it. When Nina spoke to him he didn't turn around. Then he ran out, to find some bandages, he yelled from the other side of the door.

The silence Nina had dreaded settled on the room. She lit a candle, and from the candle lit a cigarette. She stood by the window, smoking. She avoided looking at Gavilan lying on his back across the bed with his feet still on the floor, his arm draped across his eyes, asleep, she thought, she hoped. She looked for Bobby among the crowd in the plaza. The burning building brought back the memory of the burning barn and the stallion and Alejandro and all that she had tried hard to forget. Alejandro was supposed to be away at college, but he'd come home unannounced, had come to her father's farm to find her, and was looking for her in the barn when the bomb went off.

The events blurred in her mind, bled one into the other, so that now it seemed to her a single day had taken her fiancé, her home, her father and mother. She remembered Rinaldi's words: that having survived the pain of those losses, nothing could hurt her so badly ever again. But her strength seemed to her now merely a pose, a challenge to fate to try again to break her. She looked at her watch. The crystal was shattered, the hands were frozen at six after five. Was it only this morning that she and Elena had ridden together above the eucalyptus brake?

Two apparitions of Rinaldi appeared to her, the familiar one and the one described by Elena. They floated in her mind, mingling, joining, separating, mingling again. Was either one real? It was as if he'd created a ghostly double of himself, and now she sat alone in the dark and empty theater wondering how the effect had been accomplished. Rinaldi, The Great Rinaldi, the one person of whom she had been rock-certain sure. Or was Elena the magician, distracting her with reminiscences, with affectionate intimacies, with the movement of a turquoise scarf, while all the while she was pulling cards from her sleeve?

She looked down at Gavilan, recalling all she had blamed him for, and those many months she had tried to transmit her hatred to him wherever he was, to shoot him hot jolts of her hate, to hurt him as badly as she had been hurt. But the man in the bed was not the man in her mind, bore no likeness to that person whatsoever. Nothing was as she had thought it to be. Not Gavilan, not Elena, not Rinaldi, not Bobby. Why was she surprised? In murky water she had stepped off an unseen ledge. She'd been engulfed in a sea of emotion. Now her hate and anger were ebbing. She was drained.

Gavilan sat up, alarming her. His eyes were wild. He groped for his gun. "You're safe," she said. She put her hand on his shoulder. He sank back down. His clothes were damp with sweat. His hair was wet and spiky. He asked for water. She got him the pitcher. She gave him a towel and dug a comb out of her purse. He looked at it without comprehension. She put it back. She sat beside him on the bed. She dipped a corner of the towel into the pitcher and wiped his forehead. "I was wondering," she asked, concentrating on his forehead, avoiding his eyes. "This afternoon, down there by the fountain, how did you know my name?"

"I was warned you were coming. But I remembered you. From the pictures in the paper. Your fiancé, Alejandro . . ."

Nina stood, walked to the foot of the bed, looked down at him. "I could turn you in."

"Turn in a dead man?" He folded the towel, lay back, covered his eyes.

"You didn't have to tell me who you were."

"I wanted you to know the truth."

She braced herself. The second time in a single day someone had felt she had to hear the "truth."

There was a knock at the door. Gavilan gripped his gun.

"It's me. Open up."

Bobby came in with a man in baggy corduroys and a crewneck sweater and a wooden cross on a leather thong around his neck. "The padre's car's out back," Bobby said. "We gotta go. Help me pack up the gear."

Gavilan sat in back with Nina. The padre drove. Huaráz was closer, but the padre said no, there was another clinic, farther away, but where the padre knew the doctor. The road was dirt and rutted, and Gavilan, his hand cradled on his lap and his head back on the seat, seemed to pass in and out of consciousness. It was two hours and close to midnight before they stopped in front of a Quonset hut opposite a row of mud houses. The padre knocked. A light went on inside and a man wearing pajamas and a bathrobe with a cigarette between his lips opened the door. Bobby and the padre carried Gavilan inside.

A blanket on a clothesline divided the room. The front, which had a table and chairs and a cot, was the waiting room during the clinic's hours, and was where the Israeli doctor slept at night. In the back there was an examining table made from planks laid across a pair of sawhorses and covered by a blanket. Shelves holding a meager store of supplies, a low cabinet, and a metal wastebasket were the only furniture in the room. The bare bulb threw their shadows on the floor and walls. The doctor scrubbed his hands in the basin on top of the cabinet. Gavilan sat on the edge of the table, resting the bloody hand palm up on his lap. Squinting through smoke, the doctor unwound the bandage. He lifted the flap of skin, poured something over the wound. While he rebandaged the hand, he took a cigarette from the pocket of his pajama top and lit it off the old one, flicking the stub into the wastebasket. Nina asked for a smoke, accepted it, and stepped back beside Bobby and the padre. She looked for a place to drop the match. At the bottom of the wastebasket there was the smoldering butt and a fetus covered with ashes. She slipped the match into her pocket and, still reeling from the sight, pulled Bobby by the arm outside. She threw her cigarette away. She was crying and Bobby put his arms around her.

"Don't you dare fall apart on me," he said, holding her at arm's length. "I'm counting on you." He hugged her. "It's all over we get caught with him. They find out who he is, we're cooked. He's too out of it to travel. He can't stay here, and we can't go back to Marcara, the place was full of Guardia." He drew her close again. "I was supposed to go up to the mountains with him. I'm not cut out to stand over a stove all my life. This was my chance, goddammit. What are we going to do?"

"Go. Leave him."

"No."

"The padre will take care of him. You and I can go away."

"You don't understand. This was my chance."

She pulled out of his embrace. "We can go away together."

"You lived up here. You must know somebody. A friend, a relative. *Some*body. It'd just be for a day or two. Till he's strong enough to travel. Nobody has to know who he is. We can make up a story. He's our trekking guide. It was an accident. He cut himself with his knife."

She had turned away. "Nobody treks this time of year." There was no conviction in her voice.

The gash took thirty-five stitches. No tendons were cut. Gavilan sat through it without saying a word. The doctor handed them bandages and dressing in a rumpled brown paper bag. He told them how to change it, how often, how and when to take the stitches out. Gavilan slid the sleeve of his sweater down over his wrist, put on his coat, and eased himself off the table. "We gotta go," he said. "They're waiting for us." He took three steps toward the door before his legs buckled and he staggered against the examining table, knocking the planks off the sawhorses. Bobby helped him to the cot. Gavilan struggled to get to his feet. Wasting time, he repeated. He had to get back, they were waiting for him to get back.

The padre looked to the doctor, who, divining his meaning, shook his head no. "Impossible," he said. "Just bringing him here has jeopardized the clinic. They'd close us down if anyone knew. I've worked too hard. You know how they are, the merest suspicion is reason enough. He can't stay. I'm sorry. He can't."

The car swung through the gate and headed down the long row of poplars guided by red reflectors on the fence posts. They stopped in the turnaround and shut off the engine. There was a light on upstairs in the house. "Wait here," Nina said. She climbed the steps to the porch. Other lights came on. Nina went inside. Five minutes later she returned to the car. "I told her he was Bobby's guide," she said. "He cut his hand on a knife."

Bobby and the padre carried Gavilan into the house and up the stairs to the bedrooms on the second floor. Nina showed them the way. Passing the open door to Alejandro's room, she saw his suitcase by the door, clothes tossed onto the bed, a textbook opened on the desk, as if he'd been studying and just stepped away, for a drink of water or to answer the phone. She led them into the guest room, turned back the sheets. Bobby and the padre eased Gavilan onto the bed. Elena came in with an armload of blankets.

Gavilan asked to speak to the padre alone. When he heard the others descend the stairs, he told the padre to get word back that he would be late. He made the padre promise to get word back to the men in the mountains, and then he fell asleep.

In the morning Elena stopped Luis before he got out of the truck. She told him to take the day off. No explanation was offered. It was none of his business and he asked her no questions, not even who the big gringo was drinking coffee up on the porch.

Bobby hadn't had a Sunday off in so long he couldn't sleep in, even after the day he'd had on Saturday. First he checked in on Gavilan, who was sleeping soundly and whose dressing and bandages Bobby noticed had recently been changed. Next he knocked on Nina's door, and getting no answer, opened it a crack and saw the bed was empty and made. Downstairs Elena was in the kitchen having coffee. She poured a cup for Bobby, telling him that Nina had gone out early for a ride. She told Bobby to make himself at home, and that if he wanted anything to eat he was on his own. Bobby asked if anything had been planned for dinner and when Elena said no, Bobby volunteered to cook. The kitchen is yours, she said as she left on her way to the stables.

He checked the refrigerator and the freezer, which were both well stocked, as was the pantry. He fixed himself some toast to have with his coffee and sat down to plan a menu. He hoped cooking would take his mind off yesterday, and the uncertainty in front of him. Cooking, when it was for four and not fifty, was relaxing for him. He considered the options for dinner. In the meantime he thought he might make some muffins. In a big blue ceramic bowl he mixed flour with baking powder, salt, egg, oil, and orange marmalade instead of sugar, which he couldn't find, and put the tin in the oven, thinking they'd be ready about the time he was ready for his second cup of coffee. He wished he had a newspaper because he wanted to see if there were anything about the bombing. He'd given a roll of film to Enrique Moon to get to the stringer in Huaráz. He took his coffee onto the porch.

Nina had slept poorly. Gavilan had been the only one awake

when she got up. He looked pale and weak. Seeing him there, injured and vulnerable, she found it hard to believe all that had been imputed to him, but she couldn't wholly accept Elena's accusations, either. She decided she would watch Elena closely.

She saddled Araby and allowed the horse to choose the path, letting him go wherever he wanted as long as it was away from the house. The morning was cold and gray, with low clouds that threatened rain, and she was alone except for a few steers grazing on the sparse, dry brown grass. She didn't want to be alone. She hated to be alone, and she could never understand people who said they had to be alone, who needed time to themselves, to think or to straighten out their lives. She would have much preferred to have someone to straighten her life out for her, to think for her as her father had done, and as Rinaldi had done, but now there was no one she felt she could trust, not completely.

Araby heard it before Nina did. He picked up his ears at the sound of the steady beat of the blades. At first it came from down the valley and then closer, until seemingly it was everywhere. Suddenly a helicopter dipped through the clouds directly above them, hovered a moment as if to get its bearings, then wheeled and, skimming the fences, flew toward the house at Mirasol.

Bobby was back at the table with his coffee, waiting for the muffins to finish. He had settled on fried chicken and sweet potatoes, which he thought he'd candy, fresh baked bread, and pepper slaw, so that was it, dinner was set, and maybe he'd round it out with a pie for dessert from those big Chilean apples in the bowl on the table. It wasn't until the helicopter was almost over the house that the noise finally broke into his consciousness. He looked up as if he could see it through the ceiling. Then he went to the windows facing the horse ring, but he couldn't see on account of the clouds. The noise receded up the valley and he went back to his coffee. He was wondering about the possibility of finding a fresh chicken— there were only some wings in the freezer—when the sound of the copter grew louder. He went to the window again and this time he saw it flying low toward the house, hovering above the horse ring before it settled in a whorl of dust.

Bobby watched a soldier jump out, and then another before he bolted up the stairs. Gavilan was wrapped in a tangle of sheets and blankets. Bobby shook him, careful of the bad hand, and when that didn't wake him he pulled off the blankets, shook him harder, and slapped his face. Someone had tipped off the army, he couldn't think who, maybe the doctor. It didn't matter. They were here, and he had to wake Gavilan, hide him, help him get away.

He searched the room for Gavilan's clothes, looked through the closet and the chest of drawers, looked under the bed before he remembered that Elena had taken the clothes either to wash them or to throw them away. Through the bedroom window he saw her stooped beneath the slow spinning blades and pointing up at the house. He ran down the hall to the room where he had seen the tuxedo hanging on the closet door, and there on the bed was an open suitcase, and beside it a pair of pants and a shirt, socks, and a pair of tennis shoes on the floor. Back in Gavilan's room he could see the blades of the copter drooping, and the two armed soldiers standing outside. A third man climbed down, an older man with his hat under his arm, whose hair was thinning on top, who was wearing heavy black rectangular rose-tinted glasses.

Bobby shook Gavilan hard. He pulled him to a sitting position, still asleep, and began to dress him. It was taking too long. He could hear them at the kitchen door. He draped Gavilan's half-dressed body over his shoulder before he had thought of anyplace to take him. He considered climbing out the window, then hiding in the closet, spun one way, then the other with Gavilan out cold draped over his shoulder. He thought of stuffing him under the bed, and bent over to see if there was room. Gavilan's gun thumped onto the floor. He heard Elena's voice saying, "Upstairs . . . on the bed." He dumped Gavilan onto the sheets and picked up the gun. He heard their boots ascending the stairs. He locked the door. The gun felt heavy and awkward in his hand. He'd never fired a gun. He gripped it by the barrel, hefted it, thinking it might be better as a bludgeon. He braced himself. Then, inexplicably, he heard the footsteps descending and a moment later, through the window, he saw the two soldiers trudge across the yard and climb back into the copter.

Bobby opened the door a crack. No one was there. He heard voices down in the kitchen. He crept along the hallway, looking into each room as he passed. In the master bedroom at the top of the stairs he saw the bed piled high with gift-wrapped boxes. He went back to Gavilan's room. Gavilan was lying in a heap of clothing and covers, just as he had been dropped. Bobby threw the blankets over him, tossed the clothes on a chair, put the gun back under the pillow. He heard the *thug-a-thug* of the copter's motor kicking over.

"Bobby!" Elena called him from downstairs. "Bobby! I think your muffins are done!"

He ran downstairs to pull them out, black and smoking.

"Yes, certainly, Bobby and I have met," Rinaldi said cordially in response to Elena's question. He didn't extend his hand to shake, Bobby noticed, who was himself preoccupied with where to set the smoldering muffin tin. "Just the other night, in fact," Rinaldi was saying. "Bobby and Nina stopped at the house for drinks. We had a long conversation, Bobby and I, although I don't suppose Bobby remembers much of it."

Bobby wasn't misled by Rinaldi's polite affability, but in mid-morning, in the bright airy kitchen, with Elena and without the bodyguards, Rinaldi didn't seem the menace he had seemed before.

"Elena tells me you're here to photograph the festival of Santo Rosario," Rinaldi said. Bobby wanted to deny it. Some part of him wanted to disavow all connection to this, but looking at the weak, watery eyes of the arrogant Rinaldi, at the pale flabby man with narrow shoulders and a round pot belly, who wasn't much of a man in any sense Bobby understood the word, looking at Rinaldi that way, the thought came to him that he'd like to wring the bastard's neck. Right then and there. No, not wring his neck, just slap him once, hard, across the face. Tweak his nose. Humiliate the arrogant asshole. Instead he merely nodded. "You know of course," Rinaldi continued, "that there is no longer a Santo Rosario?"

Bobby said, "Yeah, I've heard." The smoke from the muffins made a cloud above their heads. He opened the kitchen door and placed the tin outside.

"But perhaps the feast will still be held. It's possible. After all, it's gone on for years and years, through worse disasters than this. I expect it will. Especially since it has gotten so big. It no longer belonged to Santo Rosario exclusively. Other villages share in putting it on. They take turns, I think."

"That's what I was counting on," Bobby said.

"And your guide, how is he feeling this morning?"

Not as chipper as you are, Bobby thought. "Sleeping," he said.

Elena told Bobby the colonel was staying for dinner. The enmity between the two men was obvious to her, as was its cause, and she viewed it with detachment. She felt herself in possession of an objectivity and a clarity she was enjoying. A power is what it was. "Will there be enough for all of us?"

"Depends," Bobby said. "I was planning on fried chicken, I saw some wings in the freezer, but if the colonel is going to be here, that's four, and Roberto, if he's hungry by that time, that's five, and as long as I'm going to take the trouble to make it, we ought to make enough for another meal. Can we get another chicken? Fresh is always better anyway. Say, where do you keep the sugar? I looked all over."

Elena said, "I suppose I still remember how to slaughter a chicken. The sugar is right over there." She pointed to a canister.

"You?" Bobby said, impressed. He pried the lid off the canister, spooned some into his coffee. "If it were left to me, your chickens would live to a tough and stringy old age."

A horse galloped into the yard. Nina sprinted up to the house and bolted through the door, only to be brought up short by the sight of the three of them standing in the kitchen.

"Look who's here," Elena said, meaning Rinaldi. "Surprise."

Nina looked wild, sweaty, her hair every which way. She was still holding her crop.

"Hello, Nina dear," Rinaldi said.

"I saw the helicopter, I thought—I . . . ." She looked from one face to another. She was out of breath. "I didn't know what to think," she said. The smell of horses had come into the kitchen, mingling with the smell of burnt muffins.

"You're not disappointed, I hope." Rinaldi reached out to her, but Nina backed away. Rinaldi put his empty hands into his pockets.

"I've been riding all morning," Nina explained. "I'm soaked with sweat. I left Araby out in the yard. He needs to be walked. I'd better go cool him down. Excuse me." She backed toward the door.

"You can leave Araby to me," Elena volunteered. "You don't look so well, dear. Is the altitude still troubling you?"

"As I was saying," Rinaldi went on, speaking to Nina, his hands still in his pockets. "The bombing in Marcara yesterday? I suppose you didn't hear about it, either. It's the reason I had to come. An investigation is under way. I'm to be briefed this evening in Huaráz. But I have the afternoon. I was just going upstairs to change out of my uniform."

"Upstairs?" There was a note of alarm in Nina's voice that she was unable to disguise.

"He knows about Roberto," Bobby said trying to allay her fears but intensifying them instead.

"Wait for me to come back down, won't you, Nina, please. I'd like to speak with you. I won't be a minute," Rinaldi said.

"But I was just going out," Nina said.

"Elena offered to see to the horse. Wait for me, please. I have something I need to talk to you about. Your father's estate," he added.

"Can't it wait?" Nina's mind was racing. "I told Bobby I'd get him some cream. For dinner."

"Then I'll go with you. It'll only be a moment until I change."

"No, that isn't necessary. You just got here. You should relax."

Elena noticed that with her newly acquired clarity came the ability to see the humorous edge to things. She admitted to herself that she was enjoying the scene in her kitchen among the three of them. "Well, you all work out your plans," she said. "I've Araby to walk and some work to do around the stable, mucking out the stalls, and I've got a chore to do for our chef here, too." Elena walked out the back door taking a large kitchen knife with her. Rinaldi went upstairs, leaving Bobby alone with Nina.

"Oh, my god," Nina whispered.

"There's no way he can know who's really in his guest room, if that's what's worrying you. But maybe you ought to let him go with you. The less he's around the house the better. Keep him away as long as possible. Does Elena know?"

"About Roberto?"

"About you and Rinaldi."

"She knows."

"Shitfire."

"She knows, but Rinaldi doesn't know she knows."

"Hmm. So Elena, *she* knows about Rinaldi and you, and Rinaldi, *he* knows about you and me, and she *probably* knows about you and me, but he doesn't know she knows what she knows, which is to say . . ."

"Stop it, Bobby. This isn't funny."

Rinaldi called from the front hallway. "Nin*aa!*"

Bobby kissed her on the forehead. The kiss was salty. "I'm sorry," he said. "It's just until this evening," he said.

"Then what?" Nina hissed. "Are you going to take me with you? I can't go back to him, Bobby. I can't."

Rinaldi opened the driver's door for her, touched her casually on the arm, and later, driving down the highway, placed his hand on her knee. Each time he touched her she stiffened. The Land Rover handled like a truck, requiring all Nina's attention, and the engine was too noisy for them to converse without having to talk unnaturally loud, and so they didn't speak, which was fine with her.

"Nina, pull over," Rinaldi said, leaning close to her ear. "I want to talk to you. We have to talk."

"But the cream," Nina shouted.

Rinaldi pointed to where he wanted her to stop the car.

She pulled the car onto the shoulder.

Rinaldi apologized for forgetting the rodeo. "But look at this." He handed her a pair of tickets.

"What good are these now? The rodeo's gone," Nina said. She flung them back at him.

"You didn't look," Rinaldi said handing them to her again. "They're for next week in Buenos Aires. I've made the reservations. We fly out on Wednesday. The rodeo is Saturday. We come back on Sunday. Well, what do you think? Am I forgiven?"

"It's too late," Nina said.

"It's worked out for the best. What with the bombing in Marcara, I wouldn't have been able to go last night anyway. And now we have the rodeo *and* Buenos Aires. And," he paused, reaching into his jacket, "you have this." He held out a jewelry case. When she didn't take it, he opened it for her. Inside was a necklace. Diamond.

"I don't want it," she said.

"I'm in your debt. I want you to know I appreciate your coming to see Elena, even after I'd broken my promise to you. Take it. Please." He tried to put it around her neck. She batted his hands away. She stared straight ahead, clenching the steering wheel. "I know it must have been hard to see her like she is. I should have prepared you."

Nina gave him a questioning look.

"I'm sure you noticed. The place is like a mausoleum."

She stared at him.

"Well, surely you couldn't have missed Alejandro's room? She hasn't touched it since the day he died. His tuxedo is hanging on the closet door as if he were going to walk in any moment and put it on for the rehearsal dinner. And his suitcase, you saw the suitcase? Lying open on the bed just the way he left it, with the clothes he took off next to it, the same clothes he came home from school in. Do you think that's normal behavior? To leave an open suitcase and dirty clothes on the bed for eighteen months?"

"Don't speak to me about normal," Nina said.

"I wanted to have those clothes washed and put away, but she wouldn't let me touch them. Or anyone for that matter. She almost fired the housekeeper for suggesting it. I came in one day and she was holding them on her lap, pressing them to her face, smelling them, I suppose. Is that normal? And what about the pictures of him all over the place?"

"They aren't all over the place. They're in the living room." Nina found herself defending Elena. It was easier than confronting Rinaldi directly.

"Don't you think it's a little morbid in there with all those pictures of him everywhere?"

Nina didn't answer.

"I do. I think she's lost touch. I think she needs help."

"Because she loved her son?"

"Because she's behaving in an irrational manner. Because she is drinking. Because she tore up the rose beds for no good reason, and when I asked her about it, she gave me a solemn, preposterous explanation about them being some sort of Zen Buddhist garden."

"She was pulling your leg."

"No, I know when someone is pulling my leg. What about the dog? Did she tell you about the dog, Alejandro's dog, Nicky, did she tell you what she did to old Nick?"

Nina rested her forehead against the window. "She told me other things."

"She shot him, that's what she did. And do you know why? I'll tell you why. Because Alejandro *told* her to, in a dream or something. Now she claims Alejandro speaks to her. That's what she told me, her exact words. Alejandro missed his dog, she said. So she shot him. Sent him to be with Alejandro. What more does one have to know?"

Nina tried to match Rinaldi's description with the Elena she had seen and spoken to herself. She couldn't concentrate. She had to know about Alejandro and the bombing before she could focus on anything else. She had to know whether the man whom she loved, trusted, and depended on for so much had committed unspeakable evil; or if Elena, a woman whom Nina admired, was as Rinaldi described her. And what about Gavilan? If it wasn't Rinaldi, then it was Gavilan. Yet he had risked his life to save hers and now she was protecting him. There was no good answer. "I don't know about Elena," she said. "I can't think about her right now. There's something I have to know from you first." She searched for the way to begin. "I had a long talk with Elena, our first since Alejandro died. She told me . . . Elena said—"

Rinaldi cut her off. He waved his hand in front of her face. "I already know what you're going to say, and it's absolutely ridiculous. It's crazy. She told you that *I* planted the bomb that killed Alejandro, right? Isn't that what she told you?" Nina looked at Rinaldi with disbelief. "What more evidence do you need that this is a person who has lost her grip on reality? That settles it. I've been considering having her put in a hospital for treatment. I didn't want to do it, but it doesn't look as if she will be able to snap out of it on her own. It will be for her own good. She needs professional help. She doesn't know what she's saying or doing. She may do something to hurt herself. Or someone else."

Nina pictured Elena leaving the kitchen with the knife. "Are you denying it?"

"Nina, please. Elena's very disturbed. Isn't it obvious?"

Having given Luis the day off, and Sunday being the housekeeper's day off as well, Elena was left to do the chores herself. After cleaning the stalls, putting down fresh bedding, and filling the buckets with water and feed, she fed and watered the dogs and the barn cats, fed the chickens and picked out two for dinner. It had been some time since she had slaughtered a chicken herself, and she found she was out of practice. After tying their feet and hanging them upside down on the clothesline, she severed their heads. That part went well enough, but one flopped around and splashed her with blood. Then she'd lost the feel for removing the innards, so whereas at one time she could have pulled everything out in a piece, she had to reach inside several times, and was up to her forearms in gore by the time she finished. She made another mistake, scalding the birds too long, and had an awful time plucking the feathers. As a result, feathers stuck to her everywhere. She finished just as Bobby came into the kitchen. She slapped the chickens onto the counter, put the knife in the sink, and pushed a strand of hair off her forehead.

Bobby looked Elena over. "Gave you a pretty tough time of it, did they?"

Elena looked down at her clothes. "I can see where you might think it was a closer fight than it actually was," she said. Elena liked Bobby. She liked his sense of humor and she admired the way he had handled himself in front of Rinaldi, whom she was sure had been alerted by Luis. The bombing in Marcara she suspected was a convenient excuse to try to intimidate Bobby. "The smaller one was game, but truthfully, I had her all the way. Don't forget I had this—" she picked up the long bladed knife. "Helped to even the odds."

Bobby laughed.

"Have you seen the colonel?" she asked.

Bobby told her he had left with Nina. Was there anything else she could do? she asked, and Bobby said she might singe the chickens, and then, if she didn't mind, would she set the table? She knew where everything was, it would be easier if she set the table instead of him.

Nina walked into the house while Elena was setting out plates in the dining room. Feathers were still in her hair. Her faded blue work shirt was splotched with dried blood, and her arms from her wrists to her elbows were stained the same murky brown. There was blood on her cheek and forehead. Only her hands were clean.

"Did you get the cream?" asked Elena.

"Cream?" Nina had forgotten the excuse she had given Rinaldi for having to leave the house. Cream? she asked herself. What does she mean by cream? Now everything Elena said was cause for scrutiny. Nina searched for double meanings or for a lack of meaning altogether. "Is the silverware still in the bottom drawer?" Nina asked, trying to help. She knelt to open the buffet, pondering the implication of "cream."

They worked side by side setting out plates, silver, and glasses. Nina counted the settings, five—one more than was needed. "Who's the extra setting for?" she asked.

Elena stopped and counted the plates herself. "There isn't an extra," she said.

Nina pointed and counted out loud. "Me, you, Rinaldi and Bobby, that's four . . ."

"And Alejandro makes five," added Elena, folding a napkin. She was humming.

Nina set out the rest of the silverware. Her hands were shaking and it took a long time. She avoided looking at Elena. She remarked that she liked the gravel garden. She had tried to make it sound casual, but her voice cracked and she had to repeat herself.

Elena stopped setting out the water glasses. She rested the empty pitcher against her stomach. Nina fumbled with the serving spoon. She could feel Elena's eyes on her.

"Where the rose beds were?" Nina aligned a knife next to the spoon. "The Zen Buddhist rock garden?" She glanced up.

Elena covered her mouth with the back of her hand, turned her face toward her shoulder, trying to supress the laughter. "We'll need a serving spoon for the pepper slaw, too," she said, and a giggle escaped. "You'll find it in the buffet."

"Did I say something funny?" Nina was certain she hadn't. This was more of Elena's craziness.

Elena went to the sideboard and from the crystal decanter poured herself a drink. She pulled herself together. "One for you, dear?" she asked, her smile lingering. Nina said no. Elena took a swallow, then smiled again, looked down at the floor, and shook her head.

"What?" Nina asked, having already drawn a conclusion from Elena's behavior. "Tell me!"

Elena finished her drink, poured herself another, and took a sip of it before setting it down. She started to laugh again and forced it into a cough. "Excuse me, dear," she said. "I just can't help it."

Nina began to cry.

"Oh, Nina, sweetheart." Elena came to her, hugged her, patted her back. "I'm sorry, darling. I wasn't laughing at you. You don't think I was laughing at you, do you, dear?" She picked a feather off Nina's blouse.

"I don't know what to think," Nina said, unable to look Elena in the eye. She accepted a napkin to wipe her tears.

"Poor thing," Elena said. "I should have warned you. You really *don't* know what's going on, do you?"

Crying, Nina shook her head no. She blew her nose.

"I'm sorry. Please stop. I'll explain everything. You see, Rinaldi I can expect it from, he has no sense of humor, he never could tell when he was being put on. And I can't help myself sometimes. He takes himself so seriously. I should have taken your feelings into account. How would you know? But it is terribly funny, like something out of a play, the four of us together." Elena held out her hands to Nina, but Nina backed away, bumping into the buffet. "Really, dear, it's very funny. If you could see the expression on your face."

Nina attempted a weak smile.

"I suppose he told you about Nicky. And the voices from the grave?"

"You shot Nicky, he said."

"I ought to be more prudent about what I tell him. I didn't expect him to tell anyone else. For such a shrewd man, he's really quite gullible, you know, a child in many ways." And then, growing serious, added, "To be sure, a spoiled, malicious child, but a child just the same. He wants you to believe I'm losing my mind. He wants to believe it himself, I think. It's the only way he can cope with me now, and with what he has done. In order to believe his own lies, he has to treat me as if I were out of my mind. I'm not, you know, in spite of what he says."

"And the roses . . . ?"

"Had crown gall. Makes these ugly pustules for which there's no remedy, no cure. And it's contagious. I had to pull them out."

"And Nicky?"

"Old age. A gall in itself. Poor Nick. He was incontinent, always messing all over himself, and his hips were bad, he couldn't climb the steps to his bed on the porch anymore. He was suffering so, and I couldn't bear to see it—he'd been such an energetic dog his whole life and he would sort of look at me with those brown eyes as if he were asking me to fix it for him, and I couldn't. The vet recommended putting him down, but I couldn't bring myself to do it. He *was* Alejandro's dog. Every day he was spending more and more time just lying there, half the time in his own excrement. I knew the vet was right, but still I couldn't do it. Oh, Luis would have only been too pleased to do the job, but I wasn't going to ask him. It upsets me to indulge his perversity. And I didn't want to be a hypocrite about it. Nothing angers me more than someone who simply can't bear the thought of killing a living creature and eats lamb chops twice a week. It was hard to do, but it was necessary, and I only hope, should my body deteriorate to the point where I'm no use to anyone anymore, and can't control myself, like Nicky, that there would be someone with the compassion to do the same for me." Elena drained off her glass. "Unfortunately, I can't imagine who."

"And setting the place for Alejandro?"

Elena looked quizzical.

"You told me a moment ago you set a place for Alejandro."

"Did I say that? I meant what's-his-name upstairs . . . Roberto. In case he should feel well enough to come down to eat."

"You don't hear voices, then? You don't speak to him?"

"Oh, I do, all the time, though not in the way Rinaldi thinks. No seances or anything like that. But I do speak to him in my thoughts. I suppose I always will."

Bobby brought in the platter of fried chicken and joined Elena, Rinaldi, and Nina at the table. The pepper slaw, bread, and sweet potatoes had already been served. "Use your fingers," Bobby said. "It's the only way to go." He accepted their compliments. "Fresh-killed makes all the difference."

Elena informed Rinaldi that Bobby was a professional chef.

"A cook," Bobby corrected her.

Rinaldi, who had changed back into uniform, said that he already knew, that he was a great fan of Blacky's, that he ate there often. "I was by there today, in fact," he said. "On my way to the airport." He looked around the table. "Unfortunately, I didn't have time to stop. I noticed it was very crowded. A lot of government people, it seemed." He accepted the platter of chicken from Elena. He had a queer look on his face, a half-smile that quickly disappeared.

"We're always busy for Sunday brunch," Bobby said. He cut himself a slice of bread. No one was eating. Everyone looked around at everyone else, except for Nina, who stared down into her plate.

"If you're waiting for Roberto, I think you should go ahead and eat," Elena said. "I checked in on him before I came downstairs. He was still sound asleep. Those pills must be very powerful." Nina wondered how Elena could be so casual. Because she didn't have a bomb go off in front of her yesterday, she decided. Because she didn't know who was sleeping in her guest room.

Rinaldi picked a drumstick off the platter with his fingers. "Our Mr. Shafto," he said, with transparent deference, "is a man of many talents."

Elena said she'd like to see his photographs sometime. Bobby invited her to his studio, but Elena said she had no plans to go to the capital. One never knew, of course, she said, but she thought she had had enough of the city.

"Which reminds me," Rinaldi said, looking into the inside pocket of his jacket. "I brought a picture of my own to show Bobby. After dinner. It's just a Polaroid snapshot, but I'd like to see his reaction." That queer smile again, and then another bite of chicken.

Nina sat quietly. She had no appetite at all. She wondered how the others could be eating, and she looked around the room, avoiding their eyes, wanting to flee, wishing she had somewhere to go. She was the first to see Gavilan standing in the archway that led in from the hall. Then Bobby looked up, and Elena and Rinaldi on the opposite side of the table with their backs to him turned around. He looked unfamiliar—showered, shaved, wearing the clothes Bobby had tried to dress him in earlier—khaki slacks, a red-and-white-striped rugby shirt, white tennis shoes. He looked like a college kid. Bobby reached around Nina and pulled out a chair for him. " 'Bout time," he said, his mouth full of bread. Gavilan walked in on shaky legs.

"The smell," he said pointing to the platter of chicken. "It must have woke me up." Bobby quickly introduced him to Elena and Rinaldi. "Roberto Cortazar," he said, placing emphasis on "Cortazar" in order to put Gavilan on his guard. Bobby went through the story again in order to make sure Gavilan knew who he was supposed to be. "I hope you don't mind," Roberto said. "I borrowed these clothes. I couldn't find mine, and these were lying on the chair by the bed."

Alejandro's. Nina looked at Elena, whose expression remained open and pleasant, and at Rinaldi, who, sipping his fourth gin and tonic, seemed not to notice. "I'm so glad they fit," Elena said. "I'm glad someone will get some use out of them. They were my son's and I just couldn't bring myself to do anything with them, but now that I see you can wear them, you can have them. All of them, if you like. I'll pack them up for you before you leave."

Nina's eyes closed. She felt swamped by a sickening anger toward Rinaldi, and toward herself for being so easily duped. She tried to regain control of her emotions, but her thoughts were whirling. She excused herself from the table and rushed up to her bedroom. Downstairs they heard the door slam.

"I'll go see what's wrong," said Elena.

The men ate awhile in silence. Gavilan, who hadn't had a meal like the one before him in he didn't remember how long, since he had hid out with Blacky, noted his own lack of appetite with irony.

"Where are you from, exactly?" Rinaldi directed his question to Roberto, and inwardly Bobby cringed, suspecting Rinaldi was acting coy and somehow knew. Roberto, picking at the chicken, mentioned the name of a village in the mountains. He was a teacher there, he said. The colonel asked him if he knew much about the Moreno Zapato, if they were very active in that part of the sierra.

"No," Gavilan said. "I don't understand much of what it's about." He spooned a tiny helping of sweet potato onto his plate. The smells were beginning to make him sick. "Maybe you could tell me."

Rinaldi went to the sideboard to pour himself a drink. He felt expansive, voluble, and welcomed the opportunity to speak. He had a meeting scheduled with the Minister tomorrow. He considered this a rehearsal.

He took a sip from his glass. He had their attention. "Since I am in my own home, enjoying a meal with my guests"—he bowed toward each of them and raised his glass—"a delicious meal, by the way"—he raised his glass again—"I feel free to speak in a way I might not in other circumstances. Can I get either of you a drink, by the way? Brandy?"

Elena returned and slid into her seat. "She's not feeling well. A headache." Bobby pushed away from the table, intending to go upstairs. "She asked that she not be disturbed," she added. Bobby sat back down.

"A shame," Rinaldi said. "I probably won't be around to say good-bye. Tell her I hope she feels better, will you please. Now Mr. . . ."

"Cortazar."

"Yes, of course . . . Mr. Cortazar had a question: 'What,' he asked, 'is the conflict with the Moreno about?' Let me assume for the moment that unlike the press, or the ministry or the garrison, the military command, or the Indians, you, Mr. Cortazar, do not have a bias. Of course you do, but let us assume for the moment you are a disinterested party, that you genuinely *do* want to know, rather than merely to substantiate your preconceptions . . ."

Rinaldi spoke for fifteen minutes, circling the table, stopping at the sideboard to refill his glass, standing behind his chair as if it were a lectern. A glib fifteen-minute summary of the situation which Roberto estimated was three minutes of half-truths and twelve of total bullshit.

A car pulled into the turnaround, its headlights shone through the window. Rinaldi polished off his drink and buttoned his jacket. He took his hat from the buffet and bent over to kiss Elena on the cheek.

He bowed and placed his hat on his head. "I'm sure we'll meet again." His eyes drilled into Bobby's. "Mr. Cortazar . . . A speedy recovery." Another slight bow. "And now, gentlemen, Elena, my dear, if you'll excuse me . . ."

He walked out the door onto the porch and then, forgetting something, stepped back inside again. Standing in the hallway, he took an envelope from inside his jacket pocket. "Bobby . . . ?"

Bobby got out of his chair to accept the envelope from Rinaldi.

"Until the next time," Rinaldi said, and once more gave him that weird little smile.

"Yeah, sure," Bobby said. "See you around."

"Say, these things aren't too bad," Mosquevera said. He held the grease-spotted bag out to Rinaldi. "There's meat, and cheese and I think there's a chicken left, too."

Rinaldi swatted the bag away from his face with the back of his hand. The smell of garlic and grease and onion filled the jeep.

"Not hungry, huh?" Mosquevera held the pastry between his teeth while he shifted gears and guided the jeep out the driveway. Oil leaked from the empanada, dripped down his chin and onto his shirt.

Rinaldi was aware that the ignoramus Mosquevera was trying to goad him, but he wasn't going to let him spoil his mood. He only wished he could've been around to see Shafto open the envelope.

Mosquevera used his knees to steer down the row of poplars while he wiped at his shirt with a paper napkin. The jeep swerved toward the trees and he jerked it back, throwing Rinaldi against the dash. Rinaldi swore under his breath.

"Well?" Mosquevera said after a moment. He blotted the stain with one hand and steered with the other.

"Well what?"

"Was Shafto there or wasn't he?" Rinaldi only grunted. "Luis told you he was. You can count on Luis."

Rinaldi wasn't about to discuss his personal life with Mosquevera. "What kind of coverage did we get?"

"Front page. All the papers. Radio. TV."

"I got a phone call this morning. From his holiness the Minister. He's decided that it would be in his words 'ill-advised' to end martial law at this time."

"That's what you wanted."

"It's just the beginning. We need to talk. And I need a drink."

"There's beers in back. If warm doesn't bother you."

"I prefer the Raymondi."

"The curfew, remember?"

"They'll open it for me. I need a drink."

Mosquevera permitted himself a smile as the jeep lurched onto the highway. When they were cruising, he fished out a bottle of beer from behind the seat and pried off the cap on the dashboard. He took a swallow. "You gonna kill him?" he asked.

Rinaldi stared through the windshield.

"I'd kill him," Mosquevera said. "That's what I would do." He drained the bottle and pitched it out the window. He reached behind him for another. "But first I'd break his bones." He cracked open the bottle on the dash, swigged, wiped his mouth with the back of his hand. "One by one." He belched. "And I'd make her watch."

Rinaldi was seething. "Tell me what they found in the restaurant?"

"I can't believe of all the people in the world you coulda asked to deliver that package up to Luis, you pick her. I wish to God you'd explain that one to me, because"—he shook his head and laughed—"whew, man, you got your old lady up there, and your young honey, and there's this Shafto guy, and then you show up . . . Must have really been something. You all get naked together, or what?"

"You're pushing it, Mosquevera." Rinaldi summoned all the menace he could manage. "Just tell me what was found at the restaurant."

"No cash. Must have all been in the wine and the paintings, like you said."

"Blacky have anything to say?"

Mosquevera shook his head. "What about that other one? The one you captured up at the baths?"

"Nada."

"Did he say anything about their numbers?"

"Nope."

"Recruits? Supplies?"

"Unh-unh."

"Nothing at all?"

"Wouldn't I have told you?" Mosquevera tilted back the bottle. It was empty and he dropped it onto the road, where it shattered.

"Didn't he talk?"

"He talked all right. We got it down now where they want to talk so bad that ten minutes after they're dead, some of them are still jabbering away. And he told us things. All he knew. Mostly misinformation. They lie to him, he lies to us, but he *thinks* it's the truth. They told him they'd be up at San Gerais. We went up to San Gerais. There was nobody there."

"What did he say about Gavilan."

"Said he hadn't seen him in a month. That'd be about the time he was supposed to have been assassinated."

"And what does that mean to you?"

Mosquevera rubbed three days' stubble on his chin. "That we did too good a job. That it's over."

"Just because we haven't seen them in a couple of weeks?"

"It's not all that unusual for *us* not to see them. Hell, we never looked for them that hard to begin with. But the cocainistas ain't seen them either, which *is* unusual. What I think is that there's only a few of them left. And I'll tell you something else . . . I don't think there was ever more than a handful to start with. I mean hard-core Moreno."

"And this idea that there are numerous independent cells? Compartmentalization."

"Something we made up."

Rinaldi protested. "No, that's a page out of Che."

"What's the difference? We made up so much I don't remember what's real sometimes. You still call it compartmentalization when there's only the one compartment?"

"You're wrong, Mosquevera. Six months ago I estimate there were three hundred of them. I'm willing to bet there are two hundred left."

"Because we're partners here, you and me, I'm not going to take that bet. We made a lot of money out of this deal together, a ton of money. But listen to me. What you got, when you come right down to it, when you put the facts on one side and all the other stuff, the newspapers and our so-called intelligence reports on the other, what you got is a big pile of bullshit over here, and over there you got the bodies of a couple of teenagers, mercenaries, college kids, and some Indians who wouldn't know a Marxist from spit. And then you have our informants who would tell you up was down or vice versa if they thought it was what you wanted to hear, if they thought there might be a couple of bucks in it for them."

Rinaldi was shaking his head. "You're wrong. You're wrong. You're wrong. They're out there. Gavilan's out there and he's got two hundred men, and more crossing our borders everyday, and more than that in the cities awaiting his call."

"Come off it, Rinaldi. Even the Minister doesn't buy this revolution horseshit. That's for the fucks out there who read the newspapers." Mosquevera shut up. He knew that to pursue this line with Rinaldi would lead nowhere. No telling what he might do if you pushed him too far. Humor him was the way to go. Rinaldi didn't know the score anymore. He was lost in a fog. This wasn't about politics, or Indian rights, or revolution, or any of that shit. This was about money, plain and simple. The Moreno could've tromped all over the mountains for years and nobody would've bothered them. But they messed with the drugs. That was their mistake and it was Mosquevera's lucky day. Because when the government declared martial law, beefed up the garrison in Huaráz, and put them in command, it was their invitation to the ball.

The problem was, Rinaldi wasn't interested in dancing. Mosquevera had puzzled over this for months, it had been inconceivable to him, but now he'd come to accept the truth. Rinaldi wanted something other than money. He wanted to be the big shit general.

"Face it, Rinaldi. It's over," he said. He enjoyed the chance to play the rational, philosophical part.

"No. It's not over yet. Marcara changed the Minister's mind."

"Well, martial law may not be over, but let me remind you what is."

"Six more months is all I need."

"What're over are the payments from the cocainistas. *They* haven't changed their minds."

"Forget the cocainistas. I'll give you what they were giving you. Six more months, they'll *have* to give me my promotion."

Rinaldi's offer stopped Mosquevera in his tracks. "Well. Huh. That seems very white of you, Rinaldi. Huh. I guess that pretty much takes care of my concerns. Now what is it you have in mind?"

"You know how to write, don't you?"

"I know how to endorse a check, if that's what you mean."

They woke the manager at the Hotel Raymondi. In the empty bar he served the colonel a brandy and Mosquevera two beers and a couple of bags of pretzels. He brought the pad and paper Rinaldi requested, then trudged back to bed.

Rinaldi dictated an outline of the plan to nominally restore the civilian government. It was a public relations ploy dreamed up by the Ministry of the Interior. No real power would be transferred, but certain concessions were made, the lifting of the curfew for one. There was to be a fiesta announcing the decision, a parade and fireworks. The garrison was to be reduced to a skeleton force. This, of course, was not to be announced.

"Is this it? We done?" Mosquevera cleaned the wax from his ear with the point of the pencil.

"Did I tell you about all the supplies piled up in the garrison? Uniforms, medicine, ammunition? About the suspected Moreno we're holding in the stockade? What about the fireworks? You got it all down? This is confidential information, remember. You'll be certain that it doesn't fall into the wrong hands?"

"I'll make sure. As soon as I finish my beer I'll take care of it. Anything else while I'm taking notes? You want me to sit on your knee?"

Rinaldi ignored the provocation. He was feeling better already. The Minister says it's over. Mosquevera says it's over. What threat could two dozen Moreno be to a well-fortified garrison, even if it were undermanned? "Yes, there is one more thing," the colonel added. "Santo Rosario."

"There ain't no Santo Rosario."

Rinaldi told him to put the pencil away. Then he explained what he wanted done.

"Wait a minute." Mosquevera stared at Rinaldi in disbelief. "Jesus, I wish I had another beer. This gringo, the guy out at the ranch, is going to be at Santo Rosario even though there ain't a Santo Rosario, and you want us to go back up there again, on the day of the feast, if there is a feast, and do what?"

Rinaldi told him again.

"No way. Unh-unh." Mosquevera shook his head. "I got no beef with this guy. She's *your* woman, not mine. You take care of it. I ain't going way the hell up to no Santo Rosario. After what we did last time those fuckers up there would just as soon throw rocks at us as look at us."

"It'll be no big deal. Masquerade as Moreno. You know, like before. The ignorant bastards won't know the difference."

"I don't think so, Rinaldi. That particular charade is getting stale."

"Oh, come on, Captain." Rinaldi drained off his glass and stood up to leave. "It's the army they hate. The Moreno they'll welcome with open arms."

OHMIDARLIN

After three hours the hike for Nina had become a test of endurance. After six it became an ordeal. The warm, yellow late-afternoon turned cool at dusk. Night was cold, moonless, dark. The path was a trench between canyon walls, uphill, ceaselessly, endlessly uphill.

Too much city life for this *caballera*, she thought. Too many cigarettes, too much sunbathing and spectating. Before she had moved to the capital she might have hiked this path just to see the sunset. Her thoughts began to drift and she forced them back to the present. The acute awareness of her physical pain was preferable to the other kind. She began to count her breaths to keep her mind focused. She knew, of course, that the readjustment to altitude took time, and that in a single day they had gone from sea level to Mirasol at five thousand feet, and now they were hiking higher still, yet these symptoms—headache, dizziness, shortness of breath—took her by surprise. Me, she thought, who used to laugh at the soft city women who fell to *soroche* in the mountains.

Other travelers were merely footsteps and shadows, insubstantial, moving out of the night and merging back. No greetings were exchanged. For Nina, nothing seemed to warrant the expenditure of a single breath more than what was required to put one foot in front of the other. She craved the air, which she took in sips and gasps, in deep double lungsfull, wanting to satisfy her need, and failing, the demand far exceeding supply.

Barking dogs, the thud of hooves, insects, the smack of Bobby's stick on the donkey's back, these were the sounds she heard over the constant wash of the stream that flowed beside the trail. The rasp of her breathing joined the chorus of nighttime noises, and when she stopped to rest, which as the night wore on she did more and more, she heard the pounding of her heart.

Gavilan had promised they'd be stopping soon. Where they were going was "just up ahead," he'd said. He'd said that two hours ago. Her relief had turned to apprehension, and then to doubt, disappointment, and finally anger. After she had convinced herself that they had been deceived, that Gavilan, for no reason other than malice, had lied, when her doubts about his reliability in the simple matter of the distance between two points had joined with her greater doubts in a confluence of anger, toward Gavilan, toward Bobby, Rinaldi, toward this trail, cigarettes, the night, the dust, blisters, the dogs, and the brute of a donkey which would take not a single step without coercion from the stick, when her frustration and wailing discomfort had overwhelmed all other thought and feeling and sensation until there was only the pressure encircling her chest and the hot stabs of anger, just then she heard his voice from the darkness say, "A quarter mile further, no more."

They turned onto a hillside. The steep path climbed through a pasture. She heard cows cropping grass before she saw them, so still and dark was the night. She stopped to let the heaving in her chest subside. Her head swelled with dull pressure, her pulse raced, her throat burned. She was at once both damp with sweat and chilled. The sounds of the others grew fainter and for a panicky moment she thought they'd left her behind, but Gavilan was waiting. He extended his good hand and pulled her to her feet. Four days ago standing made him dizzy. Now she was the dizzy one.

She hadn't allowed herself to believe him, but what he had said was true: they'd arrived . . . somewhere. A mud house. A fire inside. She could see the flicker through the doorway.

A boy came out of the house, unloaded the donkeys, and drove them into the field. Bobby put the packs under the eaves with the sacks of food and supplies they had bought for Gavilan down in the valley. Nina rested with her back against the house. He draped a jacket over her shoulders. She was shivering, her teeth chattered. From his canteen he gave her water, which was warm and tasted of plastic, then sat down and put his arm around her. They sat that way until the boy returned. He looked at Nina before he went inside, and a moment later came back out with a blanket that smelled of smoke and donkey, and handed it to her before he ran off again down the hill.

Gavilan came out of the house and sat on the other side of her. Things were bad inside, he explained. He told them about Julia, about the baby and the clinic in Huaráz. Now Julia was in labor, and something was wrong, Gavilan didn't know what. They had sent the boy, Augusto, to get the *curandera*, but Gavilan didn't know if there would be time.

Nina had witnessed the birth of plenty of calves, had even pulled two or three out herself when a leg was caught or when they were turned a funny way, but she knew nothing about assisting in the birth of a human. Bobby helped her to her feet. The stars spun and she leaned against the wall. When the whirling stopped, she felt her way inside. She had to stoop or bump her head on the beams. Did the floor really slope as steeply as it seemed?

A man and a woman knelt beside a pile of blankets in the corner of the room. A baby slept wrapped in a shawl on the woman's back. Behind the man peered two small copper faces. Nina paused in the center of the room, waiting to be invited closer.

That they requested her assistance was an indication of how desperate the situation was. Nina knelt in the space that they made for her. The pile of blankets groaned. She pulled back a corner, afraid of what she might see. Firelight fell on a dark round face.

She was a delicate thing, a child herself, fifteen, or sixteen at most. Pain squeezed her eyes shut and pulled back her lips. Her teeth were small and very white. Nina reached to brush the hair from the girl's damp forehead, and as she did the girl's eyes opened. Seeing Nina the girl reached for her mother, who spoke to her and hugged her and eased her back down. The girl turned her face to the wall.

Nina stroked the girl's hair, saying Julia, Julia, softly, patiently, and in time Julia turned her face back to where Nina could see the lines of tears streaked on her dusty cheeks. She found the girl's hand and held it beneath the ponchos, blankets, and burlap sacks that all smelled of animal and smoke.

The woman looked to Nina, who didn't look back for fear what her face might reveal. She called for Bobby to bring the canteen. She wet Julia's lips, which were dry and ridged, and cleaned her face and placed a wet cloth on her forehead. She held Julia's head and put the canteen to her mouth. She kept track of time between the contractions.

It was an hour before the *curandera* came. She knelt opposite Nina on the other side of the girl, and laid a bundle on the girl's swollen stomach. The idea of putting anything at all on Julia's stomach made Nina gasp, and when she did the *curandera* looked away from her work. Her eyes were very dark and very shiny. Nina had never seen eyes like that, a gaze so penetrating. The *curandera's* hands went back to unwrapping the bundle, but she kept her eyes on Nina. She jutted her chin and cocked her head as a way of asking Dominga who the gringa was.

Nina spoke for herself in Quechua.

"La Perla, at your service," the *curandera* said. She smiled at Nina's command of the language. Each finger of her right hand was ringed with a narrow silver band. Her face was lined, her lips were cracked, but her voice was like a young girl's. And she wore no hat. All Indian women wore a hat. Nina grew agitated watching her, at the way she looked, like every other Indian woman and like none of them. The way she stared at Nina, how she spoke and moved, none of it seemed right.

The *curandera* turned her full attention to Julia. She lightly touched the girl all over her body—her forehead, eyes, cheeks, neck, and then, reaching under the blankets, her arms, chest, and belly, her legs and feet.

Nina's anxiety grew. She wanted to intervene. She wished she knew something about medicine. She wished she had some authority. Her powerlessness induced an aching despair. She closed her eyes and squeezed Julia's hand as if by wishing hard, by willing it, she could transmit strength and comfort to the dying girl. She opened her eyes to see La Perla once again looking at her. La Perla's eyes were moist, they sparkled, and Nina, her cheeks growing warm, released Julia's hand. But something about La Perla's gaze was reassuring, as if La Perla somehow understood what Nina had been trying to do, and approved.

Held in La Perla's gaze, Nina felt a soothing calm, but no sooner was eye contact broken than her apprehension returned. Abruptly, La Perla reverted to being simply another Indian woman, the same as Dominga, the same as Julia would be if she survived—wrinkled, long-suffering, old before her time. Nina's heart pounded. She was frantic for some explanation. The altitude, that's what it was! And the stress! No one would deny that she'd just been through some very stressful days. No wonder she couldn't think rationally. Under these circumstances, who could? The special qualities Nina had ascribed to La Perla, the turmoil she had experienced in her presence, were the effects of stress and *soroche*, nothing more.

La Perla arranged the bundle's contents on Julia's body. Her every act was precise and deliberate. She lit six candles and placed them around Julia's head. She had coca leaves, flour wrapped in a square of paper, a bottle of murky liquid, a bottle of oil, and a razor blade. Alongside Julia she put another bottle Nina guessed was *trago*, and a handful of puma teeth, and several dozen short green twigs tied in a bundle. She emptied the contents of a small leather pouch into her palm. It looked like decomposing leaves.

The men and boys were asked to leave, and some minutes were spent removing Julia's clothes without exposing her to the cold night air. La Perla handed Nina the twigs and asked her to put them on the fire. Then three times La Perla chanted the name of the ancient Inca Atahualpa. Her voice, high, sweet, and melodious, and to Nina mismatched to her age and appearance, provoked another wave of anxiety. La Perla noticed Nina's discomfort and mimicked her in a way Nina thought was hilarious.

The twigs smoldered on the coals, making a cloud of acrid smoke. Nina's eyes burned and watered, her throat burned and she coughed. They all did. "What's she trying to do?" Bobby asked after he'd been allowed back in. La Perla explained that the smoke was a screen to protect them from the girl's illness. Bobby couldn't stop coughing and left again. Nina could hear him coughing outside.

La Perla positioned them around the girl: Gavilan next to Nina, Dominga and Antonio at the girl's feet. The boys stood behind their parents. Bobby watched from the doorway. La Perla passed a bag of coca, and they chewed the leaves mixed with white powdered quicklime. She opened the bottle of *trago* and poured a jar for each of them. Reciting something Nina couldn't understand, she spilled the remainder onto the floor. It soaked into the dirt. She answered before Nina could ask that she had invited the beings who live in the earth to attend the healing. She said they would be insulted if they were not invited, and since these spirits were spiteful, if they were going to be present, it would be best if they were drunk. Alcohol brightened their mood. She laughed at her own explanation. Her laugh was infectious and despite the sick girl, her own fatigue, and the *soroche*, Nina laughed too. The *trago* had made her giddy. La Perla leaned over the girl's body and they drew into a conspiratorial huddle. "The *abuelos* are what you might call mellow drunks," she whispered. "If they're loaded, they won't be too interested in taking advantage of the girl." She allowed her body to slump and her face muscles to relax in a way that perfectly mirrored the posture and manner of someone who had had too much to drink. "They are easy to trick when they are drunk, and they can't carry out their diabolical intentions." She winked at Nina.

Antonio jumped to his feet, hurled his jar of *trago* against the wall, smashing it to pieces. "Bullshit," he roared. "Bullshit!"

Dominga tugged at the sleeve of his sweater, telling him to sit down, but Antonio pulled his arm away.

"The *abuelos!* Damned if it isn't always the *abuelos.* Or if not them it's the *wamanis* in the stream or the *apu* in the mountains. Or the other devils, the *pishtaku.* What about the bastards at the clinic? That's what I want to know. What are you going to do about them? How're you going to stop them from carrying out *their* diabolical intentions?"

La Perla stared at Antonio. Antonio stared back. Nina could see nothing in the *curandera's* face except perhaps surprise, but Antonio was defiant.

"It's bullshit, all of it," he said again and turned and left the house.

Gavilan followed Antonio out.

La Perla spoke softly to the oldest boy, Augusto, telling him to bring her a guinea pig from where they were penned inside the wall. A pregnant female, she said.

Antonio stormed back in followed by Gavilan.

"Dominga!" He was furious. "We're not going to waste a *cuy* on this crazy ceremony, are we? You know she's going to kill it. You know that, don't you? And then she's going to act as if it were overwhelmed with Julia's sickness, when really she killed it herself by strangling it or breaking its neck. It's all an act, you know that, don't you?" He stood over his wife.

Dominga looked at her hands in her lap.

"Dominga?"

Julia moaned from the pain of another contraction. The guinea pig squealed.

"Dominga, damn you! Answer me!"

Gavilan took Antonio by the arm. "You don't want to make it harder for Julia," he said gently. He guided Antonio toward the door. "Maybe La Perla *can* help her. Forget about the doctors in Huaráz. Come outside with me."

Antonio allowed himself to be led a few steps, then pulled out of Gavilan's grasp. "Who are you to tell me what I can and cannot do inside my own house!" He picked up a stick from beside the fire. They used it for a poker. It was half the length of a broomstick, charred and pointed on the end.

No one saw where it came from, only that in the next instant Gavilan was pointing a gun at Antonio's chest. "She'll die unless she gets help. We can't just let her die." As he pulled Antonio toward the door, Augusto dove at Gavilan's legs. He held Gavilan around the ankle, trying to topple him, screaming for him to let his father go. Bobby pulled Augusto away and held him until Gavilan had marched Antonio outside. Bobby blocked the door with his body. All three brothers pummeled his legs with kicks and punches in order to force their way through to their father. Bobby protected himself as best he could.

"Boys!" It was their mother. "Stop it! Come here! I need you." The two youngest brothers, breathing hard and fast, trembling, their clothes disheveled, sat down by their mother. Augusto never quit. He was swinging and jabbing the poker at Bobby.

"Augusto! Put that stick down! Right this minute! I need you here!"

Augusto dropped the poker. Bobby quickly stooped to pick it up and tossed it out the door. Glowering, the boy came back to his mother's side.

The guinea pig squealed and wriggled while La Perla probed its belly with her fingers. She passed it through the smoke from the smoldering twigs. It became quiet and passive. Then she touched its head to Julia's forehead, slowly pressed each part of the animal to the corresponding part of the girl.

Julia's screams became whimpers, then moans, then she was quiet. Her eyes were open now, she was conscious, responsive, almost tranquil. Her contractions were more frequent and lasted longer, but miraculously she seemed not to be in pain, and she was holding Nina's hand firmly in her own.

By the time La Perla had touched the foot of the animal to the foot of the girl, the animal was, as Antonio had predicted, dead. She pinched it by the skin behind its neck, letting its limp body dangle. She sent Alberto into the pasture for cow dung.

She sliced the animal open with the razor, throat to tail. Among its organs she searched for evidence of Julia's illness. In its brain she found a greenish lump, an indication of jealousy. She placed the lump on the dung. She scraped gummy tissue from the hide that she said was caused by a cold. Lesions on the heart were caused by fright. Splinters in the leg were the work of *abuelos*, who probably did it at a time Julia had slept in the *puna* hut.

The tiny dead babies, each no larger than a thumbnail, she placed on the dung with the other matter. She examined the animal's every organ thoroughly and systematically. The carcass was cleaned, rubbed with oil, and dusted with flour. Then she wrapped it in paper with coca leaves and the *trago* bottle, which still contained a swallow or two. She instructed Dominga to bury the package in the *puna*. She warned her to bury it where no one would find it, and deep enough so no animal could dig it up. The sickness should not be allowed to escape into the world again, she said.

More candles were lit and spaced around Julia. Her forehead was cool, her face relaxed. Nina continued to hold her hand. The contractions were coming more quickly.

Nina didn't know where Gavilan had taken Antonio. They didn't come back. The three boys went to sleep. Bobby had pitched his tent in the yard and returned to stand in the doorway. Dominga and La Perla kept vigil by the girl. Nina went outside and crawled into the tent where Bobby had laid out her sleeping bag. It felt like she had been asleep less than a minute when she was awakened by someone shaking her. It was Bobby. "Ohhmidarlin, ohmidarlin . . ." he was singing softly. While he sang he trained a flashlight on a Polaroid picture he was holding under her nose. Nina's eyes were slow to focus. She took the picture to study it: it was of Julia, holding a baby. "OhmiDAAARlin Clem-en-tine," he sang. "She's a real little beauty," he announced. "Clementina."

THE PRESIDENTIAL SUITE

The construction crew stood with Gavilan by the wood-burning stove at one end of the long narrow room. The gray day got grayer, what you could see of it through the small, steamed-up windows. We sat, Nina and me, our backs to the wall on a bench by a long wooden table. To finally be off my feet, getting warm, to be out of that rain and gloom . . . Nina propped up her feet and shut her eyes. Her hair was wet and stringy. A drop of water hung on the end of her nose. The men talked in low voices while the rain hammered the roof. Shitfire, what a day. Long as a semester.

They brought us soup, which we drank out of cans. The building creaked and the wind blew in through the gaps between the sheets of corrugated iron. The three bare bulbs hanging from the rafters swayed and flickered. Nina bummed a smoke, took one drag, remembered she'd quit, and stubbed it out. The men, all but the one who had collared Roberto by the stove, laid bedrolls on the floor. A man in a hard hat handed us a blanket. We wrapped it around us. We were muddy, cold, sore, glad for the thin peppery soup, for a roof, for the blanket and a floor to sleep on. The lights went out.

Roberto threaded his way among the bedrolls. "Collect your things," he said. "We've got to go. Leave them some money for the soup on your way out the door."

I couldn't believe it. I couldn't believe we were going out in that downpour again. We should've listened to him in the first place. Nina and I should have taken the long way around with Antonio, the kid, and the burros, and caught up with Gavilan later, like he recommended. But I had to be a hard-ass, take his suggestion for a challenge, which maybe it was and maybe it wasn't, and now he was making us pay. Nina was a zombie. I'll admit I'd felt better myself.

Maybe the big mistake was bringing her along. She'd begged me to take her, she had no place to go, she said, she couldn't go back, Rinaldi was there, Rinaldi was waiting. I had to take her, she said, as if it were totally up to me. Then Gavilan gave his OK, and I sure as hell wasn't going to send her back, not after what that bastard had done. I'd stuck the envelope he'd handed me at his ranch in the back pocket of my jeans. It wasn't until after I'd cleared the table from that Sunday dinner, washed the dishes, until after Elena and Roberto had gone to bed that I remembered it was there. I felt it when I sat down on the wicker chair out on the porch. Inside was the single snapshot. I leaned over to hold it in the light coming out of the open door. Despite the sloppy focus, and the flash that had made the soles of his feet in the foreground white and overexposed and unnaturally big because of the weird perspective, and everything from there on back dimmer and smaller, his head looking only as big as a grapefruit, and bruised and lumpy with his eyes swollen shut from the beating he'd taken, and the dark hole in the middle of his forehead, despite all that, it was unmistakably Blacky naked on that table. And the way that hand was holding his head, by the hair, the cuff turned up on the forearm and a watch with the face rolled under the wrist, holding Blacky's head the way a hunter might show off a trophy rack—Shit. I don't know. I should've maybe listened to Blacky. Some guys took it more serious than me or him. Rinaldi maybe was one.

Gavilan tried to tell me different, that the reason was that Blacky was a Moreno, it had nothing to do with Nina and me. I shouldn't blame myself, he said. Blacky knew the risks, he said. But I remember the look on the bastard Rinaldi's face, the queer little smile he had when he handed me the picture, and I know it's on account of me it happened. I hadn't said anything to Nina yet. She had troubles of her own.

We crossed a pass in the dark and the storm and dropped down the other side, walking downhill for the first time in two days. Lightning gave us our only view of the landscape. Gavilan was somewhere up ahead. We'd been walking an hour when we caught up with him lying under a tarp tied to some bushes five yards down off the trail. He'd been waiting for us, otherwise we'd have missed him in the dark. "Get some sleep," he said. "We have another long day tomorrow."

"Here?" I said. "Here?" To put only a couple miles between us and the construction camp in order to sleep in the open didn't make sense. "If we looked a little harder maybe we could find an even more uncomfortable place to sleep," I said. "Maybe someplace with snakes."

Roberto rolled over, but I wasn't through. I admitted I was wrong, we should have maybe taken his advice, gone with Antonio like he said, but what was he trying to prove? I told him it was unfair to Nina, she wasn't in shape for this, but it was getting to me, too, walking nonstop, all day and half the night, no time to rest, no time to cook, nothing to eat, the rain, the mud. He said I was taking things too personally again, this wasn't anything he was doing to me, he was doing it for his men. He had to get back. He'd warned me. He was days overdue already. But I wasn't going to let it rest.

"You think an hour or two without you is going to make such a goddamn big difference to your men that we had to leave that camp back there where there was a fire and a roof over our heads to sleep out here in these bushes in the goddamn rain?"

Nina caught up with us. She was wearing one of those flimsy plastic ponchos you carry in your purse in case you're out shopping and there's a cloudburst. It was in shreds. She'd started the day with a plastic scarf, the kind that folds like a map to the size of a pocket comb, but it annoyed me just to look at her, and I gave her my watch cap to wear. Now, dead on her feet, she leaned against me, but I stepped aside so she'd have to support her own weight. She looked about to fall over. I wasn't done with Gavilan. "You can sleep out here if you want, but not me, bub, no way! My tent is soaked, my sleeping bag is soaked, and I'll be damned if . . ."

"They were there," he said over the sound of the rain on the tarp.

"Who was?"

"Soldiers. At the construction camp. Looking for Moreno. It wasn't safe. They might've come back."

I was still wet and I was still angry and I had the thought maybe he was just saying that to calm me down. I was going to find another place to sleep regardless. I'd be back, I told them, and they agreed we'd move the camp if I found any better place within half an hour's walk. If not, we'd spend the night where we were.

Without that waterlogged pack to carry, the going was easier, although the rain wasn't letting up, was if anything, coming harder. I'd been walking less than twenty minutes when I saw a house off to the side of the trail and up a short rise. If it hadn't lightninged, I'd never have seen it, would have passed it by. No door, no glass in the windows, no shutters. Looked abandoned to me. "Anybody home?" I yelled. Lots of people here lived in places that looked abandoned to me.

Inside I heard something scratch across the floor, mouse, I figured, and caught a whiff of urine. I lit a match, saw a table, a candle, and nothing else, lit a second, saw a fire pit, a pile of wood, caught a stronger hit of urine, and backed out the door holding my breath. At least we would be under a roof, I thought, and we'd have a fire. Maybe the smoke would smother the stink.

Nina was sitting up shivering when I got back. Roberto was sleeping, how I don't know. Nina had that worthless poncho at least, but Gavilan had nothing for the rain. "Let's go," I said. Roberto objected, said that houses were never abandoned, that anyone traveling the trail would stop at that house. "They'd be out of luck," I told him. "I put a deposit down." I pulled Nina to her feet. Roberto caught us a few minutes later. "I don't mind you crashing with us tonight, Roberto, but we got dibs on the double bed. Maybe they'll move a cot in for you."

"You don't know what you're doing," he said.

"I know enough to get in out of the rain. What the hell kind of country is this gonna be when you guys take over? Don't know enough to get out of the rain."

They followed me inside. "This is it. The presidential suite. The complimentary bottle of Dom and fresh-cut flowers"—I struck a match and lit the candle—"are on the . . ." There was a man with a gun standing five feet away.

"I'll take that," he said. "The matches, too, if you don't mind." He spoke with an accent, Aussie or Kiwi. He had the candle in one hand, the gun in the other. "Mine are damp. I'll tell you that an hour ago I wouldn't have given much for my chances of a cigarette tonight." South African, I decided, but it may have been the bush jacket that made me think that. I backed up toward the door and backed into Nina. "No, no, no, no," he said. "Please, come in. I allowed you to leave once already tonight, and I mustn't let you slip away again." He pointed the gun to where he wanted us to stand against the wall. He searched us, found Gavilan's pistol, and sat us down on the floor. "And who might you be?"

"Trekkers." I said the first thing that entered my mind.

"You must be very hardy indeed to trek in the rain." He was looking through my pack. "Who's the photographer? You?"

"Birds," I said.

"And the gun your companion is carrying?" He reached under Roberto's sweater. "Also for birds?"

"We'd heard rumors."

"I see," he said.

"Liar!" Nina shouted so loud and so unexpected it made me jump. She pointed a finger at me. Then she ran across the room and dropped to her knees in front of him. "He's lying. They're Zapato Moreno. They killed my fiancé and then they kidnapped me. You've got to help me! Please!" She was sobbing. She had both arms around his leg. He was holding the candle over his head as if he suspected that that was what she was after, but he kept the gun pointed at us. "Please, help me! He's lying to you, can't you see he's lying to you? Don't let them take me. Don't let them!"

He shook free of her, stepped back, left her crying in the dirt between us. Nice try, Nina, I thought.

"Why don't you tell me all about it, miss . . . ," he said. Nina raised herself up and moved toward him. "From there, if you don't mind," he said.

"I am Nina Alicia Renata Isabel DeBettencourt. That one, he's Moreno. He calls himself Roberto, but I don't think that's his real name. The other one is Shafto. He's a journalist, a sympathizer. You must have read about me in the newspapers. They've kidnapped me. They're holding me for ransom. You have to help me. Please. I beg you."

Roberto didn't say a word. He leaned against the wall with his arms folded across his chest. His eyes were half-closed. He seemed bored, ready to go to sleep. Nina was sobbing and begging, groveling, a first-rate performance. She crawled over to him, clutched his leg, rested her head on his shoe. I took a step in her direction, and she screamed. He backed me against the wall with the gun.

"She's raving, you can see that," I said. I could improvise too. "She fell in the stream this afternoon, she hit her head on a boulder, she's sick, we're trekkers . . ."

Nina turned and pointed at me. "Don't you dare say I'm raving!" She attacked me like a wild woman. I held her wrists and then she kicked at me, caught me on the shin, and I had no choice but to push her away, throw her down. I threw her a little harder than I meant to, but I was getting angry, and I was already scared, and I couldn't tell anymore, I wasn't sure she was acting or not. From down on the ground, very calmly, very evenly, like a normal person, she said, "They planted a bomb which killed my fiancé. They've kidnapped me. They're going to kill me next." She stood beside him and pointed across at us.

"I don't know who you are," he said. "You might be Moreno. For all I know you may even be trekkers as you claim, but in any event, whoever you are, you've made an unfortunate blunder in stumbling in here. As a result it's going to be a long night for all of us. But at least for you it will be dryer than it might otherwise have been, and for me"—he held up the matches—"a fire, a cigarette, company . . . And in the morning, when my, ah . . . associates arrive, they'll know better what to do with you. In the meantime, if you don't mind, you can get the fire going."

He watched us from across the room. Nina sat nearby, crying. She was good all right. Roberto and I sat beside each other against the far wall. He seemed dazed, indifferent. We sat that way a while watching each other across the fire. Nina quit her sobbing routine. She appeared to be asleep. I went over to her. He waved the gun at me, but I ignored him, put my hand on her shoulder, said her name. She gave me one look and started the screaming again. She was really good, really convincing.

She scuttled across the dirt floor to where he was sitting. "Don't let him touch me!" She was hysterical. "Keep him away!" She pressed up against him.

She was getting to him. "It's all right. Calm down," he said.

"Promise me!" She had him by the front of his jacket.

He pushed her away. "Stop that screaming! I can't stand screaming." Nina stopped. He pulled down on the tails of his jacket.

"That's better." He held up his hand as if taking an oath. "You can calm down. I promise. Just no more screaming."

She hugged him. He tried to push her away, but she clung to him. In that instant Roberto was on his feet and running. He leapt the fire while the guy was trying to pull out of Nina's grasp. He swiped at her with the gun and she fell, holding her head. A step away, Roberto stopped short, the gun in his face. He raised his hands and backed off.

"That's right. Back where you were. Back up. Keep going. All the way back. Now sit down. The next person who moves gets shot." He was very nervous now. The gun shook in his hand.

Nina held her head. Blood trickled from a cut above her eye. She seemed very calm now, or more likely stunned. "Give me the gun, you coward," she said quietly. "Give it to me. I'll shoot him, if you won't. I'm not afraid. Give it to me."

"I've had enough of you," he said. "Of all of you. Sit over there," he said to Nina, pointing at a place away from him and away from us, too.

He put some wood on the fire, sat down, and took an aspirin bottle out of a pocket. He tapped a mound of powder into his hand and sucked two helpings into his nose, killing any hope I had that he might fall asleep. He grew fidgety. He took my pack and emptied it onto the table. He looked at my gear. "Nikon, eh? I prefer Leica myself."

"May I have a cigarette, please?" Nina asked.

"You'll behave yourself?"

"You do believe me, don't you?" she said. "It was in all the papers. About the bombing. About me." She combed her hair with her fingers, dragged on the cigarette.

"Sorry, dear. Where I've been, the newspapers don't deliver."

"On the radio, then?"

He shook his head. "It's all bad news. I never listen."

"Then your friends, they'll know. You can ask them. My family is very prominent. DeBettencourt. It was in all the papers."

He fed the fire. He fed his nose. Roberto had pulled his hat down over his eyes. Nina began to whimper again. "You can't. You can't let them take me."

"They'll be here in a few hours. If they're Moreno, as you claim, my associates will know. As I understand it, they've had some problems with the Moreno. They may even let you use the gun."

"You do believe me, then?"

He nodded.

"Thank you, thank you. You don't know how much it means to me." She hugged him. He never took his eyes off us. "They're horrible. They were going to kill me, I'm sure of it. I'm so relieved. You won't be sorry. I don't care anything about what business you're in. I'll do anything for you, money, whatever you want. You'll see. But you must help me. You must."

"It'll all be settled in the morning, one way or another." He took the aspirin bottle from his pocket. "Care for any?" Nina closed a nostril with a finger and inhaled. She put her arm around his shoulders.

"You see that one, the dark greasy one. I want to shoot him myself. Do you really think your friends will let me? He's a bastard, that one."

"And the other one?"

"Do what you like with him. He hasn't brains enough to be much trouble to anyone. All he cares about are his cameras. Ask him to show you his cameras."

"I've already seen them."

"Ask him to take a picture of us."

"Us?

"You and me."

"Why would I do that?"

"Why not?"

"The lady would like you to take a picture," he said to me.

"Tell the bitch to take her own fucking picture," I said. Blacky was right. I should have listened to Blacky. If I'd have listened to Blacky none of this would have happened.

"I don't think you understand. The lady says she would like you to take a picture. I'm not asking you, I'm telling you."

I picked up the Polaroid. Roberto tilted back his hat. Nina had her arm around the asshole.

"I'm not ready yet," she said.

I held the camera up to my eye. I moved them into focus, centered them in the frame.

"Take it already," he said.

"Don't rush me," I said.

"Closer," she said. "I want a close-up." I took a step toward them. "Closer." I walked to within four feet of the barrel of the gun.

"Back off," he said.

"Not too far," she said.

"Hurry up," he said.

The instant the flash popped, Nina grabbed his hand. Red flame shot from the muzzle. Roberto dived past me. There was another shot. Nina screamed. The motor whirred and the picture slid out the camera. Then it was quiet again.

He was seated on the floor against the wall, his eyes open wide, his legs stretched out in front of him. A red flower blossomed on the front of his safari jacket. Roberto held the gun. Nina had turned her back to the wall.

"Dead?" she asked. Her voice was flat.

"We'd better go," Roberto said.

"Is he dead? Tell me," Nina insisted.

"He's dead," I said.

"That's all I wanted to know."

She'd butchered chickens, eviscerated calves, drowned kittens, shot birds by the hundred, skinned game, pulled dead rats from traps, crushed a cockroach in her fist. She was raised on a ranch and she wasn't squeamish, but she'd never touched a dead body before, a human body, much less a body she had played a part in killing, and she surprised herself at how willing she was to put her hands on this one, to slide her hand into his pockets, to feel his still-warm thigh, to touch his chest through his bloody shirt. The craving she had for a cigarette was stronger than any revulsion she felt at the look and feel of a corpse. She threw the money, the passport, and the aspirin bottle on the table, and put the cigarettes in her pocket after shaking one out and lighting it. American cigarettes. On occasion she'd said she'd kill for one. Now she had, and she wasn't particularly sorry.

They were in a rush to leave. Whoever was meeting him could come at any time and they didn't want to be there when they did. Gavilan snatched the man's pack, an army rucksack full of cash, as well as the money she'd thrown on the table, the passport, and the gun. He threw the aspirin bottle on the fire and Bobby burned his fingers pulling it out.

All day long she'd been cursing the rain, but now she welcomed it. She was invigorated, glad to be out of that stale, smoky house and on the move. On little food and less sleep, with the bump on her brow where he'd hit her, still she was glad to be outside and moving. They walked through a featureless landscape, the dark closing in to where she could only sense the path under her feet and confirm the presence of the other two by the splash of their boots in the puddles.

The rain slowed to a drizzle, turned to mist, then stopped altogether. The clouds parted and scattered, and between the clouds were stars. She discovered that rhythm was the trick to the mountain paths, that a steady pace, no matter how slow, worked better than any combination of sprint and rest. She also knew that they would wait for her. Before, she hadn't been sure.

The first light showed the outline of the mountains, jagged and dark beneath a clear pale dome. Above them was the deep v in the ridge toward which they climbed, traversing an endless series of switchbacks. She passed Bobby vomiting off to the side of the trail. Gavilan was somewhere above. Fifteen minutes later, in the full light of morning, the sun astride the ridge line, she reached his stance. He sat with his back against a boulder, the rucksack at his feet.

"Nice morning," he said.

Bobby was still well below them, so Roberto was talking to her, but she checked over her shoulder just to be sure. Since leaving Mirasol he had been remote, imperious. She took a swallow from her canteen. He asked for a drink, surprising her again, and she hesitated, not because she was unwilling to share the water, but because his tone was new, friendlier. He misread her reticence.

"Never mind," he said and withdrew his hand. "I can wait. There's a river we have to cross this afternoon. I can get a drink there."

"Don't be such a jerk," she said. She handed him the bottle. He tilted back his head, closed his eyes, and swallowed. He wiped his mouth with the back of his hand.

"You were really something last night," he said. "I'm an actor myself. I know something of what's involved."

"I thought you were a trekking guide," she said.

He ignored her baiting tone. "You saved our necks back there."

Nina screwed the lid on the canteen. That makes us even, she thought. She stared off down the hill. She saw Bobby making slow progress, bent under the load on his back, and far down below him she saw specks of color move out of shadow into the sunlight. She pointed.

"His 'associates,'" Gavilan said. "Coming for this." He touched the rucksack with his boot.

"How do you know?"

"I know."

"How far are they behind us?"

"An hour. Two."

They waited for Bobby and gauged the progress of their pursuers. Gavilan broke the silence which Nina had set by her abruptness. "There's something I want to tell you. Do you want to hear?"

"Depends," she said, already on the defensive.

"When I saw you in the plaza I noticed something about you besides your . . ." he held out his hand palm up and gestured from her head to her feet. "Besides the obvious."

She brushed her hair off her forehead. She felt a knot of suspicion form in her chest, as she always did when she thought she was about to be flattered.

"There were your looks, of course, and the kind of confidence that comes from being admired, and I wondered what would happen if suddenly the admiration stopped."

His deferential tone had belied his meaning. Nina felt she had been tricked. "I've been wondering, too," she said. "I wondered if they're all as full of shit as you."

He laughed. He hadn't laughed often. Even Bobby, from two switchbacks below, stopped and looked up at them. Gavilan laughed longer and more heartily than seemed warranted by her meager sarcasm. She wondered if those slow-moving specks down in the valley could hear the laughter of this presumptuous, brave, filthy person. She couldn't help herself from smiling, too, but she didn't let him see, she bent her head pretending to examine her canteen.

"Do you always make these lightning judgments?" A tinge of sarcasm she didn't intend remained in her voice. It was becoming habitual, and she didn't like it.

"Making them, changing them," he said. "I had to change my judgment of you." He thought for a moment. "I saw you had a vision of yourself."

"Oh, this is very very deep," Nina said, avoiding his gaze.

"Let me say that I saw you were aware of some possibilities. Is that any better?"

"And what else did you see?"

"That you'd never been defeated. That was the most unusual thing about you. I don't know anyone gets to be your age—what are you? twenty-two?—who hasn't been defeated yet."

"How long did it take you to 'see' all this?"

"I don't know. It's a feeling I get."

"A feeling?" Sarcasm clung to her words. She was interested, but some part of her insisted on pretending she wasn't. Worse, she was sure the pretense was transparent.

"Almost everything worth knowing about a person, you can learn in a very short period of time," he said. "The rest is confirmation. With you there was something I missed."

"Because I'm so extraordinarily complex, I suppose?"

"You've known sadness, but not defeat. I was right about that. Sadness is a form of self-pity. Defeat implies a goal, a trial, sacrifice, suffering."

What do you know about my trials? Nina thought bitterly. My suffering. My heartache? She picked up a stone.

"And then I knew your vision wasn't clear. You sense something is out there for you, out beyond the story of your life, but you don't know how to get to it. It's there and you know it, drifting, sometimes quite close, sometimes it seems as if it were all around you, but always just out of reach."

She tossed away the stone she was holding and searched for another between her feet. "And it floats on a cloud and has wings and a halo." She pretended to pluck at strings.

"Yes, that's it! That's exactly right. It is a kind of angel," he said. He knew she was being facetious, but chose to ignore it. "And this angel is calling to you. You hear it, and you'd like to answer, to go to it, the problem is you don't know how."

"But you do, I suppose."

"That's right. I do," he said, and he laughed. "You have to fly," he said, and he laughed again so that she didn't know if she was being put on or not. "But you know you can't fly, right? It's crazy. Who can fly? Not you, you're sure of that. So you don't even make the attempt. The sad part is you think the angel will call to you another time."

"Are you finished?" she asked.

"I'm finished. It wasn't as hard to say as I thought. Did it make any sense to you?"

"Not in the least."

"Well, I tried," he said. He laughed again.

"But suppose it did. Why are you telling me this?"

"Because it's something you should know."

She shrugged. She put her canteen back in her pack.

"That's just what I'm talking about," he said. "What you just did." He stood right over her. "The most interesting subject in the world to you is yourself. You think about yourself constantly. Isn't that right? So why pretend this bores you?"

"Why don't you tell me? You're the one with all the answers." She glared at him. He looked away, sat back down against the rock. Her triumph felt empty. She shouldered her pack.

"You need to be defeated, that's all." His voice was apologetic. "I'm telling you the only thing I know, in the only way I know how to say it. You should welcome defeat, you should court it."

She was glad when Bobby dropped his pack beside them and flopped on the ground, ending the conversation. Gavilan asked for Bobby's camera with a telephoto lens. He looked at the four men slowly advancing up the trail below them. They each took a look through the lens. Bobby rolled his eyes back. "Just what a guy who's started his day at four A.M. by blowing lunch all over his shoes wants to see. Listen, Roberto . . ." Gavilan, who had already started up the trail, turned around. "About last night . . ."

"Everyone makes mistakes," Gavilan said, cutting him off. "Don't hang around long." His eyes indicated their pursuers.

They reached the ridge and dropped down the other side. They left the main trail. They followed the rim of a canyon above a green, slow-moving river. In the distance, but now not so far behind, they could see their pursuers.

The country was open, with no place to hide. On their left was the canyon. The walls were sheer with no obvious way down to the water. On their right was a barren plain, and in front, still some distance away, a steep slope of talus. In an hour a buttress rose to their right, cutting them off from the plain. The river ran unseen below and to their left. As they walked they were squeezed between the buttress on one side and the canyon on the other. The trail became a ledge, in places a single body-width wide, cut into the vertical mountain wall. Every step required concentration. By now they'd been walking eighteen hours on no sleep and no food except the soup at the construction camp. The sky was clear, the sun high and hot. What renewal Nina had felt on leaving the house early that morning was gone, replaced by anxious dread, by a thirsty, sweaty discomfort and insistent pain. With her eyes on the path, she almost walked into Gavilan. In front of them the trail had collapsed into the canyon. There was a gap, an interruption of fifty feet before the trail resumed again. Nina eased herself down with her back against the mountain and her legs across the path, her feet jutting into the empty air above the river.

"What now?" Bobby said. "We sure can't go that way." He looked out to where the trail had slid away. "And we can't go back." He indicated the four men with a jerk of his head. They couldn't see them, but they knew they were close. The gap had been narrowing all afternoon. Bobby grabbed hold of a rock on the wall over his head and tested it with his weight. It pulled out in his hand. He tried another with the same result. "Rotten," he said. "Unclimbable." He pitched it out and they watched it sail over the gorge and drop out of sight.

"Doesn't leave us much choice," Gavilan said.

"Only one." Bobby removed the rope from his pack.

"Down?" Nina asked.

"Down it is," Bobby said.

From where they were, there was a forty-foot drop to a second ledge, below which—they couldn't see how far below—was the river. Bobby tossed another rock out into the clear bright sunshine. Nina leaned over the edge to watch it. Nausea swept over her. She sat back, closed her eyes, and listened, but never heard it hit.

The problem, as she understood it, was whether the rope, 165 feet of it, was long enough to reach the bottom of the gorge. She had nothing to contribute to the discussion and momentarily wondered whether it might not be better to surrender to the cocainistas rather than go down that rope, which Bobby, apparently having decided was in fact long enough, was knotting around the single sturdy flake he found in the wall. He threw the rope out so it uncoiled neatly as it dropped and disappeared. He pulled on it. The knot held; the flake didn't budge. Next he undid the strap from his pack and retied it in a loop, which he put around Nina's waist, brought up between her legs, and fastened with a carabiner the way the corners of a diaper are fastened with a safety pin.

She watched with foreboding. Her fear swallowed her strength and her will to resist. Bobby wove the rope through a system of interlocking carabiners. He explained everything as he went along, but the words left no impression on Nina. The very thought of stepping off the edge, of hanging on the rope, of lowering herself down to the river seemed to sap the last of her strength, to leave her in limbo. He was telling her how easy it was, that the configuration of hardware attached to her did all the work. "The harness can hold a truck," he said. "Concentrate on staying upright, on fending yourself off the wall with your feet, on paying the rope out slowly." He brought her to the edge, and she stood with her back to the canyon, to empty space. "Now take a step back."

She was numb. She looked over her shoulder and down. "I can't," she said. She stepped away from the edge.

"You have to," Bobby said backing her up. "What about all those trees you told me you climbed when you were a kid? Think about them." She did. It didn't help. She was a different person then.

"They're on their way," Gavilan said.

"No choice, Nina. You got to go," Bobby said. He had her lie on her stomach with her legs over the edge. He held her hand. Her toes searched the cliff for a foothold and found a place wide enough for the ball of her foot. She held on to the rope with one hand and clung to Bobby with the other. "I'm going to let go now," Bobby said. He pried her fingers off, but she clutched his ankle. He spun away and she grabbed for the edge.

She tried to shinny back onto the ledge. Gavilan pushed Bobby aside. Nina thought he was going to reason with her. "Is your hand on the rope?" he asked. She nodded. "Feet on the wall?" Hopeful, she nodded again. "Then we'll see you at the bottom," he said, and he stepped on her fingers. She screamed and pulled her hand away. Her feet slipped and she fell. The rope slid through her hand. The friction seared her palm. She yanked hard. The rope jerked. It stretched, and she bounced, swung, and banged the wall with her shoulder and hip. She had fallen thirty feet. The harness had gathered painfully in her crotch. Her hand burned. She opened her eyes, looked up, and saw them looking down at her, saw the rope wearing a groove in the dirt where it came over the lip. The sun and the sting of sweat and tears made her blink. She looked at the red slash across her palm.

"Put your feet flat against the wall. Sit back, walk yourself down a step at a time." Bobby sounded miles away, a small voice from out of the sky. "Let the rope slide through your fingers."

She descended foot by foot. The rope held. Her feet on the wall in front of her kept her from spinning, her hand on the rope above her kept her upright, her hand on the rope below checked her speed. She reached the ledge they had seen from above. It was wide enough to stand. She could see the river now, green and slow and shimmering. While her weight was off the rope, she pulled the straps out of the crease between her legs, wiped her sweaty palms, and then backed off again. She pushed with her feet, eased the rope inch by inch through her fingers, and worked her way down to a second ledge, really just a bulge protruding from the sheer rock face. Below it, the canyon wall was undercut. The rope fell free sixty feet to the river. Without her feet on the rock to control her, she began to spin in slow circles. She was directly over the river. She was going to land in the river. She was going to swim. Thirty feet above the water, having reached the end of the rope, she learned that not only was she going to swim, first she was going to fall.

The cold was a shock. It took the little breath she had. Weighed down by her clothes and her pack, she fought toward the sunlight, but the surface came no closer. Her arms were caught in the straps. She couldn't lift her arms. She swallowed water. She choked. She was sure she was going to drown. Then something grabbed her by her jacket and pulled her to her feet. Her face broke into the sunlight. She gasped, blinked.

"Stand up," a voice said. "Stand up!"

She staggered onto the sandy beach. Antonio dropped her pack at her feet and waded back out. He pulled her floating canteen from the slow-moving current and tossed it onto the sand.

From the beach, she watched as Gavilan dropped below the bulge where the rock was undercut. He hadn't a harness and rigging like Bobby had made for her. The rope ran through his legs and over his shoulder in a way that somehow slowed his descent. He reached the end of the rope and dropped off, kicking as he fell.

He made a huge splash when he hit. Antonio and Augusto fished him out. He sat on the beach beside Nina.

"We saw them," he said, breathing hard. "Right behind us." They watched Bobby coming down. Nina worried that they would cut the rope with Bobby on it, or that they'd use it themselves to follow. Bobby seemed to be taking a long time to get down.

"Wetting it with fuel," Gavilan panted. "From his stove. Be sure it would burn."

Bobby held himself for a moment near the end of the rope. He let his pack fall into the river. He let himself go. There was a whoosh of flame as he came off. The rope burned like a fuse. Drops of burning, melting nylon plopped and steamed in the river. When his head broke the surface he was smiling.

As long as the sun stayed in the narrow slot between the walls above them, they basked on the beach. Their clothes dried on their bodies. Antonio built a fire from driftwood on a sandy bank upriver from where they went in. Bobby spread out his tent. They took the soggy stacks of money out of the rucksack and separated the bills, laying them flat and weighting them with rocks.

"How much do you suppose is there?" Bobby asked. Gavilan said it looked like a lot, but the denominations were small, some worth less than a dime. He guessed not more than a thousand dollars. Antonio and Augusto, neither of whom had seen more than a few dollars at any one time, seemed unimpressed. They didn't trust currency and themselves transacted their business only in coins. Bobby asked Nina what she'd do if the money were hers, and she said that since there wasn't enough to buy back her father's farm, or get a place of her own, or go to school, she wasn't sure. Bobby said he'd blow it all on a fast telephoto lens.

"Your cameras!" Nina said, suddenly remembering that Bobby's pack had, like everything else, gone into the river.

"Dry as a bone," Bobby said. "Wrapped them in Ziploc bags." He asked Antonio what he would do with the money, and Antonio said he didn't want it. He didn't want to happen to him what had happened to Theofilo. He explained the system by which the wealthiest men in the village were required to pay for community projects which sometimes bankrupted them and forced them to go to the sugarcane fields to work. It was their way of seeing that no one man accumulated too much wealth. If a person happened to prosper, all he could do was buy another house, or a piece of land, and there was no more land for sale.

"But suppose the money was yours to spend?" Bobby asked.

A new blade for his plow, Antonio said, and he added, a loom, a radio, and a team of oxen, if there were enough.

"What if you *could* buy a good piece of land?" Nina said. "Someplace level and fertile."

Antonio answered that if there were a piece available, a really good piece, and if he could afford it, he would forget the plow and the team. He would, in fact, forget the land altogether. He would open a store in a town instead, live like Enrique Moon, and never dirty his hands again.

Nina asked Gavilan what he had planned for it. "Guns?"

Gavilan answered her as if she had asked sincerely. It was easier to take weapons from the police, he told her, than to find a place to buy them and then transport them to the mountains. He said that the money wasn't all that useful. There wasn't much to spend it on. "What we need, they won't sell to us, not at any price. Ask Antonio," he said. They took the money not because they had immediate use for it, but because that kept it out of the hands of the cocainistas, who did.

"Where does it go?" Nina asked. "Or is that none of my business?"

"We used to get it to Blacky. He disbursed it. To the families of the men. To Padre Elio."

"Is there any left?"

"Blacky invested it."

The mention of Blacky jolted Bobby. He couldn't sit with the feeling. He had to make a joke. "Shame, shame, shame. Marx wouldn't like it," Bobby said. "What do you think, Augusto? What should we do with the money?"

"The Feast of Santo Rosario," Gusto said without hesitation. If there were any left he'd buy himself a horse, a fast one, nothing like these dusty, plodding donkeys, and maybe a knife. He could whittle a flute for Alberto.

The shadow crossed the river, moved onto the sand, fell over them, and climbed up the canyon wall. The day turned instantly cold. They drank hot tea and discussed the possibilities. Nina said that the money was in part rightfully hers, she had helped steal it, and she voted that it be given to the village for the feast. Bobby concurred. Gavilan, thinking this might be his opportunity to establish a beachhead, said he would give Viracocha the money to pay for the feast on two conditions: that they sell him provisions at fair market value when there was a surplus to sell, and that he be given the right to name a representative to oversee the planning and the expenditure of the money. Antonio said that he had no authority to speak for the village, but that as a friend of the mayor, he would pass the offer on.

Although they hadn't eaten since the soup the night before at the construction camp at San Gerais, Gavilan was insistent they eat no more than a single day's ration. They ate potatoes roasted on the coals, and cornmeal boiled with water and powdered milk. Bobby set up the tent, which by that time had dried. Augusto, squatting on his haunches, watched the yellow nylon bubble rise over the flexible aluminum poles. He tested the smooth, taut skin with a finger. Nina sat with Gavilan and Antonio by the fire. Clouds rolled over their narrow band of sky. The river turned gray and the wind ruffled its surface and stung their skin with sand.

Lit from within by a flashlight tied at its peak, the tent glowed in the darkness. The silhouettes of Bobby and the boy played on the yellow wall. Nina unzipped the door and crawled inside. Antonio followed. Gavilan stayed by the fire. Someone had to stay on guard, he said. He would take the first watch himself, although he had no intention of sleeping inside the tent anyway. He had violated his principles by not insisting they sleep outside the previous night, and he was not about to do it again.

Antonio lay on his side with his head propped in his hand, and the boy, who was eating a candy bar, lay inside the curve of his father's body. Augusto passed his father a piece of the chocolate Bobby had put out on his sleeping bag along with the rest of his supply of treats and his cameras. Help yourself, he'd told the kid, but so far Augusto had risked only the chocolate. The dried fruit, the nuts, these were too exotic.

Augusto watched while Bobby wiped each piece of equipment, explained its use, and then carefully replaced it in its own plastic bag. When Augusto reached for a light meter, Bobby told him not only what a light meter did, and how it did it, but how important it was to him, and how expensive (as much as two donkeys), how delicate, that it was irreplaceable. It was meant as a subtle warning. Augusto listened politely, got the message, but wasn't interested in the meter after all. He wanted the Ziploc bag. Bobby inflated it and improvised a balloon, which he and Augusto batted back and forth between them. When they were tired of the game, Bobby gave the bag to Augusto, which he accepted with obvious pleasure and handed to his father, who tucked it under his sweater.

A sand-laden gust hit the tent, reminding Nina of Gavilan standing guard outside. He refused her invitation to come in. Bobby made hot chocolate, which like the other treats was from his personal stash, to celebrate the birth of Julia's baby, their escape, and the reunion with Antonio and Augusto. He passed around dried pineapple. Augusto watched his father try it first before he ventured to put a piece in his own mouth. Nina took a piece out to Gavilan, who put it in his pocket. "Camilo has a sweet tooth," he said. "I'll save it for him." She left him by the fire.

"We need some more water for cocoa," Bobby said. "Who's going to the river? How about you, Augusto? Fill up the pot."

No. The boy shook his head.

"Go on. Just down to the river."

The boy refused.

Bobby raised his voice. "If you want the cocoa you got to get the water."

Nina said that she would go, but Bobby said no, he had asked Augusto.

"He said he doesn't want to," Nina said. "Don't make an issue of this, Bobby. He's just a kid. He doesn't want to. I'll go. It's no big deal."

Bobby insisted. "I gave him chocolate, I offered him pineapple, cashews, I gave him a goddamn course in photography. I even gave him a plastic bag. Now I offer him cocoa, which I am not obligated to share with anybody, I carried it all the way the hell up here myself, and all I ask him to do is walk thirty feet to the river for water for his own goddamn cup of cocoa and what does he say? He says no."

Nina unzipped the tent door. "You're making too much of this. Give the pot to me."

"Do you want the cocoa?" he said to Augusto. Augusto only glared at him. "Then go down to the goddamn river for water."

"Bobby, you don't understand," Nina said.

"I understand perfectly. He takes me for a chump. Look at him looking at me."

"You *are* a chump. He's a little boy. He's afraid to go down to the river. He thinks there are monsters in the river."

Bobby considered the possibility, then decided against it. "Augusto? Afraid? Nah. No way. He's not afraid of monsters. The kid's out here roaming around the mountains with revolutionaries, *drug* smugglers for chrissake, he does a day's worth of work a union man at home doesn't do in a week, and you're telling me he's afraid of monsters. Get real. Stubborn is what he is."

"You don't have to take my word for it. Ask him yourself. Go ahead."

"You scared of monsters, Augusto?"

The kid only glared.

"Antonio," Bobby said. "Is he? Yes or no?"

"Demons," said Antonio. "*Pishtaku.* Things his mother tells him. They grab children at night, boil them, and sell their fat in the capital. Right, Augusto? *Pishtaku?*" The boy put his face in his father's chest. "His mother told him."

With the pot bubbling and the steam rising and the smell of cocoa, the tent was a cozy place. They drank from two cups, passing them around the circle in opposite directions, each of them taking a sip of the cocoa and then passing it on. Nina took a cup out to Gavilan.

"Anything prowling around out here?" she asked. Gavilan shook his head. "No cocainistas? No *pishtaku?*"

"There are plenty *pishtaku*," he said. "You couldn't pay me enough to go down to that river at night. You've got more nerve than I thought."

She sat with her back against the canyon wall. The wind kicked sparks out of the fire, and the water lapped on the sand. She lit a cigarette with the glowing end of a stick.

"Roberto, I want to ask you a question."

"Ask."

"If you're not who they say you are, and you haven't done what they say you've done . . ."

"*Most* we haven't done."

"Then who are you and what are you doing here?"

"We're fugitives. We're trying to save our skins," he said simply.

"I would think if that's all you were trying to do that you would just disappear someplace. There are no shortages of places to lose yourself. It must be something else."

"There's no way you would understand," he said, unwilling to be drawn further into the conversation with her. He remembered the talk they'd had in the morning.

"Give me the chance. I want to know."

"Fate, then."

"Fate's not an answer."

"Some things aren't within our understanding."

"Make me understand."

"I can't. You do or you don't. A person goes through life, he sees certain things, another person sees different things."

Snow began to blow. Nina walked beyond the sphere of firelight to the water's edge. Wind through the canyon whistled and chafed the surface of the river. She returned with an armload of driftwood. A storm was moving in. She turned up the collar on her coat and moved closer to the fire. "Gavilan isn't your name. It isn't your real name, is it?"

"It's the name I'm known by."

"Who were you before you were Gavilan?"

"It doesn't matter."

"To me it does."

"Before I came to the mountains, I was nothing, a nobody."

"You won't tell me, then."

"I told you. You didn't listen." Gavilan watched the fire.

"I know that I can't continue with you and Bobby," Nina changed the subject. "I'm going back with Antonio tomorrow. He said I could stay with him and his family, and I was thinking, as long as I was going to be in Viracocha, I'd like to be of use to somebody, so I wouldn't feel like I was just running away, do you know what I mean?"

Gavilan had been leaning on the rucksack full of cash. He pulled it out from behind him and tossed it at her feet.

"Thanks," she said.

"I'm glad you asked. I wasn't sure how I was going to convince you. Now you ought to get some sleep. We're going to have to share the watch. Someone else will have to take over from me in an hour."

"I have one more question." She waited for him to give her some sign that it was all right to continue.

He nodded.

"At the hotel. After the bombing, and your hand, you said you had something to tell me, and then Bobby came back with the padre and we left in a hurry and you never got the chance. Do you still want to?"

"It's about Alejandro. His death. Are you sure you want to hear?"

She wasn't sure. "I think so."

"I—we, the Moreno—have been blamed. I think you know now it wasn't us."

Nina's thoughts shot back to the morning at Mirasol. How did he know what she knew? Then she remembered Luís skulking around, eavesdropping, lying about it, driving off in a hurry. Luís. "How do I know it wasn't you?" she tested him.

"You were with me in Marcara. You know we didn't plant the bomb that killed that little kid"—Gavilan held up his bandaged hand—"but the government says we did, says we claimed responsibility. We didn't plant any bomb at your family's farm, either. I wanted you to know."

"Why? Why was it so important? What am I to you?"

"Nothing, really. I saw your picture in the newspaper, one taken at the funeral. But I knew Alejandro, and I wanted you to know how sorry I was, and that no matter what they say, I wasn't the one responsible."

That Gavilan claimed to know Alejandro was for some reason shocking to her. She was put on guard, wary that she was about to learn yet another piece of information that would turn her world upside down, would again drive the point home that she was as easily tricked as a child.

"I—I don't understand," she stammered. She searched for some plausible connection between this man sitting by the fire and Alejandro, her playmate since childhood, her fiancé. Maybe Gavilan had been a hand on the farm, had been one of the many who'd come and gone? Was that the link? A tremor of apprehension passed through her.

"Alejandro was involved with Indian rights. At the university. He'd met with Padre Elio several times. I was at one of those meetings. I liked him. I'm sorry what happened. I wanted you to know."

"He never told me," she said. "I mean, I knew he was involved in politics, but he never said exactly . . ."

"He didn't want you to know. He was afraid to tell you. He had helped to organize the farm workers on the sugarcane plantations down on the coast. Their next target was the workers on the big haciendas in the sierra. Like his father's. And yours."

Nina had imagined nothing like this. When Alejandro had said he was becoming involved in politics, she'd assumed he meant something like student government, or the fraternity council. But organizing the farm workers? The Farm Workers Alliance? It had been the big issue among all the ranchers in the sierra, at least until the Moreno supplanted it. Her father hated the union; he believed it to be the first step in an agricultural reform that led toward a redistribution of the land and ultimately spelled the end of their way of life. For good reason, Alejandro had been vague about what kind of politics he was into. Her father would have withdrawn his consent to the marriage had he known. And Rinaldi—Her mind raced ahead. "Are you saying . . . ?" She could not bring herself to voice the question. It was bad enough that Rinaldi had been behind the bombing, but to think that he deliberately set out to murder his own son . . . "That Colonel Rinaldi . . . his own father . . . because of Alejandro's union activities . . . ?"

"No. I think it was an accident. I think Alejandro was in the wrong place at the wrong time. Padre Elio guesses he had come to the ranch to find you, to tell you what he was doing. Alejandro had told the padre that he had decided to give you the chance to decide if you still wanted to marry him. They talked about it together. I think your father's ranch was chosen because he was among the most outspoken opponents of the Alliance, and if the Moreno were tied to the union movement the ranchers would not only support martial law in the province, they would demand it. That's what I wanted to tell you. You should know Alejandro was more than you believed him to be. I think he had decided to tell you himself when —You know the rest."

"I don't know what to say." Nina stood up, brushed the sand from the back of her pants. "Excuse me—I think I'll take a walk by the water. I—"

"He was a man of strong convictions," Gavilan said. "I admired him."

"Thank you. I'm going to take that walk now," she said and backed out of the firelight.

"Where you been?" Bobby asked when Nina crawled inside the tent followed by a swirl of spindrift. "Am I glad you're back. Hurry up, zip the door, you're letting in all the snow." He spoke in English. Usually they spoke in Spanish.

"*Son las once,*" Augusto said, holding up his wrist to show Nina the watch he was wearing.

"Where did you get it?" she asked. The boy looked at Bobby. A new hole had been punched through the band, but even then, it was loose on Augusto's wrist.

"I felt rotten after I'd yelled at him like that. I forget he's a little kid."

"*Son las once y uno!*"

"Bedtime," Bobby said. Then, in English, he said to Nina, "I want to tell them it's time to go to sleep. I don't know how to say it. They don't seem to take a hint."

"Looks like Antonio is sleeping already."

"That's the problem. I don't want them to sleep in here. There isn't enough room in here."

"Sure there is." She looked around her. "We can move the packs outside and put your camera gear against the walls."

"But they"—Bobby lowered his voice—"smell. Their blankets smell from the burros. Their clothes smell. *They* smell. That isn't a problem for you?"

"Not compared to everything else, it's not. Besides, what're you going to do, send them outside? It's snowing outside," Nina said.

"Gavilan's outside, isn't he?"

"That's different. That's his choice. He's on watch. By the way, one of us has to relieve him in two hours."

"*Son las once y dos!*"

"But I don't want them in here," Bobby complained.

"*You* tell them that. I'm not going to," Nina said.

"Thanks a lot, pal," Bobby said. "I'd have thought you wouldn't object to the privacy either. I'd be doing it for you too, you know."

"Not for me, you wouldn't."

"Augusto . . . ," Bobby began.

"*Son las once y tres*," Augusto interrupted him. He had a big smile.

"Augusto, *mi amigo*," Bobby stuttered. "Nina and I, we were just talking and we decided—"

"*He* decided," Nina interrupted.

"*I* decided since it's getting so late and all, and we just had candy and cocoa, and the pineapple, it's been a long day and we—I was thinking I'd sort of like to go to sleep now, see? I have to go on watch in a couple of hours, you know, in case the cocainistas show up again, and it's been a hard day anyway, so . . . You don't mind, do you, *mi amigo?*"

"*Buenas noches*," Augusto said.

"Tell your father."

"My father is sleeping."

"I know. That's why I want you to wake him up. It'll be warm by the fire. There's plenty of wood out there, isn't there, Nina? Plenty of wood."

Antonio opened his eyes. Without saying a word, he gathered up the blankets and unzipped the tent. More snow blew in. He crawled out, dragging Augusto with him. The wristwatch came sailing inside. He left the door open.

"Hey," Bobby yelled, sticking his head outside. "It's his, it's Augusto's. I gave it to him. He can keep it. Hey, Augusto, don't you want it?" Bobby zipped up the door. "People who never bathe shouldn't be so touchy," he said.

Nina and Bobby lay side by side in the dark. The wind howled down the canyon. The tent shuddered, the nylon popped. Bobby reached out and took her hand, but she drew it away. "I don't blame you," he said. "I feel like a shitheel."

"You should."

"I can't let them sleep out there. How can they sleep out there tonight? I'm going to go out and bring them in. I'll apologize. I just wanted to be alone. With you. They couldn't take a hint. I didn't want to hurt their feelings. I'll go out and get them. We'll make room for them just like you said. I'll give the kid the wrist-watch back. I'll just breathe through my mouth. It won't be so bad. That's what I'll do, I'll breathe through my mouth."

Ten minutes later he crawled back into the tent alone.

DEAD LIFT

If nothing else, it's been an education. It's very clear to me now what photojournalism is about. I couldn't see it before, although if you think about it a minute, it's obvious: chasing unpleasantness all over the goddamn globe is what it is—wars, plane crashes, fires, floods, famine, earthquakes, all kinds of catastrophes, one thing after another. You get good, get a reputation, you get your pick of disasters. How come I didn't see that before? What was I thinking? I got no illusions about this kind of life anymore. Cooking suddenly doesn't seem so bad to me. Maybe I *was* made to be a cook. Only one reason I'm sticking this out: I promised Blacky. Plus, no way am I going to give Gavilan the satisfaction of seeing me quit.

Truth is, I don't think he can take much more of this either. How can he? It's hurting him just as bad as it is the rest of us. Has to be. A person's got to eat, doesn't he? He's got to sleep. And that isn't the half of it. If it were just the food and the sleeping out and the dirt and hiding and tramping around all night, I could manage that. The part that gets to me is that the other side has guns—artillery, tanks, jets, copters—and very few compunctions. You see where I'm going with this? Gavilan pretends it's all a walk in the park, but I see right through his act, he doesn't fool me.

I'm no stranger to discomfort, it isn't that. On Nanda Devi I spent a night on a ledge wasn't wide enough for both my cheeks. I had to tie myself on so I wouldn't roll off in my sleep. Meanwhile there's rocks big as basketballs zinging down. Other times I've had to pee so bad that to stand outside the tent in a gale with my pants down around my knees and the temperature minus two thousand was a tremendous relief. I can laugh now. Now it sounds funny. But there wasn't anybody with guns out looking for me, either. That's the difference: it's one thing to scare yourself a little on your vacation, even freeze your pecker off in the name of fun, but it's another thing altogether to take a bullet in the ass just for the sake of a photo.

Actually we've eaten every day I've been here except for twice, which makes it cornmeal and sugar fifteen times. Three times there was powdered milk, twice there were potatoes, and we had apples once, but that day there wasn't any corn. We walked nights and we worked days and we ate cornmeal and sugar for two and a half weeks. We never saw a single soldier, no army, no Guardia, no other Moreno, nobody, and even though no one ever fired a shot, it didn't seem to matter. I never relaxed. You couldn't relax. You always had the feeling that they were out there.

I lost twenty pounds. That's a guess, I haven't seen a mirror, much less a scale. My clothes are hanging on me. They're filthy. They're rags. My extra stuff I gave away: a shirt to Gavilan, the rest I gave to Emilio. I couldn't carry spare clothes in my pack after I saw what Emilio had to wear. Some of the other guys had at least a hope of *maybe* a possibility of finding some other clothes, but as tall as Emilio is, there were probably only two pairs of pants between here and the capital to fit him, and I had them both.

One thing I'll say, the weather's been good. For the last two weeks we've had almost nothing but. Here I give my tent to Antonio and ten of the next thirteen days, in the middle of rainy season, I don't need a tent. That's the world telling me something, telling me you did the right thing, Bobby boy. For the record, it was Nina who gave me the idea. A yellow tent isn't one of the better places to hide yourself, which was obvious once she pointed it out to me, and besides, did I want to sleep in a tent when nobody else had a tent to sleep in? I wouldn't have minded, to tell the truth, if it had been a less conspicuous color. I asked her to take it back with her, and she suggested giving it to Antonio instead. I was sorry I hurt his feelings, not four hundred dollars' worth of sorry, which is what it costs for a mountaineering tent like mine, but I didn't want Nina to take me for a cheapskate.

The day we reached the Moreno camp Antonio didn't stay longer than it took to unload the food off the burros, settle accounts, and take my tent. And my wristwatch. They were still pissed off and I had to practically beg them to take the stuff. He did me a big favor and took a tent you couldn't replace anywhere in the whole goddamn country. The watch was a couple bucks and no big deal. I'd give the guy fifty watches.

Nina went with them. It seems like years ago she left. We agreed to meet in Huaráz. I wanted to apologize for what I'd gotten her into, but she stopped me midway, and after that there didn't seem to be much to say other than good-bye. It started to be one thing with me and her and then it turned into something else.

Some recruits arrived the afternoon I did, and a big part of my getting through this I attribute to them. They were as unsuited to this sort of life as me, but the way Gavilan welcomed them you'd think they were Seabees, instead of five teenage kids run away from a Catholic boarding school in Cashamarca with a single .22 Winchester and one box of bullets between them.

Camp was seven men in a mine shaft. Outside the rain was hard, steady, and cold. I didn't see the entrance until we were on top of it. You had to crawl in, and once you were in there, you couldn't see or stand up straight. The walls seeped and oozed. They glistened with wet. Drops from the ceiling opened eyes in the bat shit and dust on the floor. From out of the dark at the back of the shaft came a damp, cold wind, and between the porthole of slanting rain and the darkness the seven men sat like rats in a sewer.

I took two rolls of film in the tunnel. Here's this stranger comes barging in, hello, how-do-you-do, pops a flash in your face, you'd think they might have objected, but no one did. No one smiled and no one turned away. Gavilan had given the OK. If I had it to do over again, I might have done it differently, taken it slower, but it was what I was there to do, and I was already thinking about getting it done and getting home. Each face was as empty as a cow's. They were skinny and grungy and worn, old-looking, even the youngest, Camilo, who is seventeen.

I tried lying on my back, on my side, on my stomach. I couldn't get comfortable inside that tunnel. Gavilan and Emilio talked for an hour. I was right next to Gavilan. I didn't know whether I was supposed to be listening or not, but it was so quiet, even though they whispered I overheard: there had been ten men when Gavilan left to meet me in Marcara, but his buddy got captured at the baths at Chancos, and there'd been a desertion, a man named Truegas, and a third guy, Tomás, had gone looking for food and hadn't returned. Captured or killed or deserted, nobody knew. That left seven before we came, and the kids from Cashamarca.

Emilio reported where they had been, which was nowhere, and what they had seen, which was nothing. After the briefing Gavilan crawled to the side of each man, shook his hand, and spoke to him for five or ten minutes. He spoke in whispers in each man's ear. What he said I couldn't hear. I saw him give my dried pineapple to Camilo.

We stayed in the tunnel till dark. They took turns standing guard, one above and one below the camp. If you weren't standing guard you were sleeping. Shitfire, how could you sleep in that muck? Not me. Pretty much from the start, all I thought about was when I was going to be able to leave. I didn't sleep and I didn't hear any planes pass over, even though the weather was good for flying. I was chilled, my bones ached from the damp. At dark we crawled out and stretched and washed in a stream that ran through a gully nearby. It was like being given parole. Everyone whispered. It was hard getting used to the whispering. None of it was easy getting used to. Seventeen days later I'm not used to it yet.

That first night Emilio dished out the dinner, a cup of cornmeal per man, and half a cup of powdered milk. It was part of what Gavilan brought up on the burros. When they found there was coffee, they danced. Well, they didn't exactly dance, but they were pretty damn happy just to have a cup of bitter, watery coffee. They toasted each other with cups of coffee.

There's no way to prepare yourself for the life they lead up there. It's the life of an animal. You eat when there's food, and starve when there's not. You sleep wherever you stop under whatever there is. You're alert to every sound, every sight, every move-ment—footprints, broken twigs, crushed blades of grass, a stone out of place has a meaning. Your mind can torment you.

I've made some adjustments. There wasn't a choice. I can walk forever, in the dark if I have to, and I'm not so finicky about what I eat. If there's dirt or a bug in my food—and there's always dirt and bugs in the food, it's *mostly* dirt and bugs—I wouldn't shove it to the side of my plate, if I had a plate.

Rivera holds clinics in the villages doing whatever he can without much in the way of supplies. Mostly he gives aspirin and bandages. Calixto baptizes babies. The rest of us work alongside the villagers, doing whatever they're doing that day. We've cleaned the irrigation ditches, built a house, planted seed, made bricks. I've got pictures of all of this. They teach the Indians to read, or try to, which is Bravo's job. Bravo is American, a college kid, his father is a naval attaché down here in the capital. He came to visit his folks during a school vacation and showed up here in the mountains. I've been meaning to ask him how it happened, but from what I remember of college and parents, maybe it's not such a puzzle.

If it sounds a little like Robin Hood joins the Peace Corps, that's my take on it, too. But I'll tell you this, I see them live it every day, and I see they're willing to die for it, too. That in itself is not so unusual. There're guys ready to die over dope, or messing with somebody's wife, or who's the greatest heavyweight champ, people ready to die for all sorts of silly stuff all the time every day, and do. The unusual thing is to live for what you believe. That's the difference. They live for it, and I hear that they kill for it, but I haven't witnessed any of it yet, haven't seen a weapon fired on any side. Unless you count the South African on the way up. The hardest thing to figure is how Blacky got mixed up with all this. He was a practical, levelheaded guy. The only thing he ever got philosophical on was trim.

The other thing is the Indians. They don't seem to get the gist of this program. Ever since the first Spaniard showed up, they've been jacked over. Of course memories are short when it comes to whoever it was *they* had been jacking over, but now you'd be surprised how many Indians don't give two shits for learning the alphabet.

We were helping rebuild a wall in Cashavilca. We weren't permitted to actually fit the rocks into place, that was done by the local guy, Dionysio, who you could see had some native engineering genius. Didn't use mortar, just fitted the stones together like a 3-D jigsaw puzzle. Forty foot long, three high, two foot thick, solid, straight as string, level as a table, and not a wobble in the whole forty feet. Our contribution was bringing rocks to the site. There were four of us on the detail—Gavilan, me, Bernardo, and Calixto. Ever since the basketball game—my knuckle was still purple and stiff, but Gavilan's cut bothered him and it evened out—we had this competition going. I don't think he'd ever cop to it, but I knew he was competing with me. Calisthenics in the morning, push-ups, which I took going away, sit-ups, he had the edge there, hiking, he was able to walk me into the ground when I first got here. Then it got close, or closer at least. But the crafty bastard may have been sandbagging me. You never knew with him.

The event in Cashavilca was who's gonna carry the biggest rock? Bernardo and Calixto were way out of their league; they couldn't keep the pace. It was all Gavilan and me right from the beginning. As it got later in the day, we had to go farther and farther in order to find challenging rocks. You know how weight lifters pass at the lighter weights to save their strength for the record? Gavilan and I passed on any rock smaller than a watermelon, left them for the other two. Wasn't long before we were walking fifty and a hundred yards to find something world-class to carry back. You had to carry them like babies and it turned your forearms to butter.

Toward late afternoon I wandered into this dry, weedy streambed looking for the knockout punch, some huge motherless rock, a rock so big that Gavilan, even if he could find one to match it, would never be able to carry it back, and in this streambed I came across this waist-high pile. Obviously, someone had taken the trouble to stack them there. I didn't know why, but clearly it was no accident of nature. I didn't want to tear down a monument or anything, so I called in Bernardo for a consultation. Bernardo was the go-between with the Indians. If anyone knew what these guys were thinking, it was Bernardo. They were harder to read than *Moby-Dick* to me.

Bernardo said it didn't look like anything important, but he decided to check with Dionysio to be sure. Dionysio shrugged his shoulders. We interpreted this as permission to lug the stones away. Calixto and Bernardo were already dragging ass. For every one they carried, me and Gavilan would cart off two. We carried a rock under each arm. And we hustled. Drop a load at the wall, sprint back to the pile, grab another load.

It went that way for four or five trips until the smaller stuff was all gone and underneath we found this *boulder*—the freaking Unspunnum Stone—except that you'd need more than a shot of Ovaltine to lift this baby out. The part above ground was big as a beer keg, weighed three hundred easy, maybe four hundred pounds. I walked around it a couple of times looking for handholds, testing it in a halfhearted way. I shook my head. I'd dead-lifted 450 once, this was a few years back, but as bulky as this boulder was and the way it was imbedded, there was no way I, or anybody else between here and York, PA, was going to be able to get it out.

Gavilan was watching me. "Well?" he says.

"Well what?" I say.

"Aren't you going to get it out of there for us?"

I pronounced it unmovable. "You must want to see me in a truss," I said. Gavilan wasn't going to goad me into anything. Alekseyev couldn't lift that rock out. Dr. Squat, dead-lifted eight hundred pounds, had thighs you couldn't get your arms around, even if you wanted to you wouldn't be able to reach around one of his thighs, *he* couldn't do it. I wasn't even going to try.

"How do you know you can't?"

You got to understand that I know Gavilan by now. I'm onto him. I told him take his Norman Vincent Peale someplace else.

"Go on, give it a shot," he says.

"Tell you what," I said. "I've got a little proposition for you. I'll bet you dinner that you can't move that rock even one inch."

"Where do you want to take me?" he says.

This cracks Calixto up. I had to laugh too. Gavilan could amuse you sometimes.

"My ration for yours," I say. "I'll even sweeten the pot a little. If you manage to move it at all, doesn't even have to go anyplace, just rock it a little, you can have my dinner tonight and tomorrow both."

"Deal," he says. He pushes up his sleeves, spits in his palm. This is a very big rock. Spit's not gonna help. He rubs his hands together, puffs out his chest, swings his arms. Loosening up.

When I see he is actually going through with it, I tell him forget it, the bet is off. He's trying to prove a point and the point he's trying to prove isn't worth missing a meal. I tell him I don't want his dinner, eating just the one cup of cornmeal is difficult enough. Shitfire. No one could lift that rock. I knew it, he knew it, and so did everyone else. It was a sucker's bet. I tell him this.

"A bet's a bet," he says.

First he pushes up his sleeves past his elbows, and repeats that goofy warm-up routine, the business with his chest and swinging his arms, and then a couple of jumping jacks, touches his toes. After that he walks around it a few more times, looking for the best place to attack, I suppose. I don't really know. He hasn't got a prayer, I can tell you that. Next he squats down behind it. The thing is so big he's hidden back there except for his arms, and you hear him puffing and blowing while his fingers feel around for a good place to grip.

Knowing the kind of guy Gavilan is—the kind who sees a moral in everything, the sun goes behind the clouds, there's a lesson in it, if the clouds part, it's a goddamn omen, *that* kind of guy—knowing that about him, I should've never made the bet. What a ham. He puffs, he blows, he grunts, he squeezes, he groans, he screams. The rock doesn't budge. Of course the rock doesn't budge. Doesn't take a Rosicrucian to tell you that that rock is going nowhere. If it weren't so pathetic, it would have been comical. "What'd I tell you?" I say. "All bets are off." I'm trying to let him off the hook gracefully.

Gavilan stands up, backs off. The color drains from his face.

"Too late," he says. He's out of wind. "We agreed. Witnesses." He jerks his thumb at Calixto and Bernardo, who are sitting down, themselves glad for the excuse to take a blow. Gavilan has his hands on his knees. His head is drooping. He shakes his arms from his shoulders and massages his forearms.

If you ever lifted weights, you know if you try to make a lift the first time and don't, the chances you'll make it the second or third time go way way down. Your psych is gone, is the reason. Which is not to say it never happens.

Gavilan shakes out his arms some more. A lot more deep breathing. All for show, of course. He puts his fists together and holds them over his head, smiles, a gesture of confidence aimed at Calixto and Bernardo. He dries his palms on his thighs, very deliberately sets his feet, wraps his arms around the rock, *re*sets his feet, gets his grip.

Loud grunt, big explosion of air, a scream, more grunting. Calixto and Bernardo hoot and whistle, cheer him on. The boulder doesn't move.

By this time a couple other people have wandered over—Dionysio, Rivera, some men from the village. Gavilan breaks through the circle of onlookers. He stands ten yards away with his back to us, he's shaking his wrists, getting the blood out of his forearms. Then he charges back, talking to himself, you can see his lips moving, but you can't hear what he's saying. For the third time he grabs a hold of this boulder, tries to pull it out. His face turns deep red. There's veins bulging in his forehead and in his neck. He presses with his thighs. His legs start to sewing machine. He pulls with his back and arms and shoulders. Groaning. Straining. His eyes're bulging out of the sockets, and his teeth're bared. Blood is trickling around his forearms where they've scraped on the rock. His face goes purple, a really alarming shade of purple.

Then his grip lets go and over he goes on his back.

He's lying there against the bank of the gully. He's heaving, dry heaves at first, and then he throws up all over the Orioles T-shirt I gave him. He stands up and staggers around. If it wasn't real, he's a better actor than Steve McQueen. When Rivera comes over to help him he pushes him away. Somebody hands him a canteen. He throws it thirty yards and stomps away by himself. We leave him alone. We know when to leave him alone.

Dionysio mentions he has a place for that rock if we could ever get it out. Somebody gets a pole. It's a ten-foot pole and we wedge one end under the rock and use a smaller rock as a fulcrum. Paco swings from the end and the rock still doesn't move until two more of us hang on beside him. Once we lever it out of the dirt, we roll it away and it rumbles twenty yards down the gully. I estimated wrong; it must weigh a ton. A good two thirds of the thing had been under the ground. What else was under the ground was a body. There are gray, dusty buttocks in the hole where the boulder had been.

I feel like a vulture. While they're exhuming a stiff, I'm leaning over their shoulders snapping pictures. Some part of me is saying Bobby, this is very sick, and this other part is figuring the best lens to use when they turn him onto his back. It's not like I could do anything for him now, I tell myself. It's not like he was on the roof of a burning building and I'm putzing around with shutter speeds while I could be finding a net. That's what I'm saying to myself, but I'm not convinced. I still feel like a slug. The others are giving me looks.

The grave is shallow, two or three feet of loose dirt and rubble below all the stones we'd already moved. He's buried face down, naked. When they roll him over you see he's a kid, sixteen, seventeen at most. His head is shaved, his eyes are sewn shut, his mouth is sewn shut the same way, stiched like a baseball, only the thread is black instead of red. His ankles poke out at odd angles; they're busted, nearly wrenched from their sockets.

Bernardo says this is something the Indians do, this kind of mutilation. They do it to people they think are devils, people who aren't really people at all. Somebody did it to Tomás Weiss. Bernardo says they stitched the eyes so he couldn't identify his killers, and they stitched his mouth so he couldn't reveal their names, and they broke his ankles so he couldn't pursue them. He says if they think you're a devil they stone you to death. Or club you. Sometimes they poison you, which is apparently what they did to Tomás Weiss. Whether before or after they busted his ankles and sewed him up, Bernardo didn't say.

Calixto gave a short sermon, which I heard and forgot before we had finished throwing the dirt back over the body. It took five of us to roll the boulder back up the gully and put it in place for a headstone.

From the air, Paramonga looked soft and green and furry, except where the cane had been cut. There it was brown and stubbled with the long, dry stalks of cane straw lying three feet deep in a matted tangled weave.

"You know I've climbed some mountains, don't you, Roberto?"

"Shhh. Whisper, Bobby. Whisper."

"Huascarán, Huandoy Norte, Nevada de Copa, a bunch of them, McKinley, even partway up Nanda Devi. Ever hear of Nanda Devi?"

"Can't you whisper? They may still be around."

"Once I swam from my place out in Callao down to Crescent Beach and back, five miles, I figure. It took me two hours down and four back against the current. And you know what?"

"Whisper, damn you!"

"This is the point I'm trying to make."

"They'll hear you!"

"The point is, Roberto, that this is harder. Harder than mountains, harder than swimming, harder than anything. Christ, this is hard."

"We're going to be OK, Bobby. We're going to make it."

"Who would've guessed that lying still is harder than climbing mountains? Lying in this motherless cane. I'll be a son of a bitch."

"I'm telling you we're going to be OK."

"I'm a cook. Shit like this doesn't happen to cooks. People don't shoot at cooks." After a while he said, "I'll be glad when this is over."

"It's going to be over soon, if you don't whisper."

"How's your shoulder?" Gavilan asked after an hour. An hour's quiet was too long for Bobby unless something was wrong.

"I don't know."

"Bleeding?"

"It stopped."

"You'd never get me up on one of those mountains, you know that? No way."

"Mountains are cake compared to this cane. At least nobody's shooting at you on a mountain," Bobby said, whispering now.

"Nobody ever fell off a cane field, either," Gavilan said.

"You'd like it. I'm telling you, Roberto. Climbing is something you'd like."

Gavilan and Bobby had come into the yard at the cooperative looking for a Moreno contact named Vasquez who worked in the fields. The foreman stopped them and asked who they were, and they told him a story he didn't believe. He took them into his office on the pretext of helping them locate Vasquez, but he went to call the Guardia from another room. They ran off into the fields. Bobby was shot in the shoulder. The two of them burrowed under the straw. It seemed the safer thing to do, rather than try to get back to the mountains in daylight. They heard the copter passing back and forth overhead.

"Roberto?" Bobby whispered. "I don't think I can take this anymore."

"You'll be all right, you'll see. Listen to me. Just until it gets dark. Then we'll get out of here."

"I can't lie here any longer. I got to move. I got to stand up."

"Soon."

"The fucker *shot* me, Roberto, I'm scared."

"Whisper, Bobby. Whisper."

"Roberto . . ."

"Just lie still until tonight. They're out there, looking for us right now. There's five thousand acres of cane out here. The odds are with us if we stay put. Lie still. They'll think we slipped through."

"I don't think I can."

"The hell you can't. You don't know what you can do."

"Can we at least talk? Time goes faster when we talk."

"Sure, but whisper."

"Where'd you learn to play basketball?"

"Padre Elio. Before Marcara, he worked in the barrio. He taught us the game. We had a team."

"Jesus, my shoulder hurts."

"Don't think about it. What about you? Were you any good?"

"Not as good as I was big. How about this? Here's something you don't know. What were the most points scored in a game by a high school player?"

"I remember Abel Churrusco scored fifty-two. No one else on the team took a shot the whole game."

"It wasn't no goddamn Abel Churrusco, I'll tell you that."

"I was just trying to get an idea. I'll say seventy-five."

"A hundred fifteen."

"No."

"Yeah."

"Get out."

"No shit. A hundred fifteen. Kid from West Virginia."

"Not Abel Churrusco?"

"No. From West Virginia."

"What's the most you ever scored?"

"Thirty-one. Against Friends. That was this Quaker school. Tallest kid they had was five-eleven. On his tiptoes maybe he was five-eleven."

"You know one of the things I remember?" Bobby said. "The smell of Desenex. I always loved the smell of Desenex. Let me ask you something, Roberto."

"I don't know Desenex."

"You think you have a chance of pulling this off? I mean, really. Do you think there's any chance you're going to whip the army and the police and the navy and the air force and take over the country?"

"I don't want to take over the country. I don't want to whip anybody."

"That's good, because from what I've seen so far, you guys

couldn't whip the Friends. I mean, face facts, Roberto, you got eight weapons and ten men."

"Do you know when Fidel took Cuba he had thirteen?"

"I don't know thing one about Fidel Castro."

The conversation was cut by the sound of people moving through the cane nearby. A Guardia patrol was setting up camp. Bobby's head was about two feet from Gavilan's, close enough for Gavilan to hear him say "Oh, no," under his breath. Gavilan didn't respond. He didn't want to encourage conversation. They could hear the Guardia clearly. They seemed as unhappy about spending the night out there as Bobby and Gavilan were. There were three or four of them, and except when the wind blew and rustled the straw, they could hear them as if they were sitting around the same fire.

The night passed slowly. Gavilan didn't sleep for fear he would snore or sneeze or cough or rustle the straw and alert the patrol. Or that Bobby would. But he didn't hear a sound from him all night. He remembered how restless he had been earlier. Either Bobby had disciplined himself, or he had died.

In the morning the Guardia left. By that time Bobby and Roberto had been in the cane almost twenty-four hours. Bobby whispered that he was thirsty. Gavilan was glad to hear Bobby's voice, to know he was still alive. To ease their thirst, they sucked on sugarcane. They couldn't move during the day without tremendous risk. Their best chance was to stay put until night.

"I feel better," Bobby said. "I guess a person can't stay scared forever."

"Some do," Gavilan said.

"You ever get scared, Roberto?"

"Sometimes. It's better not to talk about it."

"You scared now?"

"Yes. Let's change the subject."

"Name another time."

"When I took your legs out from under you on the basketball court in Marcara. I thought you were going to tear me apart."

"You don't know how close you came. I think I hear someone coming again . . ."

The cane was being trampled nearby. Gavilan heard Bobby whisper his name, and didn't answer.

There were ten or twenty men. They were cutting the cane with machetes. They were close, but they would have to be right on top of them to see them because they had buried themselves in the straw.

Bobby stayed quiet after that. It was getting difficult to talk, anyway. His mouth was dry. And it was safer not to talk. But when they were talking, reality was once removed. Time passed. Now the seconds dragged by. An hour passed, maybe two. It was hard to tell, especially when the sun was in the clouds.

"Roberto, can I ask you something?"

"Just ask for once instead of always asking my permission first."

"It's personal."

"Everything's personal."

"Suppose you weren't doing this. Suppose you could do anything you want. What would you be doing?"

Gavilan thought for a moment. Lots of things came to his mind, but it was useless to think about them and painful besides. His habit was to act as if whatever he was doing was what he had chosen to do, although most of the time it didn't feel like that. "Nothing comes to mind," he said.

"You never remember wanting to be anything else or do anything else?"

"If I ever did, I don't remember now."

"I wanted to be a hundred different things, but the only thing I wanted to *do* was have fun. I thought taking pictures would be fun."

"And?"

"And here I am."

"And this isn't fun?"

"You're not suggesting that this is fun. You can't be suggesting that. You're a real sicko if this is your idea of fun."

"Maybe not as much fun as climbing mountains, freezing, risking your neck to get someplace where, once you get there, you turn right around and come back down. No, not as much fun as that."

"Not right back down. Sometimes you eat a candy bar, take a picture if the weather's clear."

"Suppose *you* knew this was going to turn out OK, but before it did, you also knew it was going to get worse than it already is. Then how would you feel?"

"I don't know. This is pretty bad."

"But suppose you knew it was going to get worse. You could handle it, couldn't you?"

"Let me see if I have this straight: I got a bullet in my shoulder, the police are chasing me, not to mention the army, I haven't had as much as a glass of water in two days, I'm lying here in a sugar-cane field with a guerrilla psycho looney, and he wants to know can I handle it if it gets any worse? Is that the question? It's not something I even like to think about."

"But you have."

"Have what?"

"Thought about it."

"Yeah, I thought about it, and . . ."

"And . . ."

"It can't *get* any worse than this, bub. This is it. This is the worst."

"Can you handle it?" Gavilan repeated.

"What's my choice?"

"Right. No choice. Here you are. Can you handle it?"

"I don't know. What about you?"

"You want to know can I handle it if it gets worse than this?"

"Yeah. That's the question."

"Suppose we have to stay hidden in the straw five more days, can I handle it then?"

"That's what I want to know."

"Then they capture me anyway."

"Yeah, they capture you. Right."

"Torture me."

"Torture your ass."

"How?"

"Tickle your feet."

"They tickle my feet. Then they throw me in jail."

"Yeah, jail."

"Kill me."

"I guess, that too."

"Could I handle it if I had to spend five more days and nights in this cane field with you as my sole companion, after which I am captured, tortured, imprisoned—"

"Put in solitary confinement."

"—put in solitary, executed . . . How are they going to do it? Shoot me?"

"They're going to hang you."

"And the question is can I handle that?"

"That's the question."

"Do you think I haven't thought about this before?"

"You don't act like you do," Bobby said.

"Tell me about Nina DeBettencourt."

"Answer my question first," Bobby said.

"The answer to your question is yes."

"You're sure?"

"I said I was sure."

"Absolutely positive."

"Positive."

"Okay. I accept that. What do you want to know about Nina?"

The afternoon crawled by. They took turns sleeping in anticipation of leaving at nightfall, but in the evening the patrol returned to the same campsite they had used the night before. It meant another night and another day under the straw.

The night was interminable. When dawn finally arrived and the patrol left, Bobby and Gavilan left too. They didn't want to get boxed in another night. They crawled two hundred yards through the matted carpet of straw. Movement was noisy. The trip took four hours. Bobby didn't talk much through the day. The heat and dust constricted his throat, and talking was difficult. Gavilan asked from time to time how he was doing. His wound needed attention, and besides the hunger, thirst, and anxiety that they shared, he was in pain. Gavilan remembered something his mother used to say: to complain was bad manners, and manners were the basis of character. Bobby didn't complain, or he hadn't since the first morning. Late in the afternoon, he told Gavilan a joke about a Polish terrorist. Mentally he was very strong, Gavilan thought.

"Roberto? Don't you think it's time you settled down, found some steady work, quit this rootless way of life?"

"You mean get married . . . ?"

"Have a bunch of little guerrillas."

"Join the Chamber of Commerce."

"Now you're talking, bub. That's the idea. Try to act a little normal for a change. This stuff you're into doesn't make good sense."

"It's not that hard to understand."

"Tell me then."

"I think you already know."

"No, I don't. What are you trying to prove? I'd appreciate it if you told me. I'd really appreciate it. Seriously."

"When you get back to the capital . . ."

"Yeah."

". . . look at the pictures you took . . ."

"And?"

"And they'll tell you what you want to know. You know how it is, Bobby, don't you?"

"I don't know squat anymore."

"The camera never lies."

A PIECE OF CAKE

The elephants were gone, they'd grown out or died, and the same with the giraffes, they were stunted, leafless, nothing left but a few dry twigs, and the llamas, too, gone, every last one. Not to see them grazing on the traffic islands in the center of town was a sign to me of what had happened to Huaráz under martial law. The sculptured bushes had been the city's trademark, like the cherry blossoms in D.C.

When Nina and I had made our arrangements, I hadn't counted on the crowd in town. I was told I was lucky to have found a room anywhere, with the celebration marking the end of martial law just two days away. Truth is, I didn't care one way or the other about a room. After where I'd been the last month and the places I'd slept, a roof and a mattress had slipped a few notches on the list of things I couldn't do without. I wanted a bed, sure I did, but it was nothing I was going to sweat, which is probably why I got the room at the Raymondi. It's when you have to have a thing it's sometimes hard to get.

Something about barbershops brings in the kibitzers, I don't know what it is. It can't be only the magazines. Salon de Juan was full, none of them customers. Salon de Juan is not its name, of course, far as I know it doesn't have a name. No name, no barber pole. No dryers, mousse, or manicures either. It's four sheets of corrugated iron propped up like a house of cards. A sneeze could flatten the place. Conversation stopped as soon as I came in off the street. They looked me up and down—my clothes, my beard, my hair—I bet I was something to see. I got the feeling Juan was ready to beg off, because maybe I was too big an undertaking, but I said the magic words—Enrique Moon—and he pointed toward the chair. "Juan Silvio Guiterrez, at your service," he said. He tied the sheet around my neck, and tilted back the chair.

Right off the bat Juan found some lice, which didn't surprise me. He picked my scalp, poured kerosene over my head, soaped me up, and sent me next door to the cab stand where there was a hose I could rinse with. I've got to do that twice, walk down the crowded sidewalk with a sheet around me and my head full of lather, stand in the gutter and squirt myself off with a hose.

Whatever Juan and his buddies were discussing when I came in wasn't so interesting anymore. I'm the main attraction. I didn't want to talk about what I'd been doing, or where I'd been doing it, or how a person came to look like I did. I wanted to short-circuit any curiosity, so before someone could ask, I volunteered that I was a climber. Climbing is incomprehensible to the locals, and once I copped to it, in their minds anything was possible. Heads nodded as if my confession explained it all. A mile-wide gulf opened between us. Any further attempt at communicating with me was deemed a waste of breath.

"Yeah, we tried Alpamayo by the northwest ridge," I said. Does Alpamayo have a northwest ridge? Didn't matter. I'd become invisible. They were leafing through magazines and talking among themselves.

Juan wrapped my face in hot towels from a pot on a propane stove. Not counting coffee I might have dribbled, it was the first hot water to touch my face in a month. He stropped the razor and changed the towel. The lather was hot, too. His fingers smelled from bay rum. He scraped my whiskers away along with a couple of layers of skin. It was too late not to trust him, so I sat back and shut my eyes, about as close to ecstasy as a person could hope to get.

The after-shave snapped me right out of it. Pure alcohol with a whiff of bay rum. Talk about burn. Shitfire! My cheeks were raw as hamburger.

Juan handed me a mirror. I saw my face for the first time in four weeks. It was thin, white where the beard had been, and brown around my eyes, which made me look like a raccoon. I borrowed a comb and took out the part Juan put in, slicked it straight back off my forehead. He used a whisk broom on my clothes, but he needn't have bothered. Next stop was a new set of threads.

The store didn't have a wide selection in my size, even though I'd lost a couple inches in my waist, but what do you expect from a place that sells roofing tiles, balloons, seed, barbwire, candy, *pisco*, pots and pans, and men's, ladies', and children's clothes in a space the size of a living room?

I didn't have a robe and the hotel towel didn't go all the way around my waist. I caught myself running to the shower at the end of the hall. This made me wonder: if I was anxious about being seen semi-naked in the hotel hallway, where was I going to get the nerve to steal a car? I put the question temporarily out of my mind. In the bathroom mirror, I saw Juan was worth every bit of seventy cents he cost me, and Rivera did a decent job on my shoulder. I guess the wound wasn't as bad as I'd thought.

A shower was something I've been looking forward to, and I wasn't disappointed. The water was hot and plentiful and the pressure was strong. The room got steamy. I scrubbed my knuckles raw. I used my knife to get under my nails. I brushed my teeth with salt until my gums bled. I lost track of time. When the hot water was gone I stood under the cold.

I stretched out cool and clean on the cool, clean sheets. I put my hands behind my head and listened to the sounds from the street. There were four hours to Nina. I lay there and thought about the last couple of weeks, about Nina, and Blacky. I tried to forget Rinaldi, but you know you can't deliberately try to forget anything. I thought about Roberto, and about how I was going to get him that car he wanted. He didn't ask me to, I volunteered, but at the time it didn't seem like such a serious proposition. What was there to stealing a car? I'd seen it done on TV millions of times.

The garrison is six blocks from the center of town, where Avenida Arequipa runs into Costa Rica. It sits on about twenty acres on a level bluff above the Santa River. Chain-link fence surrounds it all. Most of the land is occupied by a rifle range and parade grounds which are marked off with whitewashed rocks. There are a couple of stucco buildings and rows of newer Quonset huts. You see all this coming down Costa Rica Street.

A pair of MPs in chrome helmets were standing by a guardhouse checking traffic in and out of the gate. I took special notice of their machine guns.

"Where you from, mister?" asked one, a little guy with pock-marked skin and a gold tooth in front. "USA, I betcha." He beamed at me, but the other, the one with the wire-rim glasses, looked grave, all business. I asked if they would mind posing for me. They minded. When I lifted the camera anyway, off came the grin and up came the weapons, and I didn't get any shots except for the two I squeezed off from my waist while I apologized, sorry, no harm intended. I asked if I could take a picture of the front gate without them and they said sure, go ahead. They stepped into the guardhouse while I ran off a Polaroid. Reconnaissance was a piece of cake.

The car was another matter, and exactly how I was going to go about it occupied me the eight and a half minutes it takes to walk back to the center of town. Stealing cars, it's one of those things like riding a bike or swimming or smoking, if you haven't picked it up by the time you're fifteen, chances are you never will. I put the Polaroid into an envelope and went back to the Raymondi. I had coffee in the bar, and left the photo on the table. That's all there was to it. Somehow it was supposed to get back to Roberto.

I still had two hours to kill before meeting Nina. I went to the shop of a photographer friend of mine, Manuel Cartagena. He had some of his work displayed in the windows, black and white por-traits which he had hand-colored, a technique so old-fashioned it had come back around again. His wife told me don Manuel was at the park taking pictures. She agreed to keep my exposed film in her refrigerator. I bought a few black and white postcards of early mountaineering in the Andes, thanked her, and left.

There's an outdoor cafe at the town's main intersection where you can sit and watch the traffic and when it's clear, see the moun-tains. I ordered beer and a glass of ice and pulled out my postcards, one of a lady in a long dress trying to step across a crevasse, and another of a man in a derby standing on top of a freestanding needle-shaped serac. To me the mountains are sneaky, treacherous places. Seracs and crevasses are loaded guns. Why anyone would treat them as lightly as this unlikely pair of climbers puzzles me, until I'm interrupted by a guy and a girl standing beside my table. I didn't recognize him at first, without the chrome helmet, but the

wire-rims and the serious face jogged my memory. Lieutenant
Roca, he introduced himself, and his sister, María. He asked if they
might join me, and I couldn't think quick enough why not. I waved
the waiter over, and ordered beers all around.

The sister was a med student. I lit her smoke and bummed one
for me. I was trying to hide the awkwardness of the situation behind formality, smoke, anything. I gave them the same story I gave
at the barbershop, but with Roca and his sister it had the opposite
effect. They wanted to know all about mountaineering. María
flicked the hair from her eye. "It's very macho," she said.

I couldn't tell whether she was coming on or putting me on.

"I've never met an *andiniste*," she said. Her hair was black, her
eyes big and blue. "Latin men don't seem attracted to risks that
can't be taken either publicly or in tight pants," she said. "Prefera-
bly both." She laughed and flicked her hair. "Except where politics
is concerned."

Blas Roca seemed at ease, enjoying himself, proud of his older
sister the doctor. I asked him about the army. He was content to let
his sister speak for him. "I was against it from the beginning," she
said. "It was strange to find myself agreeing with Father for once,
but that is what finally convinced Blas to enlist, I think, that Father
so vehemently disapproved."

"That's not true and you know it," said Roca.

"Why else would you quit the university and join the army?"

"The university." He said the word with contempt. "Demon-
strating, throwing rocks, printing leaflets one day, and then getting
drunk at the football game the next."

"But the army, Blas? The *army?*"

"Do we have to go through all this again?"

"He's a poet," she said to me, flicking her hair.

Roca said, "Other poets have been soldiers."

"You should read the poetry he writes." She looked at her watch,
stood up abruptly, announced they had to leave. They were meeting friends for dinner. Would I care to join them? I thanked her,
no. There was only an hour to Nina, although had I all the time in
the world, María wasn't really my type. Earnest conversation, coffee houses, poetry—that was more Blacky's scene than mine.

I walked to the park on the chance I'd find don Manuel. He was
at a picnic table bent over a chessboard. His Speed Graphic 4×5

was sitting on the wooden tripod beside him. I waited respectfully so as not to disturb his concentration. He didn't raise his head, ran his hand through his long, wispy strands of gray hair. After a while he said to me, "Do I remember correctly, Mister Shafto, that you don't play chess?"

"Your memory is good."

"Checkers," he said.

"Right," I said.

"For idiots," he said. His pipe was in his teeth. He separated the pieces on the board. "White or black?" He wore a bow tie and a three-piece suit. There were dark pouches under his eyes. "Forgive me my ill temper. It's my exasperation speaking. You don't know how hard it's become to find a game anymore. Chess doesn't flourish in an oppressive atmosphere."

My mind wasn't on the game. He clobbered me.

"Double or nothing?" I offered. "Let me be white this time. I play better when I'm white."

"For idiots," he said as he double-jumped my last two men.

I automatically set up the pieces again. "Don Manuel, I need some advice."

"My advice to you is give up checkers. And don't call me don Manuel. My son-in-law calls me Don Manuel and he is a little pimp."

I lost three men before I could get it out. "I'm in kind of a bind, Manuel." I had thought of confessing the whole situation, about Rinaldi, Blacky, about my promise to Roberto, but I decided the less he knew, the better it would be for him. "I need to borrow your truck." Roberto had said to steal one, but I couldn't see me doing that.

"Certainly. May I ask why?"

"It would be better if you didn't know."

"King me. Better for whom?"

"For everyone."

"I can appreciate that there are situations where ignorance is preferable."

"This is one. In fact, it would be best if you just left your keys in it. That way, if anything happens—"

"Like what?"

"Like, you know . . . anything. Then you could claim it was

stolen. In fact, that's what you do. Call the police and say it was stolen."

"Does this mean I won't be getting it back?"

"I really need the truck, don Manuel, I mean Manuel. I'll be 100 percent responsible."

"You want me to give you my truck, and you tell me I might not get it back, and you won't tell me why? Is that correct?"

"More or less."

"I think I would have to know the circumstances."

"I'm afraid if I told you, you wouldn't give me the truck."

"It's the only way I'll give it to you."

"You have my word. If you don't get it back I'll get you another."

"You can have the truck. I trust you. Now you must trust me."

I sat for a moment thinking of a way to explain it to him.

"Is it for something criminal?"

"Not exactly," I hedged.

"Ah, I see," he said as if my telling him nothing had somehow told him everything. "Politics, then. Say no more. I didn't think you were the type, but I'm not unsympathetic." He sucked on his pipe.

"You'll do it, then?"

"I became a Marxist about the same time as Marx," he said, puffing smoke.

"You'll let me have the truck?" I could hardly believe it. We weren't such close friends I'd even the right to ask. "I'll, I'll . . ." I stammered around thinking of a gesture equal to the gratitude I felt. "I'll give you my Polaroid."

He lifted an eyebrow. "Wonderful philosophy, Marxism . . ."

"Park it where you usually park it, and leave the keys under the mat."

". . . Stinks in practice, though. Anyone can see that it's unworkable. What are you going to do? Rob a bank? Never mind. You were right not to tell me. Do you still have the instruction book? If not, I'll have to write to Polaroid for one."

He didn't recognize her at first. Her clothes were the reason—dirty blue jeans, black high-top basketball shoes, the shirt-tails of her plaid flannel shirt hanging out. An old army rucksack was over her shoulder. The Nina Bobby had his eyes peeled for would be wearing black satin slacks, a gauzy blouse, and her hair would be pulled back to show off her gold hoop earrings. He imagined her sitting in the hotel lobby, her ankles crossed, smoking, turning the pages of Brazilian *Vogue*, or since he was early, he would see her stride through the doors, turning heads, her high heels rapping, trailing a scent of expensive perfume.

In the purity of her expression and the joyous welcome of her arms, his fantasies were instantly forgotten. His imagination was no match for the radiant soul he held in his embrace.

"No elephants," she said, giving him an extra squeeze. "Isn't it awful?" She touched his cheek. Her fingers were cut and scraped, and there were black half-moons of dirt caked under her broken nails. "Smooth," she said. She hugged him again. "Bay rum." She herself carried the odors of wood smoke and burro. "You look like a raccoon," she said. "A skinny one."

He assumed she'd want to use the shower in the hotel before she did anything else, but she said she had errands to run. The shower could wait. She talked while they walked through the early-evening streets.

She had been living with Antonio and his family, sleeping in the storeroom. She'd taken control of the organization of the feast, using Antonio as the go-between for her and the mayor, Theofilo, and the rest of the town. It was understood that Theofilo should have the responsibility for its planning, but he had been over-whelmed. He took to drinking earlier and earlier in the day, shrinking by steady increments his periods of sobriety, until they lasted for only a few minutes after breakfast. It was Nina, then, who, with Antonio's advice and assistance, decided the kind and quantities of food and drink that would be needed, selected the actors to play the roles of priest and general and demon, had the costumes made, made arrangements for the band and the transpor-tation of everything to Santo Rosario, and was making plans to clean up the plaza, a task for which Gavilan had volunteered the Moreno.

This was a Nina Bobby didn't know, unlike either the aloof aristocrat he had first seen in the market or any of the other facets he had come to know: the soccer fan, the kept woman, the farm girl, or the game and resourceful Nina whom he had seen during the first week in the mountains. It was more than just her appear-ance. She was sturdier, and certainly dirtier, unglamorous, but ap-pealing the way a mechanic might be when you're broke down and here he comes out of nowhere tooling down the road in his tow truck, slapping the radio's beat on the dashboard.

She talked nonstop, one sentence tumbling into the next, and with such animation that people passing them on the street turned their heads. Bobby was a little disappointed that she asked him none of the questions for which he'd already thought out his an-swers. He'd rehearsed the story of his time in the mountains to come across as even more trying than it had been for him, which was trying enough. He'd planned to remain stoically restrained, or if pressed, to trivialize it, make jokes, as if it were too terrible to be straightforward about. He would leave her with the impression his evasions were out of concern for her, wanting to spare her the true terribleness of it all, implying that she could never understand it anyway, that it required a toughness she did not possess, and a type of courage only men like him could summon. In truth, he hoped she would imagine it to be an altogether more admirable, noble, and exciting adventure than the boring, exhausting, and sometimes terrifying experience it had been for him. But she didn't ask, not even about his wound. As they walked through town Bobby massaged his shoulder, wincing, trying to provoke her curiosity. "Just a flesh wound," he was dying to say, but she never asked.

Because of the celebration, fireworks were hard to find. They looked for them all over town. But Nina had promised Augusto, and she insisted on tracking down every lead.

Bobby took pictures as they walked. For a few blocks they followed a funeral cortege, a shiny black casket carried on the shoulders of four men, with some women and children following behind. Bobby and Nina remained at a respectful distance, not wanting to intrude. Bobby knew there'd be a picture if he was patient. The casket was heavy for the four men, the evening warm, and after a while the procession stopped to rest. Bobby metered the scene. The pallbearers slumped on the casket. A mourner disappeared around a corner and returned a minute later with a tray of dripping ice-cream cones. He passed them around. They had to hold the cones away from their bodies, tilting their heads and licking fast to keep the melting ice cream off their funeral clothes, and Bobby got his picture.

Besides fireworks—an off-duty policeman sold her all she wanted, boxes of them—there were other things on Nina's shopping list: a generator to power the electric lights, toys for the children, candy, prizes. She seemed determined to spend every cent Gavilan had given her, and as they walked amid the preparations for Huaráz's own festival, new ideas came to her: paper streamers, lanterns, candles in case they were unable to get a generator, and paper plates and cups, none of which had ever been a part of the Feast of Santo Rosario before. But they'd never had so much money before.

The streets were nearly empty by the time they reached the Raymondi. Nina took her shower. She was gone forty-five minutes. Bobby undressed and then, having time to think about it, not wanting to presume, put his jeans back on. He liked the way he was looking, all the fat stripped away so the veins on his arms stood out and the cut beneath his pectoral muscles was sharp and clean and deep, and even the bottom pair of abdominal muscles rose like biscuits in a tin. And there was the red-brown scab of the bullet hole. He thought about Blacky and *his* bullet hole, and how Blacky looked on the slab, no shirt on him either. Bobby lay on the bed under the open window, listening to the sounds in the street: children running, church bells chiming the hour, and he thought about Blacky and Rinaldi.

Nina returned, wrapped in a towel. She stretched out next to Bobby. He stared at the ceiling, wanting to reach for her and not wanting to, thinking of Blacky, and Rinaldi's odd little smile. Nina ran her finger lightly around the scab on Bobby's shoulder.

"Not what you expected, was it?" she asked.

No, it hadn't been. It had been more and less, but it was not the mountains now on his mind, it was her nearness, and the shadow over him that kept him from rolling over to press himself against her, from pulling his hands from where they were cupped behind his head, that kept his eyes on the slowly spinning fan above the bed. He had to tell her about Rinaldi, the threats, about what had been done to Blacky, but he didn't know how without also revealing his fear. It sickened him that he was afraid. He groped for a way to explain it to her and to himself and still keep some of his self-respect. His fingers grew cold, and the breeze through the open window made him shiver, but between his legs and under his arms it was damp. He bent his head to smell the odor of his fear, wondering if Nina could smell it too. Her breath was steady and rhythmic. She was asleep.

When she awoke he was sitting in the casement watching the twilit streets. Without a word, he went to her and they made slow, quiet, sad, chaste love, joined lightly along the full lengths of their bodies, cheek to cheek, belly to belly, hand to hand, chafing like boats in a slip on a windless afternoon.

The night was warm. They walked through the town with her arm through his, talking only to point out sights of interest: a little boy reading a comic book on the curb under a street lamp, a saddle maker tooling a stirrup, a revival in a storefront church.

The restaurant was bright and noisy and full of people. They sat together at a long table with a dozen others, choosing from a menu of a hundred items chalked on a board that took almost all of one wall. Accustomed to no choice at all, Bobby couldn't select from the profusion. Nina ordered for him. She had to shout to the waiter, who would not or could not squeeze between chairs to get closer than ten feet away. Bobby allowed the clatter of dishes and the proximity of strangers to deter him from the promise he'd made to himself to come clean with her.

It seemed to Nina that the crowd had created a pocket of intimacy. She used it to tell Bobby about the time she'd spent with

Antonio's family, how different it was from her own. They were poor, but their lives were very rich. That sounded shallow and trite, she knew, but it was true. She compared it to a blind man who, as compensation for the loss of one of his senses, finds the others becoming more acute. Of course, most sightless people would give up their gain for the recovery of their vision, just as Antonio would give up his poverty without a second's hesitation. Antonio yearned for more, ached for it, he made no secret of his desires: a transistor radio, glass panes in his windows, shoes for the children. In that regard he was no different than anyone else she'd ever known, seeing the greatest value in what he didn't have.

She talked about her plans for after the feast. She was moving out of the carriage house in the city. She had written Rinaldi a letter. She was through with him. She'd have to get a job, she knew. She thought she might come back to the mountains to work in the clinic with the Israeli doctor. Or travel. She'd always wanted to travel. But to travel she needed money.

Bobby listened. When his food came, he found he could take it or leave it, but he took it because it was there, and because he had promised himself this meal. Nina ate with genuine pleasure, pausing with food on her fork to make a point, to tell how Marcellino, on the days he wasn't working in the fields, practiced by planting stones in straight furrows, only to dig them up minutes later, a harvest of instant potatoes. She told him how Julia would carry Clementina wrapped in a shawl on her back for two years before she would set the little girl down to explore on her own. She told him about the belts Antonio wove, and the folk songs Alberto sang. She told him how guinea pig tasted like chicken, sort of. She told him about getting falling-down drunk with Dominga and another woman one afternoon, and how raunchy the conversation had been, how Dominga had questioned her about Bobby. It wasn't that she didn't notice that Bobby was quiet and unresponsive. She thought that if she remained unflaggingly enthusiastic she wouldn't be dragged down by his mood, and maybe, like leaves swept up in the wake of a speeding car, she could take him with her for the ride.

"Interesting system they have for busing the tables," she said, trying to draw him out. Not having noticed, Bobby looked around. Nina pointed to the waifs outside the window. "Watch," she said.

When a diner had finished his meal, paid his bill, and left the table, one of the gang of kids from outside would come in, scoop the leftovers off the plates, and run back out to the street. They used a paper bag or a shoe box. One boy used the tails of his shirt. They took only the food, never plates or utensils. No one seemed to notice, not even the waiters. Although they were never chased, they were as skittish as barn cats, darting among the tables, grabbing the food, and escaping to the safety of the street. There were six of them out on the sidewalk from the ages of, she guessed, five to thirteen. It seemed they were having a pretty good time.

"Maybe you should tell Blacky," she said.

The mention of Blacky made Bobby's heart drop. He caught a waiter's attention, called out his order. The waiter didn't think he'd heard him right. He made Bobby shout it twice. *Six* pieces of cake?

Bobby paid the bill. They walked out together, leaving the cake untouched.

She couldn't stay the night, she said. She'd arranged a truck to take her back to Marcara with the fireworks and the piñata and the other things she'd bought. She had an hour before she had to meet the driver. They walked to the park. When she left he stayed on the bench by himself.

Bobby parked the truck by the warehouse on Arequipa thirty yards from the garrison gate. The first thing he noticed when he shut off the engine was that the noise from the parade wasn't as loud as he had hoped it would be. He could hardly hear the band. He eased up the door handle, slid off the seat, and shut the door softly. He walked twenty yards away from the garrison and stepped into a deep recessed gate in a warehouse wall. From there he had a clear line of sight fifty yards to the pair of MPs standing duty, a different pair from the other day. Through his 200-millimeter lens fitted with a 2X tele-extender, he could see them clearly.

He looks at his watch. 3:17. He slaps his pockets for the tenth time to be sure he hasn't forgotten to leave the keys in the truck. He had always considered himself to be a pretty cool head, but now he knows it is one thing when a party of ten shows up without reservations, and this is something else. He takes a light reading, checks to see the film is winding, double-checks the ASA, the shutter speed, and f-stop. He wipes the UV filter with the tail of his shirt. The way he's shaking, the pictures will all be blurred, especially with the telephoto, and he finds a way to brace the lens against the wall. He looks at his watch. He's not cut out for this kind of stuff, he decides.

At 3:23 Paco, Camilo, and one of the school kids, Paulo, come walking down the sidewalk on his side of the street. Bobby can see Camilo is totally wired. From what he can tell of Paco, he could be going to the corner for a paper, but Camilo is wired and Paulo looks shaky, too. Probably not as shaky as I would be, Bobby thinks. He doesn't see their guns, but he can't believe they're going in there without any guns. He guesses they are tucked in their belts or under their sweaters.

The three are past the truck and twenty yards from the corner when three others—Roberto, Bernardo, and Bravo—come down Costa Rica. Roberto has his arms around the shoulders of the other two. They are walking down the center of the street, stumbling a little, singing, handing a bottle back and forth, kicking a can. They start across the intersection, stop partway, and do an impromptu chorus line in front of the guardhouse. One of the MPs steps outside to investigate. Bernardo offers him the bottle. The MP taps his billy club against his thigh and says something over his shoulder to his partner. Both of them laugh. Roberto, tipsy, rocking on his feet, stands face-to-face with him. The MP backs Roberto off with his billy.

What happens next happens fast: a black Mercedes barrels down Costa Rica. It veers toward the gate, fishtails, and jumps the curb. Roberto dives to the sidewalk, taking one MP with him. Sliding sideways, the Mercedes careens into the guardhouse, bowling it over with the other MP still inside. By the time the first MP is back on his feet he is facing Roberto's revolver. The guardhouse itself has toppled onto its door. The soldier inside might have crawled out through one of the shattered windows, but he doesn't. He's hurt or lying low. The time is 3:25.

A motor drive can eat thirty-six frames in under six seconds, and Bobby misses what happens next changing film. By the time he has reloaded, the black Mercedes with Emilio at the wheel is moving slowly into the compound. Camilo is out in the street by himself. He has a machine gun aimed at the one MP who is flat on his stomach, his hands clasped behind his head. The other is still in the guardhouse. The time is 3:28.

There are gunshots inside.

3:41. The shooting stops. There is just the distant sound of the band from the center of town. The Mercedes rolls out, its fender crunched and rubbing against the tire. It stops in the intersection. Camilo backs up to the truck and climbs inside. He pulls beside the Mercedes, and with the motor running, crouches behind the open door on the driver's side. His gun barrel pokes through the window.

At 3:45, Bravo, Bernardo and Paco come out carrying a wooden crate the size of a small coffin. Behind them are Paulo and the other school kid, Vicente, with what looks to Bobby like a generator. After them comes Rivera—he has a new blue beret on his head, and then ten yards behind, the last one out, Roberto comes out alone.

They load the crate and the generator, climb up onto the bed, and slam the tailgate. Camilo covers Roberto from behind the open door of the truck. The Mercedes starts to pull away. Roberto is still in the street when a soldier appears in the garrison gate. Bobby sees him through his telephoto, but Camilo can't because Roberto blocks his view. The soldier kneels and raises his rifle. Roberto gives Camilo the thumbs-up while the soldier is sighting on his back.

Bobby runs out of his niche in the warehouse wall. "RO-CAAA!"

A burst rakes the street. Roberto drops to the pavement. With him down and out of the way, Camilo sees what's happening. His machine gun jumps in his hands. Bullets ping in the gravel before they climb Roca's thigh to his stomach. They knock him onto his seat. His rifle falls beside him, his wire-rim glasses hang from one ear. Bullets pop in the stucco over his head. New red medallions are pinned on his chest. He looks down at them with surprise.

Engines rev. Doors slam. Roca rolls onto his side. Tires spin and squeal. The Mercedes pulls away and the truck follows it up Costa Rica. The intersection is empty. Roca lies still. Bobby, who will not remember having screamed, turns and walks away.

The time is 3:51.

SANTO ROSARIO

New, white, clean, shiny, the radio sat on a mossy stone in a place where nothing was new, white, clean, or shiny. It was an ancient place, a place the future would never find. Here the view was backward into a dimly remembered past, and inward, away from foregone conclusions, or upward, because the sheer walls of the surrounding mountains made life in Santo Rosario the life of a toad trapped at the bottom of a well.

Goddamn lucky is what they were, thought Bobby. Did them a favor, is what the army did, driving them out of this place. Anyplace had to be better: a toppling wall, a few crumbling houses, the storeroom crumbling, stumps, mud, a rooster left behind in the rush to leave. He thought about what a long, dusty, difficult, tiresome, roundabout trip it was to Santo Rosario. He decided getting out must be a lot, lot harder. Otherwise why'd it take an army? Otherwise they'd have blown this pop stand sooner. Wouldn't take any prodding to get me to leave, he thought. Something about it, I got this funny feeling.

The transistor radio was Antonio's, a present from Nina, and it had been playing, she said, every waking moment since she had brought it back for him from Huaráz. Now, between bursts of static and intermittent silences, Bobby heard the Rolling Stones. Marcellino had stopped playing Frisbee to sit on the wall and listen. Snot leaked from his nose. Candy bulged in his cheeks. He was mesmerized. He swung his feet back and forth. The shoes were new, another gift from Nina. He hadn't tied the laces and he'd crushed the counters and he'd scuffed the toes. His new socks had slipped below his dirty heels.

Vicente and Bravo had gotten the knack. Alberto showed promise—the Frisbee was his, also a gift from Nina—but neither the
rest of the Zapato Moreno nor Theofilo had yet made much head-
way into its puzzling operation. Not for lack of enthusiasm,
though. It was almost as if at this particular spot on the globe,
something—magnetic storms or a lag in the jet stream, perhaps the
gravitational pull of the moon—some inexplicable *thing* was inter-
fering with, and in Theofilo's case nullifying, the Frisbee's normal
aerodynamic properties. It seemed harder to throw than potato
chips. It fluttered and crashed. Or it boomeranged. And to catch it,
the way it eluded them you'd think it was alive. They grabbed
empty air, they clapped their hands on nothing, they batted and
swiped and swatted at the yellow plastic dish. Each attempt met
with laughter, the falling-down-on-the-ground kind. If someone
somehow did manage to snag it, he got cheers and slaps on the
back. When Theofilo, *Tio* Theofilo as he asked to be called, with
the stateliness of drunkards and their universal sense of humor,
placed the Frisbee on his head and tossed his hat instead, he earned
himself an ovation. And Bobby, who could sail it across the plaza as
easily as snapping his fingers, who could telepathically direct its
flight to wherever it was he chose to wait for it—him they regarded
with awe.

The Frisbee got stuck in a tree; Nina volunteered to retrieve it.
She got a boost from Camilo and climbed high from limb to limb
as if she were on a ladder. Theofilo crossed himself. The Moreno
hooted. Nina got the Frisbee. Bobby got a picture.

Bobby sat down on the wall beside Marcellino, who, with a look
of rapture on his face, swayed to the Stones like a cobra to a flute.
He took Bobby's hand and rubbed it with his own. Bobby tried to
free himself—the boy's skin was like pumice—but Marcellino
squeezed and rubbed and rested his cheek on Bobby's sleeve. The
boy's head lolled and his jaw sagged. His tongue was bright lime.
He rubbed Bobby's hand and looked up at him as if Bobby were
God's own brother. Bobby squirmed inwardly. He sensed he had
somehow made the kid a promise he couldn't keep.

They had all gathered in Santo Rosario to prepare for the feast
now two days away. They had cleaned up the chapel, swept out the
houses, and cleared away the debris left by the villagers when the
army had driven them out. As much as time would allow, and as

best they could, they rethatched roofs, shored up rafters, replaced missing doors, rebuilt fallen walls. They decorated with streamers and strung the electric lights. They hung lanterns with candles. They'd hauled up as much of what Nina had bought in Huaráz as they could, leaving the rest to be brought up later. Runners had been dispatched to all the surrounding mountain villages to spread the news that regardless of the abandonment of Santa Rosario, the feast would be held this year as usual. The Moreno would camp across the stream somewhere up by Blue Lake until the day of the event. Once they got the generator going, which would power the lights, the preparations would be complete. Roberto and Nina had been tinkering with it all day.

Bobby wandered between houses down to the stream. He stepped around the entrails of the sheep that they had slaughtered for dinner and waded into the water which was cold and knee high. For once everyone was happy, he thought: the Moreno because of their success in Huaráz, the clothes, and weapons, and because of the foothold they thought they had gained through their offer to fund the feast; Theofilo because not only would the feast *not* put him into debt, as everyone had predicted, it looked like it might actually turn him a profit; Augusto because the feast fell on his birthday this year and he had come to regard it as his personal party. And if there was no expression of joy from Antonio, there were no complaints from him either, although admittedly he was harder for Bobby to read, and complaints from him were unlikely under any circumstance.

Across the stream, Bobby took the path up through the fields. Green shoots grew between the charred stalks. The ground crunched under his shoes and the wind lifted the smell of ashes. Why hadn't the army, having gone to the trouble to burn some of the fields, burned the houses as well? There wasn't much he did know anymore, except maybe that he should've stayed a cook.

He climbed to a bluff from which he could see the stream and the town, a good vantage point for shooting the feast. From this distance the village seemed not such a hopeless, godforsaken place. He imagined the picture he wanted: evening, telephoto, tight com- position, just the plaza ringed in light from the colored bulbs and jammed with people, the elements dense, compressed, flattened—

busy—the smoke giving things on the ground a hazy, dreamy, Chinese-y look.

Nah, he thought. Too predictable. He reconsidered. He'd pull way back, use a wide-angle instead, take it all in—the stream, the burnt fields, the path from Viracocha zigzagging in on one side of the frame, the path to Copa Chica zigzagging out the other side. The village itself would be tiny, inconsequential, dwarfed by the landscape, by the mountains hidden by cloud, their bulk merely suggested. Or, if he got lucky, the weather would clear and there'd be alpenglow on the peaks and a line of smoke leading the eye into a pink and purple sky. He didn't forget the fireworks. He'd improvise a tripod, hold the shutter open, get the bursts of light and the long colored streaks . . .

As quickly as he assembled it, the image fell apart. He squeezed his eyes shut with the effort to fix it, but against his will another picture, more vivid, more real, superimposed itself: the Polaroid of Blacky, Blacky laid out on the slab. Something inside himself forced Bobby to look at the picture. Blacky with a hole in his forehead. Blacky stiff and dead.

But it was not only Blacky's death which weighed on Bobby. It was the prospect of his own. He'd underestimated Rinaldi. He'd discounted his threats. Now he knew different, knew he'd never be safe. He'd have to leave, a fugitive again. He would go with Nina, not because he loved her, although maybe he did, probably he did, but because Rinaldi wanted her, and that alone was reason not to give her up. There was some satisfaction in that. Not enough to balance the anger he felt at what had been done to Blacky, or at having been made to run.

Nina congratulated herself on having gotten Augusto the knife for his birthday. She didn't know what she would have done without it. The Moreno had taken the generator from the garrison and hauled it into the mountains assuming it worked, but it didn't. The knife had Phillips and slot-head screwdrivers both, as well as two blades, a scissors, nail file, and corkscrew, and it was enough, Nina hoped, to get the thing running.

She had no wrench to pull the spark plug, but she cleaned the air filter and the cooling fins, scraped the breaker box cover, and used the nail file to clean the points, which were slightly burned and pitted. She adjusted both the idle and the mixture. She fixed the linkage on the choke to allow the valve to close completely. She adjusted the throttle. She cleaned the fuel strainers, the sediment bowl, and the breather filter. She checked the vent in the fuel tank. She checked the crankcase oil level. You don't grow up on a ranch without knowing how to work on engines.

"OK, kid," she said to Augusto, who had followed her every move. "Do your stuff."

Gusto set the choke and yanked on the crank cord. The engine sputtered, but didn't catch. He rewound the cord and yanked again. The effort threw him back on the seat of his pants, and the engine offered an encouraging *phut-phut-phut-phut* before it died. Nina poured some gas down the carburetor's throat. She turned the mixture screw a quarter turn. She thought the plug might be fouled. She checked for loose connections and frayed insulation. She discounted the condenser as the source of the problem. The odds against a bad condenser were a thousand to one.

Antonio, whose expertise did not extend to gasoline engines, stood watching off to the side. He held Augusto's old wide-brimmed felt hat. The boy was wearing Rivera's new blue beret. Augusto yanked again on the cord with no success. Nina wished she had a socket to pull the plug. Augusto yanked again.

Antonio called softly to his son. All day Augusto had been with Roberto and Nina, first sorting and stacking and storing the fireworks in one of the abandoned houses ringing the plaza—how the boy had pleaded to set one off!—and then this, tinkering with the generator. Antonio felt Augusto was somehow slipping away. He beckoned for the boy to come.

Augusto answered his father impatiently, without looking up. "As soon as I get the engine started." He unscrewed the air filter and, as he had seen Nina do, peered down into the carburetor's throat. His father called him again. Reluctantly, Augusto went.

"This is a good place for puma," Antonio said softly. "Let's you and I go set our trap."

"But I almost got it started," Augusto whined.

"If we wait any longer, it will be too dark to see."

"Maybe Alberto wants to go. Or Marcellino. Can't you see I'm busy?" He returned to the generator.

Antonio stood holding the hat. A few minutes later, after handing the hat to Roberto, he walked alone down toward the stream. Augusto never lifted his nose from the engine.

Nina witnessed the rebuff and felt Antonio's pain. They had been together—the three of them, Nina, Antonio, and Augusto— since the afternoon Antonio had fished her out of the river, and she was attuned to their unique relationship. They seemed more like partners than father and son, drawn together by mutual respect, affinity, and common interest as much as by obligation or blood. Coercion played no part that Nina could detect. The boy knew what had to be done was trusted to do it.

She tried to remember what it had been like to be twelve years old, and she recalled the chores she had been assigned to do— feeding and watering the horses, cleaning the stalls, washing the dishes—chores that she had resented. They had a maid to do the dishes, and a farm hand to tend the horses. Her work was gratu- itous, and besides, her father was always looking over her shoulder. She pictured him inspecting the stalls while she stood to the side holding the pitchfork. He had always been trying to "give" her a sense of responsibility, the assumption being she hadn't one of her own. She'd never been allowed any real participation in matters concerning the family. Her opinion was never asked, or if it was, it wasn't taken seriously.

It was different for Gusto, who hadn't the luxury of a protracted childhood, who *was* responsible and knew it, who would work all day because he was needed and depended upon. He was not play- ing at work, nor were his tasks practice or preparation for some- thing else. His contributions were real and necessary, and they were acknowledged.

"I think your father wants you to go with him," Nina said. "Go on. Maybe you'll scare up a puma."

"Everyone knows there aren't any puma anymore." Augusto pulled the cord several more times. The Briggs and Stratton en- gine was no closer to starting than it had been before. Gusto said he thought he knew what might be wrong. Did they mind if he tried to fix it?

Nina watched the boy tinker with the engine. She had done everything she could to assure the success of the Feast of Santo Rosario. It was as important to her as anything in her life had been up until then. She hadn't cared as much about the plans for her wedding.

But whatever the outcome, she knew that for her the work had been its own reward. Her weeks in the mountains had carried her out of reach of the past, beyond grief, guilt, and anger. Her headaches were gone. She'd finally gotten acclimatized. She'd given up smoking, maybe that was part of it, too. She felt fit and strong. Ready. Ready for Freddy, as Bobby would say. She'd planted, hiked miles to and from the pastures, carried water, made mud bricks and helped Antonio build an addition onto his house. Her body had rebelled at first—blisters, sore muscles—but had grown accustomed to the new demands. Calluses formed. Her muscles got hard, her body slow to fatigue. She'd gone to bed early, bone-weary. She'd slept soundly, and awakened at daybreak refreshed and renewed. She'd rediscovered the satisfaction of completing simple tasks, of adding brick to brick, of covering a row of seeds. There was the comfort of routine, and the spaciousness of time. Best of all was the righteousness, the revitalizing power, the absolute, indisputable godliness that an austere and disciplined life imparted.

It would be wrong to say the tempo of the mountains had left her little time to think, that sooner or later her ghosts would find her. But by an act of will, she had focused on the present and on the possibilities which had opened up to her. Contrary to what she might have predicted, she was thrilled to be free of Rinaldi, and in the strange way tragedy often pulls a blessing in tow, she felt free of the dominating influences of Alejandro and her father as well. Free to do or be as she chose, uncircumscribed by the expectations of others.

As for Bobby, he had been the instrument of her liberation and she owed him a debt for that. Besides she liked him, loved him, she could honestly say, in the way she had always understood that word to mean, which was to see him as he was and to accept him that way, without the neediness and complication love had always been for her in practice. As for passion, as best as she could figure, passion was a trick in the air, like rainbows, like fog. Only men believed in its durability.

From where he sat on the bluff across the stream, Bobby saw the lights go on. He heard the cheering. He could see someone dancing with Nina, he couldn't make out who. He walked back down the hillside and waded the stream which, because it was growing colder—the sun had fallen behind the ridges and the glaciers were refreezing—swirled around his ankles. In the plaza he was met with the smell of roasting meat. The sheep was on the spit and there were potatoes in among the coals.

Bravo handed him a mug of steaming coffee which Theofilo offered to spike, an offer Bobby accepted. The radio reception had improved, and they sat around the fire listening to the bossa nova show broadcast from the capital. Marcellino had chosen Paco to attach himself to. Theofilo was in a mellow, amiable mood, singing along with the radio even though he'd probably never heard the tune. He danced with his bottle, taking small, graceful steps.

It was dark. Everyone was sleeping. Ice lined the edges of the stream. Gavilan stepped carefully from rock to glazed rock. It was cold enough, he thought, without having to sit his watch in wet shoes. He climbed the far bank and hunkered down among the boulders. The night was clear and moonless and still. He had grown to like standing watch, the solitary hours while everyone slept, and he would miss them when they ended. It had begun as one thing, had become another, and was changing to something else again. What that new thing was, was still unclear. It was not defeat. They had not been made to flee. Their retreat would be orderly, they would find new ground on which to make their stand: the cities, the prisons, the schools, the barrios, the mountains—it made no difference. Territory had never been the issue.

He heard a noise from down by the stream. Instantly alert, he braced his rifle against his shoulder. From behind a boulder, he scanned the banks. It was too soon for Paco to be coming to relieve him. He stared into the darkness. There was something moving near the water, small and silent, too small and too silent to be a man. Something prowling. A puma, he guessed, drawn to the entrails. The shadow merged with the deeper shadow of a tree. Minutes passed during which Gavilan saw nothing move and heard only the trickle of water in the stream.

The hiss seemed to come from right beside his ear. Scrambling to his feet, he slipped. He banged his elbow and dropped his rifle. It clattered down the rocks and splashed in the stream. He slid over the bank and groped blindly in the shallow, icy water. There was snarling now, and a series of explosive grunts. His fingers went numb in the water. He clutched a handful of gravel, and then a round, heavy stone. He spun in the stream, searching both banks for the source of the sound.

It came from above him, suspended over the opposite bank. A puma, trapped in a sack of some sort, was fighting to free itself. A rope ran from the sack over a limb, and holding the other end, legs out straight, heels dug into the ground, was Antonio. The branch bowed and creaked under the big cat's weight. Gavilan climbed the bank and grabbed onto the rope. Others ran from the village. Augusto, barefoot, took the rope's tail and pulled behind his father. Bobby grabbed on too, and the sack rose higher into the tree. They wrapped the end around the trunk. Someone shone a flashlight on the yellow nylon sack.

"Shitfire!" Bobby said. "That's my goddamn tent!"

There was a loud ripping noise and a foreleg pawed wildly in the beam of light. The other foreleg punctured the thin nylon skin and the terrified cat broke through to its shoulder. On its back it scratched and clawed and tore at the tent. Its claws were like razors. The cat fell free. It twisted to right itself, then froze midair, caught in the flash of Bobby's strobe. All four paws hit the water at once. It crouched in the stream, baring its teeth, hissing and snarling, its eyes like glowing coals. Slowly it turned and swaggered across to the opposite bank. Its paws splashed in the shallow water. Then, with a single spring, it leapt the high bank and disappeared into the darkness. The tattered yellow tent hung in ribbons from the tree.

"Has Bobby calmed down?" Roberto asked Nina. The others had gone back to sleep. She had offered to stay with him to finish out his watch.

"I think so. He may have gotten the picture of the cat falling out of the trap. He said it would be worth the tent if he got the picture."

"He's not angry with Antonio?"

"You know Bobby. One minute he's angry at you, the next he's giving you the shirt off his back. I heard him tell Gusto he'd send him a picture of the puma."

They talked sitting among the boulders on the bank. Mostly it was Nina who talked, rambling, first about the puma, then about Bobby, then about the feast. She talked about her weeks with Antonio, and she skipped back further in time to remind him of their rappel into the gorge, how he'd thrashed in the air after dropping off the rope, the splash he'd made when he hit. Not graceful like the puma. Nothing like the puma.

Paco, coming to relieve Roberto, called from across the stream, and the two of them, Roberto and Nina, walked back into the village together. The sky was just turning light. Roberto said good night and turned away, but Nina grabbed his sleeve. "I just wanted to tell you . . ." She looked at her palm and twisted the ring on her finger. ". . . those things you told me about myself, what you said you saw in me? Remember?" She looked him in the face while twisting the ring.

"I remember," he said.

"What you said was true." Her eyes were back on her hands.

"Things have changed." He pointed at her. "You've changed."

She looked up.

He started to walk away again.

"Roberto?" Again he came back. He waited while she searched for words. "I understand now, at least I think I do, what you're doing up here, I didn't before, but . . ." Her voice trailed off.

She seemed to be finished. He nodded, said good night a second time, politely, and left Nina standing alone.

Just as well, she thought, twisting the ring on her finger. She hadn't thought of a way to finish her sentence.

VIRACOCHA FORTY-THREE YEARS

Despite the day he had spent working in the fields, Augusto could not fall asleep. His brothers had been sleeping for hours like lovers in each other's arms, and his sister and niece were asleep by his feet, but Augusto couldn't find a comfortable spot. The more he tossed, the more the blankets gathered beneath him, and the more restless he became. He lay on his side and watched his mother stirring his father's dinner. She went from the pot to the doorway and back to the pot.

Augusto rolled out of bed. His mother watched while he put on his sandals and pulled his poncho over his head. "Oh, no," she said, stepping in front of him, but he slipped around her. She ran to the doorway and barred it with her arm. "You go right back to bed. If I let you go, do you know what will happen? You won't be gone five minutes when *he'll* come home, and then we'll have to go looking for *you*. I've had enough of waiting and worrying for one night. So you go right back to bed. No arguments."

"I'm not afraid."

"Of course you're not, but *I* am. And I want you here with me."

"What if he needs help? Suppose he's hurt? And don't say I'm too young, because I'm *not*." He ducked under his mother's arm and out the door. It surprised him how easily he had gotten past her.

"Gusto!" she yelled to his back. "Gusto!" She strained to see, but he was gone, sucked into the night. She would worry, yes, but in truth she was glad he was going. Something was wrong. Her husband should have been home hours ago.

Augusto thought she'd have tried harder to stop him. When he didn't hear her behind him, he slowed his pace and considered going back. It wasn't so bad out in the open fields, but down on the road it would be darker, he knew, much darker, and where the road dropped down to the stream . . . He had walked almost a mile before he admitted to himself his mother wasn't coming to take him back after all.

He told himself that it wasn't the darkness causing those sensations in his chest and stomach. And it wasn't *pishtaku*, either, he wasn't afraid of them. Plain old worry could make you feel that way, and he was worried about his father. And there still could be a puma or two around. Santo Rosario was proof of that. Augusto stooped to pick up a rock. He couldn't see his hand in front of his face and had to feel in the dirt in order to find one of a weight and shape that suited him.

Where the path joined the road to the village, he paused and stared down the black tunnel of overhanging trees. He hefted the rock in his hand and took a deep breath. He forced himself to take a step. The air seemed like tar, black and thick enough to pinch between your fingers. He looked back over his shoulder. Forward or backward, it made no difference, it was dark either way. He held to the side of the road away from the stream, pushing against the darkness as if it were a moving current.

At first he pretended he hadn't heard it, a sound from across the road and down over the bank. Then the sound came again. He stopped to listen. Low, almost a growl but not a growl, more like a moan or a whine, but weird, unnatural, not human and not animal either. The sound rose and fell over the sounds of water in the stream. Then it ceased. Gusto held his breath. He heard the stream and the wind moving the leaves in the canopy over his head. He heard the sound again, higher now, and louder, as if whoever or whatever making it was moving closer. He wanted to run, but his legs refused. The sound was like bees, or a cat, or . . . His panic was intense. Then he thought he knew what it was: someone down by the stream was humming. His father!

He took a step in the direction of the humming, and then he thought, No, don't go, it's a trick of the *pishtaku* to lure you down to the water.

"Papa?"

The humming stopped for a second and then began again. "Papa? It's me. It's Gusto."

A dark shape rose up from the bank and lurched across the road. Augusto jumped inside his skin. He cocked his arm and stared into the darkness. "Is that you, Papa?"

" 'Course it's me. Who'd y' think? I didn't scare ya, did I?"

"A little," Augusto said, lowering his arm. His heart was pounding. "What happened?"

"Fell over the bank. Fell on a rock."

"Are you hurt?"

"Almos' broke my bottle. Here, put your hand down here." The boy felt a knob on his father's shin the size of a new potato. His fingers came away warm and sticky.

Antonio slung his arm across his son's shoulders and the two of them, stopping several times to rest, or for Antonio to swig from the bottle, walked back up the road and through the fields home. Antonio hummed the whole way.

Dominga watched him limp up to the door. She didn't know whether to hug her husband or curse him, but she came to him when he held open his arms. She said a quick prayer, then smelled the liquor and her anger rose again.

She quelled the urge to scold him while she cleaned the bruise on his leg. Augusto fed him his dinner with a spoon. The others slept. "Are you going to tell me where you've been?" she said.

"With Theofilo. *Tío* Theofilo."

"You told me you were going to stay away from Theofilo."

"I was right," he said. "I shoulda." He winked at his son and reached out to tickle him. Augusto laughed and squirmed and evaded his father's clumsy attempt to grab him. "Santo Rosario starts tomorrow night, but I doubt Theofilo'll be around to see it. The poor guy's got to leave for the coast. Got to go to Paramonga. Now izzat a reason to get drunk or not?"

"I don't feel the least bit sorry for him."

"Oh, come on, Dominga." Antonio propped himself up on an elbow. "He's not such a bad guy."

"Don't you think the boy should be going to bed?" Dominga hinted.

"Gusto's no boy. He's a man, aren't you, Gusto? He's gonna be twelve in a coupla days."

"He has to work in the morning."

"Tha's true, tha's true. Your mother's right, Augusto. A man nee's his rest."

Augusto kicked off his sandals and rolled in beside his brothers.

"And then there's the feast tomorrow night, if we're still planning to go."

Antonio put the bottle to his lips and tilted back his head. The bottle was empty, had been in fact, three tilts before. He struggled to his feet and staggered over to his wife. "Which reminds me. There's somethin' I got to tell you," he said. "Issa secret."

Dominga put a finger to her lips, tilted her head toward Augusto, who was facing them, wide-eyed.

"Gusto, go to sleep. This is between your mother and me." Augusto rolled over. He lay perfectly still, barely breathing.

Dominga wiped her hands on her skirt. "Can't this wait until the morning?"

" 'S important," Antonio said.

"Then we ought to go outside to talk. Here, put this on." She handed him his poncho. They crossed into the addition where Antonio now stored his loom, tools, the grain and potatoes. Chickens squawked, flapped, and resettled themselves. Dominga lit a candle. "What is it?" she asked. Out the doorway she could see the light from the fire in the main room of the house.

"Tomorrow—"

"Shhh!"

Antonio dropped his voice. "Tomorrow's the day."

Augusto, who had crept from his bed to stand just inside the doorway, stiffened.

"Anyway, tha's what Theofilo says." The food and cold air had sobered Antonio some, or maybe the subject was sobering. "I din't believe him either, at first. Been drinking all day when I found him, and you know Theofilo, even when he isn't drinking, can't believe half of what he says."

Dominga didn't doubt Theofilo this time either. She had been expecting something to happen for weeks. Even so, she felt compelled to argue against it, as if her logic could influence fate, as if it were Antonio who needed convincing.

"They have *guns!*" she said. "The army tried, didn't they? The *army* couldn't get rid of them, and the army has guns, too, and airplanes. If the army can't do it, who can? And don't tell me Theofilo, that fat old ewe." She was breathless. "Antonio, *you* know they're not demons."

"Don't matter what I know. Don't matter a bit."

He told her what he'd heard. From the doorway Augusto listened, stunned. Kill Roberto? No! It wasn't possible. Roberto was too smart, too cautious to let himself fall into a trap set by Theofilo. Or anyone. Besides, his father wouldn't let it happen. He was sure of his father. He could count on his father just like his father could count on him. He started to breathe again. He told himself he'd been alarmed for nothing. He stood and listened, out of his parents' sight, or so he thought, and he was, except for the shadow he cast in the yard beyond the door.

They had come back from Santo Rosario, walked all that way because there was communal work that needed to be finished before the feast. On his way home from the fields Antonio had come across Theofilo sitting against a tree. He was alone, guzzling, angry as well as very drunk, full of self-pity, barely coherent. Over and over he said that he had to go to the coast to work in the sugarcane fields, and it was all because of "them."

The "them" Theofilo blamed for his misfortune was the village council. They had queered the deal with the Moreno. It was going to cost Theofilo a lot of money and force him to get work at Paramonga in order to pay his debts. The expenses of office had cleaned Theofilo out. Faced with footing the bill for Santo Rosario, he saw no choice but to accept the Moreno's offer. He knew the deal ran against the council's policy not to supply the Moreno at any price, but he was desperate. And the more he thought about it, the better the idea sounded, until its logic seemed so clear and so right to him that he assumed everyone else in the village would also see it his way. It was a beautiful plan to have the feast at the devils' expense, and he congratulated himself for having devised it. Still, he knew better than to inform the council beforehand. He would fill them in *after* the feast. With the money the Moreno had to spend, it would be the best feast anyone had ever seen. The gringa would see to it. And he, Theofilo, mayor of Viracocha, would get the credit. They would talk about the feast for years. They wouldn't do anything to him after that, after the feast he was going to throw, with a band and fireworks. How could they?

The Moreno had given him a shopping list: a sheep, three horses, three burros, a quantity of cornmeal, powdered milk, sugar, and whatever candy and coffee, fruits, and vegetables he could find. He returned to Viracocha, his head spinning with calculations. Using the two houses he owned and his own small flock as collateral, he assembled everything the Moreno had asked for. He made the transactions in Marcará, thinking that away from Viracocha there was at least the possibility his business would remain his own.

But the council learned almost immediately and everyone knew about the gringa living up at the Flores'. The village had automatically come to suspect the Moreno were behind every unusual occurrence, and in this case they were right. The council ruled unanimously to forbid Theofilo from selling the Moreno as much as a single potato. They didn't care that he had put up his house for collateral, or that he'd paid inflated prices. And they didn't care that he had taken the risk so they would have the best Santo Rosario ever, a feast they would remember for years to come, with decorations, a band, and fireworks. The council stuck to its guns.

Now Theofilo was stuck with four horses—one lame, another blind in one eye, a third barely broken to halter—and three high-mileage burros. If he had wanted to wait another day in Marcará, he could have gotten meal which wasn't quite so wormy, but he was in a hurry, and who knew? The Moreno might *like* the worms, they might consider worms a delicacy. The people up at Copa Chica ate dog, Theofilo knew for a fact, so what would be so surprising if the Moreno liked to eat worms? Now he was going to have to eat the worms himself.

At the meeting of the council they took turns denouncing the Moreno, each member speaking more strongly than the last. No one said a word in their behalf. They didn't like the army any better, maybe even less, but they knew if they somehow managed to keep the army away, the Moreno would remain, but if they got rid of the Moreno they would never see another soldier again. It would be just like it was before the Moreno came. It was unanimous. The Moreno had to go.

Antonio finished the story. Dominga shook her head. "Did he tell you how they plan to do it?"

"Surprise them in Santo Rosario, is all I know."

"I don't understand. The army comes here, people disappear

right and left, they take what they want, never pay a dime, they drive their trucks through our fields . . . Oh, Antonio! We can't let them do it! We've got to stop them."

"What can we do? The council decided. Do you want to go against the council?"

"My brother says he could get you a job, me too, instead of breaking our backs—"

"Picking through garbage? You call that a job?"

"No. Not picking through garbage. A real job. He said—"

"Live in the barrio, send the boys to beg or steal in the streets . . . I've been to the capital, I know. Forget what your brother says."

"It's not like we have very much to lose."

"I don't understand you, Dominga. One minute you say one thing and the next minute you say something else."

"They're not what they're said to be, that's all. They're men. I know what men are, the things they're capable of, and I wish to Christ they would go and leave us alone. But they aren't demons, Antonio. I don't understand them, but they're not demons."

"Nobody understands them. That's what makes them demons."

Dominga put her face in her hands. When she spoke again the passion was gone from her voice. "You're right, Antonio. I know it. They're trouble for us."

Remembering the night his granddaughter was born, Antonio was suddenly vehement. "He didn't have to point his gun at me," he muttered. "Inside my own house."

Dominga threw up her hands. "Now I see! You're still angry over that!"

Augusto calculated that without a burro, one he would have to coerce every step of the way, or a load to carry himself, or anything else to slow him down, not even his father, he could get to Santo Rosario by morning. He didn't doubt he could make the twenty mountainous miles, but would it be in time to warn Roberto? He knew he had to make the attempt. He couldn't let them walk into a trap. As for his father—there just wasn't time to wait for him. If he were to have any chance at all of reaching Roberto in time, he would have to leave right away. With his sandals in his hand, he slipped out the door and along the wall until he was around the back of the house. Then, pacing himself for the long night ahead, checking his urge to run the whole twenty miles, he walked the dark fields.

For the second time that night, Dominga resisted the impulse to stop her son. Thinking about him, and the person he was growing into, she looked back at her husband, a blank expression on her face. "I forgot what I was saying."

"About the old witch."

"You heard her. Julia was full of *mal*. Clementina, too. What is your resentment compared to the lives of your children?" She reconsidered her decision to let Augusto go. She knew where he was going, an eleven-year-old boy, alone, at night.

Antonio's shin was throbbing. He was sick from too much food eaten too quickly on top of too much to drink. He was thinking of how tired he was. Not just from the day, and the *trago* he'd drunk —Jesus, he had a headache! —he was tired of everything. He didn't want the Moreno killed any more than Dominga did. He knew the Moreno better than anyone. Of course they weren't demons, everyone knew what he thought about that demon crap. He wasn't afraid of the council, either, she was right about that, too. He'd lived in Viracocha forty-three years and he hadn't yet found anything there he couldn't do without, or take with him if he were forced to go. He had nothing against the Moreno. He just didn't want to be the one to have to save them. He hadn't invited them here. He'd already paid his debt to them. Hadn't he saved Gavilan's life once already? Dominga knew nothing about the incident at the baths, and it wasn't any old crazy witch or even the council he had defied, it was the comandante himself, Mosquevera. He'd more than repaid his obligation for the cow and for Julia, who he was certain, if she was going to get well, would have done so without La Perla and all her candles and smoke and the loss of a guinea pig. He was tired, too tired to exert himself for men who had further troubled all of their troubled lives. And yes, he did resent having been put out of his own house. In front of La Perla, in front of his sons. But he wouldn't let Dominga know about that. "It's La Perla's the instigator," he said. "She's the one to be telling all this to, not me. She's the one who's behind the plan to kill them."

"You have to warn them, Antonio."

"It's not up to me."

"You're going to let them kill Roberto? And Bobby?"

Antonio snorted. "Big gringo jackass."

"But should he be killed for it? Antonio, they have to be warned. And you're wasting time."

"I'm tired. I've been all the way to the fields and back already today, and now you want me to go to Santo Rosario."

"You have to try."

"Are you ready to live in the barrio?"

"I'll go with you," she offered.

"You stay here with the children." He got to his feet. "I'll take Augusto. He can go faster than me. Twelve years old, and he can outwalk me already."

Dominga helped her husband up. She kissed him on the cheek. "If you want to go with Augusto, you had better get started," she said. "I'll pack you something to eat."

CUSTOMARY SURLINESS

They were an hour above Blue Lake when the trail started steeply up the final two thousand feet to the pass. Bobby followed Gavilan close enough to allow them to talk.

"It's over my head, Roberto," he was saying. "I just don't understand it, man. I've been here six weeks and I still don't get it."

"Lots of things a person doesn't understand," Gavilan answered. "It doesn't make those things less real or true or worthwhile."

"I mean this is the end for them."

"For Antonio? Augusto?"

"As a race, as a people, yeah, looks like the end to me."

"What was done can be undone," Gavilan said.

"Some things, maybe. But these Indians are down an alley, against the wall. They can't go further and they can't go back."

"They were driven there."

"Doesn't matter. What does that matter? It's over for them. Think about it. The culture is dead. They're history, man. Name an accomplishment that isn't three hundred years old."

"Surviving is an accomplishment here."

"Rats survive. Cockroaches survive."

"What's the point?"

"Everything has its time, man. Dinosaurs. Greeks. Clothes wear out. Machines break down. Face it, Roberto, they've had their day. You think they were any more generous to the people they conquered? Any kinder? More compassionate? Shitfire, I read a whole book about them: these are the folks that sacrificed virgins, cut them open, ate their hearts while they were still beating. And then, after doing all that, they pitched the bodies over a cliff." Bobby whistled like a falling shell. "That tells you something right there, doesn't it? Tells you all you need to know."

Blacky would have known what was coming, Bobby thought. Blacky would've picked up the cue. But the straight line Bobby needed from Gavilan wasn't forthcoming. Bobby had to supply it himself.

"What'd they have to go and kill them for? Didn't they ever think of asking nice? They coulda tried taking 'em out to dinner, a coupla margaritas, maybe a little toot . . . Girls are girls, am I right? But nooo, not these guys. Right away they go and kill them. A waste of a perfectly good virgin if you're asking me. Ate the hearts! Can you feature that? Eat a beating heart? Raw? Then, as if that weren't enough, the jerks go and toss the best parts away."

Bobby waited for some response from Gavilan. Blacky would have laughed. But all he heard were footsteps behind him in the dark. "Shitfire, Roberto. The problem is they've been sealed off up here too long. Isolated forever. Lookit England. All downhill since the XKE. Inbreeding's the reason. Same deal here. They got to get out of these mountains, man, mix it up with the rest of us. They need some new blood. Spike the gene pool a little. Shoes, change hats, new threads, new tunes. It's obvious. Even to them. They're leaving in droves. The capital's full of them. The ball game's over up here. I know it, *they* know it, everybody knows it. How come you don't know it?"

"How come you don't know this lake you're so hot to photograph has been photographed about a thousand times already? It's on every calendar they ever made."

"You know what you are?" Bobby answered. "I'll tell you what you are. You're the Boy Scout helping the old lady across the street who doesn't want to cross."

"The fact that it's a cliché and everyone knows it's a cliché doesn't stop you from getting up at two in the morning to walk up there to photograph it again."

"These people are dinosaurs, man. They didn't adapt. Don't get me wrong. I don't want to see any harm come to any of them. Some of them I even like. How can you not admire a guy like Antonio? Shitfire, the guy's terrific. And Augusto, talk about the all-time great kid. I wish my kid was like Augusto. But that doesn't change the fact that these Indians are on the skids, and damn straight I'm gonna do it again. At dawn if we get there in time."

"The best you can do is make an imitation. A copy of an imitation."

"Listen, man. I'm just hitting all the squares, taking them in order. One at a time. I'm not like you. I'm not one of these people who blazes new trails. I didn't invent photography. I didn't discover landscapes. Everything I know or think came from somebody else. When I learned to cook, I followed a recipe. You see something you like, you copy it. What's wrong with that? I mean, you don't think you invented revolution, do you? Or do you?"

They walked for a while, allowing the gap between them to widen, Gavilan falling back, Bobby walking with a purpose to reach the ridge before sunrise. He had a thousand feet more to climb and still the only light was the stars. He would make it, he knew.

An hour later he sat on his haunches behind a pile of rocks on which he had set his camera. He tucked his bare hands under his armpits and pulled up his collar to keep the wind off his back. The wind was blowing over the pass, and a higher wind was blowing plumes off the summit of Alpamayo. He watched the snow on the peak record the changes which morning made on the sky. The lake turned from black to blue to green to turquoise. He shot a roll of film before Gavilan reached his perch.

"Was it worth it?" Gavilan asked.

"This was a test. I'm gonna come back, and I wanted to check the scene, see if it's worth bringing some heavy equipment up here."

"You gonna move the lake to where it catches the light a little better?"

"Like you said, my man, this picture's been taken a thousand times. There's nothing I can do to make it new. But there is something I can do that no one else can: lug one of those big mothers up here, an 8×10, or maybe I can convince Polaroid to loan me one of their 20×24's. I could camp up here, stay up here, live up here, and when the sky is right and the light is right, when the lake is just the right shade of blue, and glassy like a mirror, when it reflects the summits like you said, and there are dark thunderheads maybe, and the sun comes in low underneath the clouds and the snow catches fire, I'll be here with my 8×10, and I'll make the biggest, sharpest print of this view anybody has ever seen. A mural. A goddamn billboard. It'll look like you're there yourself."

"It'll still be the same picture."

"But bigger, better," Bobby said. "Mine."

Gavilan left, saying he wanted to reach the stream before the sun thawed the glaciers and made the water rise. He told Bobby to hurry the others along. Bobby sat and watched the sky brighten. Already it was warm, unusually warm, even up on the pass. Nina passed him and the other men passed, climbing the last hundred feet. Dressed in new fatigues under their ponchos, carrying new weapons, bellies full for a change, spirits high in anticipation of the fiesta, they waved or shouted good morning.

Señora Mendoza pointed to the boy under the blankets. "I didn't know what it was at first," she said. "I thought it was a dog on the path, but I came closer and it didn't move and I saw it was a boy. We brought him back and put him to bed. He started to thrash around and he talked, sort of in his sleep. Ernesto told you?"

La Perla nodded.

"I think his name is Roberto. That's the name he kept on saying. After Ernesto left to find you, he quieted down again. It scared me. I thought he had died." She crossed herself.

La Perla recognized the boy as the oldest son of Antonio Flores. She pulled the blankets off to examine him. There were no marks on his body, no obvious injury. She looked at his feet, which were cut and swollen. One foot was blistered across the instep where the strap from his sandal had worn the skin away.

"He was wearing only the one sandal when I found him," Señora Mendoza said. "The other one was tucked inside his jacket. Here." She held the sandal by its broken strap.

La Perla wrapped him in blankets and cleaned his face with water. She carefully washed his feet and cleaned the sores. While they were waiting for water to boil, Augusto woke.

"Well, Gusto," La Perla said. "You're a long way from home."

He looked around. He tried to get out from under the blankets. With one hand La Perla pressed his shoulder down. He wriggled under her weight, but hadn't the strength to free himself. He struggled until sweat glistened on his forehead and upper lip. He began to shiver. La Perla wiped his face. She asked for another blanket. Gusto tried again to get up, but La Perla pinned him down. Then he closed his eyes.

Into a cup of hot water La Perla put a pinch of the contents of the small sack she pulled from among her skirts. She let it steep. A few times Augusto opened his eyes, but he didn't try to stand. "Drink this," she said. She held his head. The aroma made him wince. He struggled in her arms. He was no match for the strength of the *curandera*. She held his nose and when he opened his mouth to breathe, she poured some tea down his throat. Then she rested her weight on his chest until he became too drowsy to fight.

"Here," she said to Señora Mendoza. She handed her the pouch. "When he wakes up, make him another cup of tea."

"When will that be?"

"I don't know. A while."

"And if he resists?"

"Don't force him. Give him something to eat."

"Will he be hungry?"

"He's come a long way."

Bobby climbed the last few steps to the pass and slipped through the slot between the rocks that led to the northern slope. The sun bored through. Its heat pressed against him. He paused for a moment before the stupendous vista of mountains, blue sky, and valley; then, with his eyes slitted against the brightness of the sun on the snow, he pushed on down the trail.

Some distance below the ridge, he caught up with Nina. He sat beside her shoulder to shoulder in the heat of the sun. The sun had climbed opposite them and its light had followed them down. Meltwater gushed alongside the path. They dipped their shirttails in the water and cooled their faces. They splashed water on their necks and poured water over their heads. There was no shade, but the uphill side of the rock was cool against their backs. After they had been sitting awhile, a shadow fell over them. Bobby opened one eye. It was Camilo and Emilio. Camilo had new green army fatigues and a new machine gun, but Emilio still wore the blue jeans and Coors T-shirt Bobby had given him. There had been nothing in the booty from the garrison Emilio's size. They sat next to Bobby, pressed their sweaty backs against the cool boulder, and stretched out their legs.

"I got an idea," Bobby said, his eyes still closed. They were all too hot and tired, Bobby knew, too hot and tired to ask him what his idea was. He went on without prompting. "Picture this. A recruitment poster. We use Camilo as a model. Stand up a minute, will you, Camilo?"

"Fuck off," Camilo answered, pressing his damp neck against the coolness of the rock. "Damn, it's hot. Too late in the year to be so hot."

"C'mon, Camilo. I'm serious," Bobby said. "Handsome guy like you, we'll fill the ranks in no time flat."

"Yeah, but what do we do with a thousand teenage girls?" Emilio came right back.

Bobby opened his eyes, sat up straight, stared in disbelief. "You gotta be kiddin' me, Emilio. You're puttin' me on, right? You guys want to run the country, and you're asking *me* what to do with a thousand teenage girls? Shitfire, Emilio. You just lost my vote. Now, c'mon, Camilo. Stand up for me."

As hot as he was, Camilo played along. He walked up the trail, turned, and walked back, mimicking a model on a ramp.

"Great," Bobby said. His camera was where it always was, around his neck, and he put the viewfinder up to his eye. Camilo stood at attention, staring into the distance. "Wonderful. They'll be tripping over themselves to enlist. Growl a little for me, Camilo. Look ferocious. What do you think, Nina?"

"I think you tried the same routine on me. I think Camilo should be careful not to drop his keys." She hauled herself to her feet and started down the trail. "Hope it's cooler in Santo Rosario," she said.

"See you guys down the road," Emilio said. He hoisted his pack and followed her.

Bobby kept his eye to the viewfinder. "*Hasta luego,*" he said, and to then Camilo, "Do that spin for me again, will you? That's it. Beautiful. Beautiful. One more. And one more. And just one more."

* * *

Antonio was hot and hung over. His head hurt, he was hungry, thirsty, tired. His legs were stiff. His feet were swollen. He had all but forgotten the Moreno. He was worried about Augusto.

He searched among the crowd in the plaza for a familiar face. The glare hurt his eyes. He saw the streamers and lanterns and the string of electric lights. He wondered for an instant where the generator was. He spotted his neighbors on the far side of the plaza by the stone wall. *"Con permiso,"* he said. The crowd turned to him like fish to chum. It tightened around him.

Someone grabbed the lapels of his coat: Dominguez, the big man. "What do you want?" The people at the edges of the crowd stood on tiptoe and strained to hear.

"I'm looking for my son," Antonio said. He was hoarse, his throat dry. Sweat dripped off his forehead.

"What?"

"Looking for his son." His answer was relayed to the fringes.

The crowd pressed closer, grew dense, compact. Antonio tried to push his way out, but they were too close for him to even raise his arms. He could feel their breath on his face, smell their breath and their bodies. The crowd moved, and Antonio, his arms pinned to his sides, was carried along. He stumbled, but was too tightly hemmed in to fall. A hand swiped at his hat, missed. Someone spit at him, and then it rained spit, and he had strings of spit hanging from the brim of his hat. He had the urge to go limp, to collapse.

"It's Flores!"

The mob backed off. Someone handed him a rag, one of his neighbors. He wiped his face.

By the time Gavilan reached the stream, the sun had been sitting on the snowfields for several hours. Cold, gray, and silty, swelling with meltwater, the stream had climbed the banks. The rumbling was the current rolling boulders down the streambed underwater. At the rate the water was rising, Gavilan guessed the others would have to find another place to cross. Would serve them right, too, he thought, to have to scramble a mile or two along the banks to find another ford. It wasn't that he hadn't tried to get them moving. But then there was the eggs and bacon and coffee Nina had brought, and it being the day of the fiesta, he didn't press too hard. He looked back up the trail to see how close they were following—

they were way back up the slope—then looked at the stream, gauging how high it would be by the time they arrived.

He waded in, holding his rifle over his head. The water was up to his crotch. The rocks were slippery, the current strong. The cold made his bones ache. Midway across, he stepped in a hole, lost his balance, and in seconds was washed thirty yards downstream, where the current slammed him into a boulder and pinned him on the upstream side. He hauled himself out. He'd been foolish to make the attempt, and now he was stranded on top of a boulder fifteen feet from shore in the middle of a rapid. Worse, he'd lost his weapon. He looked to see if any of the others were coming. He thought to wait for help, but he knew that the longer he waited, marooned on his little island in the roiling current, the harder it would be to reach the bank, and so he eased himself back into the channel. Again, the icy current swept him away. It swirled him around and tumbled him over. He knocked his head and bruised his shins before being shunted into an eddy.

The bank was steep and muddy. Breathless and shaken, he grabbed the exposed roots of a tree. His feet slipped out from under him and he pulled himself out on his belly. He was wet and tired and dazed from the bump on his head, which was bleeding. He sat on the bank, panting, touching the bump on his scalp.

On the path toward the village, he stopped and leaned against a tree to catch his breath and allow the dizziness to pass. A small black and white dog was sprawled on the path, asleep. Beside him was a piece of red rag. The dog awoke, saw Gavilan, and snatched up the rag in its teeth. It planted itself in the path and growled. As Roberto stumbled forward, the dog retreated, then circled around behind. It nipped at Roberto's heels. A kick sent it rolling off the path. It yelped, righted itself, growled, and bared its teeth. It followed at a distance, the bit of red rag still dangling from its mouth.

He came to a house and leaned against a wall. His wet pants were plastered to his thighs and his shirt to his skin. He was dizzy again. He touched the bump and grimaced. Blood matted his hair in spikes and was smeared over his forehead and down his cheek. His head throbbed. He slid down the wall to rest. His fingers were sticky with blood and he wiped his hands on the back of his pants because of the mud caked down the front of his shirt and on his thighs. His side pocket bulged from the water trapped inside, and he unbuttoned the flap and collapsed the bubble, which sent the cold water over his crotch and leg. He leaned against the wall, which was warm from the high hot sun, and closed his eyes.

When he opened them again, his pants had dried stiff and the mud on his shirtfront was beginning to crack. His scalp was tight, his headache intense. He pulled himself to his feet and steadied himself against the wall. Behind him he could hear the roar of the stream and he knew that it had risen even higher. His men were still somewhere behind him. They would have to find another ford, he knew, upstream where the bed was narrower, or down, maybe in the canyon, where he remembered a log had wedged between the walls.

He stood in the shade between houses and saw the crowd in the plaza. His head hurt, but he wasn't dizzy anymore. He climbed a low stone wall to get a better view. The sunlight made him squint. Malice from the mob focused on two men trapped in the center. One was Antonio Flores. Roberto eased himself down and returned to the shadows between the houses. He wished he hadn't lost his rifle in the stream.

Eduardo Guzman, perhaps because he wasn't as drunk as the rest, perhaps because he had known Antonio since they were boys, was trying to keep his neighbors at bay. "Let's hear what he has to say. Give him a chance to speak!"

"Yeah, what's with you and the Moreno, Flores?"

"He's one of them!"

"He helped them, didn't he?"

"First we're gonna take care of them, then we'll see to you, Flores."

"You too, Guzman."

"We'll get the both of you."

The mob pressed in. Guzman, his instinct for self-preservation stronger than his loyalty to a boyhood friend, allowed himself to be absorbed. Antonio was left at the center alone. He tried to break out, but they threw him down. They taunted him. He struggled to his feet. A rock struck his thigh. He tried to speak, but no one could hear on account of the laughter, the shouts, and the jeering. His leg hurt. The sun was blinding, its heat malevolent. His lips moved.

"What did he say?" someone yelled from the back.

"He said, 'Fuck you!' " There was laughter. More jeering.

"Fuck him!"

"Augusto," Antonio murmured.

"What did he say?"

"What?"

"Gusto . . ." Antonio's chin drooped to his chest. "Augusto." Tears were in his eyes. He knew he would never see his son again. His sobs were lost in the noise of the crowd. Another rock struck his head. It knocked his hat to one side. He covered his face with his arms. Blood began to leak from his ear.

Gavilan had no doubt what was about to happen. He scanned the trail he had just descended. He could expect no help. They couldn't cross, not here, not now. He paused only a second before stepping again into the sunlight.

Their backs were to him. They were yelling and cursing. Some of them had red rags tied to the ends of their clubs and plows and hoes and mattocks which hung above the heads in the crowd. He looked for an opening in the tight mass of people. He put his hand on a shoulder. The man turned around. His face was slack with alcohol, but hard and mean just the same. Seeing Gavilan, he moved aside. One by one, stricken by Gavilan's appearance, stunned by his temerity, they made way. The cursing and shouting diminished to murmurs. By the time he reached the core there was silence.

He kneeled beside Antonio, who had curled in a protective ball on the ground. He touched Antonio's shoulder. Antonio cringed. He tried to scuttle away. Gavilan held him firmly. "It's me," he said. "Roberto." Antonio stopped struggling. He opened his eyes. "Let's get out of here," Roberto said.

Bobby and Nina stood with the rest of the Moreno at the fork in the trail. One branch dropped a hundred feet through the burnt fields down to the water, where they could see the stream was running too high, the current too fast, that they wouldn't be able to cross. Not in the usual place, at least.

They split into two groups to scout up and downriver for a ford, all except for Bobby, Nina, and Emilio, who took the other fork and climbed the bluff Bobby had found a few days before. From there they had an unobstructed view of the plaza. Below and off to the right they could see Rivera scrambling along the bank. The others were already out of sight.

There was no shade here, the sun burned directly above. Bobby took his meter and two lenses from his pack. He confirmed his guess that the "sunny sixteen" rule applied. He mounted a wide-angle lens fitted with a polarizer and looked through the finder. After shifting his aim a few degrees in every direction in search of a composition that pleased him, he rotated the filter until the sky went blue black and the snow on the peaks shone brilliant against it. He moved the village to the lower right corner of the frame and clicked the shutter, pleased with himself that he had resisted the amateurish habit he had of always putting the center of interest squarely in the center of the frame. There was a band of blue sky cut by the high white mountains, and below that brown hills checked with tiny fields, and below that the thatch roofs of the village. The plaza was crowded. Some of the people carried red banners attached to sticks and shovels and the handles of other tools. The red made a nice accent to the scene, Bobby thought.

The gray ribbon of water underlined the view. He saw none of the Moreno. No one had yet gotten across. He handed the camera to Nina.

"Very oriental," she said looking through the viewfinder. "Put the village in the bottom right."

Bobby had a moment's annoyance that Nina would offer him—the professional photographer—unsolicited advice. Worse, she was right. "Ah, yes," he said, brushing it off. "Vel-y o-liental. Vel-y special." She laughed and the irritation he'd felt a moment before disappeared. He removed the wide-angle and mounted his 300 mm lens. The 2× tele-extender doubled its reach. He asked Nina to sit in front of him so he could steady the barrel on her shoulder. The village appeared in detail now, the mud-brick houses, the holes in the thatch they hadn't repaired, the streamers, the lanterns, the ring of lights, the people, a black and white dog asleep on the path. Then something crossed his field of vision and Bobby pulled his eye away to see a bird as big as a man sail through the gulf of air below them, its shadow a giant black cross skimming along the stream.

"Condor!"

Bobby raised the lens and tried to pick the bird up in his view-finder while twisting the barrel to get it in focus. He saw a blur of sky, cloud, and mountain, and then the bird itself. He clicked off two shots even though he knew it was only partially within the frame and probably out of focus. Far down the valley it banked and soared back toward them again, giving him a second chance. This time he nailed it dead center, a background of ice, black rock, and blue sky framing the ugly vulture of a bird, its talons tucked under its body, its bald head and shiny black eye, the feathers at the ends of its enormous wings like greedy reaching fingers. Bobby clicked the shutter until, in long slow beats of its wings, the bird flew out of sight.

He loaded a roll of Ektachrome, shut the back of the camera, and watched the rewind lever revolve as he clicked off the leader. He rested the lens back on Nina's shoulder and looked through the viewfinder. "Today's my lucky day," he said. He twirled the lens barrel to bring the plaza into focus. He saw a roof, and swung the lens right, saw the sky and lowered it. He saw the stream, raised it, another roof, brought it left, saw the stone wall, steadied it, saw the crowd, the commotion, and for a long moment, while just exactly what it was he was looking at registered, he held the camera still.

Shitfire.

Emilio stepped behind Nina to look through the lens himself. In an instant he was sprinting along the bluff. Bobby handed the camera to Nina and followed. At the fork in the trail he was thirty steps behind.

Emilio raced down through the burnt fields, and behind him Bobby was running flat-out. He knew Emilio, knew what Emilio was going to do. He had to overtake him. He was ten steps behind and almost close enough to dive for his ankles, tackle him, make him listen. The trail dropped towards the stream.

"EMILIO . . . ILIO . . . ilioilioilio."

Eight behind.

"EMILIO!"

He was five behind when Emilio leapt from the streambank. Bobby had to slide feet first on the path to keep his momentum from sending him into the tumult of rocks and water which had just swallowed Emilio. The stream was a continuous boil as far as Bobby could see. Twenty yards downstream Emilio's head reappeared for a moment, before he was sucked under again. Bobby tore through the brush along the bank until he reached the spot near where he had last seen Emilio. He yelled. The sound of the water overpowered his voice. He scrambled higher on the hillside to get a better view. He could see to the bend in the stream where the canyon walls rose sheer from the water. He didn't see Emilio.

From the second he'd entered the furious, icy water, Emilio's only thought was for air. His sprint had left him nearly out of breath and the cold took what little remained. More than the helplessness, or the panic, more than the bashing he took against the rocks, he felt the ache for air. His clothes and shoes weighed him down and the current tumbled him over and the rocks battered him and the cold was like a weight sitting on his chest, crushing his chest, so that when his head finally broke above the churning surface he could do little more than gasp. He swung his feet downstream, fending off the onrush of rocks, but his shoes were heavy, full of water, and they sank, bringing him upright into the brunt of the current, which bashed him against the rocks and pitched him over sudden drops. He jolted through a series of rapids and dropped into a pool, where the falling water held him down and pummeled him, rolling him along the bottom before it finally let him go. He was swept along by the torrent, too weak and numb to do more than try to keep himself afloat.

The stream curved and funneled into a canyon. The banks drew closer together, higher and steeper. The current was swift, but the water was deeper, the rocks submerged, so that Emilio, bruised and numb with cold, was, for the first time since leaping in, able to take consecutive breaths. He allowed himself some hope. He thought that the worst was over, that he might work his way into an eddy. He thought he might still get back to Roberto. He tilted back his head and gulped the air. The high, steep, slippery walls left only a stripe of sky above him. He floated on his back. It was why he was again able to see the huge black bird as it swooped over the canyon rim, the condor, as big as a man, and why he didn't see the horizon line disappear, or the pourover, or the fallen log lodged between the walls, debris from a prior flood, normally a good four feet above the waterline, now partially submerged. And it was also why, on the following day after the water had receded to its normal level, when they found Emilio's body dangling high and dry above the streambed, impaled on a weather-burnished spike of a branch, its tip protruding through the second *o* in *Coors* printed across the back of his T-shirt, Emilio's face bore a look of such surprise.

Antonio had considered himself already dead. He did not recognize the man kneeling beside him. Nor did he understand his words. He was anticipating some new horror, more painful, more prolonged. He felt the hand on his shoulder and recoiled, tried to draw away.

"It's me!" The voice was insistent. "Roberto!"

Gavilan gently helped him to his feet. They probed the tight perimeter for an avenue out. Antonio dragged his injured leg. The crowd backed away, tramped on each other's feet backing away. Many averted their eyes. Some looked with horrible fascination. They whispered and murmured. The bolder ones stared.

Without taking his eyes from the mob, Roberto spoke into Antonio's ear. "What's going on?"

Antonio didn't answer at first. The glare. The pain in his leg

. . . Augusto. Gavilan put his ear close to Antonio's lips. "He came to warn you. Tried to warn you."

"Who came? Why?" Gavilan never took his eyes from the crowd.

"Gusto." Antonio sank to his knees. The mention of his son's name seemed to drain the last of his will. His chin drooped to his chest. With both hands on the lapels of his jacket, Roberto jerked Antonio back to his feet. He slapped him hard, slapped him again, gave him the front and back of his hand. He shook him until Antonio's jacket tore in his hands and Antonio collapsed backward onto the ground.

The circle closed in. Gavilan would not wait for it to close in on him. He lowered his head and dove into the mob. He took a blow on the head with the handle of a plow and a kick which knocked him onto his back. The world spun. He saw ragged cuffs, he saw sandals and bare dirty feet, thick calluses with lesions deep as tire tread. He covered his head with his arms. Above him the press of faces blocked out the sky.

Through his panic came the thought, So this is where it ends, and behind it the urge to surrender to the onslaught of an overwhelming force. His will still spasmed through his arms and legs, but his heart veered off on a course of its own. In rapid successive beats it plunged through anger, self-pity, despair, apathy. Suddenly he felt the ground tremor beneath him and the kicking stopped and the sky opened above him like a deep blue iris. Colored streaks crisscrossed the sky. The noise was thunderous. The villagers crouched and held their ears. Roberto brought himself to his feet.

Rockets tore through the roof of a house on the fringe of the plaza. Smoke billowed from the smoldering thatch. It poured out through the door and windows, and through the smoke he saw the rockets ricochet off the walls inside. They hissed and whistled. They exploded with thuds and cracks and bangs. The sound reverberated in the mountains.

Roberto pulled Antonio to his feet. He steered him toward the noise and flame while the mob was frozen by this display of magic and unholy power. There was a clear, wide aisle now, and the two of them, Antonio limping, Gavilan supporting him under the arm, dragged themselves through.

Antonio's leg was aching. The smoke stung his eyes, the noise hurt his ears. He was filled with dread at what was behind him, at what lay ahead. Her. La Perla, directly in front of them, framed in the doorway in a nimbus of smoke and sparks and flame. She had something in her hand. She dangled it by the broken strap. Antonio's jaw clamped shut and his stomach rippled with anxiety. The hair prickled on the back of his neck. He doubled over, his stomach in convulsions. He moaned.

Now, except for the crackling of the burning thatch, it was quiet in the plaza. The fireworks had spent themselves. The noise, the sparks, the sprays of color, the long streamers of red and blue and green were gone. Silence rang. The sun was a force. La Perla barred their way. She held the sandal in their faces.

"You may have fooled them," she said to Roberto. Her voice was husky with contempt. He felt it auger into his gut. "You fancy yourself a demon, but I know the demons, and you do not fool me." He tried to push her aside but she slapped his hand away. "Too late to leave," she said. She was smiling. "Now you must take your medicine." She jiggled the sandal in front of them. "Like the boy," she said. She looked at Antonio. "Like Gusto." Her smile was hideous. Her black eyes blazed.

At that moment Antonio lunged for her, but she sidestepped him easily, and he fell at her feet. She smirked, and laughter came from the mob. She taunted him with the sandal. He grabbed for her ankle, and this time, backing away, she stumbled. In an instant he was on top of her, grappling with her, searching for her body amid the layers of skirts she wore. They rolled over and over. Then with one hand he had her head by her braids and there was a knife in the other.

"What have you done with Gusto?" he gasped. He jerked back her head by her braid, exposed her throat. Rocks were hefted; sticks, clubs, and axes raised. The crowd came forward. He pulled her to her feet by her hair, stood with her as a shield with the blade of the knife pressed to her throat. One braid was undone, her skirts were covered with dust, her hat lay trampled on the ground.

Someone threw a rock. It whizzed past Roberto's shoulder. Another came, and another. A rock struck La Perla in the forehead. She went limp in Antonio's arms. He let her slide to the ground, a pile of black rags. The mob closed in, wary of tricks. A rock toppled Roberto.

Antonio stood over Gavilan's body. Surrounded, he pirouetted with the knife. He slashed the air, kept them at bay. He wiped the sweat from his eyes. He felt detached, a witness to this, without a stake in the outcome. His leg no longer hurt. He couldn't feel his legs at all. Nor the heat, nor the fear, nor the sick dread of worry he had felt for his boy. He was disappearing. His body was nearly gone. He was left with eyes, only eyes, and a thumping where his chest once was.

Over the mob he saw the bird. A rock struck him on the arm, but he felt nothing. He had no arm. He was with the bird. The bird had come for him and the two of them were high above the village. The people were specks in the dun ring of the plaza. All around were the white jagged spires he had known since he was a boy. The snowfields gleamed. He felt the rush of wind and the sun on his back and the flutter and flap of his clothing. They spiraled upward in a shaft of warm air, banked, and nosed downward in a long accelerating glide. A rock hit him in the chest, and another on the head. He felt it not as pain, but as pressure, and the pressure brought him back to the plaza, where he was on his back and looking up into the bland, stupid face of Theofilo.

Theofilo was panting. He was flushed and sweating and out of breath from running. "They're coming!" he wheezed. To Antonio the words were sounds without meaning. He watched the cracked, fleshy lips form the syllables. "They're here!"

They dragged Antonio and Roberto and La Perla's body into a house. They tied and gagged the two men, slammed the door. It was dark and cool inside. From the plaza came the first tremulous notes of a song, and then a louder chorus, and finally all the voices together, more like shouting than singing, harsh, boisterous, and unmelodious. Antonio struggled with the rags tied at his wrists and ankles. His eyes adjusted to the dark. He rolled across the floor where Roberto lay unconscious. Antonio tried to speak through the gag, but his words came out garbled. He rolled to where pieces of a broken *trago* bottle lay on the dirt floor. The singing had grown louder, rowdier. He rolled onto his back with his wrists tied behind and under him, searching for a shard large enough to grasp. He found the neck of the bottle and rubbed it against the rags that bound his wrists. He was soaked in sweat. The work was awkward. He had no leverage. His fingers cramped. He sawed, then rested, waiting for his muscles to relax. Outside, the singing stopped and shouting began.

Bobby and Nina saw the fireworks from up on the bluff. Now they watched the column of men snake its way down the path on the far side of the village. Through his lens he tried to pick out individual faces, but they were blurry, indistinct, still too far away. Never in his life had he felt so helpless. Antonio and Roberto, God knew what had happened to them, if they were alive or dead, and now the rest of them were walking into the trap. There was no way to warn them, nothing he could do. He sat behind his lens, which was braced on Nina's shoulder.

Even if they could get across, what could they do, unarmed against a mob? He was afraid she blamed him for Emilio, or worse, thought him a coward for not swimming the stream. He wanted to say that he knew about these things, that he'd been in big water before. He wanted to say, "You remember El Barro?" Of course she'd remember. She thought he was crazy to go out in waves like that. "El Barro was a walk in the park compared to how this stream is flowing," he'd say. He wanted to tell her that it wasn't a matter of courage, that no one could survive that river. But he knew how it would sound, so he said nothing, which was hard for him. He'd let her think whatever she wanted.

He counted five of them moving down the trail. He tried to pick out a face or a uniform—Rivera's blue beret, Camilo, or the hatchet-faced Pelota. He scrutinized them one by one as they moved between trees into a clear line of sight along the trail. The faces were unfamiliar. And the uniforms, they were old, torn, and dirty, and there were far too many men. He counted another group of eight, with more behind. He handed the camera to Nina.

They were coming into the village, their weapons slung over their backs, their faces painted with green and black, and they were smiling at the welcome—the songs and the waving banners. At the front of the column was a wiry man with a thin mustache. Nina recognized the face, the swagger, the wooden match stuck in the corner of his mouth.

"Mosquevera," she said.

* * *

Bobby clicked the shutter, rewound, and clicked again. The soldiers were in the center of the plaza. They suspected nothing. Their weapons were still on their backs. Singing and waving their banners, the villagers encircled them. They had lifted their banners as if in salute, and with them lifted their clubs and plows and axes and adzes, their mattocks.

First to fall was Mosquevera. The shovel blade sliced him across the back of the head. He stumbled forward and fell face down. There was a hail of stones. A soldier broke free, but his exit was sealed by a pair of men who stepped from behind a house. He turned, but there were another two behind him, a man and a woman. He tried to unsling his gun from his shoulder before a mattock handle cracked his head.

The rest stood no longer than a matter of seconds, although the beating, the raising and lowering of the clubs over the fallen bodies, went on many minutes longer.

The muscles of Antonio's forearms were a hard, tight knot. His fingers were bleeding where he pinched the shard. He had managed to fray the cloth but not to cut it all the way through. He tried not to think of his boy. He tried not to think what was happening out in the plaza. It was too late for them out there. Next they would be coming for him. Roberto was moving, moaning, coming to. Beside him was La Perla. In death her eyes had lost their lustre.

The room was dim, the door closed and the windows shuttered. Motes of dust swirled in the beams that here and there pierced the holes in the thatch. Suddenly the shouting stopped, the village fell quiet. He sawed frantically at the cloth, and then the door swung open and the sudden light made him blink. It closed again, quietly. He'd only cut partway through the rags, and with what strength remained he tried to rip them apart. The effort against the gag split the corners of his mouth. With his arms still tied behind him, he braced for his attackers.

A splinter of light glinted off the blade of a knife. In seconds the rags were off his wrists and the gag from his mouth. He embraced his son. His wrists were chafed raw. He shook the cramps from his fingers. He was crying. He started to speak, but Augusto hushed him. Together they knelt beside Roberto.

"Some fireworks, huh, Gusto?" Roberto said. He was still dazed, groggy.

"Follow me," whispered the boy. He slid the red knife into his pocket. With the help of his father he lifted Roberto to his feet, and despite the fact that one of his sandals was missing, he quickly led the three of them out of the house and down the path out of Santo Rosario.

SOCIAL REGISTER SLUT

I had hoped I'd have to go inside to get him. I was curious. Outside it was certainly nothing special: no nets on the rims, and the backboard wasn't much better than the schoolyard up in Marcará. Maybe inside it was nicer. For five grand a year they had to give you something. I had a mental picture of little thrones instead of desks and chairs. But Alberto was waiting by the curb in his shorts, kneesocks, and his blue blazer with the Notre Dame crest stitched on the pocket, and so I didn't get the chance. He heaved his leather briefcase into the van and climbed up onto the seat.

First words out of his mouth were "Where are they?" meaning the jeans and tennis shoes I'd promised to bring. They were in a paper bag with a present I'd brought for him, a baseball cap. Took him about thirty seconds to change. The cap fit like a bucket over a broomstick. Surprised me, though, how carefully he folded his school clothes and stowed them in that briefcase of his.

Because I'd come straight from the restaurant, I had to make a detour to my studio first, which didn't make him happy. With the reopening a week away, I'd been living in Blacky's old upstairs apartment, and I needed some things from my place out in Callao. On the ride Alberto hadn't much to say, just "When are we going to get there?" and "Are you sure we're going the right way?" and "We won't be late, will we?"

The pictures had just returned from the frame shop and I'd spent the morning in the restaurant hanging them. You know how it is—every decision is agony when you become an artiste. I liked it better when I thumbtacked them wherever there was space on the wall and was done with it. But framed like they were, I had to admit they looked pretty good.

The studio I had put off doing anything about, other than replacing the door they'd busted down. They didn't find anything, of course, not what they were after, but the search didn't leave a chair unturned. They knocked down the partitions, broke my furniture, wrecked the darkroom, scattered my clothes all around. They smashed both my surfboards—whether they thought I sealed the negs in the foam and glassed them over, or just from pure nastiness, I don't know. They in fact trashed everything I owned.

It was the last thing I needed. You spend eight weeks in the mountains, you'd like some cleanliness and comfort, and you come back to find your place torn up like that. Shitfire. But looking back, I shouldn't have been surprised. I should've known Rinaldi wouldn't take it lying down. After I cooled off I just wrote it off as a business expense and made an adjustment in his premium. Eventually Rinaldi came to understand my position. He respects a certain amount of ruthlessness. He's not an unreasonable man once you get to know him. Mean, yeah. Undeniably an asshole. A sicko, too, that's for sure, demented I would say, but no, not unreasonable.

I'd put the studio back together when I had more time. Next week, maybe, after the opening I'd get to it. Some things just didn't have the urgency they might have had eight weeks ago. Truth be told, nowadays anyplace that didn't smell of sheep was cool with me. And I had Blacky's apartment, don't forget, and although it also was pretty trashed—it could've been Rinaldi's work or, knowing Blacky, it could've been the way he left it—his place was smaller than mine and less of a chore to clean.

Old Alberto, though, one thing he didn't learn at Notre Dame was patience. He couldn't sit still. Had both hands up on the dashboard, his nose against the windshield, afraid I'd miss a turn, or sit at an intersection a hundredth of a second after the light had turned green. Asked a zillion questions. "If Augusto got my letter, how come he didn't write me back?" he wanted to know. I had to remind him—we were just pulling into the parking lot at Montesucre, there was no problem finding a space with post time three hours away—I reminded him that he was still the only one in the family who knew how.

"I bet I'm stronger than him." He sat up tall and puffed out his chest. "I take gymnastics. I've got a lot of muscles now, you know." He was skinny as a saltine.

"You'll see him yourself in a minute. He should be somewhere over there." I pointed in the direction of the stables.

The kid began to run. It had been a couple of weeks that he'd been boarding at the school, longer than he'd ever been separated from his family before. I yelled, Slow down, wait for me, but I understood his hurry because Nina was supposed to be there, too, and it seemed forever since I'd last seen her, although it was only a little more than a month. I trotted across the parking lot after him.

All of it seems obvious to me now. Looking back, it was the only thing to do. Rinaldi wanted me dead and was willing to go to great lengths to accomplish it. And what I wanted was to blow the country, but for a guy like me—not much dough, my visa expired—there was no place to go and no way to get there. But what I did have were some rolls of undeveloped film. The way I figured it, it was eat or be eaten, and I'd be damned if I was going to let that motherless Rinaldi take a bite out of me.

I tried to explain to Nina. I told her that it was me the platoon had come to Santo Rosario for, dressed as Moreno, or how they *thought* the Moreno dressed. The twist, of course, was that the Moreno themselves had new uniforms from the raid on the garrison—new fatigues, new boots, new everything—so that at Santo Rosario the army looked like Moreno and the Moreno looked like the army and you couldn't tell the players without a scorecard. Not that it mattered how anyone was dressed. The Indians were in such a juiced-up frenzy that whoever was unlucky enough to wander into the plaza that morning would have gotten whacked. The army just happened to get there first.

"Happened" isn't the word. It makes it sound like coincidence, and it wasn't. They had come for me, I'm convinced, and they knew I'd be there because Santo Rosario is where I told Rinaldi I'd be, taking pictures of the feast. But it was a fluke, because at the time I told Rinaldi I had no idea that that's where I'd *really* be, that that was where we'd all of us be. I'd said the first thing that popped into my head: Santo Rosario. Shitfire, wasn't even a Santo Rosario then. Remember it had been abandoned.

When the platoon didn't return, Rinaldi reported it missing. Presumed everyone dead. Ambushed by the Moreno, he said. He might have even believed it himself, because who'd ever have figured the Indians for something like that? Never one to miss a chance to blow things out of proportion, Rinaldi declared it the beginning of a new Moreno offensive. There was the usual shitstorm. Somehow the Interior Minister managed to hang on to his job. The plans were shelved to end martial law. Rinaldi got promoted to general. The man's in his glory. What better thing than being right? Unless it's to have your opponents forced to admit it. Publicly. In front of the nation. On the network news.

Nina didn't buy my theory. After all she knew about Rinaldi, she still had trouble accepting what the man could do. I was patient because of the circumstances: the massacre which took place right there in front of our eyes, not to mention the feast which didn't come off and all her work wasted—the ice, the fireworks, the goddamned generator we lugged all the way the hell up there, she just wasn't ready to believe Rinaldi had set it up for me. She claimed I was paranoid. I tried to explain that when there's that same stink in the air every time a particular person comes around, you got to believe that somewhere along the way he's been stepping in it. Rinaldi, he's been in it up to his knees.

I didn't hit on the blackmail scheme right off. After Santo Rosario, Nina and I went to El Barro. I had some money for the pictures of the Marcará bombing, and the raid on the garrison, not much, but enough to keep us for a couple of weeks. El Barro was out of the mountains and still it was nowhere. Not that I felt safe there exactly, but safer. It was a good place to lie low while I figured out the next move. Nina could think I was paranoid, she could think whatever she wanted, I knew enough not to go back to the capital. R and R is what I called it. She called it running away. We read the papers, read the lies Rinaldi was handing out, read about his promotion. We argued. We argued a lot. Finally she said she needed to get away. I said, Now who's running away? She went to the mountains to work in the clinic. She had her own stuff to sort through, she said.

Alone in El Barro is when I began to feel cornered. It got so I was afraid to go out of the house. It was the fear that got me onto the bus to Huaráz. I had to go. I had to see what I had on those rolls of film I'd stored in Don Manuel's refrigerator. Even without the Kodachrome, which we couldn't develop, between the black and white and the Ektachrome it turned out I had plenty. I caught the bus to the capital and went straight to Rinaldi's with a stack of 8×10's.

His butler leaves me waiting in the foyer. Rinaldi's surprised to see me, but he's not unhappy. He'd gone to great lengths to find me, and here I show up on his doorstep. He ushers me into the library and closes the door. He offers me a drink which I don't accept, and pours out one for himself. He offers me a chair I don't accept either. He makes himself comfortable, settles back, lights a cigar. He asks about Nina. Leave Nina out of this, I tell him. He says we can't very well, can we? Nina's at the heart of this. If you're so interested in her call her yourself, I say. He says he doesn't know where she is. You have a problem then, I tell him.

The discussion following is very short. Amazingly short, considering all it accomplishes. I do most of the talking. I hand him the pictures. They're the highlight of my presentation. They showed exactly what happened in Santo Rosario, and where you could find his "missing" platoon. The pictures were incontrovertible. I warn him if anything happens to me, I've arranged for duplicates to be mailed to every paper in town. He shuffles through them. He looks a little sick. He doesn't say a word after he looks at the pictures.

He sits in his leather armchair letting his drink go warm and his cigar go cold. He knows he's in a very bad position. He knows he has no choice. That's what blackmail's all about, isn't it? Severe, unexpected curtailment of choice. He'd lied and I had the proof he'd lied. The lofty position which he'd so recently attained turns out to be only as high as a dozen 8×10's. I ask for the money and the other stuff. Whatever I ask for I get. Like I said, he was an asshole, but not unreasonable.

Frankie Agramonte was repairing a saddle out in front of the stall. He pointed out to the backstretch where, sitting high on this big sorrel colt, running wide open and raising dust behind him, was Augusto. Alberto and I watched him come around. He was pressed against the horse's neck and they hugged the inside rail all around the turn and then he eased up and coasted down the straightaway. He stood in the stirrups and waved his whip and veered toward us at a gallop, the horse dark with sweat, still eager to run. They sidled over to the rail and Alberto jumped on behind and the two of them took a cool-down lap together. Alberto sat with his legs dangling, one arm around his brother's waist and the other holding the baseball cap from flying off his head.

I had put in a word for Augusto with Frankie Agramonte, got him the job as an exercise boy, but it was Rinaldi, ex-president of the Jockey Club, who swung the deal for Antonio and Marcellino with the management of the track. At my suggestion, of course. They were hired on as groundskeepers.

After Santo Rosario the Flores family was history in Viracocha. The capital was no small adjustment for them. They had been headed for the barrio to live with relatives, but I found them an apartment, nothing fancy, but twentieth-century—electricity, running water, two bedrooms, beds . . . I hadn't been there since they moved in, and I wondered how they were getting along, if they all still slept in a pile together. Julia, I know, liked it OK. Dominga was still shy around me, and even though we were working together, whole days would pass with nothing more than hello, good-bye, adios, mañana passing between us. As for Antonio, I never could get an accurate fix on that guy. He hadn't had much to say to me since the night by the river when I invited him and the kid to sleep outside the tent.

Which was the very same night things began to change for Nina and me. I didn't know it then, but now I see that that was the turning point for us. Used to be I thought of myself as a loner. I was disreputable and I liked it that way. A whole night with a woman was a long time to spend, and an afternoon . . . Shitfire, an afternoon could last forever. By myself I could *be* myself, was the way it used to be. But with Nina things were different. When she was away from me I missed her. She left this ache in my heart, a hole. It was like in every cornball song you ever heard. What I really missed was the me that I was when I was with her, that guy who wanted more from life than just a quick poke and Later, baby, maybe. All the time she was up there with that Israeli doctor I couldn't get her off my mind. I never write letters. I bet I wrote her fifteen. I got back two. She said she was fine, and for some reason hearing that made me miserable. She said that she felt "useful" there. I told her that she could be useful here, with me, working in the restaurant, or that there was no shortage of sick poor people in the capital if that's what she wanted to do. She thanked me for the suggestion, said I was sweet to be concerned, her way of saying no without saying no. She said that for the time being she knew the place for her was in the mountains. What she didn't know was that if it wasn't for me her clinic was out of business. The money to run it used to come from the Moreno and there was no Moreno anymore. Now it came from me. I got it from Rinaldi and sent it up there. She doesn't know and I told the doctor not to tell her.

I hope to bump into Rinaldi here at the track today. I have a little something for him. They're running the Humboldt Stakes this afternoon, and he has an entry, one of the favorites, Holy Robles. I'd be surprised he wasn't here to watch his horse run. But if I don't catch Rinaldi today, I'll catch him another time. It's interesting how conscientious he's become about returning my calls, about squeezing me into his appointment book.

I go upstairs to the dining room at the Jockey Club. Members only, but the manager extends me professional courtesy. I walk into the kitchen to say hello to the chef, a guy by the name of Fishy. Fishy tells me how sorry he is about Blacky and wishes me luck on the reopening.

The best tables, the ones next to the windows that overlook the finish line, are all reserved, this being the biggest day of the year at Montesucre, like Derby day at Churchill Downs. I take a table in back, which was not so much back as up, since things are arranged in tiers looking down at the track. It's more than an hour until the start of the first race. The waiters are setting out silver, filling up salt and pepper shakers, and there's hardly anyone in the place other than me. I can't concentrate on the racing form, too anxious to see Nina, who is meeting me here any minute if she's on time. We're going to have a drink and then meet the Flores for a picnic lunch down on the infield grass.

"The studio looks like a bomb went off," she says, coming up behind me. "How're you doing, Bobby?" She pecks me on the cheek and squeezes my shoulders.

I hadn't written her about the studio. She'd only have said it was more of my paranoia. "Burglars," I lie. A white one. I don't want to get into this Rinaldi business right off. Then, changing the subject,

I tell her how great she looks, another white lie. She looks tired, her hair is ratty, her clothes are wrinkled.

"Give me a break," she says. "You know what it's like five hours on the bus. Look at me! I went to your place thinking I might shower and change. It's not as if I can use the carriage house on Venice anymore. I didn't think you'd mind. Was I right?"

"What's mine is yours," I tell her. I mean it. She's the one. She really is.

"The key was—"

"Shhh, not so loud."

"—on the beam," she whispers. "God, what a mess!"

"Burglars."

"You already said." She asks the waiter to bring her a double Scotch.

"For breakfast?"

She lights a cigarette. She takes a swallow of the Scotch, takes another swallow, finishes it, and holds up the glass for the waiter to bring her another. Her hair, held back by a barrette, comes free and falls over her eye. She brushes it out of the way but it falls back again.

"I thought you quit." I mean the smokes.

She starts to cry.

"Hey, it's not so terrible. It's hard to quit."

She lets it all empty out. About how tired she is, how lonely. About the poverty and the disease and the mistrust and how under-supplied and underequipped and understaffed they are, so that when someone did come for help, often there was little they could do. "It's hard," she says, "not to let it get to you. Dov—Dr. Gershon—says that after a while you become inured to it. He says it makes you better able to do the work. He says that all the heartache helps no one, nor the caring nor the worrying. It gets in the way. He's right, but I can't seem to help it. It can be so depressing."

Depressing! Shitfire. What did she expect? The fucking Stockmen's Cotillion?

Over Nina's shoulder I see Rinaldi walk in with a babe on his arm. I congratulate myself for knowing my customers, but I hope Nina doesn't see him. She'd be upset. She's already upset. The headwaiter takes them to their table, one of those down by the windows. I can see where they're sitting, but Nina can't unless she turns around. Rinaldi has his back to me. The lady looks familiar, an actress, or someone from TV. I reach for the envelope in my back pocket, just to make sure it's still there.

Nina catches me looking away and says, "You probably don't want to hear all of this. I don't blame you if you don't." Feeling instantly guilty, I lie again and say of course I do. "I'd like to have another drink," she says, "but I'd better not. I'd go on and on and end up depressing the both of us. Tell me about the restaurant instead."

Those clear gray eyes lock on me as if flatwear and dishes are among the most interesting goddamn topics in the world. She lights another cigarette, an Inca. I'm getting buzzed just sitting near her. And it isn't just the smoke.

"I'd like to stay around for the opening," she says matter-of-factly. "I mean if that's all right with you."

"Yeah, sure, great," I say. What's this?

"Maybe I could even be of some help."

It's only what I've been asking her for weeks.

"A hostess or something."

Absolutely amazing.

"And would it be all right if I stayed with you? Just for a while. I'm going back to the clinic, I plan to go back, it's just that I need a little break. Would you mind?"

Would I mind?

"It would just be for a week or so. I do want to go back."

She still hasn't spotted Rinaldi, and by leaving through the kitchen on the pretext of introducing her to Fishy, a person she'd expressed no desire to meet, but to whom she was gracious anyway, I was able to make sure she didn't. On the way down to the infield I tell her I had left my sunglasses in the Jockey Club, which I had, deliberately, to give me an excuse to go back. I tell her meet me back of the pari-mutuel board. I have a letter to deliver, but I don't tell her that.

Rinaldi, I figure, has a low center of gravity, which is how come if you knock him down he rolls right back to his feet, kind of like one of those plastic punching bags they make for kids. "Mr. Shafto," he says, rolling to his feet and buttoning the jacket of his sport coat. If I hadn't been watching his eyes, I might have missed the single shot of pure hatred he fired my way. "May I present Mrs. Pello."

I say, "Hiya, Inez," and take the seat beside her.

"It's been a long time, Bobby," she says.

"You're looking good, Inez." I say. She is. Her hair is different, for one, softer, more natural, not that monument she used to erect on top of her head and anchor in place with Liquid Nails. And the dress she's wearing lets you know the rest of her is in the same fine shape it had always been in. There were plenty of things I liked about Inez. She was the kind of social register slut I've always been attracted to. But in the past I respected Moosh too much, and now, truth was I had other things on my mind, not least of which was Nina. Things seemed to have changed between us again.

"I see you two are acquainted," Rinaldi says.

"We had a mutual friend," I say.

Rinaldi looks different too. Takes me a minute to realize he isn't wearing his glasses. I'd never seen him without his glasses. I take the drink. I hadn't planned to stay, just wanted to deliver the envelope, but Inez is coming on to me and Rinaldi is beginning to burn and I couldn't pass up the chance to piss off Rinaldi. Me and Inez chat about this and that, old times, the restaurant, the Stakes, about Holy Robles and the other favorite, Forget Me Not. We don't mention Nina or Moosh. Rinaldi hasn't much to say, three words to be exact, and all three to the waiter: "Another pisco sour."

We talk for ten minutes. Inez writes her unlisted number on a matchbook cover, has to borrow a pen from Rinaldi first. Discretion never was her long suit. She doesn't seem to care what anybody thinks, and I admire her for that. People say it's because she has all the money in the world, and hanging in her dining room the portraits of grandma, the contessa, and grandpap el don Such and Such. But that kind, it seems to me, cares most what other people think. And it wasn't defiance either, which is the other side of the coin. No, Inez cared strictly for Inez and made no bones about it. It was part of her dirtbag charm.

Rinaldi, on the other hand, had drilled himself in manners like a recruit at Parris Island. Manners were a reflex with him. He can't help himself, so when I get up to leave he rolls to his feet again and rebuttons his coat. He's on his absolute best behavior. I could've told him to save the charm, if what he wanted was into her pants, charm is wasted on Inez. She once told me manners were some-thing you wore like a hat. For all her faults—Inez was as careless with your reputation as she was with her own—she was nothing if not democratic. She was unimpressed with the social distinctions the rest of the world organizes itself around. She'd give it up to anyone as long as she liked you.

She says to me, "Don't run," and pats the seat of the chair I just got up out of. "Sit down, honey. Have another drink with me." What a pisser she is. It's as if Rinaldi isn't even there. I love to jerk him around too much to leave. Inez slips her arm through mine, and below the table out of Rinaldi's sight, rests her other hand on my thigh. Her Alfredo is congealing in her plate. Rinaldi orders himself another drink.

I don't know where the idea came from, and I don't know what made me think of it just then. I must've seen it in a movie. It was a spur-of-the-moment type of thing. With one hand I'm raising my glass for a toast and with the other I'm tucking the corner of the tablecloth under my belt. Rinaldi and Inez raise their glasses. Then, "L'chaim," and I hand Rinaldi the envelope. I say to him, "You might look at this when you get the chance." I try to remem-ber the exact expression, the exact attitude he had when he handed me the envelope containing the Polaroid of Blacky, that sly little smile Rinaldi wore. I try to duplicate it. I don't know if the gesture is lost on him or not. He slides the envelope into the inside pocket of his jacket, into the pocket with his cigars, and rebuttons his coat. He starts to roll to his feet again. I say, "Don't bother," and he doesn't. "Inez—" I kiss her on the cheek.

She says, "Rinaldi's having some people over after the races. A victory celebration. Why don't you stop by?" Rinaldi's lips are a tight straight line.

"He hasn't won, yet," I say.

"Don't be silly. Of course he'll win. Rinaldi always gets what he wants." And then she winks at him. She slides her hand over his and to me she says, "I'll be looking for you."

"Thanks," I say, standing up. I turn my back, and walk away. The tablecloth tucked into my belt goes with me. Crash, bam, boom. Drinks, water, plates, silver, one Alfredo, one bratwurst, and one shrimp cocktail trail behind me for a couple of paces. I pull the corner out of my belt. I don't even turn around. Inez's high, rolling, uncontrollable laughter follows me out the door. Later on I think I should've looked to see the expression on Rinaldi's face. I got to admit, as juvenile a stunt as it was, to this day thinking about it makes me smile. Blacky would've liked it, too.

"What took you so long?" Nina wants to know. "Never mind," she says, before I have the chance to make something up. "It's me who should apologize." She shakes her head, closes her eyes, touches her forehead with her fingertips. "I've become such a bore." She hugs me. Her eyes are red around the gray, and wet.

"Forget it," I say. "Here, wear these." She puts on my shades. "We're going to a picnic."

We spotted the yellow Frisbee sailing out above the crowd in the infield and we followed it to Alberto, Augusto, and Marcellino. Nina reached into her purse and came up with a roll of Life Savers for each of them. We found Antonio with Julia and Dominga and the baby on a blanket amid a dozen different dishes on paper plates. Dominga wasn't a bad cook when she had something to work with. Everything was peppery. We ate peppery kebabs, peppery empanadas, peppery potatoes, and drank warm Inca colas. We walked to the rail to watch the horses run past, then walked back to the blanket to eat some more. Marcellino held my hand. He'd put the whole roll of Life Savers in his mouth at once and his lips and tongue were green. He seemed happy enough. He was smiling, at least. His tiny teeth and gums were the same bright Life Savers green.

Antonio was silent through the meal. Afterward he took Nina to show her the tulip beds. Augusto had the skinny on the Stakes and the two of us crossed the track to the windows to put some money down. Forget Me Not didn't have it over the distance, Augusto said, even though ten minutes to post he was two to one. Augusto had Holy Robles to win in a walk. I played him fifty dollars on the nose. I gave Augusto ten to bet for himself. We were partners—his dope, my money. He shook my hand, thanked me for putting in a word with Frankie.

Back at the picnic, Nina told me that Antonio had something he wanted to say to me. She gave me a meaningful look. I sat down beside Antonio, wondering what the look was about and why, if he had something to say, he didn't call me over himself.

Before he got it out, the announcer called one minute to post time and we all started over to the rail. As we walked, Antonio reached in his pocket, pulled out some folded bills, and put them in my hand. "For the tent," he said. I counted thirty bucks. I didn't want the money and handed it back. It was about what he earned in a week.

He pushed my hand away. "Take it," he said.

I'd forgotten about the tent already. Besides, what was thirty bucks? A new tent like mine cost four hundred if you could find one, which you couldn't.

"Take it," he said. He closed my fingers around the money and pushed my hand away. I thanked him and shoved it into my pocket.

"De nada," he said, and that's all he said as we walked to the rail to see Holy Robles win the fifty-third running of the Humboldt Stakes going away.

The evening was warm. The sandy hills behind the city were capped with pink clouds. A breeze blew off the Pacific. At Rinaldi's, cars lined the curb and the circular driveway. Chauffeurs stood in clusters and smoked and talked. Guests wandered the grounds under the banyans. The house itself was glowing; every light was lit. A stream of people swirled and mingled throughout the house, flowing from room to room, gathering in pools, spilling out onto the lawn and into the garden. Men wore blazers with emblems as flamboyant as orchids blooming on their pockets, and perfumed women in summery dresses tinkled with jewelry. Their heels clacked on the parquet floors. Tray after tray left the kitchen with canapes and glasses of champagne. The silver Humboldt Cup, large enough to sit in, brimmed with caviar.

The general himself stood by the dining room doors which opened onto the large flagstone patio. He was speaking to the Minister of the Interior, Ferdinand Carascál Ochoa de Villanueve —Freddy—and his young wife, Tatu. The general's lighter flashed toward Tatu's cigarette and then, catching someone else's eye across the room, he excused himself and left the Minister and Tatu —her cigarette unlit—awkward and alone. Rinaldi, as leader of the mountain campaign against the Zapato Moreno; as the tough, patient, shrewd, military tactician, as well as a millionaire several times over; as a horseman of renown, the breeder and owner of Holy Robles, victor in the Humboldt Stakes; as *General* Escobar Pino Rinaldi, provincial governor, whose opinion was sought on a wide range of issues, whose future no longer included a stint of any duration in La Paz, but rather, in addition to his promotion, an appointment to the Conference on National Security, where he sat beside the President himself—the great General Escobar Pino Rinaldi no longer had to kiss the ass of that shithead of an Interior Minister and his teenage disco bride. He knew it and they knew it and it pleased him greatly to remind them both of the fact.

He circulated among his guests, many of whom would never have attended a party on his invitation before. Now, as if raised in his house, as if relatives in a large, close-knit family, they drank his champagne and ate his caviar and wandered amid his rooms and his gardens, admiring his paintings of horses, and his Persian carpets, and his rose beds, acting as if their host were a much beloved uncle and not the same Rinaldi who only weeks before had been merely an overachieving thug from the streets. But quietly, between sips of champagne and nibbles of caviar, they marveled and they whispered and they smiled among themselves. Because they knew that but for the rise of a charismatic *guerrillero*, a fortuitous marriage, and a powerfully addictive drug, here was a man who would be—as those of *his* kind had always been by those of *their* kind—ignored.

"Perhaps His Eminence would like one of these?" he was saying to the bishop as he reached into the inside pocket of his blazer for one of the long aluminum tubes. "H. Uppmanns." He touched the envelope Bobby had handed him at lunch and, having forgotten what it was or where he had gotten it, pulled it out with the cigars. He held it at arm's length and squinted. He patted his pockets for his glasses. It was a recent affectation for him to go without them. Wiped years away, Inez had told him. The envelope was plain and white, sealed, without markings of any sort, an ordinary business envelope, but bulky. Hefting it, he remembered.

He guessed Shafto was squeezing him again. The man was an irritation, nothing more. His demands were paltry, particularly when Rinaldi considered how much his promotion meant, both in cash and in the priceless satisfactions his new rank now afforded him, like snubbing the Interior Minister and lighting the bishop's cigar.

An irritation, yes, and a minor one at that, but in an odd way Rinaldi appreciated Shafto's presence in his life. For one, it affirmed his sense of superiority: the gringo couldn't even blackmail right. But more importantly, Bobby Shafto had given new focus to the anger Rinaldi had carried with him for longer than he could remember. It was the single constant feature of his emotional life. He was either at odds with the world or asleep, and like others who have over a lifetime ardently pursued a desire to have finally overtaken it, he was now finding life, despite the titillation of all this attention, becoming a drowsy sort of routine. So while Bobby could make Rinaldi seethe, he was also a necessary stimulant.

Rinaldi tried to concentrate on the conversation with the bishop, but the envelope distracted him. Absently, he flipped it over in his hand. He tapped it against his thigh. He pointed with it for emphasis, scratched his chin with its corner. A begrudging admiration for Bobby Shafto entered his thoughts. Was it nerve? He remembered the night in the stable. A man with any sense would have been intimidated. Hadn't Shafto *seemed* intimidated at the time? Or was he simply too obtuse, the threats bouncing off him like darts against a metal hull? Certainly he lacked discernment. Their informant—what was his name? A busboy, Santo something—asserted that Shafto was not in any way connected with the Moreno, was in fact unaware of the position his employer and good friend occupied in the movement. Somewhat difficult to believe, but there was no evidence to the contrary. And as to the matter of the blackmail, Rinaldi's wealth was common knowledge, and yet what did Shafto demand? A scholarship for a campesino boy, a donation to some provincial clinic, a truck, a van, building permits, a little money. Taken altogether, it amounted to less than the cocainistas deposited into his accounts in a week. Of course Shafto still had the negatives, and his demands could escalate. Desire was, as Rinaldi well knew, ever-expanding.

And then there was the matter of Nina. She herself had said—when she still confided in him—that she did not believe Shafto's intentions were either serious or long-term. Shafto was a womanizer. Rinaldi recognized the type, although that bit of information was also in the file. To Shafto, Nina was just another piece of meat. What more evidence would one need to establish the fact that here was a man who did not know his ass from a hole in the ground?

He had given Shafto an ultimatum which would have discouraged most. Some who are pushed recoil. Some push back. It wasn't courage, or some principled stance, and it wasn't in any way admirable, Rinaldi concluded. It was a knee-jerk reaction, nothing more. Shafto had been prodded and this clumsy blackmail was the response of a man too myopic to see who was holding the other end of the stick.

Rinaldi's attention shifted back to the bishop, who, expelling smoke from his nose and mouth, and coughing—a polite, throat-clearing *hmm-hmm* at first which then erupted into a deep phlegmmy *hawwwck*—had turned as green as the Cuban fields. With his crucifix banging against his chest, and his soutane rustling, and the smoking cigar held at arm's length as if it were a live incendiary device, the bishop burst through the double doors into the garden. Rinaldi, masking his amusement with concern, watched him go.

An hour earlier Rinaldi had switched from champagne to pisco sours, and perhaps it was the familiar and desirable distance alcohol afforded him, the hazy, padded, insular sensation, the wrong-end-of-the-telescope perspective he had come to anticipate after he had consumed a certain amount. Maybe it was the dizzy blur the world was to him without his glasses. Or maybe this particular feeling was the result of what he believed to be the adulation of such a celebrated assembly. This, after all was *his* day. Whatever the reason, he felt a lightness new to him. The crushing weight of his ambition had been lifted, and it seemed to him that he could float, and would have too, if it weren't for the goddamned ballast he was hauling around, the envelope inside his jacket pocket. It was heavy as lead. It threw him off balance. It caused him to list. He knew he would have to deal with it, but later, not now. This was his day. For the moment he simply wanted a place to set it down.

In his library he intruded on a couple intertwined on the leather couch, immersed in passionate writhing. "Who the hell are you?" demanded the girl. She was insolent, annoyed, and breathless, her lipstick was smeary, her dark hair tousled. She was drunk. She tucked her breasts back into her dress, and dangling her shoes from a finger she threw her other arm over her lover's shoulder and sauntered out.

Rinaldi locked the door after them. He tossed the envelope onto his desk beside his glasses and poured himself another pisco sour. The letter opener felt cool and smooth in his hand, its weight reassuring. Its haft was a squat, leering, hideous Inca demon. Its blade was an oversized prick. Rinaldi fumbled slitting the envelopes: there were three of them. He aimed for the one in the middle, the most substantial-looking one. He stabbed and missed.

A thought—vague, gauzy, ghostlike—played at the margin of his consciousness. He tried to seize it, but it vanished, leaving him confused and anxious. Of its own volition, as if taunting him, the thought returned. It expanded into a premonition, attracted mass, solidified. It assumed form and shape and the sharp edges of certainty, becoming a full-blown vision so vivid and undeniable that in Rinaldi's mind the future attained all the irrevocable finality of historical fact. The image left him weak and dizzy. He sat back into the chair and closed his eyes. A powerful wave of fear swept over him, then subsided, allowing the anger in. He slashed at the envelope, tearing it open and slicing the inside sheets as well. He slammed down the opener, which thudded on the blotter and bounced onto the rug. He went to the bar and poured himself another drink, straight pisco this time, and carried the bottle back. He wiped his forehead, staring down at the papers. Shafto, that sonofabitching Shafto. He sat and rested his elbows on the desk, the heels of his palms pressed against his eyes.

They were tear sheets from the Sunday magazine. The date was tomorrow's. A glimpse was all he needed. He'd known all along it was coming. He didn't want to admit it, but he'd known. Shafto. An ass, a fool, impossible to underestimate, or so he had thought. But an ass could be an unpredictable enemy, and even a fool understood that without any loser there wasn't a winner, that regardless how strong, brave, or noble, the bull always died in the end. Having admitted the truth, he felt his boiling anger cool like a pot removed from the flame. It left him serene. A bright clarity broke through the alcoholic fog. One truth invited others. He didn't blame Shafto. Were he Shafto, he would have done the same. Money wasn't everything. It wasn't to him and it wasn't to Shafto either. What did it matter that you killed the goose when you'd eaten all the eggs you wanted, when you were sick of the sight of eggs, and now what you hungered for was flesh?

He poured from the bottle, not bothering with the ice. He put on his glasses. He pieced together the fragments. The whole story was there, and the photographs. "Exclusive to *El Observador.*" One paragraph satisfied his curiosity. He looked at the pictures. One by one he let the pages fall. Some fell on the desk, some on the floor.

Then the fog rolled in again. He felt a numbing resignation. Without anger, his will, which anger supported like bone supports muscle, went limp.

From the top drawer he took a sheet of paper and a pen. He scrawled a note and left it on the blotter. In the bottom drawer he found the revolver. He slipped it into his pocket. With the gun and the bottle of pisco he got to his feet. He steadied himself. He pulled the lamp chain. The room went black.

He'd no idea what time it was. Late, though there were still a few guests wandering the grounds. Avoiding them, he took the gravel path toward the stables. Light from the house threw his long shadow out in front of him. His feet crunched the stones. Ahead it was dark and quiet. Two guards were standing by his bench and talking. He saw the glow from their cigarettes. When they saw him they cupped their smokes and snapped to attention. Though Rinaldi would have liked to sit on that bench, it was in fact where he'd been headed, he simply nodded and continued past them down the path.

Kid Pro Quo jerked his massive head back inside his stall. Rinaldi slid the bolt on the bottom door and went inside. The horse retreated to a corner. He pranced nervously, keeping his hindquarters toward Rinaldi, watching him over his shoulder.

And what have I done to you? Rinaldi wondered. Must have been something, I don't remember what.

He breathed the air of the stall, the smell of horse and clean bedding. It reminded him of Mirasol. With the bottle curled protectively in the crook of his arm, he sat heavily in the straw and leaned back against the wall. His legs sprawled out in front of him. What little light came in from the garden reflected off the gloss of his shoes.

Kid Pro Quo whinnied and pranced. The straw muffled the sound of his hooves. His ears were up, his head high. He snorted with agitation and walked in tight circles. With a foreleg he kicked at the door. Except to tilt the bottle, the general sat perfectly still. In time the horse settled down. He hugged the far wall, an eye on the dark corner where the intruder was.

The sound of running water woke Rinaldi. For a moment he could not recall where he was. Nor had he any idea what time it was or how long he'd been sitting in the stall. His knees ached, his back was stiff, his pants leg was wet. The ammoniac smell of horse piss made him wince. He patted the damp straw around him until he found the bottle. It had toppled and only a mouthful remained. He swore. He felt the weight of the gun in his pocket. Revulsion replaced whatever he was feeling when he had taken the gun from his desk. He set it down an arm's length away.

His head ached. He knew it must be the early hours of the morning. The Sunday papers would soon be on the street. By nine the entire country would know. The phone would ring. He would deny it, call it an outrageous lie. Reporters would hound him; he would blame Mosquevera. Time would worsen things. They would ask questions, go to Santo Rosario, dig up the bodies. On the advice of his lawyers he would refrain from further comment. The ministry would relieve him of his duties pending the outcome of an official investigation. His superiors would distance themselves. He would return to Mirasol awaiting trial to live with Elena's icy, knowing silence.

Had he the strength to see it through, the whole embarrassing, rotten mess? He decided he did. What could they do to him now? He was a boy from the streets who had made his way to general. He was rich. He'd sat by the President's side. His horse had won the Humboldt. He smoked Cuban cigars with the bishop. He could see it through, whatever they would do to him now, he knew he could, but it wouldn't change the ending. Shafto had seen to that. And what good would it be if you couldn't change the ending?

His hand probed the straw for the gun. He held it on his lap. Kid Pro Quo stamped a hoof. The horse swished his tail and circled. Rinaldi emptied the chamber of bullets, all but one. The horse turned his hindquarters to him and shifted weight from leg to leg. He snorted. Rinaldi spun the chamber. Something unforseen could happen, he admitted, like Santo Rosario. Who could've predicted Santo Rosario? The violence the Indians harbored, an ambush ambushed. He almost laughed. But what were the odds of another surprise like that? Very long, he decided. It was all out of his hands. There was some comfort in that. He was tired of rigging the game. He would stand down, let luck decide.

The horse pushed against the door. The hinges squeaked. Rinaldi replaced two of the bullets; now three chambers were loaded, the other three empty. Luck ought to have an even chance, he thought. He spun the barrel again. It made a ratchety noise. Kid Pro Quo snorted and eyed the dark corner over his shoulder.

Rinaldi put the barrel into his mouth and tasted the oily metal. He watched his thoughts to mark which might be his last. Nothing came. Just as well. He had not expected revelation. He slowly squeezed the trigger. It seemed to travel a very great distance before the hammer clicked.

It was not especially loud, but in the dead quiet of the stables the click was sharp and sudden. Luck had decided. Rinaldi pulled the barrel from his mouth.

One of the soldiers standing outside later described the sound as that of a melon hitting the sidewalk. Luck had indeed decided, but Rinaldi hadn't the time to interpret the decision, or even to ascertain whether it was relief or disappointment he was feeling. As if to shoo a biting fly from a place he could not reach with his tail, Kid Pro Quo had lowered his head and tucked his hoof up under his belly. Powered by a half ton of muscle, from out of the darkness, unseen and unanticipated, his hoof rimmed with a special aluminum shoe, his rear leg recoiled, then straightened swiftly to its fullest extension. It drove Rinaldi's nose through to the back of his skull. It shattered his face like a teacup.

THE LAST MORENO

The hardest part had been finding Peregrina, not that I didn't know where she lived. I'd been to her barrio with Blacky, but I'd waited by the car while Blacky entered that maze to get her. Jesus, what a place! But the people who lived there didn't seem to mind it as much as I did, they seemed as happy or unhappy as any bunch of people anywhere, which goes to show you, fortune is dished out according to your ability stomach it.

I found Peregrina, and sure, she wanted to come back to work, and there was Julia and Dominga to help, and some of the others, and after weeks of waiting for all the permits and licenses and certificates, which would've been months even with Rinaldi's help if Blacky hadn't taught me how you had to duke them a five here and a twenty there to get anything done in the capital, we were ready to reopen. In nine hours, to be exact. Thirty-seven reservations.

I had cleaned up the mess they'd made looking for whatever they thought Blacky had hidden in the restaurant. The furniture and the piano had been wrecked, the dishes busted, the art stolen, but the neon sign was intact, which was fine because *Blacky's* was the way it started, and as long as I was running the show, *Blacky's* was the way it was going to be.

The idea of doubling the restaurant as a photography gallery was a last-minute inspiration. I got some work on consignment to cover the walls, and I had an excuse to frame and hang my own pictures, which was a reward in itself. Of course you had to be careful what you picked to hang: the picador's horse, the one gored by the bull? That wasn't a shot to stimulate your appetite, but the one of the lake I took from the pass with Roberto that morning, my wine vendor bought that one right off the wall.

The rest of the pictures would be a reminder in case I started getting ideas again. There was Enrique Luna, the aging leading man, every silver hair in place. There was a wall devoted to the Marcará market: the girl with the silver barrettes, the herb seller behind her balance scale, the tins of dyes, a ground-level shot of a piglet tied on a piece of blue yarn, and the boys on the Volkswagen with Baptismo on top holding the ball. There was a whole series of Nina, including her with the mackerel, and her rising off the chair just before she smacked me. The puma came out terrific, its legs outstretched and its claws extended, eyes reflecting yellow and as big as poker chips. I'd nailed the condor, too.

I was alone in the kitchen, a little nervous about the opening, although we had reservations clear into the following week so I wasn't going to have to eat sixteen pheasants and half a gallon of Caesar dressing myself. Dominga wasn't due for an hour, and the rest of the crew—waiters, hostess, bussers—until afternoon. I was experimenting with a pot of soup for their employee meal and went to the walk-in for cream. There on the door I'd taped the five or six clippings I'd cut from various papers and magazines—my scrapbook of Gavilan sightings. He'd been reported in Cuzco, Chama, Havana, Dacca, Sri Lanka. Sri fucking Lanka can you believe. Maybe because it was at eye level, maybe because the boldface stood out, my eyes seemed to always fall on the one headlined GAVILAN LIVES, dateline Iquitos, which is over on the Amazon side. I knew the article by heart. It placed him near a village up a jungle tributary with a name longer than the stream probably was wide. Only way in was by canoe. Didn't say how they knew it was Gavilan. There were still no photos of him, and all the ones I'd taken I'd burned. They couldn't identify him from any picture of mine. Didn't say what he was doing there, either, only that the proprietor of the bar-hotel–general store said he'd been living there in a hut a mile upstream from the village. When the reporter went to confirm the story he found the hut abandoned. Gavilan, or whoever it was, was gone and the woman—"in her twenties, tall, European, with a scar on her cheek"—she was gone, too. Gone . . .

Nina came in, sat at the counter, put down her purse, watched while I dumped a sixth pan of grilled tomato sauce into the five-gallon pot. She poured herself a coffee.

"What's cooking?" she asked.

"Soup," I said. "Got a smoke?"

"I quit."

"Again?"

"What kind of soup?"

"Ah, *chérie*, zis soup ees very special." I dropped in three deviled eggs, stirred in a handful of crabmeat. "It ees ze famous Blacky's Very Special Soup." I looked at Nina. No reaction. Zip. "A customer would say to him, 'Blacky, this soup is delicious, what's in it?' And Blacky would say, 'Eet ees very special, don't you think?' He'd never tell them the ingredients. Half the time he didn't remember exactly himself. 'Ah, yes, madame, very special,' is all he'd say." I kissed my fingertips.

Nina just looked at me.

"When Blacky did it, it was funny. I don't do the accent good. You sure you don't have a smoke? I know you quit, but maybe there's one hiding in your purse somewhere—a stale one's OK. Bent, mangled, I don't care. From the olden days."

She didn't answer. Her mind was somewhere else. I added cream, tomatoes, three-bean salad with hearts of palm, pureed the goop, was doing my best to amuse her, didn't care how it turned out. I considered dropping in my shoe just to get a rise out of her.

Nina rummaged through her purse. She didn't know about the blackmail. At least, I hadn't told her. The Santo Rosario story had made a big splash in the Sunday magazine. Maybe I should've prepared her. As it was, she probably opened the Sunday paper and it hit her in the face. Then on Monday Rinaldi's death was all over the news.

The problem is she never accepted the side of Rinaldi I knew. That I was here in the capital—reopening the restaurant, running all over town, got a new phone, anybody could find me if they wanted to—and that nothing had happened to me would be proof to her that I was paranoid where he was concerned. And the whole Santo Rosario episode? That would be "in the line of duty," so somehow acceptable, even though he'd invented this fantastic story she knew herself was a lie. She couldn't put the pieces of the Rinaldi of her past—friend of the family, protector, lover, the honorary chairman of the Red Cross Christmas fund-raising drive—she couldn't fit *that* Rinaldi together with the Rinaldi I described. Naturally, she decided my pieces were the ones that didn't fit. She never said so in so many words, but my guess is, that was how she had it wired. It worked for her, meaning she could live with it that way. She had her blind spots; everyone did. Look at Roberto.

She was pulling things out of her purse and piling them on the counter. "I'm sorry," she said, without looking up. "What did you ask?"

"About Elena . . . ? The funeral?"

"They buried him at Mirasol. 'What was, was,' Elena said, 'And no one could alter the facts.' I asked her if she was convinced she knew what the facts were. 'Quite convinced,' she said. She said she didn't believe in vengeance. 'Who was I going to hurt by spiting him now?' was how she put it."

If it had been up to me, I'd have thrown the bastard's body in the dumpster and let the garbage truck cart it away. Not that I had any ideas that Rinaldi was still in any way connected to it, though it would have been a nice finale, him slowly decomposing in a mountain of garbage—food for fat, lice-ridden gulls—and aware of it all the time. I diced a handful of sautéed mushrooms and worked the wand through the soup.

"They buried him beside Alejandro." Her hand was still inside the purse, but she had stopped rooting around in there, and her shoulders slumped and she looked up at me. "I guess I expected to feel more . . . more *something*, I don't know what. It's all so hard to believe." She sat up straight, pushed the stuff all back in with her forearm, and snapped her purse shut. "Sorry, no cigarettes."

I cracked a beer, took a swig, opened a bottle for Nina. "Pasburibbin."

"For breakfast?" she winced.

I shrugged, took another swig, and poured some into the pot. Anytime you start with tomato sauce, no matter what else you might put in, the color is always some shade of red. This was the color of bricks. "I'll make us something to eat as soon as I finish the soup. A sandwich OK for you?"

I wasn't sad about Rinaldi dying and I wasn't satisfied either. Had Kid Pro Quo waited another couple of hours to kick his brains in, had Rinaldi been around to actually *see* the shit hit the fan, *then* I would have been satisfied. Maybe.

Rinaldi had been all over the papers last Sunday, with Holy Robles on the sports page and Santo Rosario in the magazine, and the papers had been full of Rinaldi and Santo Rosario every day since. First the government denied the charges. They called his death "a tragic accident," "an unfortunate coincidence." Him they called a patriot and said some other stuff about all his civic and charitable baloney. That was Monday. Tuesday they tried to shuttle the blame to Mosquevera, who couldn't deny the charge on account of his lips were sewed together. By Thursday they gave in to the pressure and promised an investigation. "Did they give him full military honors, a twenty-one-gun salute, any of that sort of stuff?" The soup needed something. I went to the walk-in.

"They didn't strip him of his rank, if that's what you mean." She had to yell even though I'd propped open the door. I have this fear of getting locked inside, living on aspic until I freeze to death or suffocate. "He was buried a general."

I came out empty-handed. Just my luck him getting killed like that. I thought the Kid and me were *coomps*. I thought we had an understanding. And then he goes and plants that hoof of his in Rinaldi's face an hour before the Sunday papers hit the streets. "What bum luck," I said.

"It wasn't exactly luck. It may have been suicide."

I had this image of Rinaldi nailing a horseshoe onto a two-by-four and whacking himself over the head. Nina saw it coming. "With a revolver," she said, before I could make a crack. "They found it lying beside the body in the stall. They suspect the horse kicked him before he had the chance to do the job himself. Apparently he was very drunk."

"I have a theory on that."

"Theory?"

"People get premonitions, you know, about their death and stuff? When it's imminent?"

"So?"

"Accounts for all the drunks they pull out of auto wrecks. They can't face it sober so they go out and get totally wasted."

"That's ridiculous." She smiled for the first time since the picnic. A little tiny smile.

"Suppose you knew you were going to go out in a flaming head-on crash—steering wheel through your chest, engine sitting in your lap—wouldn't you rather be drunk? Kind of an anesthetic. Maybe Rinaldi had a premonition."

"If he knew the horse was going to kick him, wouldn't it be more logical just to stay out of the stable?"

"He didn't *know* it was going to be a horse. That's why he was in the stable. He thought it would be safe in the stable."

"What about the gun?"

"For protection."

"And the note?"

"What note?"

"He left a note. He knew about *El Observador*, obviously. They found a copy in the library. It had been sliced to pieces." She thought for a moment. Then she opened her purse and started rummaging again.

"What are you looking for?" I asked.

"Cigarettes." She had her head down. "You blackmailed him, didn't you?" she said, almost too softly for me to hear. She started piling things from her purse onto the counter again. "Didn't you." The second time was louder and wasn't a question. She took out a cosmetics bag and unzipped it.

I said, "Yeah, I did."

She tried to stand a tube of lipstick, but her hand was shaking and it toppled and rolled onto the floor. "And that's where you got the money for the restaurant and the van?" Her head appeared above the counter again, but her eyes were in her purse. She pulled out an address book and slapped that down. "And then after you blackmailed him you gave the pictures and the story to—"

"Sold."

"What?" She looked up at me.

"Sold. Sold. I didn't *give* them to anyone. I sold them."

She overturned her purse and shook it. Kleenex, gum foil, to-bacco flakes, a piece of thread floated down, like confetti. "You blackmailed him, then when you got from him what you wanted, you *sold* the story to the paper."

I nodded.

"You must have known . . . you might have guessed . . ." She pulled her arm across the countertop and corralled everything back in a second time.

"Listen, I could go out and get you a pack. There's a place right around the corner."

"And all the other pictures you took of the Moreno? What happened to those?" She was crying. I handed her a paper towel.

"Listen, Nina. I did those things and I'm not sorry. I'm not the least bit sorry for him."

"I understand. I shouldn't be either, I guess." She went back into her purse. "And the other pictures . . . ?"

"Destroyed."

"And you don't know where they went? Rivera? Camilo . . ."

I shook my head.

"Roberto?"

"Last I saw him he was with you. Two days after Santo Rosario."

I went back to making the soup. I fingered the leather pouch I wore around my neck, the one with the love potion from the Marcara market. I sprinkled some into the pot. What the hell? If things began to get out of hand, I still had the antidote somewhere. . . .

I took a gulp of beer, sloshed it around in my mouth. I lifted the bottle. "To Gavilan," I said.

"To *Blacky's,*" I heard her say above the sound of Dominga coming in the back.

"Are you speaking to me?" Dominga called. She entered the kitchen. "Are you speaking to me?" she repeated. "I'm sorry," she said coming up behind me, tying on her apron. "I didn't hear what you said."

"I asked if you were, ah, ready for tonight."

She nodded. "And you?"

"Yep," I said, polishing off the beer. "Ready." And I was. Ready for Freddy.

BIBLIOGRAPHY

I'd like to thank the following authors whose works were useful to me in researching this book:

Cabezas, Omar. *Fire from the Mountain: The Making of a Sandinista.* New York: NAL-Dutton, 1986.

Vargas Llosa, Mario. "Inquest in the Andes." *New York Times Magazine*, July 31, 1983.

North, Carolyn. "Taking the Guinea Pig Cure." *Princeton Alumni Weekly*, April 18, 1984.

Stein, William W. *Hualcan: Life in the Highlands of Peru.* Ithaca, N.Y.: Cornell University Press, 1961.

Szulc, Tad. *Fidel.* New York: Morrow, 1986.

Wright, Ronald. *Cut Stones and Crossroads: A Journey in the Two Worlds of Peru.* New York: Penguin Books, 1986.

ABOUT THE AUTHOR

RICK SLONE lives in Idaho with his wife, Joyce, and his son, Cary.